The Summer We Got Free

First published 2012
by BGD Press

Oakland, CA

ISBN-10: 0988628600
ISBN-13: 978-0-9886286-0-1

Library of Congress Control Number: 2012917177

The Summer We Got Free

Mia McKenzie

for Franny, Nana and Pop-Pop
and all the people, living and dead, who helped me get free

1976

Ava did not remember the taste of butter. It had been seventeen years since she had last moaned at the melt of hot-buttered cornbread on her tongue. She was not bothered in the least about it, because she did not know that she did not remember. At breakfast, when she dropped a square of butter on grits, or on yams at dinner, and laid a spoonful of either on her tongue, she believed what she tasted was butter. She did not know that she was only tasting milkfat and salt, the things that make up butter, which, of course, is not the same thing. She certainly did not know that the taste of butter was a thing that had once made her moan. Ava did not remember what it was to moan.

Standing at the green-checkered, Formica-topped table in her parents' kitchen, on a drizzly Saturday in August, Ava spread butter thickly on a slice of toast and yawned heavily. It was just after four in the morning and she was still in her nightgown, a pale yellow, plain thing, and her hair was tied up under a kerchief. She was thirty years old, but she looked and felt years older, especially on mornings like this one, when the damp got into her elbows and knees and the joints of her hands, down in the marrow, and settled there. Buttering the toast, her fingers felt stiff and unwilling.

She placed the toast on a plate in front of her husband, Paul, who smiled tiredly up at her from his seat at the table.

"You look half asleep," she told him, as she poured him more orange juice.

"I'm alright," he said, chewing slowly.

They had been married four years and this was one of their rituals. Whenever Paul took a night shift at the cleaning company where he sometimes worked, he had to skip dinner. By the time he got home in the morning he was exhausted and didn't want to eat a whole meal and go to bed on a full stomach, so Ava got up early and made him a couple of slices of toast, and she sat with him while he ate. When they were first married, he took night shifts often, but over the years that followed he had taken them only when they needed extra money for something specific. Lately, though, in the last few months, he had been picking them up after his regular shifts at the hotel, where he worked full-time. This change had come about because he had finally secured a long-time-coming promotion at the hotel, to day manager, and between the two of them they were making enough money to afford their own house, and Paul was picking up the night shifts for extra money for a down payment. Twice in the last week he hadn't gotten home until nearly dawn, and once they had only had time to kiss goodbye as Ava passed him on her way out to catch her bus to work at the museum.

"We got jam?" Paul asked.

Ava shook her head. "You asked me that already."

"I did?" he asked, his eyes red and half-closing.

"You working too much."

He rubbed his eyes and some of the butter from his fingertips left a tiny smear on his eyelid. "How we gone get a house if I don't work?"

"We already got a house," Ava said.

Paul sighed and stuffed what was left of his toast into his mouth. "This aint our house, Ava," he said thickly.

Ava took the last slice of toast from the toaster and buttered it, thinking about this house and her husband's renewed determination to leave it, which she did not share. She had lived here almost her entire life, since she was four years old. And while she could not remember very much about her early childhood here, she could remember some things, like the day, twenty-six years ago, when they moved in, when she first saw the red wall-paper, which her parents had hated, but which Ava thought, and later convinced them, was the most perfect wallpaper anyone had ever hung. It had faded in only the last seventeen years as if it had been fifty years, and a grayness now lived inside the red.

Still, Ava had grown up playing *hide and seek* under this very counter where she now stood buttering Paul's bread, and playing jacks on this floor, underneath the kitchen table with her siblings. If she tried very hard, she could almost, but not really, remember how the jacks sounded when they scraped against the linoleum, and how the ball bounced. But the luster on the tiles was gone now, and whenever you sat a heavy dish on the green-checkered table it wobbled on its rusty legs. The glass vase that had sat for years in the table's center, which had been given to her parents by Miss Maddy, their across-the-street neighbor and then-friend, had held flowers from her mother's bushes out in the backyard. Yellow roses, fat and lush as bowls of paint. Their fallen petals like paintdrops on the tabletop. But the rosebushes were gone now, too, abandoned to the mass of strangling weeds that had suffocated the rest of the flower garden, and the vegetable garden, and had even attacked the back porch, where the weeds had crept over the banisters and up through the floorboards, which were loose and uneven now, just as they were in every room of the house.

And indeed there was an unevenness about the house itself, an eccentricity in its character, an imbalance in its light and air, so that in the daytime the sunlight coming in through the windows only cast itself into certain areas of a room, and avoided others, so shadows fell in odd ways, elongated in the wrong places or unnaturally cut in half. And when a gust of sudden air, sometimes hot, other times frigid, entered or left a room for no reason, as often happened, it sometimes took a person's breath away.

But Ava had been read stories at bedtime, and lost baby teeth, under this roof. She had bled like a woman for the first time here, and for the last. And though it had been years since she had known any real joy within these walls, any bliss, years even since she could clearly remember old joys and blisses, she still felt a connection to the house, and a kinship with it.

Ava handed Paul the last piece of toast, then turned back to the counter to wipe away the crumbs there. Paul watched her while chewing. He did not understand why she felt so strongly about this one thing, about not leaving this house. Indifference was usually the most apparent feature in Ava's personality. It was a fact about her that Paul had noticed when they had first started going together, nearly five years ago now. Sitting on the steps of the Philadelphia Museum of Art, where they had both worked, eating beef stew Ava had brought from the cafeteria where she was a server, Paul had invited her to see *Buck and the Preacher* with him after work.

"Alright," she'd said.

"You like Sidney Poitier?" he'd asked her, grinning, happy.

She shook her head. "Not that much."

"Oh." His grin slipped. "Well. We can see something else."

"No, it's fine," Ava had said. "Anything is fine."

He had liked that quality in her then, because he had mistaken it for easy-goingness and he didn't like fussy women anyway, women who had to have everything just so. Over time, though, he had come to see the downside of it. It wasn't that she always agreed with him about things. She didn't. But when she disagreed she never argued, and Paul felt this was because, whatever her opinion on a particular subject, she never felt strongly about it, and certainly not enough to fight over it. In all the time they'd known each other, they had never had a real fight. Paul tried to pick fights with Ava, sometimes, when he was very angry or frustrated about something and needed a fight. But as soon as he raised his voice she would completely lose interest in whatever they were talking about and he would be left even more frustrated than when he started. It was only when it came to the subject of leaving this house that Ava was uncharacteristically vehement. Not in her tone, because she would not fight about it, but in her consistency. No matter what Paul said, no matter how much he insisted over the last four years, Ava would not even consider leaving that house.

"Don't you want something that's just for us?" he asked her now for the hundredth time, tiredly, passively, between bites of toast.

She glanced over her shoulder at him and shrugged.

When she put the butter back into the refrigerator, a little bit got on the skin between her thumb and forefinger and, as usual, she did not really taste it when she licked it away.

❖ ❖ ❖

Standing outside a darkened row house on a sleeping street, George Delaney lit a cigarette and flipped up his collar against the chilly breeze that was blowing a very light rain around. It was early August, but the last few mornings had felt more like April, wet and chilly as early spring. A glance at his wristwatch confirmed that it was just after four in the morning, which was about what he'd figured. He'd spent almost two hours in Butch's basement.

His own house was only ten blocks away and he started towards it, walking briskly past the graffiti-marked buildings that populated that side of Market Street, down cracked sidewalks where weeds punched up through the broken concrete, half-illuminated by the big, butter-yellow moon.

Even at this hour, there was some car traffic on Chestnut Street. As George waited at the corner for it to pass, he saw a man rummaging through a trash bin on the opposite corner. The way he was bent over it made George think of his father, who had sometimes poked around in trash bins, and had even perused the town dump, looking for interesting things he could use for sculpture. Once, he had found a bag full of keys, and had used them, together with the pole from a stop sign some drunk had knocked over, to make a piece he had said was about broken promises. George, then just a boy, hadn't understood the strange-looking thing.

As he crossed the street, coming closer to the man picking through the trash, George noticed that his coat was very like the one his father used to wear, a heavy black pea coat with large pockets and collar, cherished from his days in the Navy. And the man's hat was like one his father had often worn, too. Gray felt with a dark green band. George had the strangest thought that this was his father, alive again somehow, and he reached out and put his hand on the man's shoulder.

"Daddy?" he asked, in a voice so soft it was almost lost on the wet breeze.

The man turned, and it was not his father's face he saw, but his son's. George Jr.'s. Looking at him with wide, deathful eyes. George gasped and stumbled backward. But in a flash the face had changed. The old bum looked at him as if he were crazy.

"I aint yo daddy, nigga," he said, through missing teeth. "Is you drunk?"

George felt a weakness in his knees and he had to grab hold of the trash can to get his balance. As soon as he got it, he pulled his jacket tighter around him and walked quickly home.

Ava lay beneath her husband, listening to his soft moaning and watching the early-blue sky through the open curtains at the bedroom window. It was melty, streaky blue, the moon fatty yellow, the kind of moon she and her brother used to call *savory* because it looked like you could reach up and dip your finger in it and scoop yourself out a taste.

Paul shifted his weight from one elbow to the other. Ava could hear, mixed in with his moaning, the loose floorboard under the right side of the bed as it creaked with each thrusting motion he made. It had been loose for months, ever since they had brought the new dresser in and had snagged a nail in the floorboard while pushing the dresser against the wall. Paul had said he'd take care of it, but with all the hours he worked, and with all the other things that needed repairing in the house, he'd never gotten to it. *I should fix that,* Ava thought. *It's just a matter of a hammer and a nail. It won't take more than a few seconds.*

Paul suddenly stopped thrusting and squinted down at her in the dark. "What?" he whispered.

It took Ava a moment to realize that she had not just thought about the loose floorboard, but had said something about it out loud.

Paul frowned, and his frown was like a little boy's. "That's what you thinking about right now?"

"I'm not thinking about it. It just crossed my mind for a second."

"You want me to do something different?" he asked her.

"No," she said, putting her hand on his backside to let him know it was alright to keep going. He buried his face in the curve of her neck and shoulder, pushed himself deeper inside her, and groaned.

Ava stifled a yawn.

Twenty minutes later, when Paul was ready to come, he raised up onto his elbows and looked in her eyes, and Ava kissed him, softly biting his bottom lip the way she knew he liked, so that he came with a shudder, just as a loud crash and the tinkling sound of shattering glass rang through the house.

"What the hell is that?" Paul whispered, getting out of bed and fumbling for his drawers in the dark. When he got them on, he said, "Stay here, baby," and crept out into the even darker hallway.

Standing at the top of the stairs, he felt a draft coming up that should not have been there. The light switch at the top of the steps that controlled the lamp at the bottom hadn't worked for years, since before he'd even moved into his wife's parents' house. Peering down the staircase into the foyer, tilting his head to one side, he tried to catch any sounds coming up from the dark rooms below, but the house was quiet. He went slowly down the stairs, almost all of them creaking loudly underfoot, the sound filling up the dense quiet. When he got to the bottom, he flicked on the lamp, squinting against the small light that filled the foyer. Nothing looked out of place.

When he stepped into the living room, the curtains at the front window moved, and just at the same time he heard the front door open in the foyer behind him. He quickly pressed himself against the wall.

"Who's that?" he called out, wishing he had put on his pants. "I got a gun," he lied. "And I'm a pretty good shot, too. My daddy taught me. He used to take me out to the woods and let me shoot—" He stopped, frowned to himself, wondering why he was telling his life story to somebody who was breaking into his house, and why on earth he had called himself a *pretty good* shot.

Someone grabbed his shoulder. He turned, ready to fight, and saw George Delaney, his father-in-law, standing there.

"Jesus, Pop," he said.

"What you doing?" the older man asked him.

"We heard a crash," Paul said. "I thought somebody was in here."

George crossed the living room and flicked on the overhead light. "The window's broke. I could see it from outside, coming up the steps."

The curtains hanging at the front window billowed a little in the small breeze that blew in. Paul went to the window and pulled back one curtain, and saw that half the window was shattered. Large and small pieces of glass covered one side of the worn, orange sofa that sat in front of the window.

"Goddamnit," Paul said. "Not this again. I thought they was finished with all this." He peered out into the dark street. "You see any of them out there?"

"They was gone by the time I walked up."

There was a brick lying on the floor just by the coffee table, and George picked it up. On one side, in dark-colored marker, was written: *Do not make a treaty of friendship with them as long as you live.*

He frowned and handed it to his son-in-law, who took it, read it, and shook his head.

"What the hell that supposed to mean?" Paul asked.

"It's from the bible," George said. "Deuteronomy."

Sarah came down the stairs then. "What happened?" she asked, pulling her robe tighter around her against the cool air coming in.

"Nothing," George said.

Sarah went to the window and pulled back the curtain. "It don't look like *nothing*, Daddy," she said, eyeing the broken window and all the glass, and trying not to stare at her brother-in-law in his drawers.

Paul held up the brick. "Somebody threw this."

"Good Lord."

"Not exactly," he said, and the three of them looked around at each other and laughed, all tired-sounding and with an underhint of something deeply sad, but still not nearly as disturbed as the laugh that joined theirs then, a loud, crazed, unhinged kind of laugh that made them all go quiet.

It came from the woman now standing halfway up the stairs, peering over the banister at them, a tight grin drawn across her face, a shock of gray-streaked hair sitting uncombed on top of her head, the housecoat she wore buttoned wrong, so that she looked lopsided and disheveled.

Sarah hurried over to the stairs, saying, "Go on back to bed, Mama."

Her mother, Regina, continued down the stairs. When she got to where Sarah was standing, she seemed to notice her for the first time. "Move, goddamnit. How I'm s'posed to bust that preacher upside his head if you blocking my way?"

"Pastor Goode aint down here," Sarah said.

Regina peered over the banister at Paul and George in the living room. "Well, y'all aint came down here at four in the morning for a game of pinochle," she said. She looked right at her husband then. "You coming or going, George?" she asked him, because he was the only one fully dressed.

"Go back to bed, Regina," George said.

She stared at him, not moving an inch, with an icy glare that made the cool air coming in through the broken glass seem balmy.

"Fine," he said. "Then I will." He walked out of the living room, back into the foyer, and went past Sarah on up the steps, and past Regina, who put her hands on her hips and watched him go. He could feel her eyes on his back as he reached the top of the stairs. He turned up the hallway and opened a door, glad, as always, that they did not share a bedroom, and then closed the door firmly behind him.

"I'll sweep up this glass," Sarah said, walking back towards the kitchen.

"I'll help," said Paul, following her.

Without Pastor Goode's head to go upside, or George to harass, Regina lost interest in the scene downstairs and went on back to bed.

George loved and hated the sound of his bedroom door closing behind him. The catching of the latch sounded like privacy and exposure at the same time. He liked knowing there was somewhere in the house he could go without Regina being able to follow him. Even in her craziest moments, even on her hardest Saturday mornings, she never dared come into his room, never dared push him *that* far. It had been she who, long years back, had kicked him out of the bedroom they had shared. George had been angry about it then. And hurt by it, though he would never admit to that and have Regina know for sure that she could hurt him, which would surely make her try more often. When she'd kicked him out of their bedroom, saying that she just wanted to be by herself for a while, to try to deal in solitude with what had happened to their son, it had represented a change in their marriage that was different from all the other changes that had come over the years, something clear and final about the way they would go on from that point, inhabiting their house and their lives. Any love that had still lived then, any love that had still pulsed and breathed, even shallowly, between them, had died that day, that too-hot, hazy day when where

George slept, and everything else in the whole world, had been altered without his having a say. At least he liked to pretend he had not had a say. In the years that followed, though, he had developed a ginger appreciation of his solitary space, coming to know it as a refuge, a sanctuary when other sanctuaries had fallen away, where he could shroud himself, ball himself up into the tiniest thing. Still, whenever he closed the door behind himself, whenever he blocked out Regina and the world, he had the feeling that something was being revealed, too, and that was this: that George Delaney needed to hide. That he needed to become some tiny thing. That there was something to be shrouded from. And something to be tiny about.

He heard Regina walk past his door just a handful of seconds after he closed it, her slippered footsteps slowing right outside the door, and he imagined her straining to hear what he might be doing, what he might be thinking, tucked inside his privacy. He felt a sputter of hatred for her—not a surge, just a sputter—as he heard her open the door to her own bedroom.

George got undressed, shedding himself of the clothes he'd worn to work the previous morning, the slate grey slacks that were standard for city workers in the streets department.

Standing at his bedroom window, he thought about the vagrant at the trashcan and wondered why he'd gotten so out of sorts about some old bum in a brown coat. He spent so much of his mental energy trying not to think about his father, and even more of it trying not to think about his son, yet, on an ordinary morning, under a same-as-always sky, they had suddenly careened into his psyche from either side and smashed head-on into each other in his mind. He still felt rattled. He took a drag off his cigarette, the thick smoke stinging his eyes, and peered down into the quiet street below, wondering which of their neighbors had thrown the brick. It may have been Pastor Goode, but he had rarely ever done things like that himself. Skulking around in the dark and chucking bricks through windows was the sort of thing the preacher had usually inspired others to do. As he watched the street below, George saw a figure appear, coming from the corner at Fifty-Eighth and walking down the middle of the street. In the dark, he couldn't see who it was. The figure slowed its pace and looked right at the Delaney house. George frowned, and reached for his pants, in case he had to confront the brick-thrower. But the figure quickened its pace again and walked on down the street, rounding the corner at Fifty-Ninth and disappearing from George's sight.

Sarah cleaned up the broken glass, Paul moving the sofa so she could sweep behind it. When it was all swept up, he got a piece of cardboard from a box at the top of the basement stairs and taped it into the broken pane. "That'll do for now, I guess."

Sarah stared at the cardboard, a hard look of frustration on her face. She was two years older than Ava, and although there was a sibling resemblance, Sarah was thin and stick-like where Ava was thicker and curvier. She had a hard edge to her personality, too, Paul thought, that Ava did not have.

"I hate them," she said. "Everybody on this block. I hate every last one of them."

"They aint done nothing like this in two years," Paul said. "No letters. No calls. No sermons in the street."

Sarah just stared at the cardboard, looking angry and sad, and Paul patted her shoulder.

When he climbed back into bed, he snuggled up close to Ava. She, indifferent to all the commotion that had gone on, was deep in a restful sleep.

Ava awoke again at just after nine in the morning, brought out of sleep by the sound of her mother's haunted mumbling coming down the hall. Regina, who was always Crazy on Saturday mornings, could be heard from her bedroom at the front of the house, all the way to Ava and Paul's room at the back. Glancing at Paul, who was snoring softly beside her, she got up, pulled on jeans and a blouse with ruffled sleeves, and tiptoed out of the room and down the stairs, being careful not to draw her mother's attention. She went to the living room and pulled back the front curtains to let in some sunlight. The cardboard taped into the window caused her to pause only a moment before she turned and walked through the dining room into the kitchen. Once there, she opened more curtains, the rain-cleansed sunlight splashing itself onto the dull red wallpaper. She made coffee, then went into the dining room, where she got out the ironing board and iron, and set them up by the dining room table. The basket of clean laundry she had left on the table the day before was still there, and she pulled out one of Paul's work shirts and began to press it.

When her sister, Sarah, came downstairs, she walked right by Ava without a word, on into the kitchen. After a while, she came back into the dining room with a cup of coffee and sat down at the table. "Pastor Goode's up to it again."

Ava folded a just-ironed skirt and asked what had happened that morning, and when Sarah told her about the brick through the window, she said, "So, that's what that noise was."

Sarah sipped her coffee and looked thoughtful. "Just when Mama was thinking about moving."

Ava slipped a skirt over the top of the ironing board. "If Mama was ever willing to move, we'd have been gone years ago."

Sarah shook her head, "Only 'cause they tried to force us out. Scare us out. She didn't want to give Pastor Goode the satisfaction. But when they stopped, she started thinking about going. I saw her reading the paper one day, a while back, and she had circled some things in the real estate section. She don't want to be here no more than they want us here."

Ava knew that Sarah was wrong, that Paul had been the one circling things in the real estate section. Sarah wasn't a person you could disagree with casually, though. She took any contrary opinion, no matter how reasonable, or gently expressed, as a personal attack. So, Ava just kept on ironing and said nothing more.

A little while later, their mother came down the stairs, still looking disheveled, with a sweater on over her nightclothes and a large sunhat on her head.

"You gone do some gardening, Mama?" Sarah asked her.

"I think my tomatoes is ready," Regina said, heading for the back door.

There were no tomatoes. There wasn't even a garden. But Regina disappeared through the back door looking determined.

"Daddy was out all night again," Sarah told Ava.

Ava folded the skirt she had just ironed and laid it on the table with the other pressed garments.

"Where you think he go all the time?" Sarah asked for the thousandth time.

Ava shrugged. "Nowhere. He just don't want to be here, I guess."

"Well, that's obvious, Ava," she said, rolling her eyes. "But he got to be going *somewhere* 'til after four in the morning. You don't want to know?"

Their father spent at least a couple of evenings a week away from home. Often, after dinner, he would tell them he was going out for a while, and they wouldn't see him again for hours. Sometimes Ava heard him returning at nearly dawn. It wasn't a new thing. It had been his habit for a long time, years, though Ava could not remember exactly when it had started. "I guess I'm just used to it," she said to her sister.

Sarah frowned. "You the least curious person I know."

Ava didn't think she wasn't curious. She just didn't have the appetite for other folks' business that Sarah had.

"You used to poke your nose into everything when we was kids," Sarah said.

Ava did not think that was true.

When the doorbell rang, both sisters were startled by the sound.

"Ignore it," said Ava, sure it was one of their neighbors trying to start some more trouble. "They'll go away afterwhile."

From the kitchen behind them, they heard the back door open and shut with a thud.

"Shit," Sarah said. "Mama must've heard the bell." She hurried past Ava and the ironing board, disappearing into the kitchen.

The doorbell rang again. Ava frowned and tried to just keep on ignoring it, but when it rang a third time she put down the iron. When she got to the front door, she peered through the glass pane and saw a woman standing at the edge of the porch, her back turned, looking out at the street. She could not see the woman's face, but nothing about the back of her reminded Ava of any of their neighbors on the block. Cautiously, she pulled open the front door and pushed open the screen door, just as the woman turned and came forward, smiling, saying, "Good morning," and Ava, for no reason she could name just then, reached out with both hands and took hold of the woman's face, and kissed her.

When their lips touched, Ava tasted color. For many seconds they stood there like that, one woman with her mouth pressed against another woman's mouth, in the doorway, until, finally, the woman took a step back from Ava, just as Sarah came through the kitchen door, following an excited-looking Regina. When they got to the foyer, they saw Ava standing there with the strange woman, both of them looking oddly satisfied.

Regina stared wide-eyed, not at the stranger, but at her daughter. "Ava?" she asked, as if she weren't sure. She got close to her, peering into her face, searching, and after a moment she said, "Oh. I thought that was you."

"It is me, Mama," Ava said.

"No, I mean the other you. The first you. The one you used to be."

Sarah eyed the woman at the door. "Who are you?"

"I'm looking for Paul Holly," the woman said, sounding a little flustered.

"Oh. You a friend of his?" Sarah asked.

"I'm Helena. His sister."

She looked nothing like her brother, Ava thought. While Paul's face was round, hers was thin and high-cheekboned. His brown eyes looked nothing like hers, which were startlingly green. While he was slightly short for a man, she was slightly tall for a woman, and had long fingers, while her brother's were stubby and meaty. He was handsome, but she was strange-looking, and had very short, very kinky hair and glasses that looked bottle-thick. But the greatest difference, and the most obvious one, was the severe difference in their complexions. Paul was brown. But Helena was black.

Very black.

Black as forever, Ava would say of her, years later. Black as always.

❖ ❖ ❖

When Helena crossed the threshold into the house, Ava felt the temperature rise. The chill that had held in the corners since the previous night's rain, that had penetrated the wood floors and clung to the gray-red wallpaper like an invisible frost, melted away in a moment. Ava felt it instantly, a sudden warming on her skin, as if she had just left the shade and walked out into the sun on a hot day. She looked at her mother and sister and she was sure they felt it, too. Regina took off her sun hat and used it to fan herself. Sarah unbuttoned her housecoat and pushed up its sleeves.

"I'm sorry to drop by so unexpectedly," Helena said. "I would have called, but I didn't have a phone number." She set down the suitcase and black leather portfolio she was carrying.

For a moment, they all stood there, hot and silent. Then Sarah, who was grinning at Helena and almost bouncing on her heels, said, "Aint this something? Paul's sister."

Helena looked uneasy, with all of them standing there watching her, especially Regina, who was peering at her as though she were a strange plant that had suddenly sprouted up in the middle of the foyer. "Well," Helena said, "I mean…is Paul here?"

"He's sleeping," Ava said. "I'll go get him up for you." She moved towards the stairs.

"Sleeping?"

"Yes. He worked all night."

"Oh," she said. "Wait. Don't."

Ava stopped.

"I really shouldn't have come without calling. But I didn't have a number."

Regina squinted at her. "You said that already."

She frowned. "Did I? Well, I just hate to wake him if he's been up all night. To tell you the truth, I think seeing me will be enough of a shock to his system without him being half asleep on top of it."

"Don't wake him, then," Sarah said. "He'll probably be up in a little while. Why don't you come in and wait?"

That idea made Ava feel suddenly lightheaded. She leaned against the wall and tried to steady herself.

"I wouldn't want to put y'all out," Helena said.

"You wouldn't be," Sarah insisted. "Would she, Ava?"

Ava tried to say, "No, you wouldn't be," but her words came out all jumbled.

Sarah frowned at her. "It'll be nice to have company. Won't it, Mama?"

Regina was still peering at Helena, her eyes moving over the woman's face. "Black, aint you?"

Sarah put her hands over her face. "Oh, God, Mama."

Helena gave Regina a strained smile and said, "Is something burning?"
They all sniffed the air.

"It's the iron," Ava said, and she hurried out to the dining room, glad to
have an excuse to get away.

She found the iron face down on a pair of Paul's work pants. It had
scorched through at the edges, melting a triangular black burn into the ma-
terial. She turned off the iron and stood there looking down at the ruined
slacks, the hard smell of singed polyester in her nose.

She did not understand what had happened in the doorway. The feelings
that had rushed through her the moment she saw Helena, feelings she could
not name and did not recognize, still lingered, and she found it hard to
breathe in the suddenly-hot house. She closed her eyes and inhaled deeply,
trying to get more air into her lungs. She could hear Paul's sister's voice
floating in from the foyer. She slipped out into the kitchen, but the voice
followed her, and after a moment Helena came into the kitchen, with Sarah
leading the way and Regina following half-interestedly behind. Ava moved
to the counter and wiped away some crumbs that weren't there.

"This is my sister, Ava," Sarah said. "Your brother's wife."

There was a flash of surprise in Helena's eyes when Sarah said the word
wife, then she smiled, the most tense, uncomfortable smile Ava had ever
seen, and said, "It's good to meet you," holding out her hand for Ava to
take.

Ava came forward and took Helena's hand and tried to say, "It's good to
meet you, too," but the words came out all jumbled and wrong again.

"What's the matter with you?" Sarah asked her.

Ava didn't answer. Instead, she offered Helena coffee, very slowly, so
the words came out right, and Helena said yes, she would like some, and
that she took it black. Helena sat down at the table and Sarah sat beside her.
Ava got a mug from the cupboard and filled it, and her hands shook a little
as she handed it to Helena.

"How long has it been since you saw your brother?" Sarah asked. She
was perched on the edge of her chair, her whole body angled towards
Paul's sister.

"Eighteen years."

"Paul told us you got split up after your mother died. Sent to different
relatives."

"Oh," she said. "Well. We did get split up. I was twelve. Paul was fifteen."

"Have you been in Philadelphia all this time?"

Ava had never known Sarah to be so friendly to anyone. When she had
first brought Paul around, five years ago, Sarah had looked him up and
down as if he were the most shiftless-looking Negro she had ever seen. It

had taken her months to warm up to him and it was at least a year before Ava could say for sure that Sarah even liked him.

"I was here until I was seventeen," Helena was saying. "Then we moved to Baltimore. I've been there ever since."

"But you back here now?"

She shook her head. "I'm on my way up to New York. I just stopped by Philly so I could see Paul."

"Well, he'll be up soon," Sarah said again.

Ava looked at the clock. It was only ten-thirty. Paul wouldn't be up for hours. "Maybe I should wake him," she said.

Sarah glared across the room at her. "You should let the poor man sleep, Ava." Then she smiled at Helena. "We was just about to start breakfast. We'd love to have you."

Helena glanced at Ava, then shook her head. "I really don't want to put y'all out anymore than I already have."

"You haven't," Sarah said. "You family. Aint she, Ava?"

"I guess so," Ava said.

Sarah beamed, making her sister's strained smile look all the more uneasy.

George had not heard the doorbell. Deep in sleep when Helena came, he had been dreaming a familiar dream, an old dream, about an abandoned factory by a train track, and he awoke feeling shaken and disoriented. He could smell breakfast cooking and could hear the very faint sizzle of cooking grease, and he remembered where he was, and that it was Saturday morning, and he settled himself deeper into his mattress and put his pillow over his head. He did this upon waking every Saturday morning, to block out the sounds of Regina's craziness coming down the hall, wafting under his door like cigarette smoke and filling his space like a toxin. He could remember, though it had been a long time ago now, that Saturday mornings in this house had once been happy. In their first years on this block, when their family was unbroken. George would always sleep in and Regina would, too, when she didn't have to work too early. They would give themselves those two or three hours not to worry about Ava and what she might be up to. Falling in and out of consciousness, they would whisper to each other, "You think everything alright?" "Sure, I don't smell nothing burning." "We should get up and check on them, huh?" "Yeah, in a little while." These things sometimes said while cuddled close. Other times, as in summer, when the room was hot as hell, said from as far apart on the mattress as they could get. Often, the sound of screaming, or glass breaking, or even suspicious quiet, would finally pull them reluctantly from their bed.

That was a long time ago, though. A death ago. But lying there now, George was again struck by a suspicious quiet, and wary of what he did not hear. Regina's mumbling was not wafting under the door, was not bumping up against the pillow he had over his head. George removed the pillow and listened. He knew she must be in the house, or out in the backyard, because she refused to go any farther than that on Saturday mornings. He got out of bed and went to the door, opening it a crack and listening. He could hear the faint sound of voices coming up from the kitchen and he thought one of the voices had an unfamiliar lilt to it, but that was a ridiculous thought to have because nobody ever came inside that house. George stepped out into the hallway and stood at the top of the stairs. Now he was sure of it. There was someone other than his family in the house. He couldn't make out anything that was being said, but all of the voices sounded calm, conversational, so he knew it could not be one of their neighbors.

He got dressed and brushed his teeth and hair, and when he got downstairs Sarah was coming out of the kitchen, and she was being followed by a woman. When they saw George, they stopped, and the woman smiled at him, with straight white teeth against the blackest skin he had ever seen.

"Morning, Daddy," Sarah said.

"Morning. Who we got here?"

"This is Paul's sister. Helena. Helena, this my father, George Delaney."

"It's good to meet you, Mr. Delaney," she said.

Her green eyes were striking against her skin and they met his with a kind of purpose George wasn't used to and didn't like, as if she were trying to see into and underneath him.

"You, too," George said, looking away from her at his daughter. "If this Paul sister, where he at?"

"Still sleep."

"Well, where y'all going?" he asked.

"I'm just showing Helena where the bathroom is."

"It's right at the top of the stairs," George said. "It aint the Taj Mahal, Sarah. It aint like she gone get lost."

While Helena found her way to the bathroom, George followed Sarah back into the kitchen. Ava was at the stove, stirring a pot of something steaming. Sarah went to the counter and started cracking eggs.

"It's so exciting having company," she said. "After all this time. The last person who came over here for a meal was Paul. Maybe she'll end up staying, like her brother did."

"Paul stayed for Ava," Regina said, from her seat at the table. "What in the world his sister gone stay for?"

"Black as the day is long, aint she?" George asked, taking a seat at the table.

Regina paused to glare at him a moment, not for any particular reason, just on general principle, before she pulled a pack of cigarettes, along with a book of matches, from her housecoat pocket.

"You want coffee, Daddy?" Sarah asked.

"Yes, thank you," George said. Then, "I didn't even know Paul had a sister. Did you know he had a sister, Ava?"

"Yes."

"Well, she don't look nothing like him. I aint never seen anybody so black in my life. Y'all ever seen anybody so black?"

They all shook their heads. None of them had ever seen anybody so black.

When Helena wasn't in the room, Ava felt a little better. Steadier. More like herself again. The strange emotions that had risen to her surface unswelled. For a few minutes. When Helena came back, the moment Ava turned to put the butter on the table and saw her coming through the kitchen door, she felt a trembling, and the butter dish shook in her hand.

When breakfast was ready, they all sat down to eat, and Ava sat on the other side of the table from Helena, at the other end, putting as much space between herself and their guest as she could.

Sarah was grinning around at all of them.

"What you so happy about?" George asked.

She shrugged. "This is nice. We don't hardly never eat together like this, sitting at the table together like a real family, the way we used to. Usually everybody take a plate and go their separate way."

"This is a nice house," Helena said.

Regina laughed. "Child, this house look like something out of a goddamn horror movie. But it's nice of you to say so."

"How come the hedges aint been cut yet?" George asked. "That front yard's starting to look as bad as the back. Paul was supposed to do that yesterday."

"That boy been working non-stop," Regina said. "He tired. Them hedges can wait."

George frowned. "They high as my collar already. Tomorrow's Sunday. I don't want people walking by on they way to church seeing it like that."

Regina put down her fork. "Why you give a damn what them people think about the hedges?"

Ava saw Helena looking from George to Regina and back.

"Paul aint had a day off in what?" Regina looked at Ava. "Two weeks?" She waved a dismissive hand at George. "Them hedges'll be fine for another couple days. If you don't like it, go cut 'em your damn self."

George glared at her. "Why you always—"

"So, what's in New York?" Sarah asked Helena, loudly.

George frowned and stabbed his fork into is eggs.

"Work," Helena replied. "A friend of mine got me an interview in a couple of weeks at a school in Harlem," Helena said. "Teaching art."

"You an artist?" Regina asked.

"I'm not that much of one. But I know enough to teach children."

"I love art," Sarah said. She was sitting so far out on the edge of her chair, she looked ready to tip over.

"Since when?" George asked.

"I always have."

"Ava the one used to paint," Regina said.

Sarah frowned. "That was years ago."

Helena looked at Ava. "You paint?"

Ava shook her head. "I just did it a little when I was a child, I guess."

Sarah raised her voice just a notch higher than Ava's. "Was you and Paul close growing up?"

Helena nodded. "We were best friends."

"Like Ava and Geo," Regina said.

Helena looked at Ava again.

"My brother," Ava explained.

Sarah folded her arms across her chest. "He was my brother, too."

George got up from the table, taking his only-half-empty orange juice glass with him to the refrigerator, where he got out the jug and very slowly poured himself some more. Watching the dark yellow liquid as it streamed heavily into the glass, he wondered how long Paul's sister would be visiting and hoped it would not be too long. He didn't like the disruption, the uncomfortable conversation, or the curiosity in that woman's eyes.

"Does your brother live here, too?" Helena asked Sarah.

"Yeah, he do," Regina said. She looked from Ava to Sarah. "Where's your brother? I know he aint still sleep at this time of day."

Ava and Sarah did not have a brother anymore, but neither of them said a word and hoped the moment would pass without incident. It didn't.

"I better go wake him up," Regina said, standing.

Sarah and Ava both stood at the same time. Ava moved quickly to the kitchen door and stood in front of it.

"Where you going, Mama?" Sarah asked, standing directly in front of Regina. "Why don't you sit back down and finish your breakfast?"

"No. I just said I'm gone go wake Geo up. Is you deaf, girl?" Regina grabbed her daughter's shoulders and tried to move her aside. She was bigger than Sarah, but the younger woman held her ground.

"You want to go back outside and see about your tomatoes?" Ava asked.

Regina ignored Ava, her face growing strained and lined with the effort of trying to move Sarah, and Ava knew that any second her mother was going to snap and get angry and start screaming, or worse.

"How about some peppermint tea, Mama?" Sarah asked.

Regina stopped suddenly. She blinked. "Oh, yeah," she said, releasing Sarah's shoulders. "That sound good."

They were relieved to have figured out the One Thing. There was always something, one thing, that Regina really wanted at any given time. Ever since their mother had gone Saturday Morning Crazy, identifying that one thing was the only way they could get her to stop doing something they didn't want her to be doing and get her to do something else.

Sarah hurried to the stove and put on just enough water for one cup of tea, so it would boil faster. Ava helped Regina back into her chair.

Still at the refrigerator with his orange juice, George, though he tried not to, could not help remembering how often he *had* gone into his son's room on mornings like this, before school or church, to sometimes physically pull him from his bed, because the boy, from the time he was ten, refused to get up on time. "How you gone hold down a job if you can't get your ass out of bed in the morning?" George had often asked him. "Lemme tell you something, boy. It's always gone be somebody trying to lock you up, or kill you, and aint nobody ever gone give you nothing, so you better get ready to do for yourself, and that means getting up when it's time to get up. You hear me?" But the boy had never learned. He had overslept, and been late for school, on the last morning he ever saw.

1950

When the Delaneys came to Radnor Street, on a Saturday in early fall of 1950, on a cloudy morning, several of their new neighbors stood at their front windows and watched them with a kind of interest that most of them could not quite understand. It was an interest that kept them rooted in place behind windowscreens, almost unable to look away from the young family, but which, at the same time, made them hesitate to go out and say hello.

Maddy Duggard peered through her front window from across the street as they unloaded a car full of their belongings and through the steam coming up from her morning coffee she assessed them. The woman looked to be in her early twenties, though the coat she was wearing, a pretty purple dress coat with beige cuffs and a high, stylish collar, gave her an air of some maturity and sophistication, as did the way she walked and the way she held her shoulders. The man was thin and sandy, and he grasped their moving boxes with hands that were almost too large for his thin frame. A little girl sat on the front steps of the house, and two smaller children, a boy and girl, ran around on the porch. It was mostly the smallest girl who Maddy watched. Each time the child's mother took a box from the back of the old pickup they had parked out front of the house, and carried it inside, the little girl followed her. Each time the child disappeared into the house, Maddy found herself staring at the doorway in anticipation, until she appeared again. There was something about that little girl that intrigued Maddy, though she couldn't put her finger on exactly what it was. She did not know that a dozen of her neighbors were standing at the windows of their own houses, also watching this child, and trying to put their fingers on just that same thing. She also did not know the reason she remained at the window, and did not immediately go out and introduce herself to the family, as any good Christian, and any good neighbor for that matter, would. Standing there, she told herself that she *would* go over, in just a minute. She told herself that for half an hour.

Through the window, she saw Malcolm Hansberry, her two-doors-down neighbor, climb over the banister of the house that separated theirs and knock on her front door. "Come on in, Malc," she hollered.

"You been watching them, too?" Malcolm asked when he saw Maddy at the window. "That explains why you aint ready."

She looked at him, then remembered. "Oh shit! The leadership meeting."

Malcolm took her place at the window while she went to throw something on and pin up her hair. He had spent several minutes staring out of his own window at the new family moving in and it was only because he had to get ready for the meeting at the church that he hadn't gone over and introduced himself and offered to help with the boxes. At least that's why he figured he hadn't gone over. Pastor Goode always asked that they be on time for the meeting and Malcolm didn't like to keep people waiting when they were expecting him. It was bad manners. So, he had watched the young family while dressing, so as not to lose any time. There was something about that littlest girl, he had thought, standing at his window, and now thought again, standing at Maddy's window, that made him feel happy as he watched her running around, something that reminded him of the very tops of very green trees, something that recalled for him the yellow taffy his favorite aunt used to make. That something made him want to go over and say hello to the family, made him eager to do so, but still he stood there.

Maddy came back a couple of minutes later and soon she and Malcolm left the house and walked down the front steps to the sidewalk, headed for the church. Looking over at the small girl running around in circles, her arms outstretched as though she were pretending to fly, both Malcolm and Maddy felt a strange, almost physical tug, like the feeling of being moved by the wind at your back, only this wind seemed not to push but to pull, and without either of them suggesting it to the other, each altered their course mid-step and crossed the narrow street.

"Well, hi there," Maddy called as she approached the pick-up truck.

The children's mother, who was pulling a box from the bed of the truck, smiled and said, "Good morning." She was a little bit taller than Maddy and built like a country girl, with broad hips and thick calves. Her hands were elegant, long and thin. She had a wonderful face, with cheekbones cut like a cliffside, and her dark skin was the most flawless Maddy had ever seen.

"I heard somebody bought this house. I'm Maddy Duggard. I live right here." She pointed over her shoulder to the white house she and Malcolm had just exited. "This here's Malcolm Hansberry."

"I live in the green one," he said, pointing to his own house.

"Nice to meet you both," said the woman, smiling, revealing a little space between her two front teeth. "I'm Regina Delaney."

She had a heavy southern accent that sounded Alabama-esque to Malcolm and Georgia-ish to Maddy. "Where you from?" Maddy asked.

"Georgia."

"Thought so."

"But we been up here about five years now," Regina told them. "We was living over on Highland Avenue. And y'all?"

"I'm from here," Malcolm said. "Maddy's from Chicago."

"I moved up here two years ago with my husband and our children. My husband moved back a year and a half ago," Maddy said, smiling.

"Was that a good thing?" Regina asked.

"If that's my only choice, I'll say good, but really it was a *wonderful* thing," Maddy said, and all three of them laughed.

The children came down off the porch to investigate their new neighbors and Regina told Maddy and Malcolm their names and ages. Sarah was six, long-limbed and pretty, and she smiled politely at them. Ava and George Jr. were four year-old twins. George Jr., who was nicknamed Geo, was chubby-cheeked and had a quiet curiosity in his eyes as he looked up at Maddy. "How are you?" he asked her, not in the way children usually asked that, not as if he were simply saying words he had learned to say when greeting someone, but with a kind of attention and concern that Maddy had never felt coming from a child. The question felt so genuine that Maddy could not give a standard answer such as *just fine* or *good, thank you, baby*, without feeling as if she were lying, so she said the truth, which was, "I think I'm mostly okay."

Ava had large, heavy-lashed eyes and her knees were covered with scabs, some of them freshly picked-at. Up close, she was even more transfixing. There was a hum about her, almost a glow, almost a whisper, but neither of those things entirely; something unnameable that seemed to radiate from her. It warmed them up in the chilly autumn air and caused a little laugh to come up out of Maddy, unexpected.

"Oh," Maddy said. "I felt so happy all of a sudden."

Ava grinned at them, revealing the same small space between her two front teeth as her mother, and said, "Y'all got cookies?"

"Ava, go somewhere, please," Regina said.

Ava frowned up at her, then skipped away, back up onto the porch, and both Maddy and Malcolm watched her as she went. Neither found it easy to look away from her. When Regina leaned down into the truck bed to retrieve another box, Maddy and Malcolm each grabbed one, too, and followed her up the steps.

The layout of the house was the same as every other house on the block. They entered into a small foyer that led to a short hallway, off of which there was a living room, a dining room, and, at the back of the house, a good-sized kitchen. Stairs led from the foyer up to the second floor. Neither Malcolm nor Maddy knew who had owned the house before, because no one had lived in it since either of them had been on the block, but whoever they were, they sure seemed to like red.

"I never seen so many red walls," Malcolm said.

"It's one of the reasons we settled on the house," said Regina. "Ava loves color. The more of it she can get, the happier she is. If it aint no color on the walls, she'll put some on them, with crayons, or my lipstick, or whatever she can think of. This way saves us a lot of headaches."

The kitchen door swung open and the sandy man with the large hands waved at them as he came into the foyer. "Morning."

From her window, Maddy had judged him to be four or five years older than his wife and up close that estimate seemed right. He was tall and narrow-shouldered, nice-looking in spite of having big, almost bulgy eyes, and he had a smile that was friendly and seemed to hold back at the same time. He said his name was George Delaney, and Maddy and Malcolm introduced themselves.

"What brought y'all up here from Georgia?" Malcolm asked them.

"Oh, you know," George said. "It's more opportunity up here. White folks down there do everything they can to keep us from having anything."

Maddy shrugged. "White folks up here aint much better."

"They aint *much* better nowhere," George said, and they all laughed and nodded agreement on that.

"What y'all do for work?" Maddy asked.

"I'm in the streets department," George said.

"Working for the city?" Malcolm said. "That's a good deal."

"Regina works for some white folks out in Springfield, but it's a little far from here. Y'all know anybody closer to this area looking for help?"

Malcolm didn't, but Maddy thought she might know somebody. Jobs were hard to come by, though, and she thought a favor like that might be better saved for someone she knew longer than a few minutes. Just as that thought was occurring to her, Ava ran by at full speed towards the kitchen and Maddy felt warmed up again. "I know a lady over in Bala Cynwyd looking for kitchen help," she said. "I'll introduce you to her."

"Oh, thank you," said Regina, looking thrilled.

There was a tap-tapping on the screen door behind them and they all turned to see what looked like a little white girl standing with her face to the screen, her hand cupped over her eyes, trying to see inside. "Hello!" she called. "Is Maddy and Malc in there?"

Regina went and opened the screen door. The grown woman standing there was not white, but light-skinned with dyed red hair, and she was so short that she barely reached past the doorknob.

"Oh. Hi. I'm Doris Liddy. How you?"

She had seen Malcolm and Maddy making their way over to their new neighbors and had come over to remind them that they were due at the church. "Pastor hold a meeting every second Saddy morning with the leaders of the church groups," she explained to Regina, once she had been invited in. "Maddy and Malc is co-secretaries of the events board. I'm vice president of the women's group. Y'all been over to the church yet?"

"We planning on attending service tomorrow," George told her.

"Oh, good. It's always good to know God-fearing folks. In the city, you never know how people is, and I don't trust nobody that don't go to church."

"Doris, you don't hardly trust nobody that do," Maddy said.

Doris shrugged. "Well, like I say, in the city you just never know." Doris really never knew about people in the city, the country, or anywhere else. She was a naturally suspicious person and she expected that wherever people were gathered wrong-doing was taking place in some form or another. Her mother always used to say that the only thing more suspicious than a whole bunch of coloredfolks together in one place that wasn't a church was one white man by himself, anywhere. She never said how suspicious a whole bunch of white men were together, because she didn't have to.

Ava ran in from the kitchen, sounding all by herself like a herd of cattle on the wood floor, and Doris feared the little girl would run right into her and knock her down, before she stopped abruptly beside her mother. She looked up at Doris and didn't say anything.

Doris had also been among the dozen or so residents of Radnor Street watching from windows as the Delaneys moved in. She, too, had been unsure about going over to say hello, but unlike Maddy and Malcolm, she knew exactly why. It was this child. There was something about this child, something about the way she played, that Doris didn't like. It was in the way she ran, so fast and uncontrolled. It was in the reach of her arms as she spun herself around, unconcerned with bumping into things. It was in the spring of her knees as she jumped up and down on the sidewalk, not caring that if she fell it would be a hard landing. In all her movements, there was no restraint. She played as though she had no fear of falling. Doris had known that quality in younger children, babies just walking. But by this child's age, fear was supposed to have taught itself to her, and should have been present in her play. But it wasn't. That seemed to Doris to be disrespectful. To whom, she had not decided. God, maybe. Or her parents, whose job it was to keep her safe. How could you keep safe a child who played without fear? Doris didn't like it. She didn't like it from the start.

She had been raised, though, not to insult people, or their children, in their own house. So, when Maddy smiled down at the child and said, "Aint she something?" Doris nodded, without saying just what she thought that something was.

"Well, I'll be sure to let Pastor Goode know we got another nice, God-fearing family on the block. Matter fact," Doris told them, "I'll ask him to make some time to meet y'all before service tomorrow."

"That's nice of you," Regina said.

George nodded. "We happy to have such friendly neighbors."

A strange thing happened when George said the word *we*. He did not look directly at his wife, but only glanced emptily in her general direction, almost as if the word and the reality were not really connected in his mind, and Doris would have almost been confused as to what "we" he was even talking about if Regina hadn't nodded in agreement and smiled when he said it.

1976

George was glaring at Regina across the kitchen table. Regina was muttering to herself. Sarah was talking with her mouth half-full of food. Ava was sipping her coffee and looking bored. This was the scene that Paul walked in on and it was perfectly familiar, the same sort of thing you'd witness walking into the Delaney kitchen on any Saturday morning, though sometimes George would be sneering instead of glaring, Regina would be screaming rather than muttering, Sarah would be talking with her mouth entirely full rather than half-full, and Ava would be looking distracted rather than bored, which was the subtlest of differences.

He was still half-asleep and groggy, his exhaustion like a fog in his brain, and when he came into the room he did not see, at first, what was different about the scene, what was anything but familiar. It wasn't until he had blinked a few times that he realized that Ava didn't look bored at all, but rather uneasy. It was only after he had rubbed some of the sleep from his eyes that he saw that Sarah wasn't talking with food in her mouth, but rather laughing. He had to listen more closely to hear that Regina wasn't muttering to herself, but was speaking calmly. And it wasn't until he took a few more sluggish steps and could see down to the other end of the table that he realized George was not glaring at Regina at all, but at a woman who Paul was sure he was imagining, a vision from some half-finished dream.

"Paul," Sarah said, "you up."

Everyone at the table turned and looked at him.

"You got company," George said.

His sister stood up and took a few steps toward him. "Paul. I know I'm the last person you expected to see."

She had barely changed in twenty years. She was still built like a twelve year-old. Thin and flat-chested, with knobby knees beneath the hem of her skirt. Her black black skin was black as ever, her hair kinky and as short as his own, and he could almost swear that the black, horn-rimmed glasses she wore were the same ones she'd had at twelve. She couldn't be real, he thought. He shook his head, and waited for the dream to fade away.

"Paul, what the hell's the matter with you?" Regina said. "You going nutty or something?"

Paul looked at his mother-in-law. "What?"

"It's your sister. Aint you gone say hello?"

The sleep-fog lifted and Paul stared wide-eyed at Helena. "It is you," he said.

She nodded.

"Aint this something?" Sarah asked.

The smile that pulled across Paul's face felt tight, almost painful. "Yeah, it's something, alright."

"I know you weren't expecting to see me," Helena said again.

He shook his head. "How'd you know where to find me?"

"I asked around the old block. Somebody knew somebody who knew where you lived." She smiled. "You look just the same."

He was sure he looked nothing like his scrawny, fifteen-year-old self. He looked around at all of them at the table, at their half-eaten breakfasts. "How long you been here?"

"Not long. I didn't want to wake you, and Sarah said you'd be up soon."

He wouldn't have gotten up at all, would have slept for hours more, if not for the fact that the temperature in the house had risen so much that he'd woken up dripping sweat and couldn't get back to sleep.

"You hungry?" George asked. "Ava, get the man something to eat."

"That's okay, baby, I aint hungry," Paul said to Ava, who hadn't moved anyway. "Where you been living?" he asked his sister.

"Baltimore," she said. "After Uncle Reese died, Aunt Vicky moved down there to be closer to her family, and she took me with her."

"Uncle died, huh?"

She nodded. "Stroke."

"That's a shame," he said, and wondered if he sounded sincere.

"She on her way to New York," Sarah said. "For a teaching job."

"You a teacher?" he asked. "A real one?"

"Sure."

"You went to college, then?"

She nodded.

This time his smile came easy.

"Y'all sit down," Regina said. "You know I don't like people hovering around the table like that."

Helena took her seat and Paul went and grabbed an extra chair from the dining room and placed it next to Ava. "I'm surprised anybody from the old block knows where I am," he said. "I aint been back around the neighborhood much since right after I turned eighteen. Without you and Mama there it aint feel like home no more. Which was real bad for me, 'cause I was dying for a little bit of home right then."

"Well, it looks like you found it," Helena said, glancing at her brother's wife. She asked how long Ava and Paul had been married and what they both did for work. When Paul said they'd both worked at the art museum, and that Ava still did, Helena said, "I tried to get a job there when I was a teenager. My best friend worked there and she talked me up to her boss. He hired me over the phone. But when he saw me, he changed his mind. He said I was so black I'd distract people from the art. He said that to my friend, not to me. He told me he'd forgotten he'd promised the job to somebody else."

George looked down at his plate.

Sarah shifted her weight on her chair, then reached for her coffee.

Paul remembered the trouble his sister's skin had caused them as children, the fights he got into almost daily in her defense, the fights she got into herself.

"Does my brother ever talk about me?" Helena asked Ava, glancing at Paul.

"Of course I do," Paul said. "That's a silly question."

"I aint heard you mention her but two or three times," Regina said. "In what? Five years?"

"Mama, drink your tea," Sarah said. "It's getting cold."

When they were done eating breakfast, Helena went to use the bathroom, and the second she was gone, Sarah cornered Paul at the sink, where he was stacking plates. "Aint you gone ask your sister to stay?"

"What you mean, stay? She on her way to New York for a job."

"Yeah, and she said that interview aint for two weeks. I know she'd like to stay for at least a few days. You aint seen her in nearly twenty years. You'd feel awful if you let her go away from you again so soon."

"Sarah, stop telling people how they supposed to feel," George said. "If Paul don't want her here, that's his business."

"It aint that I don't want her here—"

"But they ought to spend at least a week catching up," Sarah said.

"Three seconds ago it was a few days," George said, "now it's a week?"

Paul shook his head. "I won't have no time to spend with her. I'm working every day and almost every night."

Sarah waved a dismissive hand. "I got the weekend off, and Ava's off Monday. We can take care of her when you aint here. Can't we, Ava?"

Ava shrugged. "I don't know. I guess. If that's what Paul wants."

He mistook her unusual uneasiness for her usual indifference and in this matter it was welcome. He didn't want to be pressured about this. It wasn't that he didn't love his sister, that he hadn't missed her, but he knew it seemed that way. Sarah was peering at him and he knew she was wondering why he was so reluctant. It just wasn't right to see your only sister again after so many years and not be happy. It wasn't that he wasn't happy. It wasn't that.

❖ ❖ ❖

Paul opened the windows in every room, and the back door, trying to lure a breeze. He had never known it to be so hot inside that house. It was always cold in there, even in summer. He sat with his sister at the kitchen table, smoking and listening to her tell about Baltimore, piecing in some of the parts of her life that he had missed. George had said he was going to read the paper and left. When Ava and Sarah finished cleaning up, Ava left, too, mumbling something about housework, but Regina and Sarah stayed, and it was mostly Sarah who asked questions and engaged Helena, while Paul listened. She told them how she had put herself through college while working for a doctor's family, helping the wife, who was sickly, with their four children. After she had finished school, she had started teaching third grade and had taught it for four years before leaving.

"Aint you gone miss your students?" Sarah asked her.

"Yes. But it was time to move on," she said. "And I've always wanted to move back to New York. I lived there for a couple of years when I was in my early twenties." She looked at her brother then. "What about you, Paul? Have you been in Philadelphia all this time?"

He nodded. "I thought about moving somewhere else after I...well, when I turned eighteen. But everybody I knew was here, and I guess I aint much of a wanderer."

"A little wandering can be good for the soul, I think," Helena said. "But so can the places you know, the places that know you."

"I don't know about Philly being good for nobody's soul," Paul said. "But the cheesesteaks is good."

They all laughed at that, including Regina, who was still sitting at the table. They looked over at her and it was plain that she wasn't laughing with them. She was still staring down into the cup of peppermint tea that Sarah had reminded her to drink half an hour ago. She hadn't looked up from it in all that time. They heard her say something that sounded like, "Maddy, I miss you."

"Is your mother alright?" Helena whispered.

Sarah shook her head no and glanced at the clock on the wall above the kitchen door. "But she ought to be pretty soon."

"Paul, why don't we take a walk," Helena said. "Would you mind, Sarah? If I had a little time alone with my brother?'

"Oh. I guess not."

Paul frowned. Walking was the last thing he felt like doing. Next to being alone with his sister.

There was history in the peppermint tea. There was years ago in it. Staring down into it, Regina could see people and things long gone. Right there on the surface of the tea, she could see the kitchen reflected, but it was not the kitchen where she now sat. Gathered around the table were her children, all three of them together as they had not been in almost twenty years. A younger incarnation of Regina herself stood by the stove, watching them, and the lack of worry, the absence of fear in that Regina's eyes made the Regina sitting at the table want to call out to her other self, to ask her how she dared look so unafraid when the end of the world was coming. She opened her mouth to say something to her, something like, "Why don't you see?" but the image in the teacup changed then, and instead of her children around the table she saw Maddy's face. Her old friend, smiling and laughing, the way Maddy always used to, as if she'd just told one of those raunchy stories she always liked to tell about her good for nothing ex-husband, the laughter causing her shoulders to shake as she threw her head back. "Maddy," Regina whispered to her, "I miss you, girl." But the Maddy in the tea could not hear her. Regina hunched down closer to the cup and watched the image on the tea's surface change again. Reflected there now was the main sanctuary of Blessed Chapel Church of God, on a Sunday, packed with worshippers, all of them on their feet and clapping as the choir sang, feet stomping and tambourines shaking and arms reaching up in exaltation. The light through the stained-glass windows threw sunstreaked color on the heads of the congregation, who sang and shouted about the glory of the Lord. Regina could not hear the song, but the movement of the bodies sounded to her like *His Eye Is On the Sparrow*. It had been Geo's favorite hymn and Regina could remember, back when he was in the children's choir, the way he would lift his voice and close his eyes at the refrain. *"His eye is on the sparrow, and I know he watches me."* When this image also faded from the tea, no new scene replaced it. Regina sat there at the kitchen table, still staring into the cup, and she could feel her head clearing now, her mind coming uncluttered. As she came back to her sanity, as it moved through her with purpose, like a spirit coming through a dark house out into the day, she got up from the table and left the kitchen, walking through the foyer and up the stairs to her bedroom, and she could still hear Geo's voice, singing those words that, now, after everything, only mocked him. *"I sing because I'm happy. I sing because I'm free."*

Regina emerged from her bedroom a little while later and when she walked by the bathroom she saw Ava on the floor, on her knees, scrubbing the bathtub. She leaned against the doorframe and watched her daughter, who was sweating in the warmth of the small space. When Ava paused to wipe sweat from her brow, she saw her mother there and she knew immediately that Regina had changed. "You back, Mama?" she asked.

Regina nodded. "I'm back."

To anybody who didn't know Regina, she would have been unrecognizable from only a few minutes ago. Her hair was combed now, and held in a neat bun at the back of her head. She had changed out of her tattered housecoat, into a plain cotton dress, all the buttons of which were fastened correctly. The most stark difference, though, was the look in her eyes. It was steady now. Clear. Almost Normal.

"Didn't Sarah clean that tub yesterday?" Regina asked.

"Did she?"

Regina nodded.

Ava sighed, then looked thoughtful. "Mama, what did you mean before, when you said you thought I was the one I used to be? Do you remember saying that, at the door?"

"I think so," Regina said. "But I was probably just talking nonsense, Ava. You know better than to listen to anything I say when I'm like that."

"I know. But the way you looked at me, it was like you really saw something."

"I don't know what I thought I saw, but maybe I was thinking about how you was when you was young."

"What do you mean? How was I?"

"You remember how wild you was. How happy."

"Was I?" Ava asked. "I don't remember that."

Regina shrugged. "Well. People change. Girls grow up."

Still, Ava thought, she should be able to remember being wild and happy. She was only aware of ever being exactly as she was now. That bothered her, although she wasn't exactly sure that there was something to be bothered about. In the doorway with Helena, though, just for a moment, she *had* felt wild. And happy.

It was still early, not yet noon, but the sun had burned off the morning chill and the air outside had become warm and soft. Paul and Helena walked down towards Fifty-Eighth Street, towards the park at the end of the block.

"You lied to your family about where you went when we split up," Helena said.

Paul stopped walking, looked at her. "Y'all talked about that?"

"I didn't tell them where you really went, if that's what you're asking."

He was relieved. "I don't want them knowing nothing about it. Juvie was the worst time of my life and I don't want to think about it, let alone tell nobody."

"Even your wife?"

He didn't answer.

"Will you tell me about it?"

He took his hands from his pockets and folded his arms across his chest. "If I was gone tell anybody, it'd be you. But I'm not."

They walked on, farther down the block, and Paul noticed people on their porches looking out at them. Audrey Jackson and Lillian Morgan, older ladies who had lived on the block for decades and who Paul knew had been friends of his in-laws long years ago, now only stared and whispered whenever Paul or anyone in his family walked by, and today was no exception. Vic Jones, the burly, middle-aged bus driver who lived across the street and always had a menacing look to offer any one of the Delaneys, leaned over his porch railing, his arms folded across his chest, his eyes narrowed. Paul remembered the brick through the window, which had been pushed from his mind by his sister's arrival.

"Well, then tell me about Ava," Helena said. "What's she like?"

"She's steady. Easy. She aint all moody and emotional like most women are."

"Really? Hmm. I thought I sensed some...complexity in her."

"Ava?" He shook his head. "I wouldn't ever call her *complex*. With Ava, what you see is what you get. There aint too many surprises."

"Oh," Helena said. "I wonder what gave me that idea."

"Well, what about you? You aint never got married or had kids or nothing?"

"I don't know about 'or nothing,'" she said. "But no, I never got married or had kids."

"You still got time. You aint but thirty."

The park was almost empty of people, but the few who were there, sitting on the scattered benches, stared openly at them as they walked by. The looks Paul usually got from his neighbors, looks of disapproval and disdain, were now accompanied by double-takes at his sister, and outright gawking. Paul glanced at Helena, who seemed to notice but not to be bothered about it, and he realized how used she must have gotten to being stared at. It had always bothered her as a child, but over so many years she must have learned to ignore it.

As they circled through the park, Helena suddenly asked, "Are you happy, Paul?"

He shrugged. "I love my wife, and I got steady work, so, yeah, I guess I'm happy as I can be. What about you? You happy?"

She shook her head. "No. I'm not. But I'm trying to be."

"Seems like you doing alright, though," he said. "Better than a lot of people I know."

She frowned. "Do you know how much I have come to hate that word? *Seems*. People use 'seems' to keep from having to really know anything. They just decide how something seems and they don't have to look any deeper, or go any further, or ask any uncomfortable questions."

"Hold on, now," he said, stopping at the end of a path, "I aint seen you in almost twenty years and you aint been here two hours yet, so if I aint asking the right questions fast enough, you can feel free to just come on out and tell me why you here, why you showed up after all this time. You aint got to wait for me to ask."

She looked surprised and a little hurt. He wasn't trying to hurt her, but he didn't know how to communicate with this woman who was his sister, but who he did not know. She sighed, and shook her head slightly as if answering a question that had not been asked. "I don't feel like walking anymore," she said.

"Me, either."

They abandoned their walk and went back to the house and when they reached the bottom of the stairs Helena caught sight of the broken window. "What happened there?"

He walked past her up the steps. "Some kids messing around out here, I guess," he said, because that was the last thing he felt like explaining right then.

Helena's train was leaving at two. Ava came downstairs to say goodbye. She'd spent the last hour in her bedroom, thinking about what her mother had said. She thought that maybe if she looked at Helena again, really looked at her, she would see what she had seen, and feel what she had felt, that first moment at the door, and would understand it. She stood before her now, in the foyer, and although she still felt a little bit lightheaded, a little bit off-kilter, she did not feel the thing that had surged up in her and made her kiss a strange woman on the mouth. She frowned, a little disappointed.

"Well," she said to Helena, "have a safe trip."

"Thank you, Ava."

"Promise you'll come and see us again," Sarah said, looking unhappy, and Helena promised she would.

Paul had offered to accompany his sister to the train station down at Thirtieth Street and now he grabbed her suitcase and portfolio and walked behind her out the door.

They made it as far as the front porch before Ava rushed out after them. "Stay a few days," she said.

Both Helena and Paul turned and looked at her. She could not read the look on Helena's face, but Paul looked confused.

"Y'all can really catch up," Ava said. "Wouldn't that be nice, Paul?"

Paul hesitated. Then nodded. "I guess so."

"It's not too much trouble?" Helena asked, looking at Paul, not Ava. "Y'all have room?"

"We can make it work," Ava said.

Sarah looked ready to shit with excitement. "This is wonderful!" she shrieked. "You can take my room, Helena, and I'll sleep with Mama."

Helena insisted she was an easy guest and that she didn't want them going to any trouble for her. "You'll probably forget I'm here," she said. But it did not turn out that way at all.

❖ ❖ ❖

"What's Baltimore like?" Sarah asked Helena. They were sitting on the back porch steps now, drinking iced tea and smoking, because the kitchen had become too hot for habitation.

"It's not that different from Philadelphia," Helena told her. "Smaller. They have good seafood. Especially crab legs."

"Ooh," Sarah said.

Paul rolled his eyes. Sarah was spreading it on thick. What was so special, all of a sudden, about crab legs?

"What do you do, Miss Sarah?" Helena asked.

"You mean for work?"

"Sure. But also tell me what you do for play. What makes you happy when you do it."

Sarah was not used to anyone showing any real interest in her. She had spent her life from aged two to fifteen being stuck in the shadow of Ava's specialness, and the years since stuck in the shadow of Geo's death, and she could not recall, in all of her adult life, ever being asked what she did that made her happy. She told Helena that she worked at a bank as a teller and had for several years. As for what she did that made her happy, she said there was nothing.

"But there must be. Think harder."

She thought harder. "I don't know. I like to knit. I make sweaters in the winter."

"Does that make you happy?"

Sarah shrugged. She felt disappointed that she couldn't come up with anything, not because it meant that there was nothing in her life that made her happy, which there wasn't, but because she feared she couldn't hold the interest of the only person who had shown any interest in her in a very long time. Worried that Helena would think she was unworthy of her attention, she blurted out, "I used to love a man who was happy about fire."

Helena clapped her hands together, delighted. "Tell me."

"It's silly," Sarah said.

"That's all the better," Helena assured her.

Paul, who had never imagined that Sarah had loved any man, leaned forward a little on the step.

Sarah hesitated. She had never told anyone about the man before. "This was years ago," she said. "Back in sixty-nine. When I used to work way down in Old City, at the bank on Chestnut. At lunch time, in the summer, I used to walk down to Penn's Landing. There was a man I always walked by. A street performer. A fire-eater. People was always gathered around him, watching him do his tricks. At first, I never stopped. I thought it was stupid, I thought he should go get a real job. But every time I walked by, I'd see the fire out the corner of my eye and wonder how he did it."

Helena was holding her iced tea, but she wasn't drinking it, and she looked mesmerized by Sarah's story.

"One day, after I had walked by him, I was sitting on a bench eating my lunch and it started to rain, so I ran and stood under this awning. It wasn't raining hard, but I didn't have no umbrella, and I didn't want my hair to get wet and have to go back to work looking like a drowned rat. From where I was standing, I could see him doing his fire thing. He wasn't but twenty feet away. The crowd had left soon as it started raining, so it was just him there by hisself and he kept performing. I watched him. The way he held the fire, the way he was so gentle with it, you'd have thought it was alive, and fragile. He sort of caressed it. He looked at it with a kind of love in his eyes. I watched him juggle his batons, and not one of them went out in the rain. Then he opened his mouth wide and ate the fire from every one of them. It was so wonderful that I started clapping. He turned around and saw me there and he smiled. And, Lord, was he handsome. Scruffy-looking, like an alley cat, but he had a sweet face. He bowed a few times and I knew he wanted me to give him some money, so I threw a few coins in his hat. After that I would stop all the time and watch him do his fire tricks, and I'd stand at the back of the crowd."

"Did you ever talk to him?" Paul asked.

"No. That one time, I'm sure he was just glad to have somebody to perform for and be able to make a little bit of money in the rain. But he never paid me no mind when there was a whole crowd of people throwing money in his hat."

"Seem like you would have tried to talk to him, if you liked him so much," Paul said. He had always thought Sarah was a pretty woman, if a little skinny, and he knew for sure that men were interested in her, because sometimes when his buddies from work saw her they'd ask Paul if she was going with anybody. Whenever they'd smile at her and try to start a conversation, though, she would act cold and unfriendly. She never believed Paul when he told her they were interested in her, no matter how much he assured her that they were.

Sarah shrugged. "It wasn't nothing but a silly little crush. I left that job a year later and I aint really thought about him since," she said, which wasn't true.

"We had a cousin who juggled," Helena said. "Remember, Paul?"

He nodded. "Just oranges, though, and they wasn't on fire."

When, a few minutes later, Paul went inside to use the bathroom, he found Ava in their bedroom, sweeping under their bed, and he accused her of avoiding his sister."I'm not avoiding anybody," she told him.

"You the one asked her to stay," Paul said.

"I know."

"Then what's wrong? Why you acting all—" he started to say *nervous*, but it wasn't a word he had ever used to describe Ava before, ever, and it felt strange even to think it. Nervousness required a level of worry, of concern about things, that Ava just didn't have. "Strange," he said, finally.

"I'm not acting strange," she insisted, and continued to sweep under the bed.

Paul sighed. Maybe it was him. Maybe the surprise of Helena's appearance and the fact that he had barely slept in twenty-four hours was making him see things that weren't there. He felt suddenly overwhelmed with tired and he sat down on the bed. For a few moments, he watched Ava sweeping, watched the ends of the straw broom as it scratched against the worn wood floor. "Ava, I lied to you about something," he said, without knowing he was going to say it.

"About what?"

He continued to watch the broom ends, noticing the way they caught in the cracks that had split into the wood after so many years of nobody taking care of the floors.

"When me and my sister got separated, I didn't go live with my cousin like I told you. I went to jail."

She didn't even look up from her sweeping. "Jail?"

He nodded. "Well, juvie."

"Why? What for?"

He sighed a long sigh and shook his head. "Baby, I aint ready to tell you all that yet." He knew she would not press him, though some little part of him wanted her to. He rubbed his eyes with his fists, like a child.

"You need to rest," she said.

He nodded, lay back on the bed, and was asleep.

When Ava got to the back screen door, she saw Helena alone out on the back porch, sitting on the top step, smoking, her head leaned back against the wooden porch railing, staring out at the overgrown yard. Paul was wrong. She hadn't been avoiding his sister. She had been trying to think of a way to talk to her, to broach the subject of what had happened at the door that morning. Now she stepped out onto the porch. "Where's Sarah?" she asked Helena.

"Your mother needed something, so she went inside to help her," Helena said. "Where's Paul?"

"'Sleep."

"Oh," she said. "Good. I thought he was going to pass out on the steps here a little while ago. Does he work nights a lot?"

"A lot lately. He wants us to get our own house," Ava said.

"*He* wants?" she asked. "You don't want that?"

Ava shook her head.

Helena took a drag off her cigarette. Smoke filled the air between them and then blew away on a warm breeze.

"I'm sorry about what happened this morning," Ava said. "At the door. I haven't really been feeling like myself today."

Helena grinned. "Who have you been feeling like? Someone who kisses strangers who show up at their door?" She shrugged. "Well, stranger things have happened."

"Stranger things have happened to you than showing up on the doorstep of the brother you haven't seen in twenty years and being kissed on the mouth by a woman you've never seen before who turns out to be his wife? Baltimore must be a lot more interesting than it sounds."

Helena laughed, but Ava didn't really see the humor in any of it. Helena seemed to realize that and said, "I'm sorry, Ava. I'm not making fun of you. You've just looked very serious and concerned since it happened and I'm trying to lighten the mood a little. It was odd. But I'm sure there's a simple reason for it."

Ava had not considered there was a simple reason. Thinking about it now, she could not come up with one, either. "Like what?"

"Maybe you saw Paul in me and were drawn to that. And you...reached out...in a way that seemed strange afterwards, but was just a natural impulse at the time. An embracing of the qualities of my brother that are in me."

Ava did not think that answer was at all simple. Or at all true, for that matter. She was sure she had not seen Paul. Paul had never inspired that kind of behavior in her. She thought about saying that, but changed her mind. She wanted to know, wanted to really understand, what had happened, and why, but she did not want to push. Especially since Helena seemed so unconcerned about it. They may as well have been talking about the weather, with the way she sat there, smoking her cigarette and casually flicking the cinders into the ashtray at her feet.

"Anyway, it was just one moment, and it passed, so you don't need to feel embarrassed about it, or nervous."

But then Ava saw something. Still with that amused look on her face, Helena leaned down to tap her cigarette ash into the ashtray. And her hand shook. No, not shook. *Trembled.* She looked up at Ava and for a moment her façade of unconcern failed and Ava saw a flash of worry in her eyes.

"Now, speaking of my brother," Helena said, "why don't you come sit down here and talk to me about him." She patted the weather-worn step beside her. "Would you?"

Ava did not want to talk about Paul. Still, she came and sat down on the step.

Helena picked up the pack of cigarettes that was by her feet and offered her one.

Ava shook her head. "I don't smoke."

She looked surprised. "Paul smokes like a chimney. You don't mind it? I think I'd hate to be with somebody who smoked if I didn't."

"My parents smoke," Ava said. "My sister. I'm used to it."

"But you never picked it up?"

"I don't get addicted to things."

"Ever?"

Ava shook her head, no.

Helena took another long drag off her cigarette. "Then, you're lucky."

There was the ring of an ice cream truck bell in the distance and it almost reminded Ava of something, only the memory, whatever it was, was distant and faint as the bell and she couldn't settle on it.

"How did you meet Paul?" Helena asked her.

"At the museum. He used to work there, too."

She nodded. "That's right. You said that. Did he find you standing under a Caravaggio, or something very romantic like that?"

"He found me in the cafeteria, serving macaroni and cheese."

"And how'd you know he was the one?"

"The one?" Ava asked. "I didn't."

Helena laughed. "I'm being silly, I guess. I haven't seen my brother in a long time. I just want to know that he's found love and that it's all soft and romantic, and that he's happy and taken care of."

"I don't know how soft and romantic it is," Ava said, "but we take care of each other."

"No children, though? Do you mind if I ask why?"

"I don't mind. I can't have children. I stopped bleeding a long time ago."

"I'm sorry," Helena said.

It had happened when she was twenty, suddenly and for no reason her doctor could discern. It had never been a source of great upset for her, because she had never thought much about having children and she told Helena that. "I don't think about children anyway."

"What about Paul?"

Ava's first thought was that Paul was fine about it. When she had told him, back before they were married, he had said it didn't matter that much to him and she had taken his word for it. But sitting there now, thinking about it, she felt unsure. "Now that I think about it, sometimes he seems disappointed."

"*Now* that you think about it? You never thought about it before now?"

It was an absurd question. Of course she had thought about it before. When she tried to recall when she had thought about it, though, or just what she had thought, she could not. And the fact that she could not remember ever once having considered her husband's feelings about having children, or not having them, made her feel uneasy, and ashamed, which were two more things she couldn't remember ever feeling before, even though she knew she must have.

Helena was watching her, curiously, her head tilted slightly to one side the way Paul's did when he was trying to figure something out.

"Of course I've thought about it," Ava lied.

Sarah came out of the house then, smiling and looking eager, holding an ice cream cone in each hand. When she saw Ava, her smile melted a little around the edges like the ice cream did around the sides.

"I didn't know you was finished cleaning, Ava," she said. "I only got two."

Ava didn't care and she said as much.

Sarah handed Helena one of the cones, and as Ava watched them both licking the cool treats, she remembered sitting with her siblings on the front steps, eating ice cream, which had been her favorite thing, a thing she had craved and begged her mother for every time the ice cream truck came around. She remembered how she had loved the sweetness, had held each bite in her mouth until it melted into nothing on her tongue. She remembered how she had savored each and every lick.

"It's a nice day out," Sarah was saying.

Ava noticed she sounded happy, which was unusual. Unusual for Sarah to sound happy and unusual for Ava to notice.

"I don't know why it's so hot inside the house," Sarah continued.

"Don't you like ice cream?" Helena asked Ava.

Ava shook her head. "No," she said, and she recognized the strangeness of her words as she said them. "It doesn't really taste like anything to me."

Regina had gone to the kitchen to take out the frozen meat for that night's dinner, to let it thaw, and she saw through the window her daughters sitting out on the porch with Paul's sister. As she watched them, George came in and stood beside her at the sink. "You back?" he asked.

"I'm back."

He peered out the window. "She still here? I thought she had a train to catch."

"She's staying a little while. To catch up with her brother."

George frowned.

"I'm glad," Regina said. "Look how happy Sarah looks. And Ava. I aint seen Ava so interested in anybody or anything in seventeen years."

George shrugged. "I don't know what they think is so interesting about her. I don't like her. She rubs me the wrong way."

Regina waved a dismissive hand at him. "She a nice girl."

"How you know what kind of girl she is? We don't know her. Her own brother don't even know her. He aint seen her in twenty years. Who knows what she came here for?"

She rolled her eyes. "What you think she came here for, George? To swindle us out of our family fortune?"

"Why you always got to have a sarcastic answer for everything?"

"Because you looking for a reason not to like her."

"Why would I?"

"Because she here. Because she seem to want to know us, and deep down you think it's something wrong with anybody who want to be around us, who don't treat us like Pastor Goode and the rest of 'em. You was the same way with Paul when he first started coming around."

"That's ridiculous," George said, and he believed it was. He didn't like the woman because of her questions. Watching through the window now, as she talked to Ava and Sarah, he saw that same searching in her eyes as she had when she looked at all of them. He wondered what it was she was searching for and, no matter what Regina said, he felt sure she wasn't there just to catch up with her brother. "How long is a few days?" he asked.

Regina shrugged.

George sighed and shook his head, just as Helena's eyes met his through the window.

1950

Blessed Chapel Church of God stood near the corner of Fifty-Ninth and Radnor, right at the end of the block, and both Regina and George felt good about living on a street with a church. It was another reason they had chosen the house. They were both still a little uneasy about living in the city. The block they had just moved from, and the neighborhood that surrounded it, over in southwest Philadelphia, had been plagued with crime. In the five years they had been there, there had been a murder only a few blocks away from their house, and several muggings, two of them at their own corner. And while they both believed that the good Lord watched over them no matter where they were or what they were doing—or, at least, while Regina believed that; George felt there were some places the Lord would not go, some things the Lord would not watch—they both felt that having a church right on the corner made the street safer. The very first Sunday after they moved onto Radnor Street, they went to join Blessed Chapel.

It was a large church, twice the size of the church they had attended for the last five years and four or five times the size of the church they had grown up in, down in Hayden. It was made of stone and mortar and stood two stories high. It had a huge, cool, sunken basement with several rooms, including two changing rooms for choir members, two classrooms, a kitchen where meals were cooked and sold on Sundays and holidays, and a chapel and altar, behind which there was a baptismal pool. On the upper floor, there was a large, main chapel, where Sunday service took place. It had thirty pews and two choir boxes. The carpeting in the sanctuary was dark red and lush. There was a large pulpit, with an organ and a piano. All the windows around the main chapel were stained-glass and each depicted a scene from the New Testament: the baby Jesus in a manger, the Last Supper, the Crucifixion, Resurrection, and Ascension. Behind the pulpit, there was a small room where the pastor could wait before going out to deliver his sermons.

"It's good to meet a nice, church going young couple," Pastor Ollie Goode told Regina and George, sitting in the little room behind the pulpit. They could hear the voices of children rising up from the basement where the youngest Sunday School students were taught, singing *Jesus Loves Me, This I Know.* "What church did y'all go to down in Hayden?"

"Deliverance," George said. "You probably aint heard of it."

"Reverend Michaels' church?"

"That's right," George said, looking at Regina, who also looked surprised.

The pastor sat back in his chair and smiled at them. He was a handsome man, around forty, balding and virile-looking, with penny-colored skin and hazel eyes, and dimples in his cheeks that appeared when he smiled, which he did often. "Maddy Duggard says y'all got three little ones."

Regina nodded. "We got a six year-old and four year-old twins. They down at Sunday School."

"That's wonderful. I got one of my own." He pointed to a framed photograph of a boy around the twins' ages, grinning at the camera. "They sure are a gift from the Lord," he said. "Even when they running you ragged, which is most of the time." He had a deep, soft laugh that reached up into his eyes.

George asked about the size of the congregation at Blessed Chapel, and Pastor Goode said they were over three-hundred now.

"You a young pastor for a church this size," George said.

"I was a junior minister until my father passed last year. It was sudden and I think the congregation wanted somebody in the pulpit that reminded them of him. Truth be told, I almost said no. I was worried I wouldn't be able to fill his shoes. But Linda—that's my wife; you'll meet her—she reminded me that when the Lord calls, whenever and wherever he calls, we must answer."

Service that first Sunday was magnificent. Later, years later, Regina remembered thinking of it just that way. *Magnificent.* The congregation was full and friendly and people stopped on the way to their seats to greet the Delaneys, to welcome them to the church and to the block. They were a sundry group, from the elders who had been leaders of the church since it had been built in the 1920s, and who now claimed the front rows of pews, their shoulders straight and dignified in their Sunday bests, the women in their black or brown or, more often, stone-gray wigs, and the men, whose canes often matched the colors of their dark suits, to their grandchildren, who made up the young adult choral, and who, no matter how much they were fussed at about it, always slouched in the pews, their legs stretching out into the aisles, their attention focused more on each other than anything else. The bulk of the congregation, though, was the generation that linked them, men and women who were Regina's and George's ages, with small children. These were the Liddys, Doris and Dexter, who lived next door to the Delaneys, with their two children, Sondra and Evan, and who spent all their free time involved with the church; the Browns, Sam and Alice, who lived across the street with their teenage daughters, Antoinette and Lonette, and who were both ushers at Sunday service; the Ellises, Charles and Lena, he a deacon and she a deacon's wife, and their son and daughter, David and Marlene; the Mitchells, Hattie and Ernest, and their children, Louise, Mary, and Carl, also next-door-neighbors of the Delaneys, and Sunday school teachers every single one; Jane Lucas, a young widow with a small son, Rudy, who lived a few doors up from the Delaneys and was a teacher at the elementary school a few blocks away; and Maddy Duggard, whose husband had taken off and left her with two children, Jack and Ellen, and whose mother, Henrietta, was helping her to raise them; and besides them a dozen more, most of whom—though the Delaneys did not know it—had been peering through their windows as they had unloaded their belongings the previous day. Most of them still did not understand what it was that had made them hesitate for just over half an hour that first morning. Doris was among the few who could name it, who could attribute it to the lack of fear she saw in the four-year-old Ava, but even she could not say exactly why it made her so uneasy. Whatever the reason was, once the ice was broken with the new family, once Maddy and Malcolm and Doris had all gone over, most everyone else on the block made their way over, too, their hesitation giving way to the happy, warmed-up feelings most of them got from watching the little girl. Vic Jones, who was Malcolm's half-brother, had been the next to stop by, and he had been followed by Grace and Eddie Kellogg. By that first night, the Mitchells, Jane Lucas, Maddy's mother, Henrietta, and a dozen more had come. Once they were with the Delaneys, drinking coffee in their kitchen, tasting the cobbler Regina had thrown together, or sharing something they had baked and brought over as a welcome, most had quickly forgotten their strange hesitation. Up close, the good feelings Ava inspired had been doubled, tripled in some cases. Grace Kellogg found that the little girl's laugh somehow reminded her of the pajamas she had worn as a child—thick, feet-in pajamas that had kept her warm in the drafty house her family had lived in for many years. Looking into Ava's eyes, Jane Lucas remembered the smile of her love, her young husband, who had died in the war. When Ava tripped and fell over the edge of the rug while running by at full speed, Chuck Ellis lifted her up and in that moment he was sure he smelled morning, though it was six in the evening at the time. These were the people who made up the congregation of Blessed Chapel and who went out of their way that first Sunday to make the Delaneys welcome, rearranging themselves on the fifth pew from the front to offer the family good seats, close to the pulpit and the choir box, the latter of which was filled that morning with members of the Women's Choir.

They opened the service with song, a slow song that got everybody settled, and then an elderly deacon led them all in prayer, before, finally, Pastor Goode appeared and began the sermon. He spoke about friendship, about home and community, and the soft light through the stain-glassed windows fell against his dark robe so that it glowed like embers. When the choir sang again, the song was bigger, and livelier, and everyone got up out of their seats and sang along, clapping their hands and stomping their feet, shaking their tambourines. The floor shook beneath them. Their voices soared.

When the service was over, Regina and George took their children up to meet the pastor. They waited at the back of a small crowd of folks offering their compliments on the sermon, or asking the pastor for his prayers, either for themselves or someone they knew who was going through hard times. When Hattie Mitchell asked him to pray for her mother, who had fallen ill the week before, Pastor good took Hattie's hand. "I been praying for her ever since I heard," he said. "And me and Linda gone stop by your house tomorrow evening so we can all pray together. Until then, know that the Lord is with you, and no matter how bad things seem, he will always make a way."

When the Delaneys got to the front of the crowd, Regina introduced the children. Pastor Goode shook Sarah's hand, and Geo's, but Regina saw him hesitate, just a fraction of a moment, before reaching out for Ava's. When he finally did, he did so smiling, but Ava, either because she had sensed his hesitation, or for some other reason altogether, did not take the pastor's hand when it was offered. Instead, she folded her arms across her chest. The pastor's smile faltered and Regina saw a flash of anger in his eyes.

"Ava, what's wrong with you?" George asked. "You know better than that."

Pastor Goode chuckled. "Oh, it's alright. She's probably just tired after the long service. It's my fault for droning on so long."

Regina and George laughed with him, assuring him that the sermon had been wonderful, the best sermon they'd heard in years.

"Well, I'm glad y'all are here to receive it," he said. He reached out and patted the top of Ava's head and grinned cheerfully at her.

Many years later, though, Regina would think back on that one moment, and the flash of anger in the eyes of that preacher, and she would wish she taken her children and walked out of there right then, and never joined that church.

1976

Ava had trouble keeping her eyes off Helena. Sitting at the dinner table, listening to her husband's sister talking about some of the places she had been and some of the things she had seen in the last many years, Ava found herself staring and wondering what it was about this person, this woman who seemed unextraordinary except for the extreme blackness of her skin, that had made her behave the way she had at the door that morning. She could not understand it. Helena seemed smart and friendly and funny, joking with Sarah and Regina and reminiscing with Paul, but there was nothing about her that struck Ava as particularly special. And though Ava did not think of herself as someone who noticed specialness in people, she thought there should be something about Helena that stood out to her, something that explained it. But there wasn't. She began to feel that she had imagined it all. As if what had happened at the door that morning had been a strange hiccup of emotions, coincidental to Helena's arrival and completely unrelated to it. She considered that for several minutes, and then Helena turned, in the middle of a story about her third grade class back in Baltimore, and looked right at Ava, right into her eyes, and Ava felt an urge to reach out and touch her that was so extreme she had to push herself back farther in her chair and grip the sides to stop herself from getting up and doing just that. Helena did not appear to notice and continued with her story, looking away from Ava, at Sarah and Paul and Regina and George, and in a few moments the feeling passed.

Just as they were finishing dinner, the sky opened up, and rain like a torrent drummed hard against the open windows of the kitchen. Paul and George rushed to close them, while Ava and Sarah cleared the table. Ava saw, through the window, a heavy flash of lightning across the sky, and then thunder shook the house.

"Somebody better close the upstairs windows," Regina said. "'Fore it's water all over the floors."

"We'll get 'em," George said, and he and Paul hurried out of the kitchen.

Ava watched Helena carry a stack of plates to the sink.

"You don't have to do that," she said.

"I'm glad to." Helena took the glasses Ava was holding and placed them in the sink with the plates. "It's really coming down," she said, watching the rain through the window, as lightning cut hard again across the sky.

The lights in the house flickered and went out.

"Shit," Sarah said.

There was some lingering daylight, but not enough to see by inside.
"You got your matches, Mama?" Ava asked the outline of Regina that
she could make out in the half-dark.

Regina took from her pocket the book of matches she was always carrying for cigarettes and struck one. In the light of the small flame, Ava
watched her move to the counter and open a drawer, taking out two candles. She handed them both to Sarah, who held them while Regina lit them.
Regina then took one of the lit candles for herself. "It's a few more of these
in the dining room," she said, and she and Sarah went to get them, leaving
Ava and Helena in the kitchen, in the dark.

At first, neither woman spoke. Ava could hear Helena's breathing,
which was as nervous and loud as her own. Then Helena said, "We seem to
be having the strangest effect on each other, don't we?"

The lights flickered on, just for a moment. In the sudden brightness,
their eyes met. The next second it was dark again. Then lightning flashed
through the window and Helena screamed.

Sarah and Regina came rushing in, followed by Paul and George, all of
them carrying lit candles.

"What's wrong?" Paul asked.

Helena pointed at the window over the sink. "There's someone there."

Standing out in the backyard, looking at them through the window, was
a middle-aged man in a dark bathrobe, standing under a large umbrella. He
squinted at them through thick glasses, not the least concerned, it seemed,
that he'd been caught peering into their house.

Paul pulled the window open and yelled, "Mind your own goddamn
business!" and Ava could hear the raw anger in his voice.

The man looked right at Helena and said, "You know who you keeping
company with? The devil's in this house!"

Paul yelled, "You better get the hell away from this window right now,
fool, 'cause if I come out there you gone see the devil for sure."

"We aint scared of you!" the old man yelled back. "We got the good
Lord on our side."

Paul made a move away from the window and towards the back door,
and the man quickly moved away from the window, climbing over the
fence that separated their backyard from the one beside it, and disappeared
into the next house.

"Who was that?" Helena asked, sounding shocked.

"Dexter Liddy," Ava said. "He lives next door."

"Is he crazy?"

"Out his damn mind," said Paul. "Just like everybody else on this
street."

"They aint all crazy," Regina said. "They misled, mostly. And a little stupid, too."

Helena shook her head. "I don't understand. Misled by whom? About what? About the devil being in this house? That's sure something to be misled about."

"And a long time to be misled about it, too," Regina said.

George frowned. "She don't need to know about this."

"How you plan on keeping her from knowing it?" Regina asked her husband. "You think that preacher gone just let us have a nice visit? Now I think about it, she's what that brick musta been about."

"Can't be," said Sarah. "She hadn't even got here yet."

Regina thought about it, then looked at Helena. "Was this morning the first time you came by here, honey?"

Helena shook her head. "No. I came by yesterday, early in the evening, but nobody was at home, so I went on over to our cousin Tyrone's place and stayed the night there."

Regina nodded. "What I tell you? Goode musta seen her. Or somebody else saw her and went and told him. With them suitcases, they musta figured she was coming back. That brick was a warning."

"What did it say again?" Paul asked, trying to remember.

Sarah frowned. "Something about not making friends with us."

Regina nodded again. "Mmm hmm."

Helena looked back and forth between them all. "A *preacher* threw a brick at somebody?"

"At all of us," Paul said. "He threw it through the front window. Or told somebody else to. That's how it really got broke."

"Why?"

"Because everybody on this street got something against us," Regina said. "Been that way ever since my son died. You saw that church across the street?"

Helena nodded.

"Well, the preacher I'm talking about is the pastor over there. Has been for the last twenty-five years. He had a son, too. Same age as mine. They died together. Then his wife died not even a year later, from the grief. And he blamed us for all of it. He been trying to get us off this block ever since. And he managed to turn all the rest of these people against us, too, including that fool who was just looking in here."

"When you say 'died together'—what does that mean?"

Ava felt a rush of heat move up her neck and along her scalp. A picture flashed in her mind, of her brother and Kenny Goode, lying dead on a hot sidewalk, on a smoldering Saturday morning. The image cut through her like lightning through the hazy sky. She felt dizzy and she held on to the counter to keep her balance.

"Now, look," George said, "this is family business. Any stranger that come by here don't need to know about it."

"Hold on, Pop," Paul said. "It aint no cause to be rude."

"And she aint a stranger," Sarah said. "I mean, she's Paul's sister. She's family."

"We don't know this woman from Eve! And since when y'all so eager to talk about all this? Aint nobody in this house had a word to say about it in years."

"Who we supposed to tell?" Regina asked. "Each other?"

"I didn't mean to pry," Helena said.

George stood up and moved towards the door. "I'm going out for a while."

"In this weather?" Sarah asked him.

"I got an umbrella," he said.

When he had gone, Regina looked at Helena. "You gone have to excuse my husband. He don't hate nothing much as he hate the truth."

Helena didn't say anything for a long moment, and Ava was sure she was still wondering how the two boys had died together, but she didn't ask again. "These people have been harassing you for...how long?"

"Seventeen years," Regina said.

"Why do you stay?"

"This our house. Houses don't come easy, you know. Aint nobody gave this one to us, we had to work every day of our lives to get it and to keep it after it was got. Besides, we aint done nothing that we ought to leave for. Pastor Goode might think he God, but last time I looked he was just a man."

"But bricks through your window?" Helena asked. "Is it really worth it?"

"It don't happen all the time," Sarah said. "Nothing's happened in the last couple of years."

"The thought of us having company, being connected to the world, like normal folks, musta got them all riled up again," Regina said.

"If my being here is causing trouble for you, I can just go on up to New York like I planned."

"Oh, don't do that," Sarah said. "I mean, it aint no reason for you to go."

"Sarah's right," said Ava, whose head had begun to clear again.

Regina nodded in agreement. "We been dealing with that preacher and all the rest of these fools for all these years. A few days aint gone bother me none. But I can understand if you don't want to have to deal with it."

Helena looked like she was thinking about it. After a few moments, she said, "I can deal with a little scandal, I guess. It won't be the first time."

"These lights ever gone come back on?" Regina asked.

"They out on the whole block," Paul said.

"Well, that's good. 'Cause if it was just our house, *I'd* start to think the devil was in here."

They laughed, small, uneasy laughs, all except Ava, who laughed a real laugh, a laugh that went on after everyone else's had finished. Her laugh grew louder, and it had the unbound sound of a child's, giggly around the edges and saturated with a kind of silliness that did not really fit the moment. It grew eager and full and caused her shoulders to shake and her body to bend slightly at the waist, under the weight of it. She felt wetness around her eyes and the muscles of her stomach ached. She could not remember ever laughing so hard. She was aware that they were all looking at her strangely and she did not understand why they weren't laughing, too. It was hilarious, what her mother had said, although she wasn't sure what about it had struck her as being so especially funny. Probably the way Regina had said it, with that half-crazy look of hers. That thought made her laugh even harder. Suddenly she felt out of control of it, and with that out of control feeling there came a weakness, both in her knees and in her bladder, and she knew that if she didn't stop laughing she would wet herself, but still she could not stop. She felt only slightly more control over her legs than her bladder, but she thought she could make it to the bathroom if she ran fast. Still laughing, she pushed herself hard off the counter and raced out of the kitchen. She ran through the foyer, feeling her way in the darkness, and up the stairs, and barely made it to the toilet. She was still giggling, her jaws sore from it, the urine coming out of her in a staggered stream as her abdominal muscles continued to contract with her laughter. She remembered, suddenly, laughing at her brother as he made faces at her across the dinner table, laughing uncontrollably, a feeling of bliss filling her up. The memory jolted her and she began to feel in control of herself again and the strange laughter quieted, leaving her exhausted and out of breath.

Helena barely slept that night. Sarah knew this because she was awake for hours herself, listening to their guest moving around on the creaky floors of the bedroom Sarah had offered her for the duration of her visit. Even after midnight, she could hear Helena walking the length of the room, her feet making different sounds on the area rug by the bed than on the places where the floor was bare. Sarah wondered what she was doing in there. Probably thinking about what she had been told at dinner, about Geo and the pastor's boy, and the years-long feud. She had been relieved when Helena said she would still stay, in spite of all of it, but now she worried she might change her mind. Maybe tonight, while they were all asleep, she would slip out, quietly, just the way she had come. How could Sarah blame her if she did? Without a very good reason not to, anyone would stay away.

Around one in the morning, Sarah heard something being loudly un-zipped, and she knew it must be the large portfolio Helena had brought, which had been leaning against the dresser when Sarah had gone in to say goodnight hours earlier. Sarah pictured it lying open now, its contents—drawing paper and pencils, she guessed—strewn about the bed, and Helena taking her time deciding what picture she might make. Sarah wanted, more than anything, to slip out of the bed where her mother lay snoring beside her and peek into the next room, or, better yet, to knock and be invited in. She imagined herself sitting cross-legged at the top of the bed while Helena sat at the foot with her drawing pad in her lap, talking more about Balti-more, sharing morsels from her life, and Sarah tasting, devouring. She did not want to disturb Helena, though, to interrupt, so instead she closed her eyes and wished for morning.

It came, warm and smelling like mid-summer in the city, like scorched air and hot sidewalks. Sarah's first thought upon waking was of Helena, and she listened, trying to hear her stirring in the early light, but there was no sound coming through the wall now. She went downstairs and started the coffee and, through the back window, saw Helena sitting alone on the back porch, smoking and staring off into the tangled weeds that had been rosebushes and a vegetable garden long years ago. When the coffee was ready, she took a cup out to Helena, smiling and saying, "Good morning," as she offered it to her.

"Good morning, Sarah," Helena said, taking the coffee. "Thank you." She looked tired and pensive, and a little bit troubled. "I was just sitting here listening to the music."

The music she was referring to was the usual Sunday-morning sounds coming from Blessed Chapel, the pre-service rehearsal of the choir, which, Sarah knew, could be heard a block a way in all directions. It rose up in the air and hung over Radnor Street like smoke.

"They always did have good music," Sarah said, sitting down beside Helena on the steps. "We used to sing in the children's choir when we was kids."

"Do you miss the church?"

Sarah nodded. "I always liked church. Ava and Geo only went because our parents made them. But I liked it. The music, the bible stories, even the sermons. And the feeling I got being so close to God. I felt like he could see me, like he knew who I was, when I was there."

"But you never joined another church, after your family left this one?"

She thought it was nice of Helena to use the word *left*, instead of the words, *was thrown out of*, which were truer. "There's a church over by where I work," she said. "Sometimes I go to their evening prayer service. But it aint the same as the church you grow up in." Sarah remembered Sunday mornings at Blessed Chapel, the sounds of praise songs, the smell of bibles, and all of them sitting there on their usual pew, all together like real family. "You go to church?" she asked Helena.

She shook her head, no. "We weren't raised religious. Our mother never went, so we didn't either. I studied the bible quite a bit, when I got older. I wasn't ever all that impressed with it, to tell you the truth."

"Well, it aint for everybody, I guess," Sarah said.

"Can I ask you something?"

Sarah nodded, eager to be asked something.

"Why do you stay in this house? I mean, I can understand your mother feeling so attached to the home she worked so hard to have, but why do you stay?"

"Where else I'm gone go?"

"Well, anywhere," Helena said.

"But where, exactly?"

Helena looked unsure.

"The little bit I seen of the world don't impress me any more than the bible does you. Maybe 'anywhere' aint for everybody, either."

"You remind me of Paul," Helena said. "When we were kids, he always hated the idea of growing up and going out on his own. He just wanted to stay close to what he already knew, which wasn't even good. I always thought he was afraid that the rest of the world wasn't any better, and that at least our pain was pain he was used to, and he didn't want to trade what he knew for something he didn't know that was just as bad, or even worse. I guess I'm not surprised he ended up marrying into a family like yours."

Sarah wished the conversation would turn back to her, and away from Paul, and she was willing to wait patiently for that to happen. Helena was quiet now, probably lost in some memory of her brother.

"Do you want to see their wedding pictures?" Sarah asked, feeling torn between spending their time talking about Paul and risking being shut out of Helena's thoughts altogether. "I can show them to you."

They went inside and found Regina in the kitchen, pouring herself some coffee. When Sarah told her they were going to look at photos, she said she'd join them and followed them into the dining room. Sarah went to the china closet, the top shelves of which were filled with fancy dishes that hadn't been used in seventeen years. In the lower compartments, she found the dust-covered photo albums and hauled them out onto the dining room table.

Helena sat down at the table and Sarah sat beside her, moving her chair closer so that they could look at the pictures together, while Regina stood over Sarah's shoulder. Sarah sorted through the albums and pulled out a small white one, with a large pink heart on its front. She opened to the front page, to a photograph of Ava and Paul holding hands, Ava in a simple white dress and Paul in a dark blue suit.

"They got married down at City Hall," Sarah explained.

"That's the dress I wore at my wedding," said Regina.

Helena smiled. "It's lovely."

"Don't Paul look handsome?"

Helena nodded.

When they got to a photograph of the whole family sitting together in the living room after the ceremony, Helena pointed at an old woman and asked who she was.

"That's my mother-in-law," Regina said. "Mother Haley. She passed away years ago."

Helena looked at Sarah. "You look a lot like her."

"You should see her when she was Sarah's age," said Regina. "You'd think it was Sarah herself."

Regina sifted through the stack of albums and pulled out a fat blue one that was full of very old, black and white pictures. She flipped through until she found one of Mother Haley as a young woman and they all agreed that Sarah bore a striking resemblance to her late grandmother.

Ava came in then, with a pad of paper and a pencil. "Anything y'all want to add to this grocery list?" she asked them. "I'm gone stop by the store on my way home from work."

"Ava, we looking at old pictures," Regina said. "Look at this one of your grandmother."

Sarah felt a twinge of disappointment as Ava came and sat down at the table.

"Who are these people?" Helena asked, pointing to a photograph of a group of folks standing outside a very small house.

"That's my family," Regina said. "That's us back home, down Hayden. All them is my sisters and brothers. And them two is my Ma and Daddy."

"Are your parents still living?"

Regina shook her head, no.

"I can see some of you in your father. You stand like him, hold your shoulders the same."

Regina stared at the picture. "We was real close, me and my Daddy. I knew I was his favorite of all us kids, even though he never said so. I stuck to him like glue."

"What was he like?"

"Funny. He used to make me laugh so bad. And he was kind as he could be without looking weak. Down there, any little sign of weakness could get you killed. Then again, any sign of strength could get you that way, too, if the wrong people saw it. People think it's bad up here, but it wasn't never nothing compared to how it was down there."

"Paul and I spent a summer in Alabama when we were kids. Just the one. We didn't need any more than that."

"I know that's the truth," Regina agreed. "But you know, I miss it, too. Whatever bad there was, it was my home and I had a lot of love there. If I'd had my way, I never woulda left."

"You didn't want to come up here?" Helena asked.

Regina shook her head. "No, I did not. That was my husband's idea, not mine. He was set on it. He said a black man couldn't get nowhere but dead in Georgia, and some sooner than later. Said I ought to know that better than anybody."

"What he mean by that?" Sarah asked.

Regina got quiet for a moment, as happy memories of her family faded, and dark, heavy things took their place. She sighed and said, "Because of what happened to my father."

"You mean the accident?" Sarah asked.

"No, that aint what I mean," Regina said. She hesitated. She hadn't talked about it in years. Her children didn't even know the story. She had never been able to tell them. Staring down at the photograph of her father now, though, she felt compelled to tell it. "He used to sell greens and tomatoes out the back of his truck, down at the open market by our town, and I would go with him every chance I got. Everybody went there to sell or buy whatever they had or wanted. Every now and then, white men would come and try to cheat folks. Most colored down there didn't have no schooling, so they couldn't count all that good, and these fast-talking white men would math 'em so they aint know what they was owed. If you was selling tomatoes a nickel apiece, corn for a dime a ear, and a head of cabbage for a dime, the white men would say, Okay, I'll give you four cent apiece for them tomatoes, cause they look a little bit too ripe, and that corn aint worth but seven cent if it's worth a penny, and the same for that cabbage. I'll take eight tomatoes, seven ears of corn, and six heads of cabbage, and my friend here'll have the same, plus two more tomatoes, and another ear of corn, that's two dollars and thirty-one cent, I'll give you two dollars and a quarter, and he'll give you two, and you owe me ninety-five cent, and him half a dollar, and come on and hurry up, nigger, I aint got time to be waiting round here all goddamn day. Wouldn't be 'til you went home and counted what you made 'fore you knew how bad they cheated you. But my daddy was good with numbers. Better than good. He never went to school a day in his life, but he taught hisself to read and write and count. He could count faster than anybody you ever seen, faster than them white men could talk. It didn't make no real difference, 'cause he still couldn't say nothing to 'em. But after while I guess he just got fed up with it and couldn't take it no more. One day they come around to the market looking for some greens. My daddy was selling some for six cent a bunch. I never will forget the price as long as I live. They tell him they aint worth but five cent, and they want a dozen and one, and when they start trying to math him, my daddy say, 'Scuse me, sir, you owe me another twenty cent for these greens. Thirteen time five is seventy-eight, not fifty-eight, sir.' They didn't like that too much, talmbout, 'What you 'sposed to be, nigger, a math teacher?' They went ahead and paid him the other twenty cent. But soon as them four nickels touched his palm, he knew he made a big mistake. He said, 'Aw, no, never mind, y'all can have 'em for fifty-eight,' and tried to give the money back. But they aint want it back. They said, 'Naw, you keep it, smart nigger, and see if it don't turn out to be worth it for you.' My daddy set up all night with his rifle, while me and my ma and sisters and brothers was curled up under the beds at the next house. I never shut my eyes that whole night, I don't remember even blinking. After while, we heard a truck coming up the road. I felt my brother squeeze my hand, and heard my mother say, 'Please, Jesus.' Then footsteps, then banging on the door, then shots. Shots so loud it didn't even sound like guns to me, more like the sky cracking open. I never saw my daddy again. They took him somewhere and left him, buried him maybe. My brothers went and looked in the woods near our house, but they aint find him. Ma went to the sheriff, mostly just so she could say she had, 'cause she knew they wasn't gone do nothing, and sure enough they said he probly just ran off, the way shiftless niggers like to do."

When Regina finished talking, a heavy silence filled up the room.

Helena had tears in her eyes.

Sarah stared wide-eyed at her mother and after a long moment said, "You never told us that. You said your father died in an accident."

"How come you never told us that?" Ava asked her.

Regina sighed. "'Cause I don't like to think about it."

Sarah couldn't believe it. All her life she had been told that her grandfather had died when the truck he was loading slipped out of gear and backed over him. "You lied to us all this time? You just made up that other story? How could you do that?"

"I just told you, I don't like to think about what happened, let alone talk about it."

"You told Helena," Sarah said. "After lying to your own children for thirty years."

"Y'all wasn't ready to hear nothing like that when you was kids," Regina said. "So I lied. And I regretted it, too, because if I had told you maybe y'all would have known better what can happen to Colored people in this world and maybe things would have turned out different."

"I'm sorry," Helena said. "I really didn't mean to bring up bad memories."

Regina was quiet now, still staring at the photograph of her father. "It just don't seem to be no end to us getting taken away from each other, do it? I swear, if you letting your sanity rest on the well-being of any black man, you may as well go ahead and go crazy now and save yourself the heartbreak."

A few minutes later, Ava was on her way out the front door, on her way to work, when Helena came out of the dining room, holding the pad of paper with the grocery list on it. "Did you do this?" she asked, her eyes wide.

"Oh, I almost forgot it," Ava said. "Did you want to add something?"

Helena blinked, looking confused. "No, not the grocery list. The drawing."

There was a little pencil drawing of Regina, sketched in detail on the corner of the page. She was in motion, her hands out in front of her and her mouth open, as if she were speaking. Ava said. "I guess I was doodling while Mama was telling her story."

"*Doodling?*"

Ava nodded.

"But this is wonderful," Helena said. "Ava, do you know how wonderful this is?"

Ava was always doodling in the corners of pages. Every grocery list she wrote had some sketch in its margins, drawn while she waited for Sarah to decide whether she wanted to buy pork or beef for Sunday dinner, or for Paul to make up his mind about milk or orange juice. She never thought anything about it, never assessed her scribblings, never even looked at them afterward. She had certainly never considered that they were *wonderful*. She looked again at the drawing Helena held out and noticed that Regina's face seemed alive with the story she was telling. Her mouth and hands suggested movement. The tiny creases around her eyes and the lines along her brow held heavy emotion. It wasn't just a scribbling of Regina, it *was* Regina.

Ava took the pad and peered close at the drawing. Helena was right. It was wonderful. Ava could see now that it was.

1953

Sarah Haley was called Mother Haley by everyone who knew her. She was called Mother Haley because of her standing as an elder in her church in Hayden, Georgia, the church that both her son, George, and his wife, Regina, had grown up in and had been members of all their lives before moving up north. Mother Haley was devoted to her church, where she had met and eulogized two husbands and raised her only son, and she believed in everything it stood for, including community and family and togetherness and, especially, judgment.

When Regina and George had moved to Philadelphia, Mother Haley had begun visiting them once a year at their little apartment. When they moved into the house on Radnor Street, she called within days to say that, now that they had more room, she was planning to visit more often. Regina assured her that it was too soon for company, that they weren't yet able to accommodate her, that the house was a mess with their belongings only half unpacked. She told her mother-in-law that for two and a half years until, finally, Mother Haley could be discouraged no longer. In the spring of 1953, she called to say that she was coming, that she had already bought her train ticket. Regina told George to tell her no.

"I can't function when she's here. She spends half her time telling me what I'm doing wrong, and the other half telling me what I aint doing right."

Mother Haley's visits at their apartment had been hard on Regina, for reasons she did not think the existence of more rooms would necessarily help. Regina always believed that Mother Haley didn't think much of her and that she imagined George could have done better, got himself a lighter-skinned, less-kinky-haired, better cook of a wife. Their relationship had always been strained, from way back, when George and Regina were first going together. Mother Haley was bossy, with other women and with men, and Regina did not take kindly to being bossed. But George could not say no to his mother. He had been raised to be an obedient child, to study on everything his mother and father told him and, as a grown man, he found it difficult to break the habit.

He met his mother alone at the train station, and the first thing she said was, "Where everybody at?"

"Regina had to stay home with the children," he told her.

"Why aint she bring the chiren out to meet me, like she usually do?"

"I don't know what to tell you, Mama," George said, picking up her bags.

"Don't make no sense. I don't know what Regina be thinking."

Regina was thinking that if she got through the week with Mother Haley in the house without snatching the woman bald-headed, she'd buy herself that hat she'd seen in a store window on Sixtieth Street and wear it to church, feeling weighed in the balance and found worthy as Job.

"Red aint no kind of color for walls," was the first thing Mother Haley said when she entered the house.

"I love them," said Regina, who had only ever tolerated the red walls before.

Mother Haley's lips twisted into a purposeful frown.

Regina fixed ham hocks and rice for dinner, and watched as her mother-in-law sniffed each bite, then tasted it with the tip of her tongue before eating it, and she decided she'd buy herself that hat if she made it through the night without killing her.

George did not seem to enjoy having his mother there any more than Regina did.

"He on edge all the time," Regina told Maddy, a couple of days into Mother Haley's visit, sitting in Maddy's kitchen, smoking and watching her friend chop onions for a meatloaf. "And he look fit to jump off any minute. He quicker to criticize, quicker to holler about nothing."

Maddy frowned. "I thought you said they was close."

"They was when he was growing up. And she still always the first person he call when he get a little raise at work, or Pastor Goode ask him to do some special job for the church. But it's something else there, too."

"Something like what?"

"I don't know. Sometime I see him watching her with a kind of meanness in his eyes, when she aint doing nothing but washing the dishes or sweeping the front porch. And she aint got to do a whole lot more than look at George Jr. before George get his drawers in a twist."

Just the day before, when Geo had run into the house from the backyard, crying, with his knee slightly skinned and barely bleeding, Mother Haley had said, "Don't cry now. You a big boy, and a big, strong boy don't cry like that."

George had frowned over his newspaper and said, "Mama, he aint a big, strong boy, he only six, and he can cry if he want to."

When George had come home later that same evening he had found his mother holding George Jr., cradling him and talking sweetly, saying, "You a sweet boy. Aint you just the sweetest thing?"

George had stormed up to her, his nostrils flared, his bulgy eyes huge. "Don't coddle him like that, Mama," he'd said, through clenched teeth. "You gone soften him up too much."

"George, what's the matter with you?" his mother had demanded.

He hadn't answered, had simply taken the child from his grandmother's arms and put him down on the floor.

"I wasn't doing him no harm," said Mother Haley, as Geo skipped off happily. "I raised *you*, didn't I?"

George had walked away.

Regina had gone upstairs a while later and found him lying on their bed, staring up at the ceiling, his eyebrows drawn tight on his forehead.

"What's the matter with you?"

"Nothing."

"She's *your* mother. You the one told her she could come stay."

"You know she don't wait for me to tell her she can do something."

"He spent the rest of that evening alone in the bedroom," Regina told Maddy. "Yelling for me to shut the children up when they played too loud."

Maddy frowned over her meatloaf. "Well, how much longer she gone be here?"

"Two more weeks," said Regina, feeling tired.

The next Sunday, the Delaneys took up one more seat than usual on the pew at Blessed Chapel. Mother Haley sat between George Jr. and his father, and spent much of the service straightening either George's tie, picking lint off either George's lapel, and reminding either George to sit up straighter in the pew, because, after all, they were in God's house, and it was bad manners to slouch on anybody's couch, let alone the Almighty's.

It was late April, and it was hot inside the sanctuary. Large fans that were mounted high on the walls re-circulated the warm air around the chapel, lightly blowing the feathers on ladies' hats, aided by the hand-held paper fans with illustrated bible stories and thin wooden handles that everyone was using to fan themselves. As many times as his grandmother told him to stop slouching, Geo had a hard time staying upright in his seat. The heavy air kept rounding his shoulders and loosening the muscles of his thighs so that he slid down more and more on the hard wooden bench. Watching Pastor Goode in the pulpit, looking debonair despite the large beads of sweat that kept forming on his face, which he wiped neatly away every few minutes with a simple white handkerchief, Geo wished the man's lips would stop moving, that the sermon would end and the music would start again. The music was the only way he could stand church on a warm Sunday.

He wasn't listening to the preacher's words, only the cadence of his voice, and whenever it seemed to build and then come down again, Geo hoped the sermon was ending. But then Pastor Goode would take a breath, and wait for the applause and hallelujahs and *yes, Jesus*es to quiet down, and he would go on. Geo reached into his pocket and pulled out a butter-scotch candy, hoping the sugar rush would help, and looked over at Ava, who was seated beside him. She was staring at Pastor Goode, unblinking, looking completely focused on the sermon. At first, Geo thought she was daydreaming about something else, but the way her head was tilted made him think she might actually be listening to what the pastor was saying. Geo decided to listen, too, to hear what was so interesting to his sister.

"Devotion to the Lord is key to our salvation. We got to follow the teachings of our savior, and spread his word, every day of our lives. It aint always easy, living by the word, because the devil tempts us every day. But to live any other way would mean damnation. First Corinthians seven thirty-five: *I am saying this for your own good, not to restrict you, but that you might live in a right way in undivided devotion to the Lord.* And devotion to the Lord also means devotion to the church, because in here his word is never forgotten. Out there, it's easy to forget, to be led astray, but within these walls you always face to face with your creator, and any child knows that it's harder to do wrong when you know your Father is watching."

The longer Pastor Goode preached, the more the corners of Ava's mouth turned down, until she was frowning so openly that their mother, who was seated on Ava's other side, nudged her with an elbow and whispered, "Stop looking so evil." Ava sat back on the pew and folded her arms across her chest.

When service was over, Mother Haley said she wanted to meet the pastor, so they all went and stood in the line of people waiting to thank Goode for his wonderful sermon. The Liddy's were among them—Doris, her husband, Dexter, and their daughter, Sondra, who was a year older than Ava and Geo. Doris fawned over the pastor so long that Maddy said, loud enough so Doris could hear, "She see the man every day, she can't have that much new to say to him. Lord."

The pastor greeted George and Regina warmly. In the last couple of years, since they had moved to Radnor Street and joined Blessed Chapel, George and Regina had become favorites, it seemed, of Goode's. He was always talking about how smart and capable they both were and always asking them to help out with one or another church event or activity, which they always did, happily.

When George introduced his mother to the preacher, Mother Haley smiled like a teenage girl. "You a real gifted preacher."

Pastor Goode put a hand on George's shoulder. "Brother, you are truly blessed to have so many beautiful girls in your life."

Mother Haley giggled. *Giggled.*

Pastor Goode reached down and put his hand on both Sarah's and Ava's heads. "That means y'all little ones, too," he said.

Sarah thanked him disinterestedly.

Ava, who always reacted to the pastor the way she did to Doris Liddy, from a feeling that she was not really liked by either of them, stared up at him and said nothing.

"Say 'thank you,' Ava," Regina told her.

Instead, she said, "I don't think people should be devoted to the church."

Mother Haley put a faux-lace-gloved hand over her mouth and looked ready to faint.

George grimaced. "Ava, don't—"

"Wait a minute, now," said Pastor Goode, putting up a hand to stop George interrupting. "Exactly why is it you think that, little Miss Ava?"

Ava did not appreciate being called *Little Miss*. Little Misses were girls who sat with their hands in their laps and their ankles crossed so that the lacy edges on their Sunday socks scratched together. "Because people can't fly if you always telling them they shouldn't."

The pastor laughed. "You got quite a little imagination."

She knew he did not think people could fly. To accommodate his ignorance, she rephrased it in a way he could understand. "Nobody can think for theyself if you always telling them what to do."

The pastor's lips pulled across his face in what Ava thought was supposed to be a smile, though there was no humor or joy in it. "People need guidance. They need to know how to walk in the light of God. The bible tells them how to do that and the church tries to keep them on that path."

Ava did not like the idea of anybody trying to keep her on a path. Her parents were always doing that, always telling her what she should or should not do, what was proper and what wasn't. It made her feel like she couldn't breathe sometimes. And she knew that if you couldn't even breathe, you sure couldn't fly. She decided right then that the purpose of church was to keep her on the ground.

When they got home a little while later, George sent Sarah and Geo upstairs and sat Ava down in the kitchen. It was the only room downstairs without red walls and he always chose to lecture her there, a fact not lost on Ava.

"I told you a hundred times if I told you once," George said, standing with his palms flat against the kitchen table, with Mother Haley standing on one side of him and Regina sitting in a chair on the other side, "you aint supposed to question your elders."

"Why not?" It was the question she always asked and for which she had never yet gotten an answer that made any sense to her.

"Because you supposed to respect them."

"Why can't I do both?"

George frowned. He hated arguing with this child. He knew he had to do it, that it was necessary, because she needed to learn the right way to behave, but she asked questions like an adult would ask, an adult who was smarter than he was, and that always threw him off. He had no answer for that question that would support his argument, so he ignored it. "It aint respectful to challenge the pastor in front of his congregation, Ava. Especially since you a child and you don't even know what you talking about."

"I do know what I'm talking about," she said.

"Stop talking back to your father!" said Mother Haley.

"Ava, go upstairs and change out of your church clothes," Regina said.

On her way out of the kitchen, Ava heard her grandmother saying, "Lord, I swear that child aint got no discipline. George wasn't never allowed to talk back to his father like that. What y'all teaching that girl?"

Summer came and went quickly that year, in a burst of haze and heat, and fall arrived earlier than expected, a thoroughly unwanted guest. Taking its lead, Mother Haley arrived for her second visit that year, right at the end of September, when the air was cool and crisp and smelled shockingly like distant snow.

That was when George first stopped going home after work in the evenings. Instead, he went over to Blessed Chapel for the evening prayer service, led by Deacon Charles Ellis. Charles, who everybody called Chuck, was only a couple of years older than George, and had immediately befriended him when the Delaneys joined Blessed Chapel. Chuck was a quiet kind of man, slow-talking and easy-going compared to other men in the city, and George liked being around him. One evening, just a few days into his mother's latest visit, George arrived early to the prayer service, and found the church freezing, and Chuck asked him if he knew anything about heating.

"A little," George said.

They went down into the basement and George helped Chuck mess with the heater, adjusting knobs and banging here and there with a wrench until it clicked on.

"You a life saver, George."

"I don't know about that."

"Trust me. Some of these older folks like to get pneumonia if it get below sixty-five."

For the rest of that week, George helped out in any way he could with the evening prayer services, adjusting the heater when it was too cold or warm in the sanctuary, bringing out cushions for the worshippers to kneel on, helping the older folks down onto their knees at the altar when it was time for the final prayer, and then up again when they were through. During the services, George watched Chuck closely as he read scripture and called souls to testify and delivered the prayers. He had such a gentle way about him, a kindness in his voice and demeanor that George felt brought to calm by.

One evening, after service was over, George hung around while Chuck talked with a few people who needed further guidance and comfort. Then, when everyone else had left, they sat and talked awhile about how the service had gone.

"People like listening to you," George told Chuck. "I can tell. You a real good speaker. How come you don't preach?"

"The Lord aint called me to it, I guess," Chuck said. "What about you? You got a good speaking voice. I bet you be great reading the scripture, or leading prayer."

"I don't know about that," George said.

"Well, you just let me know if you want to give it a shot one of these evenings."

It was near eight o'clock by the time George got home and when he walked into the house, his mother said, "Where you been?"

"Prayer."

"What you been praying for that got you smiling from ear to ear like that?"

The grin on his face dropped away. He thought he saw Regina glance at him from her seat in front of the television.

"Nothing," he said. "I was just thinking about something funny, something Sister Kellogg said after the service."

"What she say?"

"You won't understand it if you wasn't there."

As he moved to go up the stairs, Regina said, "Your dinner's on top of the stove. Aint you hungry?"

"No. I'll take it for lunch tomorrow," and he went on upstairs.

Later, when Regina came up, he said, "It was something about the pews."

She paused in putting cream on her elbows and looked at him funny. "What you talking about?"

"What Grace Kellogg said. It was something about how hard the pews is. She said they make them like that so when the preacher tell us we all going to hell, we can feel like our backsides is already there."

Regina laughed. "That Grace is a mess."

"Yeah, she is," said George.

When they climbed into bed, George put his hand on the back of Regina's head and kissed her mouth. Regina put her arms around his shoulders and held him to her. She kissed him again, pulling him down on top of her. George reached down under the covers, and grabbed the hem of her nightgown, and pulled it up over her head. He kissed her throat and shoulders and breasts, and, at first, Regina liked it, but after a while, when he had gone no further, hadn't even taken off his drawers, she reached down and took hold of his penis, which was only half-erect, and stroked it with her palm and fingers, until, finally, he removed her hand and pushed himself inside her. Regina closed her eyes and tried to enjoy the physical pleasure, and to ignore the disappointment that was flooding through her, the same as it always did whenever her husband made love to her, the emotional disappointment that had been constant, almost since the beginning of their relationship.

Long before they were married, George had been a friend of Regina's three older brothers, for years, since they were all children. He and Regina had never been close, but they had always been aware of each other, if vaguely. When George, at the age of twenty-two, had begun to court Regina, who was seventeen then, she had been surprised. He wasn't bad looking, and some of her girlfriends even thought he was sexy, but Regina had always thought of him as a skinny, distracted boy, always staring off into nothing, his bulgy eyes always squinted in consideration of some thought in his head, rather than any conversation going on around him. He was a surprisingly ardent suitor, though, and, once she had decided to give him a chance, she had found that she liked his sense of humor, which was cutting and sarcastic, and the way he liked to talk for hours about picture shows and music, rather than spending all their time together trying to get between her legs like most men did. In fact, George had proposed marriage before they had even slept together, and Regina had told him they would have to do that first, because she couldn't imagine marrying a man she didn't like in bed. After a sweaty, clumsy time out in a tobacco field, Regina decided to definitely not marry him. He was a bad lover, tentative and timid, at times unable to keep an erection. She was a pretty girl, who liked, and was liked by, other boys. She had had two lovers, and both of them had been better than George, and she didn't think she needed to settle.

"Regina, that aint no good reason not to marry him," her friend Frances had told her. "If God meant that to be the test, he wouldn't have made it a sin to have sex outside marriage. You aint supposed to know nothing about that going into it."

Regina had been brought up in the church and taught that sex before marriage was sinful. But she knew hardly anyone who didn't do it. And while she always joined in gossip about girls who gave it up to any boy who looked at them sideways, she thought doing it with somebody you were going with was perfectly reasonable. She looked it up in her bible and found nothing to support Frances' claim. There were scriptures warning against adultery, incest, homosexuality, and bestiality, but normal sex outside marriage was never even mentioned as a sin. The question of whether or not to do it was already moot, though, and the question of whether or not to marry him became equally pointless when she realized she was pregnant.

To her surprise and delight, George became a better lover after they had been together a little while. He was good at reading her and figuring out what she wanted. He learned the terrain of her body and could explore it with confidence. But the better he got at pleasing her physically, the more Regina felt him switching off emotionally. Whenever she had asked him about it, he'd said he didn't know what she was talking about, and sometimes he got angry, and over the years she had stopped asking. Their marriage was mostly good in every other way, so she had decided not to dwell on the one thing that didn't seem to work.

Lying there beneath her husband now, she pushed from her mind images of things she did not want to see, and let pleasure carry her away from doubt.

Near the end of that same week, Deacon Henry Ellis, Chuck Ellis' father, died unexpectedly, and everybody from Blessed Chapel grieved along with their family. George watched through the front window as a seemingly endless stream of condolence-givers rang Chuck's bell, all of them carrying covered dishes that no doubt contained cobblers and casseroles of all sorts. George wondered why death always called for food and guessed it was because it was the one way everyone knew to comfort each other, to say the things they couldn't always think of words for. When his own father had died, years ago, when he was fifteen, their neighbors in Hayden had brought so many cakes and stews and pots of greens that he and his mother had eaten for weeks, once they had been able to eat. George remembered how his friend, Dale Jefferson, who had never cooked anything in his life, had tried to make candied sweet potatoes, and had brought them over to George one afternoon while his mother was resting. They were terrible, overcooked and flavorless, but sitting there at the tiny kitchen table, eating them with Dale, George had felt that everything Dale could not say to him—could not say because they were supposed to be men and there were things men could not say to each other—was spoken in the scent of the sweet potatoes, which, even if nothing else was right about the dish, was perfect. Standing at his front window now, George watched as Chuck came out onto his porch to greet Malcolm, Vic, and Gladys, who were all carrying casserole dishes.

George left the window and went into the kitchen. He searched the cupboards, and the refrigerator, trying to think of something he could make. He and Regina were already planning to take over a yellow cake she had baked, but now George wanted to cook something himself. George knew how to cook. His mother, who had kept him close to her throughout his early boyhood, had taught him to cook and clean and sew. His father had argued with her constantly, saying that a boy ought to learn what a man needed to know, but his mother always got her way.

George found a pastry crust that Regina had frozen and remembered that Chuck loved shepherd's pie. He checked the clock. It was near three and Regina wouldn't be home until after five. His mother had taken the children to the playground in the park down the street and he was sure they would be back within the hour. He didn't want to be caught making a shepherd's pie, didn't want to have to answer his mother's questions about why he was making it. He needed to cook something simpler, something faster. He found sweet potatoes in the bottom drawers of the refrigerator. He could candy them and take them over to Chuck before his mother returned.

He filled a large pot with water, and set it on the stove to boil. He preheated the oven, then peeled the sweet potatoes, quartered them, and dropped them into the boiling water. Every little while, he checked the time. When the sweet potatoes were soft, he drained the water, then mashed them, put them into a large bowl, and added generous amounts of butter and sugar, stirring it all together with a large wooden spoon, adding cinnamon and nutmeg. He then poured the sweet potatoes into a baking dish and set them in the oven. The candied smell filled the room. Despite the chill outside, he opened all the windows and the back door, to let the warmth and the aroma waft away. Fifteen minutes later, when the sweet potatoes were nice and browned, he took them out of the oven and set them on top of the stove to cool, while he cleaned up all evidence of his effort, washing the dishes and wiping down the counter. It had only taken him forty-five minutes, but it wasn't fast enough. He heard the front door open and the children bounding into the house, followed by his mother's voice, saying, "Ooh, Lord, it's chilly in here." Cursing under his breath, he quickly put the top on the baking dish and set the sweet potatoes in the refrigerator, back behind the previous night's leftovers, and closed all the kitchen windows, just as Geo ran into the kitchen, saying, "Daddy, we climbed all the way to the top of the monkey bars!"

George waited for a chance to slip out with the candied sweet potatoes, but his mother gave him none. She sat in the kitchen all afternoon, smoking and listening to the radio. When Regina got home, she and Mother Haley heated up the last night's leftovers, while George played cards with the children. When the aroma of candied yams rose again in the air, George hurried into the kitchen and found Regina placing the baking dish on the table, with the other heated-up food.

"Regina, that's—" He stopped. He knew that if he told her that he had made the dish for Chuck, she would think it was strange. He had never made anything to take over to any of their other grieving friends. Regina always cooked something, and she had already made the yellow cake to take over after dinner. It would seem odd to her that he had gone out of his way to make another dish.

"What?" Regina asked.

"I made them sweet potatoes," he said.

"Oh," she said, surprised. "I figured your mother made them."

Mother Haley looked up from the greens she was seasoning. "I thought Regina made 'em."

"No, I did," George said.

"Well, that was nice. I forgot those sweet potatoes was in there. I'm glad they didn't go bad." She stuck a serving spoon into the baking dish. Then she called for the children and they all sat down to eat. George watched as she scooped out some of the candied yams for each child, then a little for herself, before passing the dish to his mother, who took an extra large helping before passing the dish to George.

George set it back down on the table. Watching his family eat the sweet potatoes, hearing their lips smack and the unusually loud squunch of their throats as they swallowed, seeing chicken and collard greens crowd against the sweet potatoes on their plates, so that they looked less golden brown, and their sweet, cinnamon aroma was drowned out by the smells of the other foods, George felt sad and very tired.

After dinner, George and Regina went over to Chuck's with the yellow cake Regina had baked. When George saw Chuck he thought he looked unglued, like a torn apart thing trying to hold itself together. Chuck took George upstairs, away from everyone.

"He wasn't proud of me," Chuck said, sitting on the bed he shared with his wife.

"What you mean? He was always bragging on you," said George, leaning against the dresser.

"He was? What he say?"

"When you got the Buick, he went around church all the next Sunday telling everybody how good you was doing for your family."

Chuck nodded. "Yeah." He was quiet for a long moment, then, "You think any man ever feel like he what his father want him to be?"

"I don't know. Not this man."

The half-cracked bedroom door opened wider, and Lena, Chuck's wife, poked her head in. She was a little woman, short and very thin, bony, with tiny wrists and ankles, and no hips or breasts to speak of. George thought of her as barely a wisp of a person, not particularly womanly in any way, not particularly anything really. When he had first met her, right before service the first Sunday they'd attended Blessed Chapel, when Maddy had introduced George and Regina to the couple, George had almost not even realized she was standing there beside her husband. When Maddy had said, "This is Deacon Ellis' wife, Lena," George had almost not understood who she was talking about, until Chuck had put his arm around Lena's shoulders and she came into focus, came into being almost.

"Pastor Goode and Linda is downstairs," Lena said. "They brought us a meatloaf. Come on down and say hello."

"We'll be down in just a minute, honey," Chuck said.

Lena lingered a moment, George thought, before going back downstairs.

Chuck turned back to George. "We wasn't close, me and my father. Now that he's gone, I feel like I missed out. Like I should have tried harder. You know what I mean?"

George nodded, but didn't say anything. He felt for Chuck and wanted to be of some comfort to him, but he hated thinking about his own father, and all the ways he had not been the right kind of son. He wished he had the sweet potatoes to give to Chuck. He wished he had a way to say the things he wanted to say.

"I'm an orphan," Chuck said, and laughed. "I'm past thirty years old and I still think of it that way. An orphan. At least you still got your mama. Cherish that, George. It means something to have somebody in the world who you came from."

"I guess," George said. "But living up to her expectations is just as hard as living up to his was."

Chuck nodded. "They always the people we want to understand us the most. But we always think they can't."

"I know she can't," George said.

"Well," was all Chuck said to that.

George sighed. "I'm a good son. I got a good job, a wife, smart, good-looking kids. I go to church. I do everything I'm supposed to do."

"You think your mother don't know that? Or maybe it's yourself you trying to convince."

"What you mean?" George asked.

"I don't know," Chuck said. "Just sometimes I don't think you like yourself much, friend."

When they got up to go back downstairs, George asked Chuck, "You think there's anybody that can really understand us?"

"The Lord can."

George smiled, and nodded, but he didn't really believe that the Lord could understand him any better than his mother.

The block party started at nine in the morning, and lasted until after dark. Although it was meant to be a party for the block, and not for the church, almost everyone in attendance was a member of the church's congregation, because almost every family who lived on the block attended Blessed Chapel. The one and only exception were the Caseys, who lived five houses up from the Delaneys, in a house they rented. Ruth Casey was Dexter Liddy's half-sister, and she lived in the house with her three sons.

Doris had very little good to say about her sister-in-law. So little, in fact, that what good she did have to say could easily have been mistaken for none.

"She always need something from us," Doris told Regina, Maddy, and Grace Kellogg, who lived on the next block but came over for the party, as they all sat in the shade of Regina's porch, drinking iced tea. "If she don't need to borrow money we aint got, then she need Dexter to spend time with her children that he don't have."

"It's hard raising boys without a father," Maddy said. "I'm always worrying that mine aint gone turn out right."

"Compared to them three," Doris said, nodding towards Ruth's sons, who were roughhousing in the street, "all y'all children is angels. Them boys is hoodlums in the making. Aint got a lick of good sense between them."

"They just kids, Doris," Grace said.

"The smallest one aint no older than Sarah," said Regina.

"I know it," Doris said. "And he the worst one. Lamar. I got to hide my purse every time he come in my house. But what you expect, when she don't even take them boys to church? Aint no child ever turn out right that didn't know the Lord."

Regina, Maddy and Grace all nodded in agreement.

"Just listen to that music she got playing," Doris said.

Almost all the music that was playing along the street, wafting out from record players set near the open doors and windows of many of the houses, was gospel. But from the Casey's open window, Louis Jordan's *Aint That Just Like a Woman* blasted out into the street, and most of the teenagers and children on the block stood near the Casey's steps, dancing along to it. Doris' seven year-old daughter, Sondra, was among them.

"Sondra!" Doris yelled. "Get your little behind over here right now!"

There was nothing little about Sondra's behind. She was the biggest seven-year-old Maddy had ever seen, built like a solid wall, wide and dense. But Maddy refrained from correcting Doris. "Ooh, I love that song!" she said instead, snapping her fingers.

"Me, too," said Regina, tapping her feet.

Grace laughed.

Doris rolled her eyes at all of them and got up and left the porch. They watched her hurry over to her husband, inserting herself into his conversation with his sister.

"Who y'all voting for?" Maddy asked, when Doris was out of earshot. She was talking about the vote for block captains, which was taking place that day. The Pastor and his wife, who had been block captains for the last five years, were stepping down because running both the block and the church was getting to be too much.

"Well, I don't live on the block, so I aint voting for nobody," Grace said, "but Pastor want y'all to vote for Doris and Dex."

"Well, that makes sense," said Regina. "Doris and Dexter do a lot for this block, and for the church. Who else is running?"

"Nobody," Maddy said, waving a dismissive hand. "It aint never been a thing you run for. We just decide who we like and vote for 'em. You can vote for anybody. Even me."

"Oh, Lord," Regina said, laughing. "This block would go to hell in a hand-basket in a week."

Maddy leaned over and smacked her on the arm.

As the day wore on, people cast their ballots, pushing folded pieces of paper into a slot that was cut into the top of a shoe box that sat on a table full of condiments, next to the mustard. Maddy had almost forgotten to vote, and only remembered when she went to get pickles for her third hamburger, around three in the afternoon. She was about to write "Doris and Dex" when Ava ran over and stuck her hand in a large bowl of potato chips, then turned and ran off again. Maddy laughed and was filled with the same warmth she always felt when Ava was near her. She turned back to the ballot and, without thinking, started to write "Ava" but just before the pencil scratched against the paper she realized that was silly, as Ava wasn't but six years old. Instead, she wrote "Regina and George," and when she folded the paper and stuck it in the top of the cardboard box, the warm feeling was still with her.

Near sundown, somebody thought to count the votes. Everyone gathered around and Linda Goode made the announcement.

"We got ourselves what they call an upset," she said. "Forty-six for Doris and Dexter Liddy; and fifty-one for George and Regina Delaney."

There was murmuring in the crowd. Doris's smile was like something painted on, rigid and emotionless. Pastor Goode looked like he didn't understand what had just happened. Regina couldn't believe it. She had never even thought about being block captain, and she was sure George hadn't, either.

For a moment, it seemed that nobody knew what to say. Although more people had voted for George and Regina than for anybody else, it was as if each person who did had expected to be the only one. After all, the Liddys were the Pastor's choice: he had all but appointed them the new captains. The Delaneys had been on the block less than three years.

Then, suddenly, Dexter Liddy shouted, "See what happens when Negroes get the vote? You never know who we gone put in office!"

The crowd erupted in laughter.

All except Pastor Goode, who, Regina thought, looked a little less than amused.

1976

Ava got to work at ten. The museum's cafeteria, which opened at eleven on Sundays, and closed at four-thirty, was empty except for the three cooks. Ava was responsible for buffet set-up on weekends. The cooks, who got there at eight, had already made the afternoon's food by the time she got there, but the buffet, with its shiny aluminum and plastic sneeze-guard, was still empty. Ava went to the back corner of the kitchen and grabbed a small white bucket. She filled it with hot water and dropped in a disinfecting tablet, which turned the water blue and fizzy. She got a clean dishcloth and plunged it into the water, and then wiped down the buffet. She then poured the dirty water into the large drain in the floor of the kitchen. The aluminum bins, out of which the food was served, were stacked along one wall, and she began grabbing them and placing them in the empty slots of the buffet. When there was a bin in every slot, she went back into the kitchen, where the cooks had placed the day's food in large containers that they had left on the tabletops. "Got 'em all ready for you, Ava," Silvio, one of the cooks, a skinny Italian boy with acne, said when he saw her. Ava grabbed one container of meatloaf and one of corn and carried both to the buffet, where she dumped their contents into separate bins, then returned to the kitchen for the chicken wings and the mashed potatoes. It took a few trips, but in a short while she had got all the bins full of food. She carried the empty containers back to the sinks and set them aside for the dishwashers. Next, she got the plates of desserts, the cakes and pies and brownies, all of which had been pre-sliced by the cooks, and set them on top of the buffet. Lastly, she grabbed a stack of "Sunday" menus, and placed them by the plates and utensils at the start of the buffet.

As soon as the cafeteria opened at eleven, customers started trickling in and Ava served them. The whole time, through every spoonful of cauliflower and plastic-gloved handful of tater tots, she thought about the drawing. Whenever she had a free moment, she took it out of her back pocket, unfolded the yellow page and stared at it, its angles and shadows, the way it seemed to breathe on its own, as if she had not just drawn it, but had birthed it, a miracle on the page, a thing she could almost not believe she had actually done, and absently, thoughtlessly, at that, a doodle on a grocery list. Where had it come from, this easy talent?

"You don't have macaroni and cheese today?" It was Richard from the ticketing desk, on his lunch break.

Ava shook her head, no. She folded the drawing, stuck it back into her pocket, and scooped him up some cream corn.

When her shift was over, she decided to walk through the museum and out the front instead of out the back like she usually did, even though cafeteria workers weren't supposed to. She walked through the cafeteria, down a corridor, out into the Great Stair Hall. She had worked at the museum since she was seventeen, but she had rarely ventured out of the cafeteria, because the paintings and sculptures in the rooms that surrounded her had never seemed especially interesting. She had gotten a job there only because a job had been available, or, at least that's what she had thought.

In the Great Stair Hall, she was met by the late day light coming in through the large, high windows and skylights, casting itself onto the Greek-temple-like, ceramic-glazed columns. As she descended the wide marble staircase, there were, on either side of her, huge, high-ceilinged exhibition rooms, and as she passed by them on her way down, she glanced inside, catching only glimpses of the art within them, seeing only colors and angles. When she got to the bottom of the stairs, she turned and went through a large archway that opened into the museum's American collection. At this time of the day, near closing, there were only a few people roaming the galleries.

Ava stood in front of a wall of drawings and her attention was pulled to one in particular, a charcoal drawing made around 1940, of a man at a grinding wheel, his large hands holding some instrument to the wheel, his body slightly bent at the waist so that he leaned into the work. His face was created in curves and shadows, with a broad nose and thick lips, and the set of his brow, deeply troubled in charcoal, along with his slightly rounded shoulders, suggested the weight of the world around him, which was hidden in charcoal shadow.

Ava moved from that room into the next, taking in images of farmers in cornfields and urban skylines, and drops of heavy color splattered on enormous canvases. Turning a corner into a green-walled room, she came upon a painting titled "In the Boudoir: (Before the Mirror)" showing a dark-haired woman standing before a looking glass, seeing herself reflected in odd shapes and contours, and mismatched colors, so that the woman in the mirror—faceless, without eyes or mouth—looked little like the woman standing before it, whose skin was made in gold, and whose cheeks were blushed. The only thing that was the same about both the woman and her reflection was the way their arms raised high over their heads. Ava sat staring at the painting for a long while, her head tilted slightly to one side, her eyes moving along the angles, the strange curves of the woman's neck, back, buttocks, and thigh. The color seemed to enter Ava, the red filling her view like blood or sunset, the blues racing through her, cooling her skin in the already-air-conditioned room. She thought again about who she had been, before, and wondered when the woman in the mirror had become different. The obvious answer was that it had happened after her brother died, though Ava did not now remember anything that had felt like a change within her. The days and months that had followed Geo's death seemed now like a blur of wailing and screaming—and not her own, but Regina's—and the hazy memory of a dull aching inside herself. She could not remember crying, could not recall, even as she sat there trying, the sting of the loss, the overwhelming grief that she knew she must have felt. Or had she? If his death had numbed her, changed her so completely, maybe it had happened quickly, in a moment, and she had never had the chance to feel much of anything at all. She wished she could remember.

Staring up at the gold-skinned woman before the mirror, Ava willed herself to recall the day Geo died. She knew it had been hot, the thick of summertime, a muggy August morning, a Saturday. She had been thirteen, with barely-combed hair and eyes flashing fire, standing in the church parking lot at Regina's side, staring down at the boys lying on the scorching asphalt. She felt a kind of shock, a confused disbelief, flooding through her young self, but not the heartache and grief that should have followed. She remembered now that it had surprised her even then. Standing there she had wondered why it did not rip through her, why she did not fall to her knees as her mother did, why she did not clutch her chest and tear her hair, why she did not die herself when she saw him there. Instead, she had stood aside as Regina lifted Geo from the ground, with a physical strength that made a liar of her small stature, and carried him up the street home. Regina had laid Geo on the sofa, and wept beside him, on her knees, while Sarah shook and cried beside her, and George stood in the kitchen doorway, watching in silence. Ava had knelt next to her brother and looked into his eyes, which were still open, but all she had seen there, in the deep brown, was her own reflection.

Ava opened her eyes and the colors of the woman before the mirror seemed lusher, deeper than just moments ago, as if some filter had been removed and she could see it purely now. The reds and blues, greens and golds, that had already filled her up now overflowed and, just for a moment, she felt she was drowning in color.

She got off the bus a few stops before home and pulled out the yellow sheet of paper once again, this time to examine the grocery list. Inside the store, she grabbed a wire basket, and was in the produce aisle, squeezing tomatoes, when she heard a familiar voice call her name, and looked up to see Sarah walking towards her.

"What are you doing in here?" Ava asked. "It's my turn to do the shopping, I have the list."

"We came to get some crab legs," Sarah said. "Helena's gone cook them up for dinner."

"Is she here with you?"

Sarah nodded. "In the seafood section." She looked happy, grinning widely. "We spent the whole day talking. She's so interesting, Ava, so independent. She told me about all the places she's been to, all the different kinds of people she's met. We had a real good time."

"That's good," Ava said.

"Mama wants okra to go with the crab legs," Sarah said. "Help me pick some out; she don't never like the ones I get."

When Sarah said *mama*, Ava was almost sure she sounded annoyed, though detecting the nuances in the tones of people's voices wasn't something she was good at. She was usually completely unaware of her sister's irritation or upset until Sarah came out and said she wasn't happy about something.

She helped her sister pick out the okra, checking for color and firmness.

"Sarah?"

"Hm?"

"Do you remember what I was like when I was young? When we were children? Before Geo died?"

A shadow passed over her sister's face. "Of course I remember."

"Tell me what I was like."

"Why?"

"Because I don't remember."

"What you mean, you don't remember?"

"I don't remember being different than I am now," Ava said. "But I was. Wasn't I?"

Sarah folded her arms across her chest. "What you trying to do?"

"I'm not trying to do anything," Ava said. "I'm asking you a question."

"You can't stand it, can you? You can't stand it that somebody's paying attention to me."

Ava just looked at her sister. She had no idea what Sarah was talking about.

"You don't remember what you were like? That's ridiculous, Ava."

"I guess it is, but it's the truth. Why would I say it if it wasn't true?"

"To remind me."

"Of what?"

"Of how great you was. Of how everybody loved you best, even Mama and Daddy. Of how nobody ever knew I was even there—"

"That's not what I'm doing," Ava said.

Sarah's face turned suddenly worried and sad. "Ava, please let me have this. I need this."

"Sarah, I don't know what you're talking about! I am *not* trying to take *anything* away from you!"

Both women were startled by the force in Ava's voice. Some people turned and looked at them. Some of the fear in Sarah's face disappeared, but she still looked unsure.

"I think something happened to me, maybe after Geo died, maybe *because* he died. And I changed," Ava said, her voice calmer now. "Did I?"

"Yes," Sarah said.

"Right after he died?"

Sarah thought about it. "No. Right after he died, you were like you always were. Except that you didn't cry. You started painting more. All the time, all day long sometimes. Grandma yelled at you for hanging the dirty ones up everywhere."

"The *dirty* ones?" Ava had a flash of herself, naked on canvas.

"And then you stopped."

"Painting?"

"Yes. And after that you started acting different. The pain of what happened caught up with you." Sarah frowned. "You saying you don't remember all that?"

"That's what I'm saying," Ava said.

Sarah stared at her for a long moment, then said, "Well, what happened to him changed all of us. You was the closest to him, so it was bound to effect you the worst. After mama, I guess." She shrugged. "Why should you want to remember any of it? I wish I could forget." She sighed, and held out her hand. "Give me half of that list, so we can get out of here."

Ava tore the grocery list in half, and gave Sarah the half without the drawing. Sarah walked off towards the back of the store and Ava continued adding produce to her basket. When she was done, she headed for the dairy section and saw Helena coming up the aisle towards her, carrying a brown-paper-wrapped package. Her skin looked even blacker in the fluorescent lighting and the contrast of her eyes was even more stark. A trace of the fascination that had been there that morning was still in her eyes as she looked at Ava, together with the worry that was there again, too, and seemed even more pronounced than before. "Your sister is around here somewhere," she said.

"I know, I just saw her. Crab legs?" Ava asked, pointing to the wrapped bundle.

Helena nodded. "I wanted to make something special for dinner. Sarah's upset with your mother, and I feel it's my fault."

Ava shook her head. "You only asked Mama a question. You couldn't know she'd been lying to us about her father."

"No, I couldn't have known that," Helena said, "but I did know there was something."

"How could you have?"

"I saw the look in your mother's eyes when she talked about her father. I saw the pain, tucked way up underneath the smile. I tend to notice things like that."

Ava nodded.

"Where's Sarah now?" Helena asked.

"She took half the grocery list."

"Oh. Well, then I'll help you with this half." She placed the crab legs in Ava's basket and they walked together down the aisles of the store, getting butter and eggs and pork chops, Helena holding the list and reading things off. When they'd got everything on the list, they found Sarah waiting in line and they bought their food and left the store, walking home together in the late daylight.

They cooked the crab legs in the broiler and Regina fried the okra. Sarah found some old nutcrackers and they used those to crack open the crustaceans. Paul was working late and George hadn't gotten home from work, so the women sat around the table together, with napkins tucked into their collars like bibs and a growing mass of shell remnants around them. There was something about breaking open the crab legs that made them all feel lively. Sarah seemed to especially like it, sometimes reaching over and cracking Regina's or Ava's food, and Ava saw Helena smiling, looking pleased with herself.

When George came in and saw them all around the table, laughing and looking happy, he frowned. "Y'all know I don't like seafood," he said, when Sarah suggested he join them.

"We didn't think you'd be home for dinner," Regina said.

"Mama fried some okra, too," Sarah said.

"And it's a couple leftover drumsticks from last night," Regina told him.

George nodded. "Alright, I'll have those."

Sarah got up to heat the chicken for her father and George took a seat at the table. He was aware of a slightly different energy in the house. Some of the heaviness that always lingered in the corners, no matter what they were doing, was a little bit less heavy. Not only did no one talk about the long-dead, but no one not-talked about them, either. The oiliness of unsaid things, which usually hung over them all like particles of cooking grease in the just-used kitchen, seemed lessened.

"This reminds me of the time we went to Savannah, not that long after we was first married," Regina said. "We went out and ate at one of them places by the water, the only one that had a colored section in the back. Way in the back, past the kitchen, almost outside, but that was alright, 'cause we could see the water from there. You remember that, George?"

"I remember I had the chicken then, too," he said.

"Savannah is a beautiful city," Helena said.

"Oh, it's pretty," Regina said. "That's for sure."

"Y'all ever been?" Helena asked Ava and Sarah, who both shook their heads. "You'd love it, Ava," Helena said. "It's an artist's dream. The old churches, the tree-lined avenues. I read somewhere that during the Civil War, the Union army surged into Savannah, intending to blow it to smithereens, but they couldn't bring themselves to do it, because it was so beautiful." She shrugged. "I don't know if it's true or not."

"Ava don't do art anymore," Sarah said.

"Well," Helena said, looking suddenly self-conscious. "If she ever decided to again." She looked at George. "You still have family down south?"

"No," he said. He was the only person in his family ever to move north. His father was already dead when he left, the victim of an aneurysm caused by high blood pressure that had plagued him for nearly a decade before he died. In those years his father had been a tense, worried person. He worked from morning until night in cotton and tobacco fields, and when he came home he shut himself up alone in the shed where he built his strange sculptures. But years earlier, when George was a small boy, his father had been different, happier. He'd worked just as hard and long in the fields, but when he came home he did so whistling, and George, sitting and waiting for him on the porch, could hear that sound coming up the road ahead of him. When he went to the shed, he always let George come with him, and he sat and watched his father making art from old tractor parts, or scraps of wood, or whatever else he'd scrounged in and around Hayden. George kept him company by singing him songs and, later, from the time he was seven or so, telling him stories he made up as he went along, about heroes and monsters and the occasional distressed damsel, while his father laughed and kidded him about his inconsistencies, saying, "Hold on, I thought the knight was Barry. Where the hell Gary come from?" George would fall over giggling. Now he took a sip of water, trying to wash down the fried okra that was sticking in his throat. He didn't like thinking about his father.

Regina was saying, "All my brothers and sisters who living is still down Georgia. They used to come and visit every few years, before it got to be a hassle."

Sarah frowned. "Aint nobody else got lynched we don't know about?"

"Girl, you better watch your mouth," Regina said. "You better remember who you talking to, and quick. Now, I told you, y'all was too young to know about that."

"We aint been kids in a long time," Sarah said. "How come you didn't tell us when we got older?"

Now Regina looked livid. "Why didn't *I tell you*? I aint *tell* you, because aint nobody *asked* me nothing in seventeen years. Everybody around here act like saying one wrong thing to me is gone send me into a fit, and I'm gone start clucking like a chicken or something."

"Saturday mornings—"

"I aint talking about Saturday mornings!" Regina said. "It aint just then. It's all the time. Y'all tiptoe around me every day of the week. Y'all talk to me just enough to make sure I don't babble back. So, why I'm supposed to think you wanna know something about me? About something terrible that happened to me four decades back, when y'all can't barely look me in the eye because if the terrible thing that happened to me seventeen years ago?"

"It happened to all of us, Mama," Sarah said. "Not just you."

"It did not happen to all of us!" Regina said, rising from her chair. "It didn't happen to *nobody* the way it happened to *me*. That was my son. I carried that boy in my body. Unless you have your own child and have him taken from you, you won't never know what happened to me."

"It's alright, Mama," Ava said, putting her hand on Regina's.

Regina pulled the napkin from her collar and dropped it on her plate, and walked out of the kitchen.

George sighed. "I guess y'all found out about your grandfather."

Ava nodded.

"How? I aint think Regina was ever gone tell you."

"We was showing Helena old pictures," Sarah said, "and she asked Mama about him."

George looked at Helena. "Boy, it aint no end to your curiosity, is it?"

"I don't see anything wrong with asking questions, Mr. Delaney."

"It don't seem right to me," he said, "coming into somebody's house and getting all in they business."

Helena frowned. "I don't think I'm doing that. I'm interested in your family. Not just in how they *seem*, but in how they *are*, and that means asking questions."

"Why the hell you so interested?"

"Because you're my brother's family now, and I'm interested in knowing the people in his life. If that offends you for some reason, then I'm sorry."

She was looking at him, in that way he hated, her light eyes searching his. He looked away from her, not wanting her to see anything that was inside him.

"Daddy, stop it," Ava said. "Helena didn't mean any harm."

"Mama the one lied to us," Sarah said.

"Well, so did I, if you gone look at it that way," George said, surprised to find himself defending Regina. "Neither one of us thought y'all should know. So, I guess you pissed at me, too?"

Sarah shook her head. "It's not the same thing."

"Why not?"

She hesitated. "I don't know."

"Because we don't expect the truth from you, Daddy," Ava said.

George felt a tightening in his gut, a squeezing. He saw contempt in his daughter's face, loathing, disgust. He blinked and it was gone, and for a moment he wondered if he'd imagined it.

"But we do expect it from Mama," Ava said.

Helena's eyes were on him and he avoided them, looking from Ava to Sarah. "That's what y'all think about me?" he asked, trying to sound amused, as if it were silly.

Neither of them looked the least amused. Sarah picked at some crabmeat on her plate. Ava just looked at him, and though he did not see loathing in her eyes, he also did not see her usual indifference there. Instead, he saw the fiery eyes of the child he remembered from long ago, back before death had changed her, had changed all of them—not Southern death, not like Regina's father, but death particularly Northern, made of hope and possibilities—and he felt weak in her gaze, and undone.

The fried okra on his plate smelled suddenly sickening, but he did not want to appear guilty of anything, so he fought the urge to get up from the table, and sat there with the nasty smell in his nose, while the others finished their dinner in silence.

George sat shirtless on the end of his bed, the cigarette in his hand half-burned-away while he neglected to smoke it, the ash dropping near his feet on the wood floor. He wondered when he had grown old. As a man who avoided looking at his own reflection, he had missed the first appearance of so many of the lines around his eyes, and so much of the graying hair at his temples and in the stubble on his face. He had never been fully aware of the softening of his chest and arm muscles and the slight yellowing of the whites of his eyes. He had become an old man without realizing it and not just on the outside. On the inside, too. At some moment—he did not know when—he had grown weary, exhausted with secrets, and all the minutes of his life had become tired lies. He remembered a time when he was not this man, when he did not sneak and lurk in shadow, when he could look his children in the eyes and not wonder what they suspected about him.

Getting up off the bed, George put his cigarette out in the ashtray on the side table and pulled on the shirt he had taken off less than an hour before. He stepped into his shoes and left his bedroom again, heading down the stairs and through the foyer, and he could hear the television set playing in the living room as he went out the front door.

Sunday evenings in the city always sound the same. Everything is hushed and slow and the faint tunes of radios create an underhum in the air, especially in summer. George walked the length of the block with his head down, as always. He did not like to look directly at his neighbors, could not bear the whispers, or the stares they still gave him even after all these years. But there were few people outside, and when he got to the corner and crossed the street, he slipped unseen, he thought, behind the church. There was a short alleyway that led along the side of the building, and George walked along it, concealed in the falling night, and came out by the back door of Blessed Chapel, in the small parking lot, and stood staring up at the church.

George had been a different man when he was part of the church, a stronger man, a man who could resist the devil because he lived so close to God, because the Lord knew him and watched over him, and helped him. When he had lost that, he believed, he had lost himself.

First checking to see that there were no lights on inside the church, George tried the back door and, just as he thought it probably would be, it was locked. He crouched down and peered into the lowest windows, the ones that led into the church's basement, where, long years ago, his children had sat through Sunday school classes, and found each one locked as well. He frowned and squinted up at the next-highest windows, the ones that illuminated the main sanctuary. There were times, in summer, when one or more of them would be left open a crack at night, for ventilation, because Pastor Goode hated the stale smell of the place when it was kept completely closed up overnight. Looking up at the windows, though, George saw not one of them ajar. He climbed up the back stairs and tried the door that led into the sanctuary, but no luck. Holding the railing, he leaned over and pressed him palm against the glass of the nearest window, but it did not give.

"They all locked," he heard a voice saying from behind him.

George turned. Standing there in the low glow from the half-dark sky was Chuck Ellis.

"I know, 'cause I locked them all myself," Chuck said.

It had been years since George had seen Chuck up close. He and Lena had moved off Radnor Street back in 1965. Since then, George had only caught glimpses of him on his way into or out of Blessed Chapel on Sundays. Up close, George could see how much Chuck had changed. He had gotten fatter, particularly around the middle, and his belly, once flat beneath his Sunday dress shirts, now strained against his leather belt. The hair at his temples was graying, as was his moustache, and his once boyish face looked pudgy and weathered. But his eyes were the same, deep brown and kind, as he looked at George.

"Something in there you need?" he asked.

George walked back down the stairs, holding on to the railing because he felt unsteady. He wanted to appear sure of himself, unbothered by Chuck's presence, but his head felt heavy on his shoulders, and he watched the ground as he walked past Chuck, and out through the parking lot, back to the street.

When Paul got home, near eleven that night, he found his sister-in-law curled up on the sofa, the light from the television set flickering along the walls of the room.

"What you doing down here?" he asked her, standing in the doorway. "I thought you was sleeping in Regina's room."

"Me and Mama had a fight," she said.

"About what?"

"You know her father, me and Ava's grandfather, the one she said died in a farm accident?"

"Yeah."

"Well, he didn't. He got shot by some white men."

"Lynched?"

She nodded.

"Jesus," Paul said. He came inside the room and sat down on the arm of the sofa, by Sarah's feet.

"She been lying to us about it all this time," Sarah said.

"Well, I can see why," said Paul. "That aint nothing you want to tell to children."

"We aint children no more, Paul."

"You still *her* children."

"That aint no excuse."

"You really that upset about it?"

"Yes. I am."

"Why? I mean, okay, she lied—that aint never good. But you aint even know the man, did you? He died long before you was born, right? So, I don't understand why you this upset about it."

"Because it makes me feel like I don't know my mother, not knowing something that important about her. It makes me feel like I don't know her at all. I sure don't know my father. Where he goes all the time, what he does. I don't know my sister, either. You know today she told me that she can't remember what she was like when she was a child, that she can't remember changing? If that's true, then I damn sure don't know her, because I thought all this time she had changed on purpose, out of grief." She shrugged. "And I don't know you, either, Paul. We might as well be strangers in this house, all of us. Living this way, cut off from people is bad enough. But cut off from each other is…well, it just makes me angry. And sad. We used to be a real family. We really did. But we stopped caring whether we knew each other or not. And I hate that. I resent it."

Paul didn't know what to say. He understood how it felt to not know your relatives the way you thought you ought to. He sighed. "So, you really gone sleep down here on this lumpy ass couch?"

She nodded.

"You want me to go get you another pillow or something?"

"No, thank you," she said, folding her arms across her chest and looking like a sad little girl.

1955

On Easter Sunday, everyone came to church in color. Most people in pastels: soft yellows and baby blues; others in bright oranges and purples. It was one of those warm Easters, smack in the middle of April, and many folks walked to the church from several blocks away, promenading past row houses with tiny front gardens that burst with new flowers that competed for attention with the women's new hats. Some of the little girls' dresses matched their mothers'; others matched the pale yellows and greens of their fathers' ties. If Jesus had been looking down on them from above, which he wasn't, he would have seen tiny dots, moving along the sidewalks, their colors bright and sure as candy wrappers, waving to each other across streets, catching up to each other at corners, and leaning out car windows, honking their horns and shouting, "Happy Easter, y'all."

Sitting in Sunday school, in the basement of Blessed Chapel Church of God, Ava listened to Sister Hattie as she read from the children's bible the story of the Resurrection, and it was mostly due to the promise of jellybeans and colorful marshmallow bunnies and chocolate that she did not challenge the logic of the tale. She knew that right after Sunday school was over and before church service began, all the kids would be given straw baskets full of paper grass and sweets. Last Sunday, after she had been "disruptive" during class, her father had told her that if she didn't behave this week in Sunday school, he would take away her Easter basket. So, when Sister Hattie said, "Jesus died on the cross for our sins," Ava concentrated hard on the muscles in her forehead, forced them to remain still, so as not to raise an eyebrow, and only smiled when Sister Hattie glanced cautiously in her direction.

"So that if we believe in him, our sins will be washed away," Sister Hattie continued.

Ava closed her eyes and tried to imagine the taste of the smooth confections coming her way, all of them soft and a little bit melty from the warmth inside the church, ready to stick to the foil wrapper as it was pulled away, ready to smudge her fingertips with sweetness that was bound to find its way onto her lacy yellow dress, like a badge of chocolate honor for holding her tongue.

"It was the greatest sacrifice ever made," said Sister Hattie.

Ava's hand was in the air before she could stop it.

"Ava, don't," Geo whispered, from his seat next to her.

Sister Hattie said, "Yes, Ava?" with a tired in her voice that had not been there a moment ago.

"But if he came back to life three days later, and then went up to heaven," Ava asked, "what did he really sacrifice?"

Sister Hattie frowned.

Later, after the Easter baskets had been given out, Ava saw Sister Hattie talking to Regina and George, glancing over at Ava, who added another jellybean to the five she already had in her mouth.

"Daddy's gone take your candy," said Geo, who was standing beside her by the altar, rummaging through his basket. "How come there aint never no—"

"Butterscotches? 'Cause only you and old ladies eat those."

Across the room, Ava saw Sondra, Doris Liddy's daughter, looking like a giant Easter egg in her pastel pink dress and matching hat. Beside her, Lamar Casey looked uncomfortable in a too-small suit.

"What's he doing here?" Ava asked Geo. "Caseys never come to Sunday school."

Geo shrugged. "He probably just came—"

"For the candy?"

He nodded.

When her parents came over, they were both frowning at Ava. "Can't you ever just behave?" George asked.

"But, Daddy—"

"Don't *but Daddy* me. Give me that basket."

Ava clutched the basket tighter and shook her head, no.

"I aint playing with you, Ava," George said. "Don't make me ask for it again."

"It's mine," Ava said.

George reached for his belt buckle. "You think I won't whip your behind right here in front of all these people?"

"George," Regina said, putting a hand on his arm. "Don't." She looked at Ava. "Give your father the basket, please."

Glaring at her father, Ava handed it over, and watched as he walked over to Sondra Liddy and gave the basket to her. Sondra grinned meanly at Ava from across the room.

"Mama, look what I did," Geo said to Regina, holding up a drawing of an Easter bunny he'd made during the last twenty minutes of Sunday school, a cute crayon sketch in pink.

Regina took it, saying, "This is wonderful, baby."

Geo beamed.

"Did you do a drawing, Ava?"

Ava, still glaring in her father's direction, held up her drawing, and Regina studied it. Unlike her brother's drawing, Ava's did not look like the clumsy crayon sketchings of a nine-year-old, but rather like the effort of a child much older. The little details, in the fold of the bunny's ear and the light, playful curve of its whiskers, were amazing.

"It's a masterpiece," Regina said.

Ava, hearing those words, stopped glaring at George and smiled up at her mother. "Thank you," she said. "I know."

The Easter Bazaar was held out in the sunshine. Right after the church service was over, the congregation of Blessed Chapel spilled out into the church parking lot, where tables had been set up, decorated with balloons and crinkly paper ribbon. Some of the tables were full of sweets, cakes and cookies and pies for sale, and others held crafts. Ceramics. Hand-knit afghans.

Regina and Maddy sat behind a table adorned with bright red balloons, with a handwritten sign that read, "Cakes, cookies and pies by Regina and Maddy." They had spent all Saturday evening in Maddy's kitchen, baking coconut cake and cherry pie, apple cobbler and chocolate brownies, and peanut-butter cookies, all of which were now outselling everybody else's baked goods.

"We should have made a second cobbler," Regina said, after selling a piece to Hattie Mitchell. "This one's already half gone."

"Save me a piece of that," George said, walking up to the table with Chuck.

"You got twenty cents?" Maddy asked him.

"You should have caught him before they passed the collection plate," said Chuck, and they all laughed. Regina watched George put his hand on Chuck's shoulder.

Doris Liddy came by the table and asked for a slice of cherry pie and, distracted, Regina grabbed the knife by the wrong end, and the blade sliced into her finger. She sucked at the pie-tasting cut and watched George, who had not noticed the accident, walking off towards another table with Chuck.

When Malcolm said, "Let me get two slices of that coconut cake, Regina," she wasn't listening, and had to ask him to repeat himself. "Coconut," Malcolm said again. "Two."

She cut him a couple slices and took his thirty cents.

Malcolm lowered his voice and asked, "Y'all hear about Grace?"

"What about her?" Maddy asked.

"Afternoon, Pastor," Regina said loudly, as Pastor Goode walked over.

Maddy and Malcolm said, "Happy Easter, Pastor."

"Same to y'all. Regina, this all looks wonderful. You sure pulled this thing together."

Regina had been in charge of planning the bazaar. It had not been a big job, just a matter of borrowing some tables and buying some decorations, at the church's expense, and getting some folks to help set up. "My part was easy. Let's just thank the Lord for this lovely weather."

"If you're able," said Pastor Goode, "I'd be mighty grateful if you'd lend a hand with the planning of next month's Mother's Day Breakfast. Hattie can't do it all on her own."

"I thought Grace Kellogg was in charge of that," Regina said.

Pastor Goode shook his head. "Grace aint part of this church no more."

Malcolm and Maddy exchanged a look.

"I need to go speak with Elder Jones," said the pastor. "Y'all excuse me?"

As soon as he was gone, Maddy asked, "Since when aint Grace a member of this church?"

"That's what I was 'bout to tell y'all," said Malcolm. "Eddie caught Grace with another man."

"You lying! Grace Kellogg? That quiet little thing?"

"You know what they say 'bout the quiet ones," Malcolm said.

"I don't hate nothing worse than being the last to know when juicy shit happens," said Maddy.

"Maddy, we in church."

"No, we aint. We only in the church parking lot."

"But I don't understand why Grace left the church," said Regina.

"Pastor had a talk with her," Malcolm said. "Tried to get her to repent, but she wouldn't. I heard she wasn't even shamed of herself. Pastor told her there aint no place here for sinners who won't repent."

"He threw her out?" Regina asked.

"Not exactly. But he let her know she wouldn't be welcome no more, I guess."

"Guess again," Maddy said, and the other two followed her eyes toward the entrance to the parking lot, where Grace Kellogg had appeared.

Sister Kellogg made her way around the tables near the entrance of the parking lot, and at first she did not seem to notice the backward glances and whispers. She said "Happy Easter" to some folks, smiling bright as that April afternoon, and they smiled back politely and said, "Happy Easter, Grace," and then shared scandalized looks once she had gone on past them. When she stopped at a table selling homemade jams, she said, "Oh, these look wonderful." Antoinette Brown, and her sister, Lonette, folded their arms simultaneously across their equally massive bosoms, and did not say a word in reply. A little wrinkle appeared on Sister Kellogg's forehead, right between her eyebrows. "Well," she said. "Y'all have a blessed day." Neither sister wished her the same.

She walked past other tables, stopping now and then to examine what was for sale and along the way her smile got less and less bright. By the time she reached Regina and Maddy's table, it was all but gone, though both Regina and Maddy chatted with her, the details of the chat unable to be heard over at the hopscotch game, from where Ava was watching. She had been playing hopscotch with her sister and Ellen Duggard when Sister Kellogg entered the bazaar, and she had watched the woman as she moved through the crowd of people, watched their strange reactions, the whispers and cold shoulders, not knowing what any of it was about. She saw Pastor Goode, standing with his arms folded across his chest, his eyes squinted suspiciously at Sister Kellogg, and she knew all this must have something to do with him. She didn't like it one bit. Sister Kellogg had been Ava's Sunday school teacher the year before and, unlike Sister Hattie, she had always told Ava that questioning the bible, questioning everything in the world, was exactly what a smart girl like her ought to do.

She watched Sister Kellogg buy a slice of cherry pie with trembling hands from Regina, then turn and walk back past the other tables, heading out of the bazaar.

"It's your turn, Ava," Sarah called to her, but Ava was already walking away from the hopscotch game. She skipped over to Sister Kellogg, at the same time that Geo, who had been playing chase with some other kids, came up to her from the other side. Both children wished her a happy Easter in unison.

When she saw them both, grinning up at her, a shadow that had fallen over her face disappeared. "Happy Easter, Ava. And Geo. Don't y'all look precious?"

"How are you, Sister Kellogg?" Geo asked her, in that way he had that made it impossible for grown-ups to lie.

Sister Kellogg sighed. "Embarrassed," she said. "But not ashamed." Neither child knew what she was talking about, but Ava put her arms around Sister Kellogg, who put one hand on each child's cheek and said, "Y'all come see me sometime, okay? I got some books for you," they both nodded, eagerly.

"Ava, you holding up the game," Sarah yelled.

Geo rejoined the game of chase. Ava went back to hopscotch, but she waited until Sister Kellogg had reached the end of the parking lot and was gone from her sight.

Regina had been watching her children from behind her table full of baked goods, and watching everybody else watching them, especially Pastor Goode. He was standing over by Minnie Jones' table and had been eyeing the twins as they talked to Grace Kellogg, with a look of benign curiosity on his face, but with a stiffness in his shoulders that Regina couldn't help but notice. She wondered what that was about. Whatever it was, it had seemed to be mutual, at least between the pastor and Ava. When Ava had opened her arms to give Grace a hug, Regina was sure she had seen her daughter look right over at the pastor as she did it, with no small amount of defiance in her eyes.

The whole house smelled of acrylic paint. Geo slid down the stairs on his butt, the way he liked to do, and landed with a soft thud in the foyer. He saw his father sitting in the living room, reading his newspaper, and he skipped over to him and climbed up onto his lap.

George frowned, took one hand off his newspaper and grabbed Geo's arm, and pushed him off onto the sofa. "You too old for that."

Geo blinked at him and rubbed the place on his arm where his father had grabbed him. Tears welled in his eyes.

"Stop crying," George said. "You aint a baby."

Geo wiped his eyes and left the room.

Ava was sitting in front of the makeshift easel their father had constructed for her out of pieces of discarded wood he had found while working around the city and had put together at their mother's request. All around her, tubes of paint were strewn, as she sat finishing a portrait of their father she had been working on since just after breakfast. Examining her work, she tilted her head to one side and tried to think what was missing.

She smelled butterscotch and knew Geo was near, and a few seconds later he appeared at her side. "Let's go make a snow fort with Kenny and them," he said.

"Hold up a minute."

Geo came over to Ava and looked at the painting of their father, with a large yellow beak instead of a nose. He shook his head. "Daddy aint gone like that."

Ava looked at him. "It's good."

"Yeah. But Daddy won't like it one bit."

Ava didn't care what her father would think about the painting. She never cared what anyone thought about her art. At school, she felt equally indifferent to her teacher's praise over something beautiful she had drawn as to her shock and disapproval when Ava made something she deemed "inappropriate," as she had when, a few weeks before, Ava had sketched the school janitor, Mr. Ennis, in a woman's dress and heels, and red lipstick. She had painted him that way after seeing him stand up to a teacher who was talking down to him and she had decided he was bold and interesting, two things she associated mostly with women and the color red. Her teacher, Miss Hoffs, had not approved, and that evening she had called the house and told Regina that Ava had been disrespectful to Mr. Ennis.

"No, I wasn't," Ava had insisted. "I painted him like that because I like him. He's brave."

"That don't make sense," Regina had said. "Men don't wear dresses, it aint natural."

Ava did not think wearing dresses was natural for anybody, but she did not argue with Regina.

"If Daddy don't get it," Ava said now, to Geo, "that's just too bad for him."

Geo had heard Ava express this sentiment before, and he thought of it as one of the things that defined her, that made her different from other people, different, even, from himself. Ava did not need or desire to be seen or understood. At school, at church, even playing on the block with their friends, Ava was never the least concerned with other people's understanding, or misunderstanding, of her. Often, when playing dolls with the girls on the block, Ava would suddenly become interested in the dodgeball game the boys were having in the street, and when the girls protested her leaving and joining the boys, insisting girls didn't play dodgeball, calling her *tomboy*, or even, once or twice, *dyke*, Ava never bothered defending herself, never insisted she wasn't a tomboy or a dyke, never extolled the virtues of dodgeball, nor the downside of dolls. She went and did what she wanted to do.

"I know what's missing," Ava said, and Geo watched as she painted bars around their father, making a birdcage that was a little too small for him.

When George came out of the living room on his way to the kitchen, he frowned upon seeing the twins. "It's snowing out," he said. "Y'all love the snow. Why y'all inside?"

"We about to go make forts in a minute, Daddy," Geo said. "Come with us."

George frowned. "Boy, you know grown men don't play in the snow."

As George passed them, he craned his neck to see what Ava was painting. "That's a nice birdie," he said. Then, squinting, he came over to the easel and peered closer. Ava watched his face, saw the corners of his mouth turn down a little bit. "That supposed to be me?"

Ava nodded.

George folded his arms across his chest. "Why in the world would you draw me like that?"

She shrugged. "I saw you sitting on the sofa by yourself, and you was humming, and you looked real small and trapped."

The frown on her father's lips turned into an angry scowl and spread to his forehead, his eyebrows drawing close together. "You shouldn't be spying on people, Ava."

"I wasn't! I was just walking by." She frowned, shook her head. "You have a paranoid nature, Daddy."

"Aint you supposed to be painting horsies and kitties, anyhow? Aint you supposed to be nine?"

She shrugged.

"Y'all go outside. Now," he said, and walked off into the kitchen.

While they were getting on their coats and hats and mittens, Regina came downstairs, headed for the front door.

"Mama, where you going?"

"Just over to the Ellis', to get my pie plate," she said, putting on her coat. She had been baking pies all week, getting ready for their Christmas party, and the house had smelled like warm fruit and butter for days and days. They followed her outside and while they hurried down the street to build snow forts, Regina crossed the street to the Ellis house and was about to ring the bell when Chuck opened the door. He was on his way out, pulling on his coat. He smiled when he saw her and asked how she was doing.

"Good, Chuck. And you?"

"Can't complain," he said. "Well, I can, but I guess I won't. I'm on my way over to the church, but you go on in. Lena's upstairs."

Regina found Lena in one of the front bedrooms and the way she was moving around in there, with her head lowered and her shoulders slumped, made Regina stop a few feet from the open door and watch her. She was straightening up the room, picking up Chuck's socks and tossing them into the hamper against the wall. She then placed a couple of pairs of his shoes neatly by the foot of the bed. The worn brown jacket Chuck always wore was thrown over a chair, and Lena picked it up, and held it against herself for a long moment, smoothing the wrinkles out of it with her palm, slowly, her mouth set in a thoughtful frown. Regina watched as she carried it over to the closet and hung it up there, then crossed back to the bed, where a striped necktie was draped over the headboard. She pulled it off, folding it carefully, bringing it up to her nose and inhaling the scent of it, her eyes closing a moment, before she finally placed it in a dresser drawer. Regina continued to stand there outside the door as Lena made the bed, tucking the yellow bedspread under and pausing to examine a loose thread that hung at the edge of the blanket. She ran it through her fingers a few times, slowly, deliberately, before finally wrapping it around her forefinger and yanking it off. She sat down at the end of the bed and stared at the thread, peered at it for a long moment, as if it were a living thing and she was waiting for it to do something interesting.

"Lena?" Regina called, deciding it was past time to make herself known.

Surprised, Lena turned and blinked at Regina.

"Chuck told me to come on up. Sorry to barge in on you."

Lena pulled the thread off her finger and enclosed it tightly in her hand. "Oh, it's alright, Regina," she said, getting up and moving to the door. "Come on back downstairs and I'll get that pie plate for you."

Regina reached out and touched Lena's arm. "You alright, girl?"

Lena smiled. "I'm fine. Why you asking?"

"You looked a little sad just then."

"I was just thinking about my mother," she said.

"Oh," said Regina. "I never met her, have I?"

"Oh, no," Lena said, shaking her head. "I was just thinking how she never married my father. And she used to always say that a woman was better off on her own, living her life on her own terms. Even if it made her life harder in some ways."

"Well, there's probably some truth in that," Regina said.

"You know, I was thinking that, too," Lena said. "But, you know what? She was dead before she was forty. That's how hard her life was."

"I'm sorry," Regina said, and could think of nothing else to say.

"Oh, it's alright," Lena said.

That was something Lena said often: that things were alright. They never really seemed to be, though, not entirely. With Lena, there was always something just a little bit off. Like the way she was never late for anything, was always right on time, but she always managed to forget something important, often showing up to bible study without her bible, or to an appointment at the veterinarian having left her cat behind at home. She was always very neatly groomed, her clothes flawlessly pressed, her shoes without a scuff. But there was always one strand of hair coming loose from the bun she wore, or a short run up the back of her stockings, or lipstick on her teeth.

When they got down to the kitchen, Lena offered Regina lemonade, and Regina sat down while Lena got the pitcher from the refrigerator and poured each of them a glass. As usual, it wasn't sweet enough, but Regina smiled and said, "Thank you. That's good."

"Sweet enough?"

"Oh yeah."

Regina offered her a cigarette, and they both smoked and sipped their lemonade, and a couple of minutes passed in silence. Then Lena said, "Our husbands sure do get along well."

Regina felt a rush of warmth around her ears and the lemonade tingled bitterly at the back of her throat. She nodded. "I guess they do. Chuck's a nice man; everybody seem to get along with him."

Lena smiled, nodded. "Of course. George, too. Everybody like him. But that aint what I mean. It seem to be something particular between the two of them. Don't you think?"

"I don't know. What you mean?"

"What you think I mean, Regina?" she asked, and sipped her lemonade.

"Well, they good friends. You mean that? Or something else?" Regina hoped she did not mean something else. She had spent months, years, trying not to think about something else, and she was not prepared—sitting here drinking this not-sweet-enough lemonade, in this kitchen that was spotless except for three drops of what looked like spaghetti sauce on the linoleum—for Lena, plain old Lena, who never had anything interesting to say, to suddenly start talking about George and Chuck and *something else.*

"I just get a strange feeling sometimes," Lena said. "When George is around. Like there aint no space for me in the room no more. Like I aint there. You ever get that feeling?"

Regina did not answer.

"I think the devil's trying to get a hold of my husband. You know?"

Regina shook her head. "No, I don't know. I'm afraid you gone have to say what you mean, and say it plain, 'cause I got pies to bake and children to look after, and I can't sit here a whole lot longer playing guessing games."

Lena looked surprised at Regina's tone, which was soft but slicing. She smiled. "I guess it's what you said. They good friends, that's all. Aint nothing wrong with that, is there?"

Regina got up from the table. "Do you mind if I take my pie plate now?"

Lena got up and retrieved the pie plate from a cupboard and handed it to Regina, who turned for the door.

"Regina, I'm sorry," Lena said. "I didn't mean to make you mad."

Regina stopped and looked at her, and couldn't help but feel for her. She understood the questions, the need to know. But she also felt that her life, everything she knew, depended on not asking, on not knowing. "My Ava asks a lot of questions," Regina said. "She want to know everything. I always think she gone have a hard life if she keep that up. 'Cause what if, once the questions get answered, it aint nothing left to hold on to?"

Lena just stared at her.

Regina turned to leave again, and again Lena called out to her. "Regina, what you think it would feel like to be free?"

"What you mean, free?"

"I mean, to be able to live your life just the way you want to, to be just who you are. To not have to do what anybody say you ought to do, not white folks, or the bible, maybe not even God. What you think that would be like?"

Regina had no idea what Lena was talking about.

A little while later, as she was crossing the street with the pie plate, and the taste of sour lemons in her mouth, she saw Ava, dancing in the snow, laughing, and she laughed herself, feeling warmer out in the sunshine, and waved to her daughter.

Everyone came to the Delaneys' Christmas party that next Saturday. Most people brought cakes and pies and other desserts to share, and some brought libations. Maddy and her mother brought peach cobbler and beer. Chuck and Lena came with their two kids and brought one of Lena's not-sweet-enough coconut cakes, plus a couple of bottles of George's favorite cheap wine. "This so cheap, the vintage is *next* year," George said, and they all exploded in laughter. Christmas records played. Some people danced and most people sang. The house smelled of spiced apples and nutmeg and peppermint.

Ava spent the first half-hour of the party up in her room, finishing a drawing, ignoring her father's repeated calls for her to come down. When she finally did come down, she went straight to the plates full of cookies that were set out on the dining room table. Geo came over to her, frowning, loosening his tie a little and looking like he wanted to rip it off. "Cheer up," she said, "It's just for a—"

"Couple more hours? That's easy for you to say. Dresses aint bad. But I don't know what fool thought up ties. Who wants to feel like they're—"

"Being strangled?"

He nodded, stuck his finger in the space between the tie knot and his neck and wiggled it, grimacing.

Ava saw Miss Maddy's daughter, Ellen, across the room and waved to her. Ellen bounced over and kissed Ava's cheek. Ava frowned and wiped the wetness off. "What you do that for?"

Ellen shrugged, then kissed Geo's cheek. He grinned.

"If you hoping that frog's gone turn into a prince," a familiar voice yelled, "you gone be disappointed."

They all turned and saw Sondra Liddy by the layer cake, sneering, while Lamar guffawed beside her. Ava rolled her eyes.

"I can't believe your parents invited the Caseys," Ellen whispered. "I mean, the Liddys I can understand, but the *Caseys*? They're *so* terrible."

They were terrible. Lamar especially. Not a week went by when he didn't get in trouble for hitting somebody at school, or for stealing something.

"Our Mama invites them every year," Geo said. "She says it's the Christian thing to do."

Ava nodded. "But she hid all our records and toys and stuff, and locked our Christmas presents in the closet. She's Christian, but she aint stupid."

A couple of hours into the party, the punchbowl cracked and Regina asked George to go down to the basement to look for the extra one. He frowned at her, annoyed. Vic was right in the middle of a story about some drunks who'd gotten on his bus earlier in the evening, and George didn't want to miss the funny part. Regina put her hands on her hips and narrowed her eyes at him and he decided it would be easier to just go ahead and get the damn punchbowl.

He was still searching for it when Chuck came down the basement stairs. "I was wondering where you disappeared to," Chuck said.

"Enjoying the party?" George asked him.

Chuck sat down on the bottom step and took a sip of his drink, looking pensive.

"You alright?" George asked.

Chuck shrugged. "I don't know if I am."

George went and sat beside him on the step. He knew from years of friendship with Chuck that if he just waited, he'd talk.

After a few seconds, Chuck said, "Things aint too good with me and Lena."

"Still?"

"We been talking about splitting up."

"Every marriage got problems," said George. "Y'all can work it out."

"Lena don't know if she want to work it out."

George couldn't believe it. He couldn't imagine *Lena* wanting to leave *Chuck*. Surely, she didn't think she could do better. Lena was the least engaging person he had ever known. She never talked about anything interesting, never even seemed to know what was going on. Anytime someone mentioned something that was happening in the news, like the lunch-counter sit-ins down south, which everyone seemed to have something to say about, Lena just smiled and nodded along, never saying what she thought, and George had decided she didn't think anything at all. For the life of him, he could not understand how it was that Chuck could be married to her. Even when he tried his hardest, when he tried to see one thing about her that was special, one thing that might have caught Chuck's eye, one little, tiny thing, he couldn't. Once he had asked Chuck how he and Lena had met, thinking perhaps there was some great romantic story that connected them, but Chuck told him they'd met at church, after Sunday service a few weeks before Easter in 1944. A few weeks before Easter. Not even *on* Easter, for goodness sake. And after asking Chuck several times what in the world he saw in that woman, phrasing it in less insulting ways than that, such as, "what's your favorite thing about Lena?" and "when did you know she was the one for you?" and getting answers like, "oh, she's real fun to play cards with," and "I don't remember exactly, why you asking?" George had given up, deciding it was one of those things he just wasn't meant to understand, like algebra.

"You ever think about leaving?" Chuck asked him now.

"No," George said.

Chuck looked a little surprised by his answer.

"Well, not really," George said. "Not seriously."

There were times when he thought about it. He certainly wasn't happy in his marriage. But it didn't really bother him much, because he had never been happy, not in all his life that he could remember, and he didn't imagine that he ever would be. The idea of being without Regina and his children didn't make him feel any happier, only strange and lost, and he couldn't imagine what his life would be like without them, a thirty-five year-old man with no family. It wasn't normal. It wouldn't look right.

"Well, I thought about it," Chuck said. "A lot. And now Lena thinking about it." He took a long drink off his whiskey, then looked at George. "You a good friend to me. Since my daddy died, you the only person I feel like I can count on."

George nodded, but could think of nothing to say.

Chuck reached out and put his hand on George's knee. George felt something surge up from within him, something urgent, and his heart began to beat fast, and so loudly he was sure it echoed in the quiet basement. Chuck stared into George's face, not saying anything. George put his hand on the back of Chuck's head and pulled him closer, and kissed his mouth. As soon as their lips met, Chuck pulled back, pushing George away with both hands, splashing whiskey from his glass onto George's shirt, scrambling up off the step.

Wiping his mouth, Chuck said, "Don't do that." His face and voice were full of disgust.

George felt a rush of heat from his chest up his throat and into his face. He stood up, wringing his hands, not looking at Chuck but at the floor. "I'm sorry," he whispered. "I didn't mean to—"

"I aint like that, George."

"Me, neither. I aint like that, I just thought—"

"Thought what?"

George just shook his head. He couldn't imagine now what he had thought. Still not looking at Chuck, he turned and walked quickly up the steps, out of the basement, and back to the party.

1976

George lay naked on a couch with faded stripes and stared up at a bare light bulb that hung from the ceiling directly above. Beside him, pressed against him, another man, whose nickname was Butch, lay on his side, wearing only a white undershirt, naked from the waist down, the sound of his snoring the only sound in the room.

It was near eleven at night and George had been there since ten. He had left home after dinner and met up with Butch at a bar they frequented over on Market Street. After a few beers and another few whiskeys, they had come back to Butch's house, and come down into the basement, where Butch's wife and children, who were sleeping upstairs, would not hear them. They had stripped each other naked and rolled around a little on the couch before Butch, having drank too much again, passed out. George had lain there, hoping he would wake up so they could do what they had come there to do. He didn't like just lying there with another man, even Butch, who he had known for years and liked.

They had been friends when they were both deacons at Blessed Chapel Church of God. Butch, whose real name was William Brooks, still was one. They had not been lovers when they had known each other back then. It was years later, in 1959, on his first visit to the bar they now frequented, that George had seen Deacon Brooks there. George had moved through the crowd of twenty or thirty men. A few of them had smiled at him as he passed. When he got to the bar, the bartender, who was high-yellow and bearded, looked him over, a hint of amusement on his lips.

"Where you come from?" he asked.

"Georgia," George had said.

The bartender laughed. "I mean what you doing in here? You know where you at?"

"I know where I'm at," George said. "I'm on one side of a bar and you on the other. I guess that make you the bartender, don't it? So, you gone pour me a drink or just stand there grinning?"

"Alright, man, I aint mean no harm. What you drinking?"

"Whiskey. Whatever you got that's good."

There were no empty barstools, so he stood there, with his head down, not wanting to look around, not wanting people to see him, wondering what the hell he *was* doing there, what the hell he was looking for in that place. He only knew about the bar because he had overheard two men whispering about it on the el one evening on his way home from work. A few nights

later, he'd left the house after dinner, without any of his family either noticing or caring. The bar was only a few blocks away from his house, so he'd
walked to it. In fact, he'd walked past it. Too nervous to go inside, he'd
circled the block three times before finally pulling open the plain brown
door
and entering. It was a small room with red lampshades and worn carpet on
the floor.

The bartender had put his whiskey down on the bar, and George had
drunk half of it in one gulp, closing his eyes for a moment at the sting in his
throat. When he opened them again, Deacon Brooks was standing a few
feet away from him, engaged in conversation with another man.

George's first thought was to leave the bar immediately, go straight to
Pastor Goode and expose Butch. But that might have meant exposing himself, too. So, he had decided just to leave, hurry out before he was spotted.
But in his scramble to pay the bartender he'd dropped some change on the
bar and the noise caught Deacon Brooks' attention. He'd come right over to
George, stood there looking at him, neither of them saying a word. George
thought about punching him in the face, damning him for being part of that
church that had rejected him after he had given so much. Standing there
looking at Deacon Brooks, he saw Pastor Goode and the rest of the congregation, saw their betrayal, and he wanted to lash out.

"You want to go somewhere?" Deacon Brooks had asked.

George blinked. "What?"

He moved closer, put his hand on George's hip. "I know somewhere we
can go."

While they fucked, George thought of Pastor Goode and the rest of those
hypocrites, and thrust harder, and when he came it was with a feeling of
power. Seconds later, though, that feeling was replaced by a deep loathing,
not of that church or its parishioners or pastor, but of himself. He'd pulled
up his pants and left without a word, without ever looking at Deacon
Brooks, only hearing him say, "Don't go," as George walked back up the
basement steps.

He had returned, though, and frequently, over the seventeen years that
had followed.

Lying there next to Butch now, staring up at the harsh light bulb, George
felt restless. He elbowed Butch in the back. "I'm leaving," he said.

Butch did not stir.

George got dressed and left.

Walking down Spruce Street, he heard footsteps behind him, and when
he turned to look he saw a shadow move between two parked cars. When
he passed the same man digging through the same trash bin as he had a
couple of nights before, the man grinned, holding his arms out. "Son! It's
me! Come on give your daddy a kiss!"

❖ ❖ ❖

The next morning, Ava awoke to a familiar song of summer: the melodic whirring of a box fan. She half-opened her eyes and saw it sitting in the open window of her bedroom, the early morning light that streamed through it being cut over and over by its metal blades in such quick rotation that the light appeared undisturbed except for a faint trembling. She lay there in her bed, held in half-consciousness by the lull of the fan, and tried to recall the dream she'd been having, parts of which still clung, sticky, to the edges of her brain. A dodgeball game. A fat, red, dimpled ball, almost spongy in its texture, almost juicy in its bounce. The closeness of friends. And the threat of older girls and boys who could not resist the urge to use the ball as a weapon, to try and hurt as many people as they could. She tried to remember the details of the dreamed game, the who and when, but they slipped through her waking-up mind like water through a colander. Uncatchable.

By the time she got downstairs, everyone had gone to work, and Helena was the only one left in the house. Ava found her in the kitchen, rummaging around under the sink. "I'm looking for tools," she said, when she saw Ava.

"Tools?"

She nodded. "A hammer. Some nails."

Ava crossed to the sink, opened one of the lower cabinet drawers, and pulled out a tool box. She sat it down on the floor between Helena and herself, took out a hammer and a box of nails and held them up.

"Excellent," Helena said, taking them. "I thought I'd repair some of the loose floorboards in Sarah's bedroom. I was worried I was keeping everyone up last night with my pacing."

"I doubt it," Ava said. "We're used to creaking floors around here."

"Well, it'll make me feel better anyway." She stood up and headed for the door.

"I'll help you," Ava said, grabbing a second hammer from the toolbox.

There was a moment of hesitation, only a moment, Ava was sure of that, but it hung there between them, weighty as a half a minute. Then Helena said, "Alright."

They worked from opposite sides of the room, the banging of their hammers filling up the nervous quiet. Every few minutes, Ava glanced over at Helena and tried to think of something to say as they slowly made their way towards each other at the center of the room.

"You're a good cook."

Helena looked over at her.

"Those crab legs were really good. I'm surprised you're not married. Doesn't every man want a wife who can cook?"

Helena laughed. "I'm not sure I can say what every man wants." She took another nail from the box and eyed the next floorboard.

"Why aren't you married?" Ava asked her. "I mean, do you want to be?"

She shook her head. "No. I don't."

"Why not?" Ava knew several women Helena's age who were not married, but all of them talked about how much they wanted to be. "You're not one of those women's lib types, are you?"

"Not really. That movement's not really about us, is it?"

Ava had no idea what that movement was really about. She tested the soundness of another floorboard, leaning her palm against it and pressing her weight onto it. It squeaked loudly beneath her.

"I guess I just like my freedom too much," Helena said.

Ava hesitated. She wanted to know about Helena's life. She felt she needed to understand everything about her, so that she could discover the one thing that was causing all these changes in her, but she didn't want to push too hard, to pry. "Tell me about the last person you were with."

"Why?"

Ava shrugged. "I'm curious."

Helena laughed. "Alright. The last man I was with was a science teacher at my school."

"What was his name?" Ava asked.

"Frederick."

"Frederick. The science teacher. My. He sounds...interesting."

Helena laughed. "Well, he was a little nerdy, I guess."

"So, then you like teacher types?"

"I think I like different things in different people."

"But you didn't want to marry him? Frederick?"

Helena shook her head. "Not even a little bit," she said, and they both laughed.

Later that afternoon, they walked over to Sixtieth Street, so Ava could purchase a new pair of shoes for work. The neighborhood was humming with activity, the traffic heavy, buses and cars and people moving in a steady stream down the narrow blocks. The shoe store was air-conditioned, and Ava and Helena lingered inside longer than necessary, trying on shoes they didn't intend to buy. Helena put on a pair of red heels and sat with her legs crossed and her head thrown back, like a picture in a fashion magazine, and Ava laughed, while the salespeople whispered to each other and threw Helena distasteful glances.

On their way back home, Helena asked, "What about you, Ava? Why did you get married?"

"That's what people do," Ava said.

"But what was it that first attracted you to Paul?"

Ava thought about it. "He was there."

Helena looked at her, her head tilted to one side.

"What I mean," Ava said, "is that he was always *there*. He came into the cafeteria where I work three or four times a day. Half the time, he didn't even eat anything. He just sat there in the corner, smiling at me. He did it for months, I guess—that's what he told me later—but I didn't even notice he was there for the first half of it."

Helena looked surprised. "He must be a very patient man, my brother. He wasn't that way when we were young."

"Tell me about when you were kids. Paul doesn't talk a lot about it."

"I don't blame him," Helena said. "There's not a lot of good to say."

They walked past a small store, out of which the aroma of fried food wafted, and two young men standing outside it watched them as they passed, their wide eyes fixed on Helena, as if they'd never seen anything like her.

"We had it pretty rough," Helena continued, either ignoring or not noticing the stares. "Our father wasn't around much. He'd show up once every couple of years and talk like he loved us and wanted to be with us, and he'd take us camping or skating or something, and then he'd disappear again."

"That must have been hard for you."

"Yes. For Paul, too."

"What about your mother? Paul told me she drank."

"Oh, she drank, alright. Like a fish, as they say. She drank herself to death, as a matter of fact. Very slowly, though, so she still had plenty of time to fuck up her children."

"How did she fuck you up?" Ava asked.

"She was not kind to us," Helena said, "after she started drinking. She yelled a lot. Constantly. She berated us, told us it was our fault that our father didn't want to live with us. She told me it was my fault, because I was so black. She beat us. Luckily, she was so drunk so much of the time that we could outsmart her and get away before it got too bad. Sometimes. Other times…" Her voice trailed off.

What Ava wanted to know, what she had really been asking, was in what way Helena had turned out fucked up, what was fucked up about her.

"I clung to my brother," Helena was saying, "and he clung to me."

"It's good you had each other," Ava said.

They were coming up to the corner of her block, passing by the church, and Ava suddenly remembered something. Herself, as a girl, standing in front of the church, with her brother. They were holding hands. Another girl stood before them, a big girl with a mean face, and she was angry, and her hands were balled into fists. Geo was scared. Ava could feel his hand trembling inside hers. She was entirely unafraid herself, though, even as the girl raised her fist. She saw Pastor Goode standing on the church steps. She peered at him, unsure whether he was part of the memory, watching the three kids but not intervening, or if he was really there, watching her walking by with Helena.

"Do you see him?" Ava asked Helena. "Pastor Goode? Do you see him there?"

Helena looked over at the church, then back at Ava. "Yes, I see him."

Ava nodded.

"What's wrong?" Helena asked.

"Nothing," Ava said. "Let's just get home."

Neither George nor Paul was home that evening, so it was just the four women together again. After dinner, they sat in the living room watching *The Flip Wilson Show*. At the first commercial break, Helena excused herself and went to smoke a cigarette. Halfway through the show, when she had not returned, Ava went to find her.

It was a warm night and there was barely a breeze. Helena sat on the top step, her back against the splintered wood railing. When Ava came out of the house, Helena said, "I know Paul probably asked you to look after me, Ava, but you really don't have to."

Ava sat down. "Don't you like Flip Wilson?"

"Yes, I do. I was actually thinking of one of my students. He used to do impressions of all Flip's characters. He'd come in the next morning talking like Reverend Leroy or Geraldine." She laughed.

"It sounds like you loved your job," Ava said. "Why'd you leave?"

She sighed. "It was time to move on."

"What does that mean?"

Helena laughed. "I don't know. It's the only thing I can ever think of to say. I was fired."

"Oh!"

"You're the first person I've said that out loud to," she said. "You won't tell Paul, will you?"

"No."

Helena looked at her, expectantly. "Are you going to ask me why I got fired?"

Ava shook her head. "No. But if you want to tell me, you're welcome to."

There was the sound of a door opening and they both turned and watched a middle-aged woman coming out of the back door of the house to the right of them. She was carrying a bag of trash, which she put into a can beside her back porch. When she looked over and saw Ava and Helena on the Delaneys' steps, she frowned and shook her head dramatically, before going back inside.

"That's Sister Hattie," Ava said. "She used to be our Sunday school teacher."

Helena frowned. "Isn't it strange living around these people and being so cut off from them at the same time?"

Ava didn't want to say that she hadn't really thought much about it, though that was the truth, because she didn't want Helena to give her the same look she had given her when she said she hadn't thought about Paul's feelings regarding children. So, instead, she said what she thought about it right then. "Yes, it is."

"Are you and Paul really going to move?" Helena asked her.

"I'm not," Ava said.

"Does Paul know that?"

"I've told him a hundred times."

"And why won't you?" Helena asked.

"I can't. It's just not something I'm able to do."

Helena sighed. "What happened to your brother, Ava?" she asked, the question coming out slow and cautious. "Do you mind my asking? Are you able to talk about it?"

"I don't know," Ava said. "I've never tried. I've never had a reason to."

"Not to your family?"

"Well, they were there. They know what happened."

"What about Paul?" she asked. "You must have told him about it."

"I didn't have to. Pastor Goode did it for me. I'm sure he thought it would run Paul off."

"In four years of marriage, you've never discussed it?"

"Not really."

Helena looked perplexed. She studied Ava's face for a long moment, then said, "Well, if you want to tell me, you're welcome to."

She smiled and Ava smiled back.

The back door opened and Sarah came out of the house. "Y'all missed it," she said. "He did Geraldine."

"Is it nine already?" Ava asked.

"Mmm hmm."

"It's my fault," Helena said. "Ava was just trying to keep me company out of a feeling of obligation and I talked so much she missed Geraldine." She shrugged. "Come have a cigarette, Sarah."

"I don't want to interrupt," Sarah said, already coming out onto the porch. She took the cigarette that was offered and sat down between Helena and Ava on the step. "What was y'all talking about?"

"What were we talking about, Ava?" Helena asked.

"Not talking about things."

"That's right. Is there anything," she asked Sarah, "you'd like to not talk to us about?"

Sarah frowned. Already the two of them had a private joke.

"I'm sorry," Helena said. "I'm being silly. How are you, Miss Sarah? How was your day?"

"Wonderful," Sarah said.

"As good as that?"

"Yes," she said. "I...I saw the fire-eating man."

Helena clapped her hands together. "Did you?"

"I did." She hadn't.

"Tell us," Helena said. She leaned over and looked past Sarah at Ava. "Do you know about your sister's fire-eating man?"

Ava did not know of any man who could be called her sister's anything, fire-eating or otherwise. She shook her head, no.

Now Sarah wished she hadn't said it. She had panicked when she saw the two of them together, connecting, and she remembered how interested Helena had been in the fire-eating man, and blurted out that she had seen him. And while the idea of sitting there telling some elaborate lie to Helena was one thing, because at least she would be rewarded for her deception with Helena's interest, sitting there telling it to Ava, who could rarely muster enough attention for anything to qualify as being interested, would be nothing but tiring. Already, Ava was brushing ash off her skirt and looking like she couldn't care less.

"Well," Sarah began, looking at Helena. "I took a long lunch today so I could go down to Penn's Landing and see if he was still there."

"And he was? After all this time?"

Sarah nodded. "Still in the same place and everything."

"Did you talk to him? Tell me you talked to him."

"I did. I introduced myself and asked him how he did all those tricks without burning hisself to a crisp."

Helena laughed and Sarah laughed with her, enjoying her own story.

Ava, sitting there fiddling with a loose thread at the hem of her skirt, thought she heard a strange something in Sarah's voice.

"He said it was just so many years of practice," Sarah went on.

"Did he remember you?" Helena asked.

Sarah nodded. "He said he remembered me coming around a few years ago, and asked why I stopped. I told him I changed jobs."

Ava thought maybe there was a tinny-ness in Sarah's voice, a flinty little something. It had been a long time since she had really listened to the sound of her sister's voice.

"We talked a little while," Sarah was saying. "And he asked if I'd come down and see him again when I get the chance."

Now that she really listened, Ava was sure there was a flinty little something and, thinking more about it, she remembered that, years ago, when she had regularly listened to the sound of Sarah's voice, that tinny, flinty thing had only ever been there when Sarah was lying.

"You're making this up," Ava said, suddenly, after not having spoken the whole time.

Sarah turned and glared at her.

"I can hear it in your voice," Ava said.

Sarah looked at Helena, who said, "Ava, she's not. She told me about this man before."

"I don't know what she told you before," Ava said. "But she's lying now."

"I am not lying," Sarah said, through clenched teeth.

Ava was not trying to hurt Sarah. It had not yet occurred to her that her sister was lying for a reason, and nor had it yet crossed her mind that being called out on the lie would embarrass and humiliate her.

Helena put a hand on Sarah's arm. Tears welled in Sarah's eyes.

It was only then that Ava realized what she was doing. She looked at her sister. "I'm sorry," she said.

Sarah got up and stalked back into the house, slamming the screen door as she went.

Ava felt terrible. She really hadn't meant to be so inconsiderate, so thoughtless. Still, she didn't understand why Sarah would tell such a strange, pointless lie. For attention? Was she that desperate for attention? She tried to remember whether Sarah had always been that way or if, like herself, like their mother, she had changed after Geo's death, but she couldn't. She sighed, thinking of the toll it had taken, a toll she had probably never had a chance to appreciate, and still, probably, couldn't. She felt suddenly, deeply sad.

"Ava?" Helena asked, "Are you alright?"

Ava looked at her. "My brother was murdered."

She could see the instant horror in Helena's eyes.

"He was beaten to death."

Helena put her hand to her mouth.

"I can stop if you don't want to hear," Ava said.

Helena shook her head. "No. But you can stop if it's too hard."

It wasn't hard. Ava was surprised by how easy it was to say, how it did not stick in her throat or stutter off her tongue the way she thought it would. How it came smoothly and surely. "Geo and Kenny, the pastor's son, were found in the church parking lot. Kenny's throat was cut."

Helena seemed almost unable to speak. She opened her mouth, but nothing came out. She reached out and took Ava's hand, then tried again. "Who killed them?"

"I don't know. No one was caught." She remembered the dream she'd had two nights ago, of the dodgeball game, the fight, Geo's trembling hand in hers, and Pastor Goode watching from above.

"Do you know why it happened? Why they were killed?"

"No," Ava said. And another flash. This time, only voices.

Where's Ava?

Leave my sister alone.

Ava felt a rush of lightheadedness and she leaned her head back against the railing. "I think it had something to do with me. I heard someone asking him where I was."

"When?"

"Right before, I think."

"Right before *what*?"

"Before they started beating him up."

Helena shook her head, looking confused. "I don't understand what you're saying, Ava. Were you there?"

Ava felt confused herself. "I don't think so."

The screen door opened and Paul peered out at them. "What a brother got to do to get some dinner around here?" he asked, grinning.

Sarah had wished for Helena. Prayed for her. Just a couple of weeks before she had shown up at their door, Sarah had got down on her knees and asked God to send someone. It had been the end of a bad day and she had gone to bed feeling lonelier than usual. Most of the time, she could handle the isolation. After so many years, she was used to it, and at some point she had even come to rely on it. It kept her safe from the unseeing eyes of people. But some days, and that day especially, it had been bad. She felt deeply alone, more alone than she thought any human being ought to be able to feel and still *be* a human being. She felt like a rock in a riverbed, or a leaf at the end of a tree branch, close enough to see others like her, but helpless to reach out, to speak, to hold or hope to be held. That day it had rocked her. Coming home from work on the bus, she had seen a little boy touching the hand of a little girl and it had torn at something inside her. It had made her lean her shoulder against the shoulder of the woman in the seat beside her, so desperate was she in that moment for some connection. The woman, reading a book, had not seemed to notice. When she had arrived home, Ava was there, and Sarah had gone right up to her and put her arms around her and hugged her close. Ava had been her normal self: when Sarah pulled out of the hug, she'd asked, "Did you have something garlicky for lunch?" Sarah had nodded and gone to start dinner. When the family had sat in front of the television that evening, she had looked around at every one of them and tried to feel some connection. Her mother had seemed disturbed. Her father had looked like he wanted to be somewhere else. Paul had been exhausted. They barely spoke to each other. When the show was over, George had left. Regina had gone to stare at the tiny television in her room for the rest of the evening, while Paul had pulled Ava away upstairs. Sarah had gone to bed early, having seen no reason not to. Lying in her bed, she had prayed for someone to come. It had not been a thought that had occurred to her before, that there could be someone who could show up and make it better. It was an absurd idea, because, well, people didn't just show up and make other people's lives less unbearable. She had wished for it, anyway. Once she had, the moment she had, it had become something she thought she could not do without, something she was sure she would not be able to go on without having. It had seemed so necessary that she had got up out of her bed and kneeled on the floor like she had when she prayed as a child, her palms pressed together, her fingertips against her forehead. "Please send somebody, Lord," she had prayed. When she awoke the next morning, the prayer had still been on her lips. She waited. Not because she expected anyone to come, but because she could not bear the thought of no one coming, and the only way not to think it wouldn't happen was to wait for it to happen. Days had passed. A week. Two. Then the doorbell had rung. And Sarah knew Helena had come for her.

Now she lay in bed, beside her mother, who was snoring softly. She had returned to Regina's room after Ava had called her a liar in front of Helena, and she had decided that sleeping on the sofa, exposed, unable to hide herself away, was now too high a price to pay for being righteously angry with Regina. She felt like a fool. She'd had such a good time with Helena, especially when it had been just the two of them in the house. They had talked and laughed like old friends. Now, Helena probably thought she was ridiculous. A silly liar. Or worse, much worse, Helena might not be able to see her at all anymore.

She had to do something. She lay there, trying to think what. She could not erase the lie after it had been told and she was sure Helena had believed Ava. Helena was a nice woman and probably wouldn't even mention it again, but that would be even worse, because she had been so interested in the story of the fire-eating man, so interested in Sarah because of it. Sarah still wanted that. She felt she had to have it.

She realized what she had to do. Lying there in the dark, she knew there was something, one thing, she could do to fix it, and erase the lie forever.

1956

Sarah had loved Kenny Goode from the third minute she saw him, on a Sunday morning at Blessed Chapel, only two weeks after the Delaneys had joined the church. Kenny, who had been away at his grandparents' house in New Jersey the whole week before, appeared that Sunday standing by the pulpit with his father. Sarah, who had been at Sunday school alone because the twins were both sick with colds, barely noticed the small boy in his grey suit. By six years old, she had already figured out that nobody really saw her. Ava was the one who got all the attention, and Geo sometimes, too, just because he was Ava's twin. But no one ever really noticed Sarah. Even her own parents, it seemed to her, had trouble remembering she existed when Ava consumed so much of their thoughts and energy. That day at church was different, though. Without Ava there, Sarah had her parents to herself. When the buckle on one of her Sunday shoes came loose, her mother actually noticed it and refastened it for her. As they walked together up to the main sanctuary, her father held her hand. So, she was already happy, already smiling, when Pastor Goode brought his son over to meet the new family—or just the three-fifths of them who were in attendance that day.

"This here's my youngest boy," the Pastor said. Then, to the child, "Say hello to our new neighbors, son."

That was when it happened. Kenny looked at Sarah and saw her. She could tell by the way his pupils widened and the way he swallowed hard and the way his voice shook when he said, "Hi, I'm Kenny." He was looking right at her. Not by her, or through her, or around her, but *at* her. He knew she was there, standing right in the spot she was standing in. His eyes took in her face, and the lacy edges of her dress-sleeves, and the barrettes in her hair. He *saw* her. And she loved him for it.

For a whole week after, they had been boyfriend and girlfriend, the way five and six year-olds sometimes call each other those things. From the front porch of the Delaney house, Sarah could see Kenny playing on his own porch down the street, and they would wave to each other, and giggle, smitten. When she played with her dolls, she called them Sarah and Kenny and made them kiss. When Ava asked her who Kenny was, she said, "You don't need to know nothing about it." When she said her prayers at night, in between the usual God-Blesses, she added a "God bless my boyfriend, Kenny."

The next Sunday, after Sunday school, as they entered the upper sanctuary for church service, Kenny ran right up to her, with his arms wide open, and she stepped forward into his sweet, five-year-old embrace, without the fear she usually felt when hugging people, a fear that came from knowing the hug would be brief and loose, done out of politeness so that she wouldn't feel bad when the hugger turned and lifted Ava off the ground and squeezed her as if she were the teddy bear they had loved and lost as a child. Kenny's embrace was all for her. For seven seconds, it gave her what she needed.

Then, over her shoulder, he saw Ava and he instantly fell out of love with Sarah, and instantly in love with her. He wriggled out of Sarah's embrace and ran over to Ava, bright-eyed and eager, and said, "Will you be my girlfriend?"

Ava looked the scrawny boy over. "Who are you?"

"Kenny."

She looked at Sarah, who was on the verge of tears, then back at the little boy. "You got cookies?" she asked him.

He nodded. "I can get some."

She shrugged. "Go ahead, then."

He ran off. Ava turned back to the drawing she was making in the corner of their mother's program. Sarah ran over to Regina, who was talking to Sister Kellogg, and wailed, "Ava stole Kenny from me!"

Regina looked at her. "You can't steal a person, Sarah," she said, and turned back to her conversation.

Sarah watched as Kenny ran back into the chapel with what looked like two oatmeal raisin cookies. She had no idea where he got them.

For the next three Sundays, he brought Ava cookies, which she stuffed into her mouth before their parents could catch her. When she finally got caught, and told Regina she'd gotten the cookies from Kenny, Regina forbade him to bring Ava any more sweets. Without the promise of cookies, Ava had no further use for the boy. But he was still in love with her and that was where he stayed, for the rest of his very short life.

By the time Sarah was twelve, and Kenny eleven, she had long ago gotten used to the idea that he would never really see her again the way he had for a whole week when he was five. He liked her, she knew that, but she could not begin to match the specialness of Ava, could not hope to inspire the feelings she inspired in him, and in everybody else. Sitting out on the porch with him one morning, in the spring of 1956, while they waited for the twins to get dressed so they could all play four-square together, Kenny asked Sarah if she was excited about going to junior high the next school year.

She shrugged. "I guess." She never tried to make herself more interesting in the hopes that he would see her again. In fact, she tried to be even less interesting than she really was, so that he would not feel obligated to pay attention to her out of charity.

"Me, too," he said. He was a small boy, on the runty side, but his personality was big like Pastor Goode's. Sometimes, on special youth-themed Sundays, Kenny read the opening prayer at church service, and he reminded everybody of his father up on the pulpit, though he looked like he was always on the verge of laughing. "The only bad thing is that Ava won't be there for a whole 'nother year," he said. "I don't like that." He sighed. "I think my daddy's happy about it, though."

Sarah looked at him. "What you mean?"

"He don't like Ava."

Sarah frowned. "Everybody likes Ava. Except maybe Miss Liddy, but she don't like nobody that much."

Kenny shrugged.

"Well, why don't he like her?" Sarah asked.

"I don't know. He just got a lot of rules about how people should act. He think kids is supposed to do whatever grown-ups tell them. He don't like back talk or nothing like that."

Sarah had always thought that Pastor Goode was too strict with Kenny. He wasn't allowed to listen to any music but church music, he had to wear a tie to school every day, even though nobody else did, and his curfew was a half hour earlier than the twins', even though he was a year older than they were. Whenever his father was around, Kenny always looked a little stressed.

"He don't come right out and say he don't like Ava," Kenny told her. "I just get a feeling."

From then on, Sarah watched Pastor Goode whenever he was in the same place as Ava. At first, she didn't notice anything peculiar in his behavior towards her sister. Soon, though, she began to see what Kenny was talking about. One Sunday after church, while everyone was gathered out front, saying long goodbyes to people who lived on their same block and who they would see all through the week, Sarah saw the pastor watching Ava as she sat talking to Kenny, and the look on his face was hard and strained, as if he were trying not to frown. Another time, when Sarah and the twins passed him on their way home from school, he smiled and said hello to all three of them as he went by, but Sarah was sure she saw a sneer on his face when she looked back after he had passed. It was subtle and anybody not looking for it wouldn't have been able to see it. She knew it wasn't meant for her, because the pastor was like everybody else in that he couldn't really see her. She doubted it was meant for Geo, because he was quiet and sweet and never gave anybody a reason to sneer.

Sarah wasn't sure if Ava was aware of Goode's dislike of her, but she didn't mention it to her, or to anyone else. She liked the idea that someone—and not just someone, but the pastor of their church and the leader of their community—wasn't in love with Ava, for a change, and she decided to just keep watching and see what happened.

The hottest summer ever came in 1956. At least it seemed that way to the twins. The heat came hard in May and by July it had settled in so good that the sidewalks radiated it even at night. There was no reprieve, whether in daylight or moonlight. In the mornings, even before the sun came up, the sticky air hung heavy. By sunrise it was thick as butter and it stayed that way all day, getting hotter and hotter as the day wore on. It never rained.

Blessed Chapel Church of God ran a day camp program in the summer months and Ava, Geo, and Sarah spent five days a week there while their parents worked. It was a lot like Sunday School, with bible study and sing-alongs, but there was also arts and crafts, coordinated kickball games, and swimming excursions to the public pool.

One afternoon during arts and crafts, Ava and Ellen Duggard were painting with watercolors, flowery garden scenes modeled after some of the front yards on their block, when Sister Hattie, who was the arts and crafts teacher, came by and nodded approvingly at Ava's painting. "You sure are a talented child, Ava Delaney. The Lord has surely blessed you with a gift."

Ellen nodded in agreement, and smiled at Ava. When Sister Hattie had moved on, Ellen whispered, "You're wonderful, Ava," and kissed her on the cheek.

Ava started to wipe away the moisture it left on her face, but decided she kind of liked it, and went back to her painting without complaint.

A second later, she heard, "She think she so great. Shoot. She aint nothing. She aint nothing but a stupid, nappy-headed wanna-be," and when she looked up she saw Sondra Liddy glaring at her from the other side of the room, where, instead of doing anything remotely arts-and-crafts-related, she was watching what other kids were doing and making fun. Her cousin, Lamar Casey, was at her side and Ava thought he looked sad as he sat there with his arms folded across his chest, his brow drawn tight above his eyes, staring down at his shoes. She thought of her father and the sad looks he sometimes got when he didn't think anyone was looking. Geo was like that, too. Sometimes he looked sad but wouldn't tell her why. Boys were funny like that about their sadness. She was thinking about all of that when Lamar looked up and caught her watching him. The sad look on his face changed then, morphed into something angry and mean. "What you looking at?" he asked, getting up and moving towards her across the room. He stood on the other side of the table where she and Ellen sat, hovering menacingly.

Ava wasn't in the mood for a fight. She just wanted to finish her painting, so she didn't say anything and hoped he would just go away. Instead, he picked up a bottle of black acrylic paint and squeezed it all over her painting. For a moment, she sat there in shock. Then rage surged up in her belly and she lunged across the table at him. She could almost feel the skin of his eyeballs under her fingernails, but she never made it that far. He jumped back and she missed him completely, and fell over the table onto the floor at his feet. She heard Ellen scream her name in a worried voice, and heard Sondra cackling. Lamar raised his foot off the ground, his dirty sneaker poised for a kick, but suddenly Sister Hattie was there beside him, pulling him away, saying, "Y'all stop all this roughhousing. Lamar, take a seat."

Lamar turned and sneered at her. "You aint my mother," he said, and then walked swiftly from the room.

"You right I aint," said Sister Hattie, "and it's a good thing for both of us." She shook her head and mumbled, "That boy aint got the sense God gave him."

Still on the floor, rubbing the shoulder she'd fallen on, Ava watched Sondra follow Lamar out.

The first half of July was burning hot. Whenever they weren't at day camp, Ava and Geo kept holed up in the house, lying half-conscious in front of the fan and only getting up every few minutes to stick their heads in the freezer. Finally, one day, after a dry lightning storm that had gone on for hours and killed a couple of people somewhere out in the boondocks of Pennsylvania, they awoke to some cool. Relatively speaking. Eighty-five degrees and balmy. They decided to spend that day outside.

The game that afternoon was dodgeball. Because Ava and Geo shared their street with lots of kids their age, and because they both made friends easily, there were always kids to play with. Besides Kenny, their best friends were Miss Maddy's children, Jack and Ellen, Rudy Lucas, and Juanita and Louis Jackson, who lived a few houses up from them. They were all among the kids playing dodgeball that day in the street right in front of the church. Sondra and Lamar were at opposite ends of the invisible court, each acting as thrower, as usual, because the ball belonged to Lamar. Kids ran in all directions as they tried to avoid getting hit, squealing with excitement with every bounce of the overlarge red ball.

Geo was the best at dodgeball. He had a knack for timing his dodges and almost always got out of the way in time. He was the last one standing after the first round and he raised his arms in triumph. Ava, Kenny, and all their friends cheered, then scrambled back into the line of fire for another round. This time, the first throw, from Sondra, came directly at Ava and she dodged it. The second one, from Lamar, skimmed the edge of the crowd, eliminating Juanita. The next one came directly at Ava again. Every time Sondra threw the ball, she aimed for Ava. After it had happened several times in a row, Ava screamed, "You're aiming right at me! That's not fair!" But Sondra didn't stop. Time and time again, she hurled the ball at Ava and Ava dodged it. Finally, Lamar threw the ball into the crowd and tagged Ava and she was out.

Geo won that round, too, and then a bunch of them took a break and sat on the front steps of the church, while Sondra, Lamar, and some of the other kids continued to play. Everybody was lauding Geo's dodging skills, and discussing possibly going down to Cobbs Creek later, when a whizzing sound cut through the air, and Ava looked up just in time to see the dodge ball, once again coming right at her. She ducked and barely avoided it, and it smashed into the side of Geo's head with a hard *boing*, causing him to fall off the steps onto the ground.

Ava looked over and saw Sondra standing there, grinning.

Geo rubbed the side of his head and tried not to cry.

"We were on a time-out!" Ava yelled.

Ellen screamed, "You can't throw at us when we aint playing!"

"I just did!" Sondra hollered back.

Ava glared at her. "Imbecile!" she screamed.

Sondra ran over and grabbed Ava by the arm, pushed her down onto the ground. "What you call me?"

"Did I stutter?" Ava asked, unafraid.

Lamar rushed over, looking eager at the idea of a fight.

"You think you so smart, don't you?" Sondra sneered, holding Ava down by her shoulders. Ellen ran over, and Geo and Kenny followed, and they all tried to pull Sondra off, but for an eleven-year-old girl she was large, and taller than both boys. She glared down at Ava. "You think you better than everybody."

Ava rolled her eyes. She was sick of this.

"Oh, you got a eye problem," Sondra said. "Well, I'm gone fix it for you."

Kenny and Geo looked at each other, and at Ava, who looked less concerned than either boy thought she ought to be.

"I aint scared of you," Ava said.

Sondra put her face close to Ava's. "Then you aint as smart as everybody think you is."

From her position on the ground, looking up, Ava saw something in one of the windows of the church, and she blinked, trying to focus, and saw Pastor Goode looking down, watching them. She expected him to call out, to tell them to stop all this roughhousing, but he only watched, saying nothing.

Ellen, Kenny, and Geo managed to pull Sondra off of Ava, and Ava scrambled up off the ground. Geo grabbed his sister's arm. "Come on, Ava, let's go home," he said, pulling her away, towards their house. Ellen, Kenny, and their other friends followed.

Once they were inside, Ava jerked out of Geo's grip. "Why you pull me away? I aint scared of that girl."

"She twice as big as you," Geo said.

Ellen shook her head. "Three times."

"So, what? I got—"

"Right on your side?" Geo asked.

She nodded.

"I hope right got a good left hook," Kenny said, and Ava laughed.

Geo was relieved. It was the second time in a week that Lamar and Sondra had started something with Ava, and he didn't like it.

Ellen put her hand in Ava's and said, "Y'all want to listen to records?" and since the twins had recently gotten Little Richard's *Rip It Up*, they all decided that was a good way to spend the afternoon.

1976

Though she tried, Sarah could not stop looking at the clock. From the moment she sat down behind her teller window at exactly nine that morning, she turned her head to glance up at the clock above the bank's front entrance every three or four minutes. By ten o'clock, she was already getting a crick in her neck. She rubbed it, gingerly, and deposited two fifteen-dollar checks for a customer who had a large piece of spinach between her teeth. When the spinach-toothed woman was gone, Sarah glanced again at the clock. Her pre-occupation with the time was so obvious that her co-worker, Mildred, a white girl who sat behind the window next to Sarah's, leaned over and whispered, "You got a long time to go before closing. You got a hot date or something?"

Sarah wasn't actually waiting for four o'clock. She never waited for four o'clock. She liked her job and most of her customers and liked the view out the front windows of the bank, where all day she could see Center City life taking place: meter maids writing tickets to delivery men who sneered or gave them the finger; the lines of sophisticated-looking, business-suited men and women, waiting for hot dogs from street vendors. Usually, when four o'clock came, she felt a little bit sorry.

She was waiting for noon. Lunchtime. It came later than usual. She was sure of it. When she stepped out into the August sunshine, she immediately turned and looked down the street to see if the bus was coming. It wasn't. She frowned. How in the world was she going to make it all the way down to Old City, find the fire-eating man, and be back at work in an hour? She could take a cab, but that would mean spending money she really didn't want to spend. She could walk, except that it was fifteen blocks down, and fifteen back. She checked her watch, which was always five minutes fast. It read twelve-ten, so she knew it was really only five minutes past. She decided to just start walking, and when the bus caught up to her she could take it the rest of the way.

Center City was always crowded during the day, especially around lunchtime. She moved quickly, passing the shiny, square, silver food vendor boxes that lined the streets and made the air smell like grease and coffee and fried onions. She walked as fast as she could in the shoes she was wearing. Her heels weren't high, but nor were they made for speed. She had gone four blocks when she saw the bus approaching from behind, and she got on it, and sat in the front seat so she could get right off at her stop. It seemed to take forever. When the bus got to Penn's Landing, she was the last passenger. She stepped down and the bus pulled away with a grunt of heavy, dark gray smoke.

She hadn't been down here in years, but it all looked the same. On one side, facing the Delaware River, there were the same little stores that had been there in sixty-five, including a tailor and a couple of antique shops. On the other side, near the water, there were huge warehouses and, in the water, the huge ships that lined the piers. Large brick and cement staircases linked Penn's Landing to Market and Walnut streets. From where she was standing, at Front and Market, she could see out over the river, to the Ben Franklin Bridge, and beyond, to New Jersey. She walked south, towards the spot where she remembered the fire-eating man had performed years ago.

She had decided, while lying in bed the night before, that the only way to erase the humiliation of being called a liar by Ava, right in front of Helena, was to turn that lie into the God's honest truth. She would find the fire-eating man and talk to him, just like she'd told Helena she had done.

When she saw him, in the same spot where he had been eleven years earlier, she was surprised. He was standing in the same place he had been in the lie she'd told Helena, but she realized now how unlikely it was to find him still there, and she was surprised Helena had believed it. If she had. Maybe she had known it was a lie all along and was just humoring Sarah. That thought made her even more determined and she went and joined the small crowd of people standing around the performer.

He looked different than she remembered. Shorter, for one thing. For another thing, the scruffy, alley-cat look he once had was gone, his hair and beard much shorter and well-groomed. The sweet face she remembered was harder around the edges, though, and lined around the eyes with eleven more years of life. He didn't notice her, just as she knew he wouldn't, and she stood there wondering how in the world she was going to get him by himself so she could talk to him. The lie had not only been that she had seen him again, but that they had talked. And, also, that he had remembered her and asked her to come back again. She had no idea how she was going to make those last two lies into the truth, but she could at least talk to him. She hoped. She checked her watch. It was twenty after twelve already.

His act had changed since she had last seen it. He had added some dancing and also some flips. No matter what else he was doing, though, it was the flaming batons that held all eyes as he juggled them high in the air. Sarah enjoyed the movement of the flames, felt almost hypnotized by it, and she remembered why she had come here every day for a whole year. He was wonderful to watch.

He did another flip and the crowd applauded. When he was upright again, he smiled at them all and said, "Thank you, friends, thank you very much." His voice was still light and young, happy-sounding, and he had an accent that she hadn't remembered that made him sound a little like a Kennedy. Considering how he looked and what he did for a living, it was a strange thought, and she laughed to herself.

The show went on for several more minutes and ended with the fire-eating man eating the fire from the tip of each baton. The audience applauded again, and the air filled with the sound of coins tinkling against each other as they were dropped into his hat. As the crowd thinned, the fire-eating man turned and bent down over a black case, arranging the now-fireless batons inside it. Sarah watched the back of him, standing a few feet away, and willed herself to say something. He was packing his things quickly, almost throwing the batons into the case, and dumping the change from the hat in with them, without even counting it, and Sarah decided he must be in a hurry. She shouldn't bother him now. She checked her watch and saw that it was twelve-forty. She needed to get back to work. But she stood there, staring at his back and trying to think of something, anything to say. He closed the case and put the empty hat onto his head and, without even turning around, he walked in the other direction, away from her. She started to call out to him, but no sound came. Instead, she watched him walk away and, when he turned the corner at Market and was out of sight, she turned and walked back to the bus stop.

When George clocked out of work at five and exited the city building through a side door, which let him out on Market, he was sure he saw Chuck Ellis standing across the street, right out front of the post office, looking at him. But when a mail truck pulled up it blocked his view, and when it pulled away a few seconds later, no one was there. He lit a cigarette and walked down the street in the other direction, towards the el station, feeling uneasy. When he got to the el station, he ran to catch the westbound train but missed it, the doors sliding closed just as he reached the platform. He cursed, feeling more annoyed than he should be, considering the trains ran every five minutes or so at this time of day. He sat down on a bench and took a long drag off his cigarette. A woman in a nurse's uniform smiled at him and he smiled back with exaggerated interest, then rested his elbows on his knees and lowered his head, staring down at the platform floor beneath his feet. He was tired. He'd worked a long day collecting Philadelphia's garbage and his shoulders and neck ached. His body couldn't handle hard work the way it used to. He rubbed the back of his neck with one hand and sighed.

He felt someone watching him and thought it was the pretty nurse who had smiled at him, and he looked up grinning, ready to give her the earnest, but ultimately empty, attention he always gave to women who flirted with him. It wasn't the nurse looking at him, though. It was Chuck. He was standing by the stairs that led up to the street surface and he was watching George, whose grin faded.

The el pulled into the station and George stepped up to the doors of one car just as Chuck approached the adjoining car. Once inside the train, George could see Chuck through the windowed doors separating the compartments. Chuck wasn't watching him anymore. George took a forward-facing seat, putting his back to Chuck and the adjoining car. When he got off at Sixtieth Street, he did not see Chuck as he walked towards the stairs and down to the street.

When he got to his front door, he was just putting his key in the lock when he heard footsteps behind him and, startled, he turned, and saw Chuck standing behind him.

"I think you got the wrong house," George said. "The devil's in here."

Chuck frowned. "I aint never been a part of all that."

"You aint never stopped nobody else from being part of all that, either."

"George, I need to confess something."

"Sounds to me like you need a priest. You thinking about converting?"

"I'd like to come in a minute, if I could," Chuck said.

"Nigger, you must be crazy."

Chuck swallowed hard and said, "I aint got a right to ask you for nothing. But I'm asking anyway. Just for a minute. Please. And then, if you want, I'll go and never come back here again."

"So, if I say no, you gone keep coming back?"

"I aint trying to harass you or nothing. I just need to say a few words to you, and that's all. Please."

George didn't know what to do. He didn't want to hear a few words. But he also didn't want Chuck coming back. He opened the front door and listened. The house was quiet. "Alright," he said, unsure. "For a minute. And then you got to go."

They stood on opposite sides of the living room. Chuck kept wiping his palms on his pant legs. When he spoke, his voice was shaky. "I wasn't honest with you, George. That time at the Christmas party. You know what I'm talking about?"

George didn't answer.

"When I said I wasn't like that. It wasn't true. Well, I mean…I guess I didn't know what I was like. Or I didn't want to know. Do that make sense?" He shifted his weight to his other leg, wiped his palms again, cleared his throat. "What I'm saying is, I felt things I didn't want to feel. I was scared of those feelings. But I couldn't make them stop. So, I tried to ignore them. Every time you came to prayer service, I'd be so happy to see you, but terrified, too. When I'd go home, I'd look at my wife and wonder why I didn't get that excited seeing her." He looked pained, his eyebrows drawn tight together, remembering. "Then that night when you tried to…well, I couldn't handle it. I mean, I wanted it. I felt it. But when it started to happen, I got scared. I knew it meant something. Thinking about it was one thing. Doing it was something else."

George looked away from him, down at the floor.

"I wasn't trying to hurt you, George. But I know I did."

George could feel Chuck's eyes on his face, but he didn't want to look at him. He didn't want Chuck to see the pain inside him, the pain that was always there, eating him up from the inside out, the pain of knowing he wasn't good enough, not for a woman or a man, not for his mother or his father, not for his children. The pain of being this other thing, this strange being that belonged nowhere, least of all in the company of God. He felt Chuck move closer to him, felt his hand come up and touch his back, between his shoulder blades, and then move up to his shoulders, massaging his tense muscles with strong fingers. George closed his eyes. He tried to think only of Chuck, of this man he had once felt so close to, this gentle, kind man with his soft voice and delicate-looking-but-strong hands, this man he had wanted so much and still wanted.

Chuck's hand moved from George's shoulder to his head, his fingers in George's hair, and in one moment he turned George's head so that they faced each other, and pulled him close, and pressed his open mouth against George's. George felt the heat and wetness of Chuck's tongue against his lips, and he opened his mouth and let it slide in, at the same time feeling a pressure in his crotch as his excitement strained against his zipper.

There were footsteps, and George moved away from Chuck, just as Helena appeared in the doorway. She looked from George to Chuck and didn't say anything. A moment later, Ava appeared at her side.

"Oh. Daddy. When did you come in?"

"Couple minutes ago," George said, willing his voice to sound normal. Begging it to. "I didn't know nobody was home."

"We were in the backyard," Ava said.

"Oh. Well, you remember Deacon Ellis?" George asked, now standing several feet away from Chuck.

Ava nodded. "Hello."

"Hello, Ava. It's nice to see you."

"This is my sister-in-law, Helena."

While Chuck and Helena exchanged hellos, George searched Helena's eyes for some sign of what she might have seen, what she might be thinking.

"Well, I have to be going," Chuck said.

Ava and Helena said goodbye and then went into the kitchen.

"Meet me at the church tomorrow tonight. After prayer service," Chuck whispered to George. "At the back door."

"Alright."

At the front door, Chuck peered out into the street and, seeing no one, slipped quietly out of the house.

Mother Haley had been dead four years, but she stood in the kitchen, by the stove, wearing the hat and dress she had been buried in. Regina had been at the refrigerator, taking the meat out for dinner, when the ghost appeared. Startled, she had dropped the package of ground beef onto the floor. "What in the world are you doing here?" Regina asked her.

Mother Haley glared at her and the white feather in her white hat trembled.

Regina squinted at the apparition. "Don't look at me like that, old woman." She was trying to sound unafraid, but really she was terrified. Ghosts in general didn't scare her. But this one was glowing almost red and Regina could feel a fury rising into the air, the temperature in the kitchen rising with it. "You got something to say, say it."

Mother Haley took a quick step towards Regina and just as Regina screamed, the spirit disappeared. Hurried footsteps came from every direction and Sarah, Ava, and Helena all burst into the kitchen.

"Mama, what's wrong?" Sarah asked her.

"That old woman," Regina said. "She was here."

"Who?" Ava asked. "Mama, who are you talking about?"

"Mother Haley."

Helena looked at Ava. "Your grandmother?"

"She was right there," Regina said, pointing at the stove. "She came at me."

"I saw Kenny," Sarah said.

They all turned and looked at her.

"A few days ago. He was there when I woke up."

"I saw Miss Maddy," Ava told them. She had seen the ghost of Maddy Duggard on the night she had almost wet herself laughing and she had been too embarrassed by that entire incident to want to refer back to it later. Miss Maddy had been standing at the top of the steps when Ava had come out of the bathroom.

Helena peered at her, frowning, and Ava could tell that she didn't believe in ghosts.

Ava picked up the ground beef from the floor and put it back into the refrigerator. They all sat down at the table and, for a little while, nobody spoke. Then Helena asked Ava, "Who was that man with your father?"

"Chuck Ellis. He used to live down the street."

Regina paused in lighting a cigarette. "What about Chuck Ellis?"

"He was here," Ava told her.

"What you mean, *here*?"

"I mean here, Mama, in this house."

"Deacon Ellis was *here*?" Sarah asked.

Regina leaned forward in her chair. "When was this?"

"A little while ago. Before you got home."

"He's a friend of Mr. Delaney's?" Helena asked.

"He was," Sarah said. "When we were little we called him Uncle Chuck. They was always together. Then he stopped coming around."

"Because of Pastor Goode?"

Sarah shook her head. "It was years before that. Wasn't it, Mama?"

"Well, what was he doing here?" Regina asked.

Ava shrugged. "I have no idea. They came in while we were out back."

"Well, that's good, isn't it?" Sarah asked. "I mean, one of *them* coming into this house, and not even to start no trouble? I know he don't live on this block no more, but he still go to church there. For him to come in this house at all, that must mean something."

"What?" Regina asked.

"I don't know. Maybe somebody finally figuring out Pastor Goode been wrong all this time."

"I doubt that's why he came in here," Regina said.

"Well, why then?"

Regina didn't answer. She got up from the table, feeling suddenly crowded, and left the kitchen. Up in her bedroom, she turned on the small black and white television that sat on top of the dresser, then removed her shoes, and sat with her legs stretched out on the bed. She smoked and watched the evening news, and tried not to think.

After Mother Haley appeared and disappeared again, the house was so hot that no one wanted to cook dinner. Instead, they searched the refrigerator and the cupboards for anything they could make that did not require real cooking, and settled on canned sardines and green beans, and bread. Paul was not working the night shift, so he was there in time for dinner for the first time in days. He spread butter on his bread and then passed the butter dish to Ava.

"I looked at a house today," he said.

Regina looked up from her sardines. "You been looking at houses again?"

He nodded.

She looked at Ava. "You changed your mind about moving?"

Ava shook her head. "No, I haven't."

"You will. Once you see this place and see how good a fit it is for us. It aint even that far away from here."

"Where's it at?" Sarah asked.

"Over on Pine and Fifty-Third."

"That aint but what?" Regina asked. "Nine, ten blocks?"

"That's right." Paul looked at Ava. "You be able to come and see your folks every day if you want to."

Ava spread butter on her bread and said nothing.

"Well, what's the house like?" Helena asked.

"It's nice. Not too big. Just the right size for us, I think. It's even some extra room, in case, you know, we ever had kids or something."

"Well, that's good," Regina said. "It sound nice."

He looked at Ava again. "The lady who showed it to me said she'd be glad to set up a time for us to go see it together. Maybe Saturday?"

Ava was aware that they were all looking at her, but she was watching the butter, seeing the way its color changed as it softened on the bread and how the light from the fixture above the table caught in the tiny bubbles of butterfat, making them gleam.

"Ava, I know you hear me talking to you," Paul said.

She looked at him, annoyed. "First you're looking at houses when you know I aint moving, and now you're talking about kids you know I can't have. Yes, I hear you talking, but what you're saying doesn't seem to have a whole lot to do with me."

"We *are* moving," he said. "Goddamnit. I been in this house four years, Ava, and I don't want to be in it no more."

"Maybe y'all should talk about this in private," Helena said.

He glared at his sister. "We talked about it in private a hundred times. It aint nothing else to say. We moving and that's the end of it."

"Paul—"

"Stay out of it, Helena," he said, his voice rising. "It aint got nothing to do with you."

Ava brought the buttered bread to her lips, and the heavy, fatty smell of it filled her up. The moment the butter entered her mouth, the second it melted on her tongue, she knew she had not tasted it before, not really, not in a very long time. The taste was overwhelming, cream-thick and heavy-rich, and devastating. Lush, and heaven, it caused her eyes to close and her head to fall back, and a pleasure like none she could right then remember coursed through her, starting between her legs and moving down into her thighs, and up into her stomach, spreading over every inch of her, building like a slow, hot thing, like a fever. When it reached the tips of her fingers, she dropped her fork, and only vaguely heard it clang against her plate.

"You alright, baby?" Paul asked her.

She nodded, but could not speak. The pleasure grew and she felt something deep within herself coming up, and she thought, for a moment, that it was laughter, but when she opened her throat there came a moan, long and wonderful and obscene. Suddenly, she remembered being thirteen, standing in a small, dark room in Blessed Chapel Church, in the bishop's nook, behind the pulpit, with her mouth pressed against another girl's mouth. And now the fever, high and hot, suddenly broke, through her skin and out the tips of her toes, from her nipples, which hardened and tingled, and off her tongue, the tip of which pressed against the roof of her mouth. She grabbed the edges of the tablecloth and squeezed her eyelids tight, and grunted, like an animal, like a woman, and the pleasure screamed and crested, and then, in a moment, turned her loose, leaving her trembling.

When she opened her eyes, her family members were staring at her, her sister looking mortified, her husband embarrassed but also a little excited, and her mother confused. Helena looked like she was trying not to laugh, biting her bottom lip as her green eyes twinkled.

Paul cleared his throat, but didn't say anything.

Ava took a deep breath and let go of the bunches of tablecloth in her fists. She smiled at Paul. "I'm sorry, what were you saying?"

"I…I was just asking you to come see it. The house."

"Alright," Ava said, not because she wanted to see the house, but because she felt better, in that moment, than she had ever felt before and she wanted to say yes to somebody.

The phone rang and Ava bounced up to answer it. The voice on the other end spoke in a whisper. "The Lord," it said, "will hand you over to me, and I'll strike you down and cut off your head."

Ava sighed and hung up. She returned to the table, frowning.

"Who was it?" Regina asked.

"I don't know."

Sarah rolled her eyes. "Stop being mysterious for no reason, Ava. What did they say?"

"Something about striking us down and cutting off our heads. Or maybe just mine. It wasn't clear and I didn't think to ask."

"Goddamnit," Paul said. "Why didn't you give me the phone?"

"Somebody threatened you?" Helena asked, her voice full of shock and worry.

"It's just words," Ava said, sitting down again.

Helena did not look relieved. "Have these people ever done anything? Besides throw bricks through your window? Have they ever been violent?"

"Not in years," Regina said. "And you don't want to know about none of that."

Helena looked at Ava. "Tell me."

"The worst thing they ever did," Ava said, "was start a fire."

"But it was fifteen years ago," Regina said, "and they aint done nothing like that since."

Helena shook her head, slowly, from side to side, and after a few moments asked, "Was anybody hurt?"

"Yes," Regina said, sighing heavily. "Somebody died. My friend. Maddy. My best friend." And here was another thing Regina had not talked about in years, another old thing brought out into the light again.

"Please tell me somebody was caught."

They answered that question with silence.

She looked around at all of them. "I can't believe you stayed here after that."

"I had more reason than ever to stay after that," Regina said. "Maddy was one of the only people on this block who never turned against us. Her and Jane Lucas. Jane moved away, because they didn't like it that she kept on talking to us and wouldn't give her no peace." She sighed. "Maddy stayed. And she died trying to help us, trying to get us out of the house after they started the fire. And we did get out."

"But she didn't? She burned?"

"She didn't burn. She fell down the stairs and broke her neck."

Helena got up from the table. She walked over to the stove, then paced back, looking disturbed. "Who are these people?" she asked. "Who exactly is making these threats, and throwing these bricks, and starting these fires? All your neighbors can't be arsonists."

"No, it aint all of them," Regina said. "Most of them don't do nothing more than stare and whisper. It's only a handful of them that holler things, or leave notes in the door, or make phone calls. And it's just one or two that do more than that, when the pastor tell them to. One of them is Malcolm Hansberry. He live in that green house right across the street and he used to be our good friend. The other is his brother, Vic Jones. He live down at the corner. And I know what you thinking. If I know who they is, why don't I tell the police? Well, I have told them. But since I aint never seen none of them doing nothing, it aint a thing the police can do. They got the pastor and this whole block ready to say they was doing something else when whatever happened *happened*."

"There must be *something* you can do," Helena said, sounding frustrated.

Regina sighed. "Well, if you think of something, honey, you let us know."

That evening Paul sat with Helena on the back porch, smoking, and noticed that she was quiet, pensive and distracted, her eyes burdened behind her thick glasses. Instead of asking her what was wrong, he watched her a while, trying to figure out what might be on her mind. When they were children, he had been good at doing that, at looking at her and seeing what was wrong. Back then, he knew everything about her, or mostly everything, and he could usually identify the source of any pain or upset she felt. Whether she was crying because somebody had called her tar baby at school, or was knocking things over, clumsily, because she always slept badly at night and spent the daytime in a fog. He could always tell, because he knew her. Back then. Now, sitting out on the back porch, stealing glimpses of her as she smoked and looked up at the few stars that could be seen in the city sky, he could only assume what the cause of her quiet was.

"That story about the fire was pretty terrible," he said.

She looked at him, nodded.

"That's what you thinking about?" he asked.

"No." She took a drag off her cigarette and looked thoughtful. "I was thinking about Ava's drawing. Have you seen it? The one I told you about?"

"Oh," he said, surprised. "No. I forgot to ask her."

She looked at him a long moment, then asked, "What was it about Ava that made you go to the museum cafeteria three or four times a day just to smile at her?"

He laughed. "She told you that?"

"Yes. Is it true?"

"Yeah, it's true. It's like I told you—she just seemed less complicated than the other women I was around. She wasn't always gossiping or worrying about how she looked all the time. She never tried to get nobody's attention, least of all mine, and I liked that. Then, when I talked to her, she was easy to get along with. She wasn't always trying to pick a fight or get her way."

"Easy. That's what you said before."

"Yeah. What about it?"

"Nothing. Once you got to know her, though, you saw that she was more than that, didn't you?"

"Sure."

"Like what?"

"She's hardworking," he said. "A good cook."

Helena frowned. "That's not what I mean."

"Well, what do you mean?"

"I want to know if you think Ava is different than she seemed to you at first. Less easy. Less uncomplicated. More funny, more creative. More intense."

"Not really. I mean, that don't sound like Ava. She aint really none of those things."

Helena seemed agitated now. "But she is. She is all of those things. Maybe you're not paying enough attention to see it."

"You saying I don't know my own wife?"

"No. I'm not saying that."

It seemed to him that was exactly what she was saying and he wondered where she got off, thinking she knew Ava better than he did. "I been married to Ava for four years. I knew her for nearly two before that. You just met her a few days ago. And she aint even been acting like herself lately."

"How not?"

How not? he thought. She sure had learned to speak uppity in the years they had been apart.

"Ava aint usually so...emotional," he said. "Maybe that's where you getting 'intense' from, but I'm telling you, that aint her, that aint what she's really like."

Still frowning, Helena crushed out her cigarette in the ashtray.

"Why we even talking about Ava?" he asked.

"I don't know." She sighed, and pushed her glasses up on her face. "You off tomorrow?"

He nodded. "Yeah."

"Let's go up to French Creek and spend the day together," she said. "You been there lately?"

He shook his head. "I aint been there since we was kids, with daddy. What you want to go up there for?"

"I loved it there. So did you. Remember how we used to roast marshmallows and fish and chase after deer?"

He grinned.

"Let's go," she said. "It'll be nice to get out of the city for a day."

"I'm supposed to look at another house."

"You can do that anytime," she said.

"Well. Maybe I could borrow Milky's car. Guy I work with. We could pack some food."

She nodded, eager.

"Alright," he said. "Yeah. Let's do it."

Regina sat in a chair by the window, beside the only lamp in the room, its shade tilted slightly so that her face was illuminated and her nose and chin cast light shadows. Helena sat on the bed with her legs folded and her drawing tablet in her lap, staring at her for many minutes. She had asked Regina if she would be willing to sit, so that she could make a drawing of her, and Regina had agreed.

"You gone draw me," Regina asked now, "or just look at me?"

Helena smiled. "I'm just studying the structure of your face."

"Can I talk while you do that?"

"Of course. I wish you would. It helps me catch the nuances, the lines."

"I don't know about nuances," Regina said, "but it's a lot of lines to catch."

"Oh no. For someone your age, you have very smooth skin."

"Well, dark skin always hold up better over time," Regina said.

Helena smiled. "Well, then, I guess I'll look thirty forever."

"Child, you don't even look thirty now. You look twenty, if that."

Helena got up and went to the lamp, adjusting the shade again.

"You know," Regina said, "Ava used to do this all the time."

"Did you sit for Ava a lot?" Helena asked, returning to her seat on the bed.

"I never 'sat' for her. She would just watch me doing whatever I was doing at the time. Cooking. Folding laundry. Watching television. Working in my garden. I used to tell her to quit drawing and help me prune the roses. But she wasn't interested."

Helena laughed. "Drawing while other people work. Sounds like an artist to me." She had a little pencil in her hand and she began to sketch.

Regina watched, her eyes moving over Helena's face. Whenever she looked at the younger woman, the first thing she saw was the blackness of her skin. Taking that in seemed to leave little room in her mind's eye for anything else. Looking at her now, though, really looking at her, Regina saw the way her skin glowed, the way her eyebrows and eyelashes, which were slightly lighter-colored than her skin, complimented her eyes, which were the greenest green Regina had ever seen on a dark-skinned person.

"Now who's studying who?" Helena asked.

Regina chuckled. "I was just gone ask where you got them eyes from."

"My father. Where he got them from, I couldn't say."

"Things like that can skip generations. He probably got it from his mother's uncle's granddaddy's sister."

The both laughed.

"Your husband has interesting eyes," Helena said.

"George? You think so?"

"Yes. You don't?"

"Well, I guess so," she said, considering it. "I aint really thought about it in a while, but, yeah, he do."

"He must have been a handsome young man."

"He wasn't bad."

"How did you first meet?"

"We didn't. Not that I can remember. Town we grew up in was so small, everybody just knew everybody else from the time they was kids."

"It must have been a huge change, moving to a big city like this."

George was right about one thing—this girl sure did ask a lot of questions. Regina didn't mind it, though. In fact, she liked it, even if she suspected the questions were leading somewhere. She didn't know where, but she was content to go along and find out.

"Oh, it was a change alright. I hadn't never even visited nowhere big as this. To move here seemed crazy to me. I couldn't get my head around this city for years. I wanted to go home to Hayden so many times. But George said we could have a better life up here."

"Was he right?"

Regina thought about it, then said, "Depend on what you think a 'better life' is. Yeah, I guess we did alright for ourselves for a while there. Before our son died." She wondered if this was where it was going, if Helena wanted to know more about George Jr. and how he died. But Helena didn't ask about it, she just continued to sketch and said nothing for a while.

Regina thought about Hayden. She still missed her home. She had never wanted to leave and had been sure she would be instantly miserable in Philadelphia, so far from her family and everything she knew. The first few years here had been good, though. It was only after they had moved onto this street, when George had begun to change, that everything started to go downhill. He had grown distant in the space of a couple of years and the man she had married had become like a stranger to her. He wasn't lying or sneaking around back then, but what he was doing was just as bad. He was shutting himself off from her and from their children, closing himself up, while at the same time opening himself up to someone else. Chuck Ellis. Regina had sat there and watched as Chuck had become the person George talked to and went out of his way to spend time with. She had resented it. She had left her home and everyone she knew because George had told her their lives would be better, but he had not told her that she would be living that better life without him. She was glad when Chuck stopped coming around, although she had dreaded knowing the reason why. She never asked. Instead, she had tried to get close to George again, thinking that with Chuck gone there might be space for her again. But he had only become more distant. And when Geo died, Regina had lost the strength to try anymore.

When she came out of her head again, Helena was watching her with intense eyes, her drawing hand moving rapidly on the page.

Half an hour later, Helena's hand stopped and she smiled over at Regina. "Done."

"Let me see it."

Helena shook her head. "Not just yet. I have to put some finishing touches on it first. I'll show you when I'm all finished."

"Alright, then," Regina said, getting up. "I better get myself to bed."

"Thank you," Helena said, "for sitting. And for talking."

"Well, it's nice to be talked to, instead of talked around, for a change," Regina said, and she went off to bed.

Late that night, Paul lay awake in his bed, staring at the wall that separated his bedroom from Sarah's, where he knew Helena was still up, because he could hear her moving around on the creaky floors, which, he no-

ticed, were a lot less creaky than usual. She had always been a night person. When they were children and shared the same room, Paul often awoke
in the middle of the night to find his sister sitting at the end of her bed,
reading in the little light that came in through the window from a nearby
streetlamp. Usually, it was one of the adventure books their father brought
when he showed up once every couple of years, which were full of stories
of sinking boats and dark, wave-washed caves, and jeweled treasure. Or
sometimes she would just be sitting there at the window, looking up at a
heavy moon, her green eyes alight with imagining. "What you thinking
'bout?" Paul would often ask, from across the small room. "How to get
free," she would sometimes say.

Lying there in bed now, staring at the wall that separated them, he
missed those long-ago nights, missed under-the-covers giggling and the
warmth of a sister, which was unlike any other kind, a warmth that seeped
into the fibers of blankets and held there all through even the coldest
nights. He had always felt lucky to have a sister, especially in February.

He turned away from the wall and lay on his back instead. He was tired
and he wanted to sleep. Every time he tried, the past pushed in. He didn't
like it. It wasn't the real past, anyway, it was a sweeter, happier version, a
half-lie, with all the pleasures and none of the pains. It was a trick, a false-
hood that omitted its own ugliest parts and pretended to be something it
wasn't, the way the past liked to do. Paul wasn't fooled.

He turned his body again, this time over onto his other side, his back to
the wall, and it was only then that he realized Ava was also awake and was
lying there staring at him. He saw something in her eyes, a flash of excitement, something carnal, like he had never seen in her before. She had never, not once, initiated sex with him. But now she reached out and touched
his face and moved her body close to his on the bed. He kissed her, meeting
her excitement with his own, pulling her to him and wrapping his arms
around her. They kissed feverishly, for many seconds, and then Ava pushed
his head down between her legs. Paul pushed up her nightgown and pulled
off her panties and gave her, gladly, eagerly, the pleasure she was asking
for. They made love in a fever of heat and sweat and it was like it had never been before. Ava took complete control, straddling him, then lying on
her back with her legs around his waist, and when they were done, when
she was satisfied, which took a while, they lay there in the dark, breathing
heavily, the sheets soaking wet and sticking to their skin.

"That was…" He shook his head. "I don't even know a word for it."

She was lying on her back, staring up at the ceiling, and she didn't say
anything.

"You thirsty?" he asked.

"No."

"I am." He got up, grabbed the empty cup he kept on the nightstand for water late at night. He opened the door, and peeked out to make sure the coast was clear before hurrying naked down the hall to the bathroom. He let the cold tap run for a little while, then filled the cup. When he got back to the bedroom, Ava was lying on her side, turned away from him. He took a long drink of water, then placed the cup on the nightstand as he got back into the bed. He moved close to her, put his arms around her.

She pushed him away. "I'm tired," she said.

He blinked in the dark, feeling rejected and confused.

Ava pulled the sheet up to her chin, even though the room was stiflingly hot.

Paul lay down on his back, frowning into the heavy darkness. "I killed somebody," he said, so quietly that he was sure she had not heard him and, worried that he might not have the guts to say it again if she hadn't, he made himself say it again, louder. "I killed somebody, Ava."

She turned over, squinted at him in the dark. "What are you talking about?"

"It was a long time ago," he said. "And I didn't mean to do it. But somehow that don't make it even a little bit better, even though you'd think it would."

"Who did you kill?"

"A woman. No, a girl. She wasn't but sixteen. She was hurting my sister. I was just trying to stop her."

Ava's eyes were wide in the dark.

"That's why I got sent to juvie. I was in until I was eighteen."

Ava sat up in the bed, reached over and turned on the lamp on the bedside table. In the light, her face was heavy with shock, her brow drawn tight, her mouth slightly open. "I can't believe you never told me this," she said.

"I couldn't. Knowing what happened to your brother, I didn't think you could love me if you knew."

He reached over to take her hand, but she moved away from him, getting up out of the bed. She was trembling.

Paul wished to God he had told her before now. Anytime before now, before the last few days. This trembling woman was so different from the wife he had known for four years. A few days ago, she would have been shocked, she might even have thrown him out, but she would not have stood there as she stood there now, looking at him with devastation in her eyes, shaking from head to foot with what he knew was disgust, and fear, and anger.

He got out of the bed and stood on the other side of it, stark naked. He wanted to reach for his pants, but he was afraid that if he looked away from her she would be gone when he looked again.

"Baby," he said. "Ava. It was an accident. I didn't want to do it. I didn't mean to."

"You meant to lie about it all this time."

"What would have happened if I told you? Way back, in the beginning? You wouldn't have had nothing to do with me. I didn't want you to walk away from me over something I did when I was fifteen, something I never meant to do, something I suffered over every day since it happened."

She stared at him for a long moment, then asked, "Who was the girl? What was she doing to your sister?"

"She lived in our building," he said. "Our mothers was friends and she would come over with her. She used to tease Helena all the time about being so black, make her cry all the time. When I came in that time, she was holding her down. I grabbed her, and pushed her. She fell against a glass table, right against the corner of it, and it snapped off and cut her."

Ava grabbed the arm of the chair by the bed and sank down into it. She closed her eyes and took a long breath. When she opened her eyes, she frowned and said, "Put something on, please."

He reached for his boxer shorts and pulled them on, then his undershirt. Then he sat down on the bed and watched her, waiting.

After a little while, she said, "I feel like I don't know you, Paul."

He didn't mean to laugh, but he couldn't help it.

"That's funny?" she asked.

"No. But I been feeling the same thing about you for days. And you aint been rushing to tell me what's going on with you."

"I can tell you for sure I aint killed anybody."

Paul got up, grabbed his pants. He pulled them on, and then his shirt, and moved to the door.

"Where are you going?" she asked him.

"Somewhere else."

"*You're* walking out? You got some nerve."

He ignored her, ran down the stairs, and out the front door.

Ava awoke craving coffee. It was just after dawn and the bluish light coming in through the window cast long, thin shadows along the walls, shadows that reached up onto the ceiling and stretched across the bed. From one dark corner of the room she felt a presence, a hum that was different from that of the box fan, the low hum of another soul, and she sat up in the bed and looked around the room, peering into the shadows. At first, the hum felt vague and unfamiliar, but as she sat there it grew stronger, and clearer, and she recognized it. It was Geo. All around her, heavy in the dark of the room, was the spirit of her brother. It was so palpable, and so close, that she expected him to emerge from the shadows any second, and she climbed out of the bed and stood in the center of the room, and waited. The dark seemed to breathe around her. Outside the window, the sky continued to lighten, and the shadows shifted and crept, and reached out for her.

"Geo," she whispered. "Are you here?"

No answer came. Daylight spilled into the room, erasing the shadows, and with them the murmur of his presence.

She went downstairs to the kitchen, where Sarah and George were already up, finishing their breakfast before leaving for work. She went straight to the coffee pot and poured herself some, then stood there with her nose inside the cup, thinking that the coffee smelled much richer than usual. "What kind of coffee is this?" she asked.

"It's Maxwell House. Like it always is," Sarah said. "You the one bought it."

Helena came in and said good morning to all of them. Her hands were dirty and she went and washed them in the sink. She was wearing a thin-strapped top and her shoulders were bare and Ava noticed the delicate bones that went from her shoulders to the base of her throat, where little beads of sweat had gathered, looking like tiny drops of coffee against her black skin, and Ava wondered for a moment what they might taste like. Helena seemed to feel her staring and glanced at her. Ava held the cup of coffee out to her. "Smell that."

Helena sniffed the coffee.

"It smells different?"

"It smells like coffee," Helena said.

Ava put her nose back in the cup and breathed in the dark aroma, loving it.

"You're up early," Sarah said.

"I was doing some work in the front yard," Helena told her.

George frowned. "What kind of work?"

"Turning over the soil. I'm going to plant some flowers there. Your wife told me last night how much her flower gardens used to mean to her and I thought I'd do it as a thank-you for your hospitality."

George wanted to object, but he couldn't think of a reason.

"Paul and I are driving up to French Creek today," Helena told Ava.

"Where's that?" Sarah asked.

"In the Poconos. We used to go up there with our father when we were kids."

"How y'all getting there?"

"A friend of Paul's is loaning us his car. Whitey, or somebody."

"Milky?" Sarah asked.

"That's it." She looked at Ava. "Is Paul still asleep?"

Ava shook her head. "He aint here."

"Oh. He left already to get the car?"

"No."

"Well, where is he?" Sarah asked.

"He walked out," Ava said, "in the middle of the night. I don't know where he is."

George looked up from his cereal. "What you talking about? *Walked out?*"

"You had a fight?" Helena asked.

"They don't never fight," Sarah said.

Ava laughed. "We do now."

The phone rang.

"That got to be Paul," George said, getting up to answer it.

Ava stared down into her coffee cup.

"Paul, where the hell you at?" George said into the phone. Then, "Yeah, she right here. Hold on."

He held the phone out to Helena. She glanced at Ava, then took it.

Ava turned back to the counter and added sugar to her coffee. She was not thinking about Paul. She was thinking about her brother, about what she had felt in her bedroom that morning. She wondered if he had really been there. With all the ghosts that had appeared to them in the last few days, it seemed likely that he would show up at some point. But he had not showed himself, as the others had, and Ava wondered why. And, too, she wondered what seeing him would do to her, what memories it would unlock, what emotions. Perhaps seeing him would bring it all back.

"Alright, I'll meet you over there," Helena was saying into the phone.

Ava sipped her coffee and wondered what would happen if Paul did not come home, and whether, in that case, Helena would leave, too.

The temperature reached ninety-seven degrees by eleven o'clock and through the front window of the bank, Sarah watched people moving slower up and down Chestnut Street, their feet almost dragging on the concrete sidewalks, their images blurred by the wavy lines of heat rising in the air. Around noon, thunder rumbled, and the sky opened, and sheets of rain slid down the bank's large windows, obscuring Sarah's view, so she could see only watery, distorted, umbrella-shaped images hurrying by. The storm moved through quickly and the city steamed for hours afterward, the air moist and heavy, but cooler than it had been that morning.

Sarah took the bus to Penn's Landing at one, hoping to catch the fire-eating man at the end of his performance, so that she could talk to him when no one else was around. When she got there, though, she found him just starting, lighting fire at the tip of each baton while the small crowd watched. The rain, Sarah thought. It had forced him to start later. She stood there watching the performance, the juggling and flipping, enjoying it as much as she had the last time, but still seeing no opportunity to talk to him.

She checked her watch. There was no way she would be able to stay until the end. She felt frustrated. At this rate, she would never be able to make her lie the truth, and Helena would never see her again.

"For this next part," the fire-eating man was saying, "I'm gone need a brave soul. Any brave souls in the crowd today?"

Sarah had never, ever, not once in her whole life, thought of herself as brave. But she needed to get closer to him. So, she stepped forward. When he smiled at her, she was sure he remembered her from years ago. Positive. But a second later, she told herself she was crazy, that he couldn't, because no one ever remembered her.

He bowed and offered her his hand, saying, "Come and stand right here beside me, young lady."

She took his hand, which was warm and rough-feeling, and stood beside him.

"What's your name?" he asked.

"Sarah."

"Ah, yes, Sarah, that's right," he said, nodding. "Sarah, you sure you brave enough for this?"

"I aint brave at all. I don't even know why I came up here. I must be out my mind."

"Well," he said. "In lieu of bravery, insanity will do."

Everyone laughed, except Sarah. What in the world was she thinking, getting up here like this? All because her little sister had embarrassed her? She was thirty-two years old, for Christ's sake; she wasn't a child anymore.

"I changed my mind," she said.

The fire-eating man grinned at her and whispered, "Don't worry, pretty girl. I aint gone hurt you none." Then he moved and stood beside her. Sarah watched as he picked up the flaming batons again. "Ladies and gents, sisters and brothers, friends and best friends, I give you Sarah, the Brave."

Some people clapped.

The fire-eating man got close behind Sarah, very close, and whispered, "I need to get close to you as I can for this, but don't worry, I don't mean nothing untoward by it."

She stood as still as she could and did not breath. She felt his chest press against her back, and he reached around her and extended his arms out on either side of her, so she could see his hands, in which he held three batons, all of them still on fire. He bent his elbows and Sarah could see the definition in his light-brown arms. Slowly, he began to juggle the flaming batons, not three feet from Sarah's face. She watched them, wide-eyed, and at first she was afraid. But something about the warmth of the fire so close, and the heat of him, stole the fear from her. She stared at the flames, as they rose and fell and licked the summer air, and at his large hands as they caught the batons, over and over, until the movement, the rhythm of it, of him, seemed to fill her like a fire in a hearth and, without thinking, she leaned back into him. Her sudden movement caused him to drop one of the batons. It smacked against the ground at their feet. A collective sigh of surprise moved over the crowd.

"Oh," Sarah said, looking down at the baton, which was still on fire. She turned her head and looked at him. "I'm so sorry. I moved."

He grinned at her, the lines around his eyes deepening, and said, "It's alright. It's good to be moved sometimes."

French Creek State Park was a couple of hours from Philadelphia and a welcome reprieve from the city. It was heavy with forest. Dense with oaks, hickories, maples, poplars, and beech trees, and here and there you could see mountain laurels and rhododendrons. Wetlands and pristine streams flowed through rich, damp creek valleys.

Paul and Helena parked Milky's Datsun in a lot near a ranger station and, carrying a bag full of sandwiches they had bought at a store on their way up, and a blanket, they walked together up into the forests.

"It smells the same," Helena said, breathing deeply.

Paul breathed in, too, and the green-smelling air filled his lungs. "It sure is better than car exhaust," he said. He pointed to the lake in the distance. "Remember we went canoeing out there?"

She nodded. "I remember those orange life jackets, and seeing fish swimming around us."

As children, they had come here a handful of times with their father, up until Paul was ten, when he had stopped coming around. They would put up an old tent that Paul was sure his father had found in a dumpster somewhere, because it smelled like old produce, and they would camp for two or three nights. Around the campfire, their father would tell them scary stories while they roasted marshmallows and ears of corn. Their father would always bring whiskey, and at some point he would pass out, and Paul and Helena would sit up looking at the stars, amazed at how many could be seen out there, and re-tell each other the same stories their father had just told, changing them so that the monster or serial killer died at the end, so they could get to sleep without fear of anything coming after them. In the mornings, they would fish and cook their catchings for breakfast over the campfire. Their father had a knack for open-fire cooking and those fish were still the best Paul had ever tasted.

They found a spot on the side of a hill overlooking the lake and put down the old blanket they had brought along. Helena lay on her back, with her fingers laced together behind her head, staring up into the clear sky. In the trees around them, birds called in high and low voices.

"I used to dream about this place sometimes," Helena said, "when I was in Baltimore. It didn't really look like this, you know, the way things don't look like they really are in dreams, but I knew it was supposed to be this place. I'd just be wandering around out in these woods. I could hear you and Daddy in the distance, but I couldn't get to you, as hard as I tried. I'd just go around in circles until I woke up."

"I had a dream about that girl last night," Paul said.

Helena looked over at him.

"I aint had one in a while," he said. "Years."

"Years?" she asked. "Lucky you. I've never gone that long without one."

"What you dreaming about it for?" he asked. "You aint got nothing to feel bad about. You aint do nothing wrong. I'm the one killed her."

"It was an accident."

"The judge never bought that," Paul said. "I don't know if I ever did, either."

"What do you mean? You meant to do it?"

"No. But calling it a accident don't seem right, either. I was angry. I was so full of anger back then. I was gone hurt somebody, at some point. If it wasn't her, it woulda been somebody else. I used to think about killing somebody. Some fool make me mad, I'd think about it. I thought about killing our daddy. If he'd ever showed up again, I might have."

"No, you wouldn't," she said. "I don't care what the Commonwealth of Pennsylvania says. You are not a killer, Paul."

He sighed.

For several minutes, neither of them spoke. Paul continued to watch the lake, where a few small boats moved on the water, and waited. He knew Helena would ask him about juvie again and he decided maybe he could talk about it a little. The past few days with Ava had made him think that keeping the past all locked up inside you might just mean letting it eat you from the inside out, taking little bites over years, until, maybe, one day, you just went crazy.

"Was juvie as bad as I imagine it was?" Helena asked, finally.

Paul shook his head. "You can't imagine it. However bad you think it was, it was worse. You might think I aint a killer, but some of them boys was killers for sure. Some of them was worse than killers."

"Worse?" she asked. "What's worse?"

"Worse is somebody that gets his kicks from hurting people. Not killing them, that's too final. Nothing left to torture if somebody already dead."

Helena fell silent again and Paul thought maybe she was afraid to go on asking questions, afraid of what the answers might be.

"It was this one gang of boys," he went on, "called theyselves the Slammers. Went around beating on younger guys when the guards wasn't paying attention, which was always. They busted me up the first night I was there. I wasn't no little punk, either, I was a tough enough kid. But they was meaner than me by a lot. They liked to see people hurting. They liked it on their own, and being in there, they found other boys who liked it too, and then they really had fun with it, made it a team sport. They used to burn kids. Hold them down and stick a lit match to their nipple, or somewhere worse. Or they'd put you in a headlock and squeeze until you passed out. They did that to me a couple times. Once, they held me down on the floor and held my mouth shut, and poured water over my head, so I felt like I was drowning. I always fought them, though. I never stopped fighting them. I had black eyes and busted lips. A couple times I got taken to the infirmary with broke ribs." He sighed. "The Slammers wasn't the worst in there, though. They'd kick your ass, but they wouldn't—" He stopped.

Helena sat up on the blanket. "Wouldn't what?"

Paul watched a broad-winged bird alight onto a thin branch above them.

"This one gang, the Rippers, was a bunch of boys from some projects in North Philly. They used to go into boy's rooms at night and do things to them. All night long, any night, you could hear it. The moaning and the whimpering. One night they came for me. I tried to fight them, but they knew how to hold a boy down. I was lucky, 'cause one of the guards came in and stopped them before they had really done anything. But after that, I knew I had to get in some kind of gang myself, or I was gone get fucked or killed, or both, real fast. I joined up with these boys from southwest. Remember Kareem? Used to live across the hall from us?"

Helena nodded. "With the one small ear?"

"Yeah, that his crazy mama burned half off. He was one of them, and he remembered me and got me in with them. Milky, the one whose car we drove up here, he was one, too. It was seven of us altogether. We called ourselves the Southwest Seven. We wasn't that creative."

"Were you safe then, with them?"

"It aint no such thing as safe in a place like that," Paul said. "But I was less of a target. And that came for a price. I still had to fight. All the time. I had to fight for my boys, help protect them so they would help protect me. I still got beat and cut and damn near killed, but now somebody had my back, so the bruises and scars was divided between us. But none of us was safe.

"All I thought about while I was there, the whole three years, was getting out and getting home. And staying home. It wasn't until I got out I realized home didn't exist no more. Mama was gone. You was gone."

"I wasn't gone," Helena said. "I was still there, living with Auntie and Uncle when you got out. I kept expecting you to show up. Expecting you to come find me."

"I did," he said.

"What?"

"I did come. First thing I did when I got out was go to Uncle's house. I was so happy to see him when he opened the door, happy to see anybody that looked anything like family. I asked for you. He said you was at school. I asked if I could wait and he said no. He looked at me like I was dirt. I told him I was gone come back when you was home. You know what he told me? He said if I cared anything about you, I wouldn't. That I couldn't do nothing but ruin your life. That you was a good student, and a good girl, and you aint need no ex-con, killer for a brother, dragging you down."

"Why did you listen to him? He was a fool if he said that."

"You can't understand. What being in a place like I was in can do to your mind. You spend every day getting told that you aint nothing. That you worse than the lowest nigger crawling the face of the earth. You ruined your life early and got it out the way, so you might as well just drink up, or smoke up, or shoot up, and wait to die. Aint no way nobody can love you anymore. You aint who you was. You aint that boy that your mama held. You a ex-con, a killer, a piece of nothing, and you a damn fool if you think different. I used to be Uncle's favorite. Remember? But he looked at me like he didn't know me. He couldn't love me no more after what I did. I know he saw in my eyes what those years in there did to me, too, and he didn't want it in his house. That made me know what I was told all those years was true. I wasn't nothing. They was right. So, I left, and I aint come back."

"Where did you go?" Helena asked him.

"Nowhere worth naming," he said. "I just rolled with guys I knew inside who had got out, too, guys in my gang. We cheated people, and robbed them. Sold smack. Any old fucked up thing you can think of, I did it. I never got caught, though. I always thought that was funny. Getting sent in there for something I never meant to do, and then coming out and getting away with all sorts of shit I did on purpose. It was years before I got it together. I don't even know how it happened. Just one day I got tired of feeling like the scum of the damn earth and decided not to be. By the time I got a real job and pulled some kind of life together for myself, and went back to find you, y'all was gone. And wouldn't nobody tell me where."

Helena was in tears and Paul had a hard lump in his throat. She moved closer to him on the blanket and put her arms around him. He swallowed the lump in his throat and took a deep breath, the fresh air soothing him. "It's alright," he said. "It don't matter now. We here together now."

They spent all morning and afternoon out there. They ate their lunches, huddled close, and talked about old times on the lake, fishing, and swimming, and building campfires. Late in the afternoon, Paul suggested they hike further up into the hills.

The terrain was steep and they both got out of breath within minutes. They looked at each other and laughed. "We old!" Paul said.

They walked further into a thick of high trees.

"You hear that?" Helena asked him.

Paul listened. It was the rush of a waterfall.

By the time they found it, having gone around in circles like Helena in her dreams, it was getting late, but they both wanted to sit a while and enjoy the sounds and sight of it. It was small, but lovely, the heavy white water rushing against dark rocks that jutted out of the side of a hill. Helena took her shoes off and dipped them in the cool stream at the base of the fall. Paul sat beside her, his shoulder leaned into hers.

"I told Ava," he said.

Helena nodded. "I thought so. I guess she didn't take it well."

"For anybody else, I'd say she took it great. For Ava, she damn near threw me out on my ass."

"She said you left."

"I did," he said. "But only so I could feel like I had some say in it."

"You're going back, then?"

He nodded. "Where else I'm gone go?"

Helena checked her watch. It was near six and it was already getting chilly. She put her shoes back on and they started walking back down through the trees. The downhill slope of the terrain was tricky to maneuver in some places and both of them slipped a few times. They were at the lake again, coming down a hill of lush mountain laurel, when Paul lost his footing and fell.

"Helena!"

She turned and saw that he had fallen and came back the few feet, kneeling beside him.

"Are you hurt?"

He grimaced. "My ankle. I twisted it." He couldn't walk on it easily. He tried, holding on to Helena, but after several feet, he said, "Stop, stop. It hurts. I need to sit a minute."

She helped him down onto the ground, then stood and looked out past the lake. "Is that the ranger station? Maybe I can run down and get somebody."

"Don't *run* down," he said. "You might end up like me."

She frowned.

"Just come on and sit here with me a minute," he said. "I'll get it together."

She sat beside him on the rocks and grass, folding her arms around herself in the chilly air. Paul put his arms around her and she rested her head on his shoulder.

"Do you think it'll be alright?" Helena asked. "Between you and Ava?"

"I think so," he said. "It might take some time, but I think we can get past it."

"Good," she said.

"You like her?" he asked.

She nodded. "I do like her, Paul."

He smiled. "I'm glad."

She put her arms around his waist.

After a few minutes, Paul said, "Alright, we better get the hell out of here 'fore they find us froze to death on the side of this hill. Or eaten by a family of bears."

His ankle hurt like hell. Every step was agony. But he gritted his teeth and, leaning on his sister, made it back to the ranger station. The ranger on duty asked him if he wanted an ambulance and Paul said no, so the ranger got his first aid kit and bandaged his ankle, noting that it looked more strained than sprained to him. They got back to Milky's car and Helena drove them back to the city.

When Paul came home hopping on one foot, with his ankle bandaged, everyone rushed to his side, looking concerned and asking questions about what had happened. Everyone except Ava, who hung back and watched from the doorway of the dining room, as George helped Helena get Paul situated on the sofa.

"What in the world happened to you?" Sarah asked.

"He hurt his ankle out at French Creek," Helena told them.

"Lawd," said Regina. She grabbed a couple of pillows from the other end of the sofa and propped them up under her son-in-law's injured ankle.

"What was y'all doing up there, anyway?" George asked. "Climbing mountains?"

"Hardly," Helena said.

"We wasn't doing nothing but walking," said Paul. "When we was kids, we used to run all up and down there and never got a scratch. Now I damn near kill myself *walking*. I guess I'm getting old."

"Ava, what you doing over there?" George called to his daughter. "You don't see your husband over here hurt?"

Ava came and stood beside the sofa and looked down at Paul's ankle. "Is it bad?"

"Not too bad," Paul said. "I just twisted it."

"Well, good."

"It coulda been a lot worse, though. If I'd sprained it, I might have got stuck up there and then who knows what. Right, Helena?" he asked, looking at his sister.

"I guess," she said.

He looked at Ava again. "I might not be here for you to glare at right now."

"I'm not glaring," Ava said, though she was unsure whether she was glaring or not. She still felt angry and disgusted by what Paul had told her last night, about what he had done. Seeing him hurt, she felt some sympathy for him, and was glad his injury wasn't worse, but she did not know what, exactly, she felt about his return.

"You don't look worried, though," he said, sounding agitated. "Matter fact, you looking at me like I'm some strange man who just wandered in here and put his feet up on your couch."

"Y'all come on in the kitchen and let's get dinner started," Regina said, and Sarah, Helena, and even George, followed her out of the room.

"You just said yourself it's not bad," Ava reminded Paul.

"But when you saw me come in you aint know how bad I was hurt."

"If your sister brought you here, and not to the hospital, you can't have been very hurt," she said.

He frowned. His ankle throbbed.

"You want some aspirin?" she asked.

"No," he said, out of spite, even though he did want some.

On the drive home, he had been sure that whatever anger she felt over what he had told her would give way to love and nurturing when she saw that he was hurt. She had never doted on him, not in all the time they had been together, which never bothered him because he knew it wasn't her nature, but whenever he was sick or hurt she would tend to him, bringing him medicine and food and checking to see if he was feverish by pressing her lips against his forehead, a thing he loved and always responded to, no matter how sick he was, by putting his arms around her. He knew she had no reason now to check him for fever, but he wished she would, wished she would at least touch him, would at least come near him, instead of standing on the other side of the coffee table looking indifferent. "I guess you don't even want me here," he said.

"I never said that. I didn't throw you out, Paul. You left."

He folded his arms across his chest. "I don't remember you trying to stop me."

"After what you told me, I didn't mind seeing you go," she said.

He took a deep breath and closed his eyes. He was tired of this. Tired of saying he was sorry for this thing he'd done half his lifetime ago. Tired of feeling like shit for it. "I'm sorry for what I did," he said again, looking up at her. "I been sorry for it for eighteen years. And I'm sorry I didn't tell you about it. But it aint nothing I can do to change it now. I can't go back."

"I know that," she said.

"Can't you forgive me?" he asked her. "Aint I done enough for you, Ava, been enough for you, taken care of you enough, loved you enough, that you can forgive me for this thing?"

She thought about his love and about the kind of husband he had been. In all the time they had been together, he had never once treated her badly, never abused her, never neglected her, never left her. He had been attentive and loving, and he had also given her time and space to herself, almost never crowding her or demanding her attention. He was the only man she had ever been with, so she had no one to compare him to, but she believed he had been a good husband and that he was a good man. Still, looking down at him now, lying there with his ankle bandaged and a look of sincere regret on his face, she felt unable to move past it.

"I don't know," she told him. "I need some time, Paul. It's only been a day."

He nodded. "Okay. You're right. I can go back to Tyrone's, if you want me to."

She wondered what Helena would do if Paul went back to their cousin's. "I don't mind if you're here," she told him. "I just don't want any pressure."

"Alright," he said. Then, "You tell your folks about what I told you?"

"No."

"Then, I wish you wouldn't. I mean, I got to tell them sometime. But I'd rather wait and see if you and me can patch things up, first. I don't want everybody hating me at all at once."

She knew he wanted her to say that she did not hate him, but instead, she said, "I'll let you tell them, then. But don't wait too long. They deserve to know."

On the second floor of the museum, several rooms back from the Great Stair Hall, in a tucked-away room into which few visitors seemed to find their way, Ava stood before a small etching of two little girls. They were peasants, it seemed to her, dressed in modest clothing and, according to the plaque on the wall beside the drawing, they were from the Netherlands. One girl was older than the other, who was very small, just a toddler. The older girl held out a toy to the younger, a doll, and the smaller girl reached for it. Ava studied the details of the etching, its shades and lines, a broom leaning against a wall in one corner of the room, a jug and basket of laundry in another. She considered the posture of the two girls, the older one holding the doll on some kind of circular hook and the smaller one reaching with one hand. The longer she looked at it, the more she thought that the older girl was not, in fact, holding out the doll for her sister to take, but was only holding it in place, unconcerned with the younger child's desire for the toy. Or perhaps even holding it back, Ava thought, away from the little child's grasp. Ava tilted her head to one side, squinted at the scene, wondered.

After a few minutes, she got up and walked through that room and into another, then out into a larger room, where the painting of the woman in front of the mirror was hung. There were a few people in this room, but not many, and there was a muffled quality to the sounds of the museum, the footsteps and whispers all far-away-sounding. Ava sat down on a bench and stared up at the painting, not thinking, not trying to remember anything, just sitting and viewing. After a while, she felt someone watching her, and when she turned, Helena was standing a few feet away. She blinked, at first thinking she must be imagining her.

"I didn't mean to lurk," Helena said, coming closer, her voice echoing softly in the high-ceilinged, wood-floored room. "You looked like you were thinking about something, and I didn't want to disturb you."

Ava patted the empty bench beside her and Helena came and sat down. There was a little dirt under her fingers and Ava knew she'd been planting flowers for Regina.

She had not decided whether or not to tell Helena about the things that were happening to her. She did not know if she could explain it right, if it would even make sense, or if she would seem like even more of a crazy person to Helena. Seeing her there, though, she wanted to. She thought it might help to know what Helena thought about it, and, too, she felt a desire to confide in her.

"My mother told me that I used to be different than I am now," Ava said. "That I used to be wild. And happy. When I was a child. I don't think I'm that person anymore."

Helena nodded, thoughtfully. "Most people aren't the same as they were as children, Ava."

"I guess. But just in the last few days I've been feeling a lot of things I haven't felt in a long time. Remembering things I'd forgotten."

Helena looked at her, and Ava knew what she was thinking.

"Since you came," Ava said.

Helena peered at her and the look in here eyes was cautious. "Do you think that's a coincidence?"

The question surprised Ava. She shook her head, vehemently. "No."

"But why? Why would my being here cause you to remember?"

"I don't know," Ava said, sighing, feeling suddenly very tired again. Her head hurt. She rubbed her temples with the tips of her fingers and looked at Helena curiously. "What are you doing here, anyway?" she asked.

"Oh. Well, I hadn't been here in such a long time. I felt like being around art today, so I came."

"Have you been here long?"

"A couple of hours. I timed my visit so I could leave with you."

That pleased Ava and she smiled, and the pain in her head got worse, a sharp stabbing in her right temple. She closed her eyes.

"Ava, are you alright?" Helena asked, and Ava felt her hand on her shoulder.

The pain subsided quickly and Ava nodded, opening her eyes. "I have a headache, but I'll be alright. Are you ready to go?"

"Before we do, I'd like to show you something."

Ava followed her out of that room and into another, and through several more, until they reached a small room with dark yellow walls. In one corner there was an expressionist painting of a train station, with people rushing along the platform towards a waiting locomotive. The scene was painted in rich colors, dark reds and browns and blacks, and everything in it seemed to be in motion.

"It's lovely," Ava said.

"I was nine," Helena told her, "when I first saw this painting. I was on a school field trip. I remember wondering where the train was going. I hoped it was somewhere very far away." She looked far away herself for a moment, then she smiled at Ava. "It was the first time I was ever moved by art. It made me want to go places, and see things."

"Well, you've done that," Ava said. "And you'll be on a train again very soon." Ava wondered if, when she left, the memories she had sparked would leave with her.

"Should we go?" Helena asked.

Ava shook her head. "Not yet. Let's stay a little longer."

They sat there on the bench, in the emptying gallery, close together with their shoulders touching, and the weight of Helena against her made Ava feel warm all through her body, and steadier than she had all day.

That evening, when George got to the back entrance of Blessed Chapel, Chuck was already holding the door open and peering around for him. When he saw him he smiled and said, "Wait there while I grab my things," and started to shut the door, but George pushed it open and entered.

He hadn't been inside Blessed Chapel even once since Pastor Goode had thrown his family out of the congregation. He looked around the small room they were standing in, a room where Sunday School classes met, and thought how everything looked the same.

"My car's right outside," Chuck said. "I thought we could drive up to Fairmount Park."

George walked past him, further into the church. From the small back room, he entered the larger basement area, where a small stage and a baptismal pool were located. The sound of his shoes against the tile floor was familiar and he remembered all the Easter breakfasts and Mother's Day luncheons he had attended here. He stepped up onto the stage and looked down into the empty pool where the twins had been baptized. He went up the back steps to the main floor of the church and into the main chapel. The familiar smell of bibles, and air perfumed by so many years of ladies in their Sunday bests, made his nostrils tingle in the dark. He found his way behind the pulpit by touch, remembering every square inch of the place, where each pew began and ended, which steps led where, and with the flick of several switches he raised the lights. Not much had changed in all those years. The colors, the dark wood of the pews and the lush red of the carpet, had lost some luster, but not much. The stained glass windows, through which no light shined at this hour of the evening, depicted the same new-testament bible stories as they always had. The annunciation. The sermon on the mount. The crucifixion. The ascension. The resurrection. The black, hard-back bibles, and the red, hard-back hymnals, sat neatly in the racks on the back sides of the pews. He ran his finger along the top edge of a hymnal and stared up at the choir box, remembering the music. The drums and cymbals, the piano and the tambourines, whose sounds had coursed through his veins like blood every Sunday for so many years.

George sat down on the cushioned deacon's pew, in the same spot where he had sat when he was the youngest deacon in the church, and stared up at the empty pulpit, over which hung the statue of Christ on the cross. He stared at the place where Pastor Goode always stood. He was not one of those preachers who moved around during the sermon, pacing the pulpit like a lion in a den. He stood behind a podium, like a lecturer, a teacher, commanding all eyes to one spot. George had loved Pastor Goode's sermons, he had been riveted by the rising and falling cadence of his voice and comforted by the way the word of God filled the chapel like a warm breeze, and even envious of the Pastor because God had chosen him to spread his gospel. Even when the sermon mentioned things that made George cringe inside, full of shame and secret pain, especially then, he had felt safe in the blanket of his voice and the shelter of this holy place.

He wanted to feel that again and he closed his eyes and asked the Lord to reach out and touch him, to help him feel connected. But no feeling of safety came. He opened his eyes. Staring up at the empty pulpit, he felt empty, too. Lost. Abandoned.

George got angry and was filled with the need to strike out, to smash something, to break every window and crush every tambourine. But he knew he could not. So he sat there and waited for Chuck.

When Chuck came and sat down beside him on the deacon's pew, he asked. "George, are you alright?"

He wasn't. But he didn't know how to begin to say all the ways he wasn't. And anyway it seemed pointless to try. Because he did not believe there was anything he could say, or anything that could be said to him, that would make him alright. He believed he would always be this way, always tortured, always afraid, always lonely and ashamed. And he believed, too, that he deserved to be.

"I haven't prayed once since I was made to leave this church," he said.

"Why?" Chuck asked.

He didn't answer.

"Come on. Let's get out of here," Chuck said, taking George's hand.

"No," he said. "Let's stay."

"Stay?"

He nodded. "Whatever we gone do, let's do right here."

Chuck shook his head. "No. I can't."

George folded his arms, and sat back on the pew. "It's here or nowhere."

Sarah had made great progress turning her lie into the truth, but she still needed the fire-eating man to ask her to come back again. She returned to Penn's Landing, this time later in the day, right after his performance ended, thinking she would catch him packing up, but instead she found him on a nearby bench, eating his lunch.

He smiled when he saw her approaching and said, "Sarah the Brave! You missed the whole show!" He stood and gestured towards the seat beside him. "Join me," he said, then waited until she was seated before he sat down again.

She had no idea what to say. She had spent the whole day at work trying to come up with something, some topic of conversation that might interest him, but she had no clue what a fire-eater might be interested in besides eating fire. He was sitting there staring at her, though, smiling and looking like he was waiting for her to say something.

She swallowed hard and said, "Hello."

He seemed to like that. His smile turned into a grin. "Hello, yourself." He held out his sandwich to her. "You hungry? It's not anything but peanut butter, but you welcome to share it."

"I'm allergic."

"To peanut butter?"

She nodded. "To peanuts altogether."

"Oh, that's a shame," he said. "A real shame. I love peanut butter myself. What if we was to get married? Would I have to give it up? I mean, I like my ladies dying for my kisses, but not literally."

She figured he was trying to be funny, but she did not believe in laughing at people's jokes just to make them feel good, so she didn't.

He laughed to himself a little, and sighed, and took a bite of his sandwich. He looked out over the water and didn't say anything else.

She wanted to run away. She was embarrassing herself and she knew it. Still, she was determined to turn her lie into the truth, determined to fix what she had broken so that Helena would see her again.

"How long have you been doing this?" she asked him.

He looked at her, blankly. "What? Eating lunch? About ten minutes." He grinned.

He was corny. Silly. But suddenly she felt the corners of her mouth pull the other way around and she smiled, too, surprising herself.

"I been eating fire for dimes and quarters for twelve years," he told her.

"Do you have a real job?" she asked.

He laughed. "A real job, huh?"

"Sorry. I didn't mean to—"

He waved a forgiving hand. "Aw, it's okay. I'm used to it. I aint met a woman yet who thought juggling fire on the sidewalk was a real job. Considering how much I like doing it, it probably aint. But, yeah, I got a real job. Working security down in south Philly. What about you? Where you work? Close by?"

"I'm a teller," she said, "at the Bell Savings on Chestnut."

"You like it there?"

She nodded.

"You live in West Philly?"

"Yes," she said. "How did you know that?"

"'Cause South Philly's full of Italians, and North Philly makes 'em a lot rougher than you. West Philly ladies are always the nicest. You grow up there?"

She nodded. "We lived in southwest when I was real small, then we moved when I was six."

"Oh, yeah? I live in southwest. Over on Kingsessing." He raised his arm and pointed southwest. "I grew up in Boston. I guess you can hear my accent. I've lived here a dozen years, though. You ever been to Boston?"

She shook her head. "I never really been anywhere."

"Well, when we're married, I'll take you there," he said, and grinned again.

She looked at him, searched his face for the disconnect, the distracted glance out at the water, or at some passersby, that would confirm for her that he was just going through the motions, humoring her. She searched for it, but she could not see it. All she saw was his crooked grin and a warm glint in his eyes.

"You a pretty girl," he said.

She looked away from him, down at her hands.

"I guess men tell you that all the time, huh?"

"Sometimes," she said. "But I don't believe them, and I sure don't believe you."

"You don't believe me?" He sounded taken aback. "Why not? You don't think you pretty?"

"I do think I'm pretty," she said. "I just don't believe you can see it."

"Why not?" he asked, sounding half amused and half put off. "I got eyes, don't I?"

"Everybody got eyes. That don't mean everybody sees."

He shrugged. "Well, why would I say it, then, if I didn't see it?"

"Habit," she said. "To be nice. Because you think that's what I want to hear."

"Oh," he said, scratching his beard. "So, you got me all figured out, huh?"

She nodded.

He stared at her, his brow squeezed into a tight frown. "Lord, girl. What in the world happened to you to make you think like that?"

She didn't answer. She looked out at the water. After a moment, she felt him move closer to her on the bench.

"Look here," he said, and when she didn't turn her head, he put his hand on her cheek and turned her face toward himself. "I don't say a whole lot that I don't mean."

He was looking into her eyes and, again, she searched for the disconnect, for the lie in what he was saying.

He tilted his head and leaned in to kiss her.

She got up from the bench and walked quickly away. She heard him behind her, scrambling to follow, stumbling over the case that held his batons, the change inside of it jingling loudly.

"Wait a minute!" he called, hurrying up to her and taking hold of her arm, carefully, gently. "I'm sorry," he said. "I was just trying to show you I meant what I said, and I got carried away. Seen too many movies, I guess. Women in movies seem to like being kissed by strange men a lot more than they do in real life. You ever notice that?"

"I have to go," Sarah said. "Really. I can't be late back to work."

"Okay," he said. "Okay. But look here. Sunday is my last day out here. I'm not gone be eating fire for change no more. I got a promotion at work. Assistant Security Manager. It's full time. And they don't want me out here doing this. It don't look good, you know?" He looked sad, and Sarah felt a little sad for him. "Come back again, will you? To see my last show? We can go get something to eat together after."

Come back again, will you? It was what she had gone there to hear him say.

He was looking at her, waiting. She searched his eyes a last time, and though she saw no distance in them, no hint that he did not mean every word he had said to her, she still could not believe him.

"Will you?" he asked her again, hopeful.

"Alright," she said.

He beamed. "On Sundays, I usually finish up around four."

"I'll be here," she said, and she turned and walked back to the bus stop.

When Ava got off the bus at her stop, Helena was there at the corner, holding a paper sack. She waved at Ava, and said, "I went out and got some food for dinner, and I saw your bus coming up the block, so I stopped to wait for you." She smiled and Ava felt happy. After the bus went past, they crossed the street together and walked up Fifty-Ninth.

"I wonder," Ava said, "what you must think of all this craziness."

"To be honest, I'm not sure I know what to think," Helena said. Then, after a moment, "Do you really believe your mother saw a ghost the other night? And that you saw one?"

Ava nodded. "Yes."

Helena looked skeptical.

"Let me ask you something," Ava said.

"Why am I still here?"

She nodded. "Yes. With everything that's happened. Why are you?"

"Because I came to Philadelphia for a reason," she said, "and I haven't done what I came to do yet."

"You came to see Paul."

"Not just to see him," Helena told her. "To tell him something. Something I haven't managed to tell him yet."

"What?" Ava asked.

Helena looked surprised. For a moment, she seemed to be thinking about it, considering whether she should tell Ava. Then she said, "I think I'd better tell Paul first."

They were coming around the corner onto Radnor just then, and they saw a small crowd of people standing on the church steps, Doris Liddy, Hattie Mitchell, and Clarence Nelson among them, all of them surrounding Pastor Goode, who, from the looks of it, was leading a prayer. Ava couldn't hear what he was saying until they got closer. "Lord, we need your help. We need your guidance. Show us how to do what must be done in your name. We believe in you, Lord, and we ask that you show us the way to cast out these evil people, as we have been trying to do for all these years."

"Oh, wonderful," Ava said.

When Goode saw her, his eyes narrowed, and he pointed at her with a shaking finger. "Lord, strike down this evil woman before me. This nonbeliever. This blasphemer!"

Helena stopped at the corner, and before Ava could stop her, and tell her there was no use, she yelled back at Pastor Goode, "Did you ever stop to think that if God wanted them gone, he'd have made it happen by now? It's been seventeen years, for Christ's sake. What's he waiting for?"

Goode's eyes, and the eyes of everyone standing on the steps, fixed on Helena. A hush fell over them, a strange sudden-silence, as if a television set had been turned off.

Ava put her hand on Helena's arm and they continued down the street.

"You don't know," they heard Goode calling out behind them, "who you keeping company with. And if you do, then you just as bad as they are. And the Lord *will* punish you."

1958

When Maddy's mother died expectedly in the spring of 1958, Maddy asked Regina and George if they would allow Ava to attend the funeral. "Y'all know my mother loved that child," she told them. "She said whenever Ava was around her she felt good. You know, her father was a sharecropper, and lots of times, when she was a child, she would go with him out into the fields, and whenever they could take a little break, they would lay on the ground side by side and look up at the sky, and her father would tell her that his own father, my mother's grandfather, had been a slave, but that his daughter, my mother, was free, and there wasn't nothing so humbling to her as that. Because it made her understand that her own freedom wasn't nothing but chance, and having the good fortune to be born when she was. Anyway, she used to say that Ava reminded her of those times, laying there watching the sky with her father, and feeling free. I know she just a child, but I think it would mean something to my mother if she was there when she's laid to rest."

Ava had never attended a funeral. She was twelve and no one she knew had ever died, at least no one she knew well enough to mourn. Once, the summer before, she had slipped into the church during the funeral of Mother Somebody-or-Other, just to get a glimpse of the body in the casket, because she felt she was an artist and that an artist needed to see things like that. Hidden in the pastor's nook, she had been able to view the corpse from just fifteen feet away. It had looked bloated and strange, with skin the color of nothing she could recall ever having seen in the living world. Oatmeal, maybe. Oatmeal with too much milk. Gray and just wrong. But seeing the body had inspired her, and she had drawn dead people for a week after, much to her parents' extreme chagrin.

"You don't have to go," Regina told her now. "If you don't want to. I don't much like the idea of you going to a funeral. Death shouldn't be invited into a child's life."

Ava had liked Miss Henrietta, who had once given her a book of art, full of glossy photographs of famous paintings and sculptures. Unlike the books she checked out from the school library, this one was new, and its crisp pages smelled of ink and color.

She did attend the funeral, and sat at the back of the church, in the last pew, with her drawing pad. All during the viewing, and then the service, she sketched the scene in the church, the flowers, which were all shades of yellow; the mourners with their heads bowed, gloved hands reaching out to touch the shiny wood, or the pearl-colored satin lining of the casket; the stiff-shoulders of Miss Henrietta's relatives, the dragging of their feet on the plush red carpet of the sanctuary, which, Ava thought, showed their discomfort with death, their resistance to the ceremony of it; Sister Hattie at the organ, playing songs that sounded like moaning, her body hunched over the keys, her foot against the pedals; the people sitting in rows on the pews, some of their shoulders touching, some not, some of their heads leaned together, others, it seemed, with theirs intentionally leaned apart; Ellen in her severe black dress and patent-leather shoes, staring blankly at her grandmother's coffin; and the light through the stained-glass windows, which was low because it was an overcast January day; and Pastor Goode, as he stood in the pulpit, giving the eulogy, looking solemn.

"Sister Henrietta knew that the best kind of life you can live is a life connected to the church. She lived the last years of her life in this church, and we should take solace knowing that, although disease ravaged her body, in her last days she had the love of God and the help of the church and its people to bring her comfort."

When the service ended, some of Miss Henrietta's out-of-town relatives, large men with several chins each, carried the casket down the aisle and out of the church to the waiting hearse. Ava stood on the church steps and watched. When the hearse pulled off, there were a few minutes of lingering, as people decided how they would get to the cemetery, who would ride with whom, and what route they would take. Ellen waved to Ava from her mother's side, as everyone came up and hugged Maddy, and most everyone said some variation of, "She's with the Good Lord now."

When Maddy saw Ava, she put her hand on top of her head and, smiling, said, "I saw you back there, drawing up a storm."

"I hope you aint offended," George said. "I told her it wasn't proper."

"I wouldn't have it no other way," Maddy said. Then, to Ava, "Show me what you made. I'd like to see it."

Ava hesitated. It occurred to her that Miss Maddy would not like what she had drawn. She was twelve now and she understood that people had their own ideas about what was proper. While their ideas almost never coincided with hers, she knew that people tended to be attached to them.

"Come on, now," Maddy said. "It aint no need to be shy."

Vic and Malcolm came over then, and Malcolm said, "You ready to go, Maddy?"

"Just a second. Ava about to show me what she was drawing in the church."

Some other people heard and craned their necks in Ava's direction.

She opened the drawing pad and held up the drawing.

They all peered down at it, unblinking. For a second, Ava thought she saw wonder in their eyes, pure awe, but a second later Malcolm's mouth twisted into a disgusted frown, and Vic shook his head from side to side, as if not believing what he was seeing. Sister Hattie said, "Oh, my Lord."

They were naked. Every single person in attendance at the funeral, even Miss Henrietta herself.

Vic looked at her. "Why would you do this? Why would you show Sister Henrietta this kind of disrespect?" He looked around at the others. "What is wrong with this child?"

Miss Maddy was still looking at the drawing, and looked like she was still deciding what she thought. Pastor Goode appeared at her side, and when he saw the drawing he clenched his teeth, glared at Ava, then took the drawing pad and closed it.

"Give it to me," Ava said. "It's mine."

"Shut your mouth," Goode whispered.

There was venom in his voice, revulsion, and it made Ava angry. "You shut *your* mouth," she spat back.

Sister Hattie and several other people gasped. Regina and George, who had both been talking with the Liddys, rushed over.

"What's the matter?" Regina asked. "What's happening?"

"He took my paper," Ava said.

"This child has been drawing filthy pictures inside this church," said Goode. "And at a funeral, no less."

"It is not filthy!"

The pastor handed the drawing pad to George, who took it and opened it. When he found the drawing, he closed his eyes and then opened them again, as if expecting it not to be there anymore. Regina stared at it a moment, and Ava was sure she saw wonder in her mother's eyes, before Regina looked down at her and said, "Ava, go home."

Ava went down the church steps and crossed the street.

"What is wrong with that child?" Vic asked, looking from George to Regina.

"We're sorry, Maddy," George said.

Maddy shook her head. "It aint nothing to get all upset about. Ava's a good girl."

"Why would she do something like that?" Vic asked. "At somebody's *funeral*?"

"She don't mean no harm," Regina said.

"*No harm*?" He laughed, bitterly. "You got to be kidding me, Regina."

"Where a girl that age learn to think like that in the first place?" Malcolm asked. "Drawing naked people? Naked *men*?"

"I held my tongue about that child long enough," said Pastor Goode. "I always knew it was something not right about her—"

"Not right?" Regina asked. "Hold on, now, Pastor—"

"—but I thought as long as y'all kept her in line, she would straighten out." He looked at the drawing again and shook his head in disgust. "But it seem like y'all aint got no control over her at all."

"We know she wild," George said.

"Oh, she more than wild," said Vic. "Drawing this filth. And talking to the pastor like she did. It's too much."

"Y'all need to get that girl in line," Malcolm said. "And y'all need to do it fast."

Ava was lying on her bed, staring up at the ceiling, when George came in the room and said, "You gone apologize to Maddy, and to the pastor, and to everybody."

"I aint apologizing," Ava said.

"You gone apologize, or I'm gone whip your ass so bad you aint gone be able to sit down for a week."

She sat up on the bed and glared at her father. "What for?"

"You know what for!" he yelled.

"It aint a filthy picture!" She yelled back. "It's art! Every artist draws naked people."

"I don't give a shit what every artist do! You aint a artist, goddamnit, you a twelve year-old girl! And you ought not be drawing things like that!"

"Don't tell me what I am," she said. "I get to say what I am."

The whipping was severe, worse by far than any Ava had ever gotten before. She tried not to cry this time, squeezed her eyes shut tight and clenched her teeth and willed herself not to cry, but it was no use. With every lash of the belt, pain seared through her, and it seemed to not only come from her legs and her backside, where the belt landed, but from deeper inside of her, way deep down in the places where the art came from, up under her ribs, near her heart, and in the pit of her stomach, and even lower, where she thought her ovaries must be. She felt sick when it was over, and she ran to the bathroom and vomited undigested oatmeal. The grayness of it made her want color, made her need it, and she ran into her bedroom, desperate for paint, and found her father there, gathering up her art supplies.

"You can have them back when you apologize," George said.

She shook her head, wiped vomit from her mouth. "I'll never apologize."

"Well, then, you won't never get them back."

The next Sunday at church, everybody was talking about what Ava had done. Before the family had gotten to their seats on the fifth pew from the front, George heard pieces of three different conversations referring to the incident.

"That's art," he heard Lillian Morgan saying as they passed her in the vestibule. "You go into any museum and you gone see stuff like that hanging on every wall."

"This aint a museum," Audrey Jackson reminded her. "This a church."

"You ever heard of the Sistine Chapel?" Lillian asked.

"I don't know about no sixteen nothing. But I know I don't want nobody drawing nekkid pictures of me when I'm lying dead in my coffin."

Regina glanced at George. "Wasn't neither one of them at the funeral. They aint even see the drawing."

George frowned. "Most of the people in here aint see it. But I bet you they got plenty to say about it anyway."

He wasn't wrong. Moving through the center aisle, on their way to their seats, he heard Bobby Smith whisper, "If a daughter of mine ever did something like that, I'd kill her."

When they got to their pew, Maddy was already there, and she rolled her eyes at them. "Y'all believe these people? It was *my* mother's funeral, and I aint even upset about it. Where they get off being so insulted?"

"I can understand where they coming from, Maddy," George said. "The ones that seen it, anyway."

Maddy waved an unconcerned hand. "That child got a gift. She ought to use it."

Regina put her arm around Maddy's shoulders.

Out of the corner of his eye, George saw Chuck and Lena Ellis moving along the side aisle, making their way to their usual seats. He tried not to turn his head, but couldn't help it. He watched Chuck shaking hands with Vic Jones and wondered what opinion he might have about Ava's drawing, whether he was among those who whispered about how George and Regina didn't know how to control their child. It was hard for him to imagine it, because Chuck wasn't that sort of person, or at least George didn't think he was. They never talked anymore, never did more than exchange handshakes and polite hellos, and the obligatory shallow chit-chat when in a group, in the three years since George had made that terrible mistake at the Christmas party. George had been the one to distance himself. A few weeks after it happened, Chuck had pulled him aside during a break at the leadership meeting, and said that they were still friends, good friends, and that they shouldn't let some drunken misunderstanding end all that. But George hadn't been drunk, and Chuck hadn't misunderstood him, and there was no way he could see to go back. He felt saturated with shame, wringing wet with it, every time he thought about what he'd done, every time he played over in his mind the look on Chuck's face, the shock and disgust. Watching Chuck now, as he greeted his friends and neighbors, happy, smiling, George envied him the humiliation he didn't have to carry around, the guilt he didn't have to feel, the loathing of himself that he didn't have to know.

Mixed in with that envy, too, was another feeling, a longing that was ever there, a pining that would not stay away no matter how many times George chased it like a stray dog from his mind.

"You listening to me, George?"

He tore his gaze away from Chuck and blinked at Regina. "What?"

Her eyes followed the path that his had taken and she frowned when she saw Chuck at the end of it. "I was talking about Ava," she said, returning her gaze to him. "Our daughter. Or maybe you got other things on your mind?"

Weeks passed and Ava grew miserable without color. He had taken her paints and her chalks and her crayons, and all she had left to make art with were the pencils she used for school. She drew pictures on the pages of her composition books, but they were colorless, and soon her craving for yellow and blue and, especially, red, became unbearable. She spent as much time as possible staring at the red walls, and watching the blue sky and the orange sunset, but seeing color wasn't enough, she needed to use it. One day, while playing with Ellen and Juanita, she fell and skinned her knee, and the blood that beaded on her skin was beautiful, and it filled her with pleasure. Later, she took a needle from her mothers sewing box and pricked her finger, and used the blood to color a small drawing she had made. A week later, her fingertips were raw and red from being pricked and when Regina noticed and asked what had happened to her hands, and Ava told her, Regina told George to give back the art supplies.

"No," he said, over his newspaper. "She aint apologized."

"And she aint going to," Regina insisted. "I can tell you right now, your anger aint gone outlast hers. You ought to know that child good enough to know that."

But he did not want to give in to Ava. He believed she knew that what she had done was wrong, and that her refusal to apologize was just stubbornness, pure defiance for the sake of itself. He agreed with Goode that Ava needed to be kept in line and he blamed Regina for always giving in to her. Children needed discipline and, even more, they needed to understand how the world worked, and know that their survival depended on following the rules.

"This aint a game I'm playing with Ava," George said. "I'm trying to teach her right from wrong. God forbid you'd take my side and support me on something."

Regina started to say something, then shook her head and left the room, looking frustrated. George went back to his paper. A few minutes later, Geo and Kenny came through the front door, in their swim trunks, their hair still wet with harsh, chlorine-smelling water.

"How was the pool?" George asked.

"I learned to swim, Daddy," Geo said, grinning, proud.

"What you mean, swim?" George asked, chuckling. "You mean walk around in the shallow end?"

Geo laughed, too. "No, I mean *swim*. David was there, and he taught some of us how. He learned at the Y last summer, I guess. You know David, Uncle Chuck's son?"

George nodded. His kids still called Chuck "uncle" even though he hadn't been a close friend of the family in years. It had just stuck. He frowned, tried to push Chuck out of his mind. "You learn how to swim, too, Kenny?"

"Naw, he learned how to *sink*, though," Geo said.

Kenny jumped on Geo, put him a headlock. Geo put his arms around Kenny's waist and lifted him off the floor. They were both laughing, their skinny, naked arms and chests pressing damply together. George felt a sudden rush of nausea and heat and he sprang up from his chair and grabbed Geo, prying him off of Kenny. "Stop acting like a little faggot!" he snarled, his teeth clenched, shaking the boy. "What the hell is wrong with you?"

Geo stared wide-eyed at his father, blinking, confused. Kenny looked down at his feet, embarrassment bleeding into his face and neck.

Regina rushed in from the kitchen, wiping her hands on her apron, looking anxious. She looked from Geo to George. "What's going on in here?"

Geo shook his head. "We didn't do nothing, Mama. We was just wrassling. We didn't mean nothing."

Kenny shook his head, too, still staring at the floor.

Regina peered at George. "Let him go."

George glared at her. "Don't tell me what to do about my own goddamn son! You the reason he so soft in the first place! He need to start acting like a man!"

"He aint a man!" Regina screamed. She put her arms around Geo and pulled him away from George. "He twelve years old! You the one need to start acting like a *man*."

The heat that had filled George boiled in him now. He turned Geo loose and raised his fist.

Geo screamed, "Daddy, no!"

George slammed his fist into Regina's face, making a sound like bat against a ball, and she stumbled back, then dropped to the floor. Geo crouched down next to her, shielded her with his body, protecting her.

Kenny just stood there, trembling, looking too scared to move.

George looked down at Regina. Her lip was busted, bleeding. He felt the heat inside him boiling over. He couldn't breathe. He needed to get out of there. He turned and moved by them, walked toward the front door, and behind him he heard a shuffling of feet. He turned around, just as Regina swung a table lamp and smashed it against his head. The pain seared through him, and spots appeared before his eyes. He felt himself falling, but didn't feel it when he hit the ground.

A full month after he had taken her paints away, George walked past Ava's room and, through the open door, saw her sitting on the floor beside her bed with blood dripping down her arm onto the wood floor. He rushed to her side. She was peaked and shaken.

"What did you do?" he asked her.

"I was just trying to get some red," she said.

She had been trying to get some red with a steak knife across her forearm, and had nicked a vein. George cleaned the small wound and dressed it, thinking all the time how everything always seemed to be spinning out of control lately. It had been a week since his fight with Regina and in that time their physical wounds had nearly healed, but the emotional wounds that had caused them had only opened wider. Now here again was more of their own blood dripping on the floor.

"It looks like paint drops," Ava said, eyeing the beads of dark red.

George sighed. "Why can't you just be like normal people?" he asked her, and he could hear pain in his own voice, and fear.

She shrugged. "This is how I am."

George shook his head. She didn't understand. She never did, no matter how hard he tried to make her see. "One day you gone piss off the wrong person, Ava," he said, wrapping a bandage around her arm, as tenderly as he could. "It's crazy people in this world."

1976

Thunder rumbled the next evening and lightning cracked open the sky. Rain fell in fat drops, like gumballs from a broken candy machine, round and dense, making plunking sounds against concrete and window panes. With the storm came a much-prayed-for break in the heat, and Regina decided she would take the opportunity to cook a real meal for the first time in days. When she went to the kitchen, she found Helena there, cooking pork chops and potatoes. "Look like we had the same idea," Regina said.

Helena nodded. "Great minds." Then, "Oh! I almost forgot!" She hurried out of the kitchen, into the dining room, and she returned a few moments later, carrying her drawing pad, flipping it open. "I've been meaning to show you this," she said. "I finished it a few days ago." She held out the completed sketch of Regina.

Regina gasped when she saw it.

"What's wrong?" Helena asked, looking disappointed. "You don't like it?"

"That aint it," Regina said, staring at the drawing. "I just didn't know I looked like that. Is that how I look to you?"

Helena hesitated. Then nodded. "Well...yes."

Regina stared down at the drawing. It was well-done, and looked very much like her, but there was a hardness in the eyes, and an anger in the set of the mouth that made her look sick and mean.

"I'm sorry," Helena said. "Maybe I didn't get it right."

Regina put a hand on her arm. "No, you did a good job. You did just fine. I'm just preoccupied about dinner, that's all."

Regina prepared the broccoli Helena had bought. Ava, Paul and Sarah all got home in the next little while, and when dinner was ready they all sat down to eat. Soon, George arrived, and joined them. Across the table, Regina saw him eyeing Helena. Whenever Helena spoke, he found something to disagree with her about.

"This weather is a mess," Paul said. "If it aint a thousand degrees, it's pouring rain."

"Thunderstorms are what I love most about summer," Helena said.

George frowned. "I hate them. They make the humidity even worse."

"These greens are wonderful, Mrs. Delaney," Helena said.

George shook his head. "They too salty."

Regina rolled here eyes. "You eating them fast enough."

Sarah ate her food in silence. She had not told Ava or Helena about the fire-eating man, about turning her lie into the truth, when she'd gotten home from work the previous day, because coming up the street, coming up to Fifty-Ninth, she had seen them up ahead, had seen Goode pointing at Ava and hollering. She had stood back and watched, and when she saw Helena stop and confront the pastor on Ava's behalf, she knew that the fire-eating man, and the lie that had become the truth, didn't matter anymore. Helena was Ava's now. Just like Kenny.

"Sarah, why you so quiet?" Regina asked.

She shrugged. "I aint got nothing to say. I probably won't have nothing to say ever again."

George raised his eyebrows. "What's wrong now? Wait, let me guess. It got something to do with *that one*," he said, pointing a steady finger at Helena.

"Pop—"

"Don't 'Pop' me," George said. "I want to know how much longer your sister gone be here."

"Daddy!" Ava said. "Don't be so rude!"

"Maybe I should go," Helena said, standing.

"Sit down!" Ava and Regina said in unison.

Helena sat.

Regina leaned forward in her chair. "Why you want her gone so bad, George? Hmm? What she doing that got your drawers in a bunch all the time? I don't see her doing nothing but helping with the cooking, the cleaning—"

"And meddling!"

"It's not my intention to—"

"Pop, she aint doing nothing but—"

"She causing trouble, and you know it! All y'all know it! Y'all just rather let it happen than agree with me about anything."

"Causing trouble how?" Ava asked.

"Asking all these questions. Bringing up all these bad feelings!"

"Look, George," Regina said, standing up. "I made an agreement with myself a long time ago not to ask you certain *questions*. But I can't, and I won't, try to stop anybody else from asking."

A hush fell over the table. A shadow passed over George's face. "What that supposed to mean, Regina?"

Regina shook her head. She was tired of this. Real tired. "You want me to say what it mean?"

George's throat felt suddenly very dry, but he didn't want to swallow and show any sign of weakness or guilt. He opened his mouth to say something, but his voice cracked. He felt shame cut him open and slip inside him like a greasy hand, taking hold of his liver.

"That's what you want, George?" Regina asked, glaring at him across the table, "'Cause I can do that."

"What are you talking about, Mama?" Sarah asked.

"She talking the same crazy shit she always talking!" George said. "You decided one Saturday a week aint enough time to fit in all your ranting and raving, Regina?"

"I heard Chuck came by," Regina said, her voice calm, steady, anything but crazy-sounding.

George felt his shame giving way to rage and he clenched his teeth and growled at her, "I hate you. With all my might I wish you would die, right here at this table."

Ava said, "That's enough, Daddy."

"I wish you would keel over into those pork chops and suffocate in that gravy," he said, and the image flashed in his mind, causing a grin to spread across his face.

Ava felt something swelling up inside her, heaving, and she was suddenly overcome with rage, white-hot and overpowering. "I said that's enough!" she screamed.

"Ava," Paul said, reaching out and putting his hand on her arm.

She jerked away from him, angry, and stood up, still holding her knife and fork, glaring at her father.

He pointed his finger at her now. "Don't talk to me like that! I'm the head of this family!"

"You're not the head of this family. You never were," Ava said, and she was vaguely aware of an urge inside herself to reach over and grab her father, as he sat there looking defiant, and to press the knife that she was only half aware of holding into the soft flesh of his throat. "You kept yourself shut off from us all our lives. We don't even know you!" There was a raging inside her. Colors flashed before her eyes. She did not understand the fury, did not really know the source of it, but for a moment it had complete control of her, and her fist clenched around the knife, which felt heavy and purposeful, as the fork in her other hand dropped onto the table with a loud clang. Everything hushed. She was aware of people's mouths moving, but she could not hear what they were saying. Her father was sitting right beside her. She had only to lift the knife and in one movement, the narrow-minded, hypocritical fool would be dead. She closed her eyes. She did not want to kill her father. And yet she did want to kill him.

She felt a hand on her arm, close to her wrist, and a gentle touch. She opened her eyes and saw Helena standing beside her, her green eyes searching Ava's. The flashing colors stopped and the hush that had fallen over everything lifted.

Her father was staring up at her with fear and confusion in his face. "What the hell is wrong with you, Ava?"

It was only then that she realized she had raised the knife and was holding it inches from his face. She lowered her arm and placed the knife on the table. Then she moved away from the table, so quickly that her chair fell over and banged hard against the linoleum. She saw Sarah jump, and put her hand over her mouth. Ava turned and ran from the room.

George fled, too. Angry and humiliated, he left the house in a blur of cussing, hurrying up Radnor Street and away from his house and his family as fast as he could, like a grenade trying not to go off where people were gathered. The rain had stopped, but the air was heavy like cream, sticky on his skin, oppressive, and he longed for that summer to end, for Helena to leave and things to go back to normal, or whatever had passed for normal before she had come. What had happened at the table was her fault. It was her questions that had brought all these bad things to the surface again.

He walked faster, eastward first, then cut over to Walnut, then Spruce. The rain had washed the streets cleaner, but not clean, never clean, the trash and grime of the city clinging evermore to the pavements and gutters. He hated this filthy city. He always had. He had come here because he could no longer stand the south and he believed he could never have any kind of real life there. Here, in Philadelphia, he had done alright for himself, better, he knew, than he would have been able to do down there. But he had never loved this place, had found little beauty in it, and nothing compared to the forests and open skies of Georgia, where he had learned what beauty was, what nature could do if left alone to flourish. Yet, he had never gone back to visit. Not once. He had left his home and never looked back.

He found himself on Baltimore Avenue, way south, and heading east again, not really thinking about where he was going until he looked up and saw the street sign for Fifty-First. He was at the corner of Chuck's block. He looked down the street, with its tall, narrow houses, and frowned to himself. This was the last place he needed to be. Still, he kept walking, and when he approached the house where Chuck and Lena lived, he slowed down, and peered at it from across the street. The front door was open, and through the screen door he could see lights on inside. He wondered what Chuck was doing and, for a moment, he thought about knocking on the door. He knew he couldn't. A moment later, the screen door swung open, and Chuck, Lena, and another man came out onto the porch. The other man was tall, and much younger than Chuck, and George recognized their son, David. He watched as David hugged his father, holding the embrace for a long moment as they laughed over each other's shoulders, sharing some joke George could not hear. As he watched, the scene changed before his eyes, and instead of David on the porch, he saw George Jr. as a grown-up man, tall and strong, and laughing, with his arms around his own father, around George himself, who held his son tightly to him.

Tears welled in George's eyes. He wished he could go back. He wished he could change it, all of it. He wished he could see his boy again and love him better.

When the embrace between Chuck and David was broken, the two men became themselves again, the image of Geo disappearing on the sticky air. George watched them for another moment, and then walked on by.

Helena found Ava sitting on the floor in her bedroom, at the foot of the bed, with her head back against the footboard, her knees pulled up to her chin. She came in and sat down beside her, her longer legs stretched out in front of her. She didn't say anything, just sat there, with her head back, too, staring up at the ceiling.

"I'm tired of this," Ava said. "I'm tired of these flashes. Of these emotions I can't control. I need to understand what's happening to me."

"How can I help you do that?"

Ava shook her head. "I don't know." She got up and paced the floor, from the bed to the door, to the window, and around again. Though the rage from a few minutes ago had gone, other things still churned inside her, like an ever-threatening storm. She knew she could not go on like this. She knew she would go insane, if she wasn't already.

"Your mother told me you used to paint every day when you were young," Helena said. "What happened to all of them?"

"Most of them got burned," Ava told her.

"Burned? How?"

"It was years ago. I was taking them outside so they could get hauled off to the dump. They were out on the porch. Dexter Liddy climbed over the railing and threw a lit match on them."

"That's horrible."

"They were headed for the dump anyway," Ava said.

"Why were you throwing them out?"

"They were taking up too much space. I didn't care about them, so I was throwing them out."

Helena frowned. "You said 'most' of them were burned."

Ava nodded. "A lot of them I hadn't brought outside yet."

"You took those to the dump?"

"No. After the first pile got burned, Mama and Mr. Liddy got into a shouting match. After that she made me keep the rest. They're still down in the cellar."

"When's the last time you looked at them?" Helena asked. "That day?"

"I didn't even really look at them that day."

Helena stood up. "Let's look at them now."

"Why?"

"I don't know," she said. "Maybe seeing your paintings, and remembering what you felt when you made them, will bring it all together again."

The cellar was cooler than the rest of the house by several degrees and it smelled of damp earth and old wood. They moved past broken furniture and trunks spilling out old things and came to a closet beneath the stairs. Ava opened it and tugged a string hanging down from the ceiling, and a light bulb burned on.

The whole closet was full of paintings. Dozens of them, all stacked in piles.

Helena reached in and grabbed one from the nearest stack, a one foot by one foot square of canvas affixed to a wooden framework. She held it up to the light. It showed people at an outside gathering on a city street, eating and laughing, calling out and waving to each other across porches, and playing double Dutch and ball games in the street. On one end of the block, the heavy trees of a park reached over into frame and, at the other end, a church stood, stone gray and solid-looking. In the background, row houses loomed in strange angles that jutted forward, so they, along with the church and the park, seemed to surround the people on all sides and almost extend out from the canvas.

"It's amazing," Helena said. "It feels like being on a city street, looking up and around and seeing almost nothing but buildings, nothing but bricks."

Ava stared down at the painting. There was a confined feeling to it, with the park and the church holding everything in. But the people seemed unaware of being trapped, the language of their bodies loose and open, their arms extended in greetings to one another, their laughter almost audible off the canvas.

Helena held up another painting, this one of George with a beak for a nose. She stared at it, her face flushed with wonder. She held up a third painting, a self-portrait of Ava as a young girl, stark naked and holding a red-dripping paint brush. The colors, like in all the paintings, Ava thought, were well-chosen. There was a lushness, a density of pigment, that pleased the eye. And, too, there was a quirkiness about the paintings, an underhint of humor alongside some trouble or grief. All of them were like that. Strange and bold and flushed with color.

"Why did you stop?" Helen asked her.

"I don't remember why."

"Try."

Ava looked at the painting of herself holding the red dripping brush and tried to think, tried as hard as she could to remember. "I tried not to stop.

But after a while, I just couldn't do it anymore. Whatever it was that made me want to paint, I couldn't feel anymore."

"And you never felt it again?"

"No," she said.

"What was it you felt?" Helena asked her. "Can you remember the feeling of wanting to paint?"

Ava shook her head. "No," she said, and she noticed that the room felt smaller suddenly, and warmer.

"Try, Ava."

Ava could feel a tightening in her chest, and her breath coming slower. "I can't remember," she said. "I can't remember." She felt her throat closing. She could not get air in. She felt Helena's hands on her face and heard her voice saying, "Ava, what's wrong?"

The room was getting smaller and smaller, the air thicker. She felt dizzy and she grabbed hold of Helena's arms and tried to keep herself up, but her limbs were going numb and she couldn't feel Helena there. Her knees buckled. She crashed hard onto the cool floor.

Ava heard footsteps pounding against the cellar stairs and when she opened her eyes, Helena was bent over her on the floor, her face close, her hands on Ava's cheek and forehead. "Ava, can you hear me?" Ava could feel Helena's breath on her lips.

"What the hell happened?" It was Paul, standing over them now, looking panicked. Behind him, Regina and Sarah were making their way down the stairs.

"What's the matter with my child?" Regina asked, looking a little crazed.

"She collapsed," Helena told them.

Regina rushed to Ava's side, crouched down on the floor beside her.

"I'm alright," Ava whispered, trying to sit up.

"What you talking about, *collapsed*?" Paul asked, as Helena and Regina helped Ava into a sitting position.

"She fainted, I think," Helena said.

Ava's head throbbed. She put her hands on either side of it and held them there.

"Can I get you something?" Helena asked. "Water?"

Ava nodded. She felt shaky.

Helena sprinted up the steps, her hard shoes like hammers on the old wood. Ava closed her eyes. She felt arms around her shoulders and knew it was Paul. She felt Regina's hands on hers. No one said anything.

In a few moments, Helena was back. "Drink this." Her hands shook on the glass.

Ava took Helena's hand. "It's okay. I'm alright."

Helena nodded, but she looked afraid.

Ava drank the water, then said, "I need to lie down."

Paul took the glass and handed it back to Helena, then bent down and lifted Ava off the ground. He carried her up the basement stairs and all the way up to their bedroom, and laid her down on the bed. Regina soaked a washcloth with cold water and pressed it gently against her daughter's forehead. Helena and Sarah stood in the doorway.

"Y'all don't need to hover," Ava said. "I just got a little lightheaded. I'm alright now."

Paul was sitting beside her on the bed, staring at her with a strangely eager expression. "You aint...I mean, could you be..."

She squinted at him through the throbbing in her head. "What?"

"Pregnant?"

She shook her head and the throbbing worsened.

He frowned. "How do you know?"

"I can't be pregnant, Paul."

"The doctor said it aint no reason why not."

"I am not pregnant!" There were half a dozen tiny explosions in her head then, and she closed her eyes.

"Ava, calm down," Regina said.

Paul frowned. "Then what's wrong with you, Ava? 'Cause *something* sure as hell is. And don't give me that 'I'm fine' shit again."

She didn't answer him. She wanted him to go away and leave her alone.

Paul stood up. "I'm calling the doctor."

"They're gone at five," she said.

"Well, I'm calling tomorrow."

"I'm not pregnant."

"Maybe not," he said. "But something's wrong, and I want to know what." He sat back down on the bed again. "You need anything?"

She shook her head, no.

He leaned over and kissed her cheek, leaving his lips pressed against her face for a long moment, and she felt suddenly claustrophobic, and put her hands against his chest and pushed him away. He looked hurt and got up and walked out of the room.

"He just trying to help," Regina said. "He worried."

"But I'm fine," Ava said. She looked from Regina to Helena and Sarah in the doorway. "Please stop hovering. Really."

When they left, she closed her eyes.

It had been the look in Helena's eyes that made her swoon. It was the same look she had seen there days ago, when Helena had brought her the sketch on the grocery list and, in her eyes, Ava had seen the greatness of the drawing. This time, though, it had been much more intense. In Helena's eyes, in that moment, there had been a captivation that Ava recognized, though she had not seen it in so many years. It was the look Miss Maddy had given her at four. The look Kenny Goode and Malcolm Hansberry and Sister Kellogg, and everyone else had all given her, all those years ago. It was the reflection of what they had all seen in her, what they all recognized in her from the time she was a small child, and in that moment Ava had seen it in Helena's eyes, too. This time she had seen that *she* was great, not just the paintings, but Ava herself. That she was extraordinary. And, for no reason she understood right then, seeing it had caused her to fall.

Standing at the bottom of the stairs, Ava could hear her family in the kitchen, the usual dinner preparations underway. Quietly, she moved through the foyer and opened the front door, slipping out of the house without making a sound. She walked quickly down the front steps onto the sidewalk and walked down the street, passing neighbors who watched her with curiosity and dislike. When she got to the steps of Blessed Chapel, she paused, and looked up at the stone structure, its stained-glass windows catching the light of the late day. She pulled open the front doors and stepped inside.

She did not have to go looking for Pastor Goode. He was right there by the altar, as if waiting for her.

1959

Ava sat in the bishop's nook, behind the pulpit at Blessed Chapel, across the desk from Pastor Goode, who was writing frantically on a pad of paper, his eyes narrowed, his lips twisted in concentration. She sat watching him, and after a couple of minutes he looked up at her, smiled. "Well," he said, setting the paper aside. "That's Sunday's sermon done."

She had gone there because her mother had informed her that the pastor wanted to see her. She had no idea why. Now she blinked at him, waited.

Goode cleared his throat. "You a smart girl, Ava. I always thought so."

Ava just stared at him. She had never forgotten what he had said at Sister Henrietta's funeral, that she had the devil in her. She knew he believed that. She'd known by the look in his eyes when he said it.

"And you are gifted," he went on. "Talented like no child I ever knew. I can't deny it. It would be a sin to deny it, because that's God-given talent, and denying it means denying the work of the Lord."

"The Lord?" she asked. "Last year you said it was the work of somebody else altogether. What's *the Lord* got to do with it now?"

"I spoke in haste that day," he said. "But since then, the Lord has allowed me to consider things differently. I heard about what happened with you and that art contest the city had."

It had been a contest for amateur artists, all Colored and all living in West Philadelphia, sponsored by the arts and culture department of the city. Ava had entered one of her paintings and Regina had taken her down to where the competition was taking place. There had been a hundred other artists and Ava's painting had been chosen the best of them all. But the judges had assumed that Regina was the artist, and when they discovered it was Ava, they insisted the contest was not open to children, and gave someone else the prize. There had been a very short article about it in the Philadelphia Daily News and, as a result, an art school in New York City had invited Ava to enter the painting into their annual competition for Colored artists in the tri-state area. Regina had already agreed to take Ava up to New York next month for the judging. Since all that had happened, nearly a month ago, most people on the block had come up to Ava and expressed disapproval of the arts and culture department and their actions, but Pastor Goode had not been among them. She wondered why he was pretending to care now.

"There's a way you can use your talent to serve this community right here," he said. "I'd like to have a mural painted on the back wall of the church. Something beautiful and uplifting. Something that will call souls to our church and to the Lord. I'd like you to paint it."

"I don't do religious art," she said.

"You an artist, aint you?" he asked. "Don't all great artists have religious works? What's the name of that one who did the Sistine Chapel?"

"Michelangelo."

He nodded. "Exactly."

Ava had spent hours looking at photographs of the ceiling of the Sistine Chapel, studying every inch of it. That, and Leonardo da Vinci's Virgin of the Rocks, painted in the early 1500s for the chapel of the Confraternity of the Immaculate Conception, in the church of San Francesco Grande in Milan. And, Ava's favorite European painting, The Supper at Emmaus, depicting the moment when the newly-resurrected Christ reveals himself to two of his disciples, painted by Caravaggio in 1601.

"Well, maybe so," Ava said. "But why you want me to do it?"

"Because the Lord spoke to me," he said. "He spoke to me and told me that you are the person to do it."

She did not believe him, but it didn't matter. Since the scandal at Miss Henrietta's funeral, she had been trying to think of a way to use her talent to benefit the people around her, instead of always upsetting them.

"Alright," she said.

He smiled and looked genuinely pleased. "Good. I'm glad we can come together. I know you think I'm some kind of tyrant—"

"Are you?" she asked.

His smile slipped, but he got control of it again quickly. "No, Ava," he said. "I'm only trying to do the Lord's work, the way he calls me to do it."

Work on the mural started that next week. The back wall of the church was partially covered with lime plaster, creating a canvas that was twelve feet by twelve feet, bigger by far than any Ava had ever used. It was covered with a large tarp and left to dry. While she waited for the canvas to be ready, Ava sketched her idea for the mural. It would depict the congregation of Blessed Chapel, some of them on their knees at the altar. Before them, there would be a bright light through the stained-glass windows.

When the plaster was firm, but not quite dry, when she could press her thumb against it and make a thumbprint in its surface, Ava set to work transferring her sketch to the wall. Scaffolding was erected and, at the pastor's request, Vic Jones showed Ava how to raise and lower it according to her needs. From up high, she could see out over most of the block while she sketched, and most of the block could see her. Though the pastor asked everyone not to crowd her, not to distract her from her task, people passed by often, and most stopped at least long enough to eye her work. Ava was sure this was exactly what Goode had intended. With so many eyes on her, she would have a very hard time adding anything to the mural that might be considered controversial, if in fact she were inclined to try.

She sketched the scene onto the wall in pencil. It took an entire weekend, a whole Saturday and a whole Sunday. When it was done, she began painting. She worked for a few hours every day, from the time she got home from school until just before dusk. The church provided all the supplies she needed, large bottles of paint in myriad colors, dozens of brushes. While she painted the details, Geo helped her by painting the background, according to her instructions, using the colors she selected.

"We really high up here," Geo said, looking down over the scaffolding.

"We aint even six feet up right now," Ava said, painting the face of one of the churchgoers.

"I guess." He looked a little worried.

Miss Lucas came by and waved from the ground. "Y'all need any help?"

"Sure," Ava said. She lowered the scaffolding and Miss Lucas climbed on.

"This gone hold all of us?" Geo asked.

Ava nodded. "It holds four adults."

Miss Lucas helped Geo paint the background, while Ava continued to paint the faces. The next day, she came by again and helped. The day after that, Miss Maddy spent an hour filling in the color on the figures' clothing, again according to Ava's directions. Ellen, Miss Antoinette, Mr. Malcolm, Rudy, and Juanita all helped.

One afternoon, when the mural was almost finished, as Ava stood on the scaffolding, painting the cushions on the altar, Sondra came around the back of the church and stood below her, her arms folded across her chest, watching. She didn't say anything at first, but even in silence she was menacing.

"I guess you think you some real hot shit now," she said, loudly, so Ava could hear from her high perch.

Ava ignored her. She hated to be bothered while she was trying to paint, and of all the things there were to be bothered by, Sondra seemed the worst possible one.

"I wonder what would happen if one of them ropes snapped," Sondra said, and turned and walked away.

Later, Geo came and helped with the last of the painting. He stood looking up at the scene, a trace of a frown on his face.

"What's the matter with you?" Ava asked.

"Nothing," he said. "This aint what I expected, I guess."

It was a beautiful painting, lush and buoyant as anything she had ever done. But there was nothing about it that pushed, nothing that made him feel uneasy.

They finished the mural that day, and that evening, as Ava was pulling the tarp down over it, Pastor Goode came around the back of the church.

"Hold on, now. Let me have a look at it," he said.

He stood back and looked it over, his head moving up and down, and from side to side. Ava knew that the painting was aesthetically good, even wonderful, and that it was what Goode had wanted. As he took it all in, a smile spread across his face, and he nodded his approval. "It's wonderful," he said. "It's the Lord's work."

Ava knew exactly whose work it was and she had the calloused hands to prove it, but she was tired of fighting this man, so she said nothing.

"We'll be uncovering it right after morning service," he said. "I'm proud of you. You have used the gift God gave you to praise him, and that's the best use of any gift. I used to think you was out of control, that you didn't understand the importance of what I'm trying to do in this church, and in this community. But now I know the Lord has a plan for you, Ava Delaney. All you have to do is stay on his path, and you gone be just fine."

The next day, as soon as service ended, the congregation of Blessed Chapel Church of God spilled out of the back and side and front doors of the church and made their way to the back wall. It was a chilly day, a day not made for standing outside very long. The temperature had dropped overnight and there was a frostiness in the air that did not fit for May. The congregation stood close together, some of the older folks shivering. George and Regina stood at the front of the crowd, and Geo, Sarah, Kenny, and Ellen stood nearby. Pastor Goode held the rope to the tarp and Ava stood beside him.

When the tarp came down, the congregation broke into applause. Most of them had seen the mural at some stage of being almost-finished, and in the bright light of the afternoon they saw what they expected, what they already knew they liked, and they immediately offered up their approval. Even Pastor Goode clapped, at first, smiling down at Ava, eager to commend the child, for her talent, but even more for her obedience, for her compliance, finally, after all those years of rebelliousness. Her parents clapped, too, the vague hint of worry in both their eyes, which had been there all morning, suddenly gone. They looked relieved. Especially her father, who, it seemed to Ava, exhaled for the first time in a full minute. The only one who did not applaud was Geo. Not because he saw something the others did not see, but because he saw exactly what they saw. A beautiful painting, strange and eccentric in its planes and angles, lush and feverish in its curves and colors, extraordinary in its display of skill and breathtaking talent. But entirely devoid of any argument, of any challenge, of any fight whatsoever. For a brief moment, he looked on the edge of tears. Then he blinked, and Ava watched the smile break open on his face, as he saw what she had added to the mural, what she had finished painting only a few minutes before, so that the paint was still wet, and her own hands, held behind her back, were smeared with color.

Shackles.

Onto the wrists of each parishioner lining the rows of pews and on their knees before the altar, she had painted shackles.

It took one and a half seconds for Geo to see them, for the image of the mural that he already had in his mind, the image he had already made up his mind about, to be replaced by the image that was actually before him. And in the half-second that followed, everyone else saw it, too. The sound of applause vanished from the air all at once. In its place, there were gasps, then murmurs, as people turned and looked at each other, with questions in their eyes, as if they could not believe what they were seeing and needed confirmation, first that the shackles were there, that they weren't just imagining them, and then that they meant something terrible, that they weren't misinterpreting them, but that their impulse to feel offended and angry by what they were seeing was valid. When they were sure that it was, they all turned and looked at Pastor Goode, who was staring up at the mural with fear and anger in his eyes.

He grabbed Ava's arm. "Why'd you do this?"

"Get off me," Ava said, trying to wrench out of his grip.

Regina and George rushed over. "Take your hands off my child," Regina said.

Goode let Ava go and Regina pulled her away from him. He glared at them. "I warned y'all about this child. I been warning y'all for years. The devil is in this girl."

"The devil!" Vic Jones yelled from the crowd.

"Listen, Pastor," George said. "She just a little girl. She don't know what she doing."

"She know exactly what she doing!" screamed Goode, pointing a shaking finger at Ava. "Every time I look at her, I can see her mind working. She wanted to defy me, she wanted to make a fool of me and every person in this church. And why? What for?"

"I aint trying to make a fool out of nobody," Ava said, looking out at the parishioners. "I been thinking about y'all, thinking about what y'all need."

"What they need?" The pastor asked. "What you think that is? To be told they slaves?"

"To be told they're *not* slaves," Ava said. "And you're not their master."

Goode looked ready to kill her. "I aint trying to be nobody's master!" he screamed.

"You tell everybody what to do," Ava said. "What to think. How to live."

"We live according to the Lord," Vic said.

"This aint right!" Malcolm yelled. "Y'all aint never known how to control that girl!"

"She gone too far this time," said Goode. "The Lord's gone punish her for this, y'all mark my words. He's gone bring down a judgment on this girl."

"I knew the first time I saw her it was something not right about her," said Hattie Mitchell.

"Me, too," said Lonette Brown. "I just couldn't put my finger on what it was."

"She too much," Malcolm said, shaking his head. "She *too much*."

1976

The dark fell like a brick that night, the sunset coming fast across the sky, daylight giving way to moonlight in little more than an instant. Coming home, George got caught in it, as if in a sudden rainstorm. It was strange, eerie, and he walked faster up and across the streets, eager to be indoors again.

When he came up Radnor, he saw Ava sitting on the front steps of the house, alone in the spanking new dark. He felt anger and humiliation stir inside him, remembering the knife at the dinner table, but when he got closer and saw the look on her face, it dissolved, and he spoke tenderly to his child.

"Ava? What you doing out here?"

She looked at him blankly, as if she didn't know who he was.

"Ava? What's wrong with you?"

She blinked and shook her head, looking around her.

George crouched down and looked into her face. "Ava?"

He saw focus slip into her gaze. "Daddy?"

"Yeah, it's me," he said.

"How did I get out here?"

George put his arm around her shoulders and helped her up off the step and inside the house. He took her up to her bedroom and she lay down in the bed again. He stacked the pillows behind her head and rested his hand on her shoulder for a moment, before turning to go.

"Daddy?" Ava called to him, and when he turned she said, "I'm sorry."

He looked at her, amazed at how much she seemed like herself as a young girl again these last few days. "You know, when you was a child, I was always lecturing you, always trying to get you to follow the rules. I know you hated it. But I was just trying to keep you safe. That's what fathers is supposed to do. But sometimes that becomes the only thing there is between you and that child, and next thing you know you aint got no other role in they life than that. It aint nothing worse than watching your children doing things you think—you *know*—is gone get them hurt. You got to try and stop it, even if that means hurting them yourself some, 'cause at least then you know where the hurt is coming from, and you can control it. You hurt them, so somebody else don't *kill* them. Or, at least, you hope it works out that way." That's what he wanted to say, but couldn't. Not out loud, because the words were too hard to get out, the truth of it almost too much to bear. Instead, he said, "It's alright. Just don't do nothing stupid like that again."

A little while later, Helena came into the room and sat down beside Ava on the bed. "How are you feeling?" she asked.

"Alright," Ava said. "Fine."

"I just heard your father telling Paul he found you on the front steps and you didn't know how you got there."

Ava laughed. "Well. Besides that."

Helena shook her head. "I shouldn't have pushed you. This is my fault."

Ava could see the worry in her eyes. "It's not your fault," she said. "I wanted to push. I still do."

"I think you should take it easy, Ava," Helena said.

Ava shook her head. "I can't."

"Why not?"

"Because what if this is all I ever get? Just bits and pieces, outbursts and fainting spells?" A few days of it had already begun to take a toll. She couldn't imagine months and years of this.

"The rest of it will come," Helena told her.

"You don't know that. What if it stops when you leave? What if I forget myself all over again?" She got up from the bed and walked over to the window. Outside, the dark was heavy, thick clouds covering the moon. She could see Helena's reflection in the window pane, watching her from the bed.

"I won't leave, then," Helena said.

Ava peered at Helena's reflected self.

"I'll stay in Philadelphia. I won't go to New York."

Ava turned and looked at her. "But your job—"

"There are jobs here," she said. "I looked at a place out in Wynnfield. There are three schools nearby it. Maybe I'll get lucky and one of them will need an art teacher."

There was a soft rustling in Ava's chest, like fallen leaves in a breeze, and she felt suddenly warmer, as if she had just been wrapped up in a soft, invisible something. She remembered being very small, sitting in her father's lap, with her head leaned back against his chest, and George's arms folded around her. She remembered her grandmother reading her fairy tales and kissing her goodnight. She remembered her sister tending to a scrape on her knee with a tissue and some spit, carefully, gingerly, gently. She remembered what each of those things felt like—the rustling, and the warmth on her skin, the same as she felt now. The feeling of being loved. She felt a swelling in her throat, a tingling, and when the tears came they were warm on her face.

"I'm upsetting you," Helena said.

"No. I'm not upset. I'm grateful," Ava told her. "But you have to go to New York. I don't want to disrupt your life."

Sarah knocked on the open door. "Helena, Paul is looking for you."

When Helena had gone, Sarah stood there staring at Ava. "You know, I almost believed you, when you said you wasn't trying to take nothing away from me. But deep down I always knew you would."

Ava sighed heavily. "Sarah, I'm tired. I don't want to do this with you. If you want to say something, say it. I don't have the energy to break your code."

She folded her arms across her chest. "She came here for me."

"Helena?"

"Yes, Helena!" Sarah said, stomping her foot hard on the floor. "Who the hell else?"

"How do you figure that?" Ava asked.

"I wished for her."

"You *wished* for Helena?"

"For somebody to come and make it better," Sarah said, nodding fervently. "And then she came. And I was happy. But you didn't care. You did what you've always done. You took her."

"Took her where?" Ava asked. "She's still here, Sarah, she just walked out of the room not three minutes ago, you can go and talk to her right now if you want to. Instead of standing here accusing me of...I don't even know what you're accusing me of."

"It's too late!" Sarah yelled. "She can't see me anymore! All she can see now is you, just like everybody else. She don't know I exist. Maybe I don't." On those last words, her voice cracked, and she started to cry. Ava went over to her, put her hands on her sister's shoulders, but Sarah took a step back away from her. "Just leave me alone, Ava."

"You're in my room."

Sarah glared at her, anger flashing through her tears. "Everybody thinks you so great. Everybody loves you so damn much."

"Who? Who are you talking about? *When* are you talking about?"

"But I can see what you really are," Sarah said. "You are selfish. You have always been selfish. You don't never think about anybody but yourself. What you want, what you need. That's how you was with Geo, always dragging him somewhere he didn't want to go, or into something he didn't want to do. Up a tree, out on the roof, into a fight. You wasn't never scared, so you didn't care if he was."

Ava sighed and sat down on the edge of the bed.

"And when Helena came here, you saw I was happy, I know you did. But that didn't stop you from placing yourself wherever she was every damn minute."

"You're right," Ava said.

Sarah hesitated, as if sensing some kind of trick.

"I did see that you were happy. And maybe I should have backed off, and let you have more time with her. But I didn't think about that. I didn't think about you at all."

Sarah nodded. "That's right. That's what you always used to do, when we was kids."

"I'm sorry," Ava said. "For doing it then, and for doing it now. But, Sarah, people do see you. Helena sees you. And you can still have that friendship you wished for."

Sarah looked at Ava for a long moment and Ava could see that she was thinking about it, considering the possibility that these things she had been telling herself for so long were not so. But then she shook her head. "It's too late," she said again, then turned and left the room, closing the door behind her.

Ava awoke in the middle of the night to a strange smell. She sat up in bed and sniffed the air. The scent was heavy, but she could not put a name to it. She got out of bed and went to the door, which was open a crack, and out into the hallway. The smell was stronger out there and she followed it, down towards Sarah's room. The door was open and Ava went inside, and the smell wrapped all around her. She turned on the lamp by the door and in the light she saw Helena asleep on the bed. There by the window, the wooden case she'd spotted in the cellar sat on the floor, open, its contents—tubes of paint, brushes, palette knives—spilling out around it. She crouched down beside it. The paint tubes were old and dusty, some of them squeezed empty, others still plump and full. Helena had opened one of the tubes and squeezed out a drop of the paint, and the bead of color shimmered in the lamplight. Ava dipped her fingertip in it and brought it to her nose. And the smell of red filled her. It moved fast through her body like a drug, the crumbly scent clinging to her skin. She stood up and caught her reflection in the dark window. She stared at herself. Something at the back of her mind, in the farthest reaches of her psyche, stirred. She moved closer to the window and reached out, touching her oil-red fingertip lightly to the glass, and traced the contours of her face, the curve of her jaw, the slant of her nose, the shapes of her eyes and lips and brow. The tips of her fingers tingled, and the tingle moved all over her skin, as if her body were remembering something her mind did not yet realize had been forgotten. She got as close as she could to the window, her nose almost touching the glass, and looked into the deep, dark eyes of the woman looking back at her, and something unlocked, unraveled, came undone.

Ava knelt down again and took the tube of red from the wooden case and something at the back of her mind said, *Don't.* She ignored it, and squeezed more red onto her fingertips, and touched the paint to the glass of the dark window.

Stop it, Ava.

She reached into the case and took out every shade of red she could find. Using her hand as a palette, she squeezed globs of paint onto each fingertip, and down each finger, and onto her palm. With the fingers of her other hand, she painted the curve of her own jaw and she remembered again laughing with Geo at the kitchen table. Only this time the memory did not flash and go, it stayed, solid and sure as the pigment on the window. She painted her lips and remembered the smells of Christmases past and the hum of friends gathered around them. She painted her eyes and then stood there before the glass canvas, still and ghostly quiet, looking into the dark pools of paint that looked back at her, wild and happy.

She stood there before the changing canvas for hours, as the room got hot, as beads of sweat formed on her brow and nose and throat. At moments, she felt sick, nauseated, but she did not stop. At other moments, her knees felt too weak to hold her, but she stood there, shaking and pushing herself forward. Her vision blurred. Her heart pounded. Her joints ached. And still she painted.

She didn't know Helena was awake until she felt a soft touch on her arm and turned to see her standing there, her green eyes afire, her lips parted. Standing there in front of the canvas, both hands covered in paint, Ava recognized another feeling, one that filled her up and busted out of her, making her laugh out loud.

"Ava, what is it?" Helena asked her.

And Ava said, "Helena, it's bliss."

She reached out and touched Helena's cheek. When she removed her hand, there were daubs of paint along Helena's cheekbones.

"Oh," Ava whispered. "Sorry. I got paint on you."

Helena touched her face where Ava's fingers had been and examined the scarlet that came off on her own fingers. She smiled at Ava. Then she bent down and took a tube of paint from the case and squeezed out a drop onto her fingertip. She touched Ava's cheeks, leaving streaks of cerulean on her caramel skin. She traced the curve of Ava's jaw and her heavy eyelids. Ava ran her thumb along Helena's throat and along her collarbone. Helena brought her fingers to Ava's mouth and touched her lips. Ava's skin tingled, and her blood, excited as red paint on white canvas, rushed. She pressed her mouth against Helena's and kissed her, and tasted every color. Helena put her hands on Ava's shoulders and pushed her away.

Helena looked down at her hands, which were covered with paint. There was pain in her eyes and she trembled. Ava wanted to reach out for her, but she stood still, and waited. Helena looked at Ava and shook her head, as if answering a question that had not been asked, at least not in words. Then she turned and walked out of the room.

Ava sat down on the edge of the bed and stared at the spot where Helena had been. All of the emotions that had been stirred up inside her in the last few days, and in the last few hours, all of the confusion and intensity, stilled, and she felt calm, almost serene, in the quiet of the bedroom. She felt as she had as a young girl, completely comfortable in her skin, entirely at ease in her mind, and in her soul. She felt like herself again.

1959

Maddy and Malcolm noticed the change right away. They had always loved Ava, from the first moment they saw the child, and they knew that mostly everyone else on the block, and in the church, felt the same way. They all talked about her all the time, said how special she was, how different, how they had never known anyone like her, how she seemed to have been sent to them by God, to remind them of the happiest moments of their lives and the best things within themselves, and to show them what freedom looked like, how it moved and spoke and sang. But when that tarp came down, when everybody saw those shackles, something shifted.

A week after the uncovering of the mural—which had been immediately covered up again, not with a tarp this time, but with white paint—they could see the change, plain as day. Sitting on her usual pew at Blessed Chapel, a few seats down from Ava, Maddy saw June Johnson, who was sitting a few rows ahead of them, peering over her shoulder at the girl, the look on her face plainly disdainful. A few minutes later, Marilyn Porter, who was ushering that Sunday, standing by the wall with her white-gloved hands clasped in front of her, whispered something to Clarence Nelson, who was standing beside her, and they both looked over at Ava and frowned in unison. Throughout the service, it happened at least a dozen times. Some people glanced at Ava as they passed by, on their way to the restroom or perhaps the water fountain, and frowned or rolled their eyes. Others were more openly contemptuous, turning around in their seats to glare. A few times, Maddy noticed, they did not direct their sneers at Ava alone, but let their eyes graze Regina, too, and, once or twice, their entire family.

Malcolm was watching, too, though not from his usual pew. He no longer wished to sit with the Delaneys, and instead sat with his brother across the aisle, where Vic had moved his whole family, giving up their long-standing seats. Malcolm had been outraged at the unveiling of the mural. He had always liked Ava, and had even let it slide when she had drawn those filthy pictures at the funeral, telling himself that, despite his initial reaction, she was a good girl, and the good things about her outweighed the bad. But when that tarp came down, he knew in an instant that he had been wrong, and that he, and all of them, had been duped. She did have the devil in her. It was plain to see. And he refused to be fooled any longer.

Doris didn't notice the change at all. She wasn't a woman who paid that much attention to what people were feeling. But she heard plenty of whispering. On the pew right in front of her, Lillian leaned over to Rose and said, "I can't believe they had the nerve to bring that child in here after what she did."

"Girl, you aint never lied," Rose whispered back. "Soon as I saw her, I felt this rush of heat. I thought I was gone faint right there in the aisle."

Doris thought that was probably just due to the temperature inside the church, but she wasn't one to deny people their occasional dramatic flourishes. Personally, she didn't see what all the fuss was about. She had known from the first moment she saw Ava that the child was just too much.

When Pastor Goode stepped up into the pulpit, Malcolm thought he looked tired. He could understand why. A few days ago, the pastor had confided to Malcolm that he wanted the Delaneys out of the church. He didn't feel like he could throw them out, because they were still so well-liked by so many people, so much of the congregation was still loyal to them. He said it was up to the rest of them—those who agreed with the pastor and understood why there was no place for the Delaneys at Blessed Chapel until they got control of that child of theirs—to let the family know how they felt.

Now Pastor Goode stood looking out at them all, a look of intense worry on his face. "The Lord sets down a path for us from the day we are born. We may not see it, we may not understand what it is, but we can be sure it's there. God's plan for us is that we walk that path. If we walk it, it will lead us to Him and the kingdom of heaven. But the devil will try to lead us astray. He will try to convince us that we know what's good for us better than the good Lord. He will bring into our lives people who seem good at first, who appear to be of God, but who are really Satan's minions. We must not be tricked. We must believe in God's plan, for us and for our neighbors and friends and everyone we love. We must all act in service to the Lord. And, when called, the righteous among us must take an active hand in the Lord's plan."

Malcolm looked around. Half the congregation was nodding their heads and muttering, *Yes, Lord*s and *Amen*s. Malcolm wondered how many of them realized who the pastor was talking about. The other half of the congregation looked worried, disturbed, as if they were unsure of what, exactly, the pastor was trying to say, but thought it might be something they didn't like. Regina and George exchanged a look of serious concern. Farther down the pew, Ava's eyes were narrowed as she looked up at Pastor Goode. The sermon went on from there into more general-sounding and less controversial territory. When the service ended and the usual mingling and socializing in the aisles began, Malcolm noticed that, like him, quite a few people kept their distance from the Delaneys, their usual greetings, their hugs and kisses and hand-shakes, not offered. Some people said hello but withheld the attention they had always showered on Ava, some of them only smiling, or barely smiling, in her direction, others not acknowledging her at all. All this Malcolm was sure Ava's parents noticed, too. When Elder Smith walked right by them without a word, he saw Regina and George frown at each other. Right after that, though, Deacon Brooks came up and shook George's hand, hugged Regina, and put his arms around all three siblings, and his usual post-service conversation, about the traffic he'd had to endure on Baltimore Avenue on his way to the church that morning, commenced. Jane Lucas was as friendly as always, as were many other people, but it seemed to Malcolm that Ava's admirers had been cut by more than half, and were continuing to diminish by the hour.

After service, as the Delaney family made their way out of the church, Regina noticed that Geo wasn't with them. "Where's your brother?" she asked Ava and Sarah, sounding tired and stressed.

"Bathroom, I think," Sarah said.

"Ava, go get him, please."

Ava frowned and turned back into the entrance.

Sarah leaned against the door and watched her sister as she headed for the steps that led down to the church basement, where the restrooms were. Sondra was standing at the top of the steps, off to the side a little, laughing with her friends, and when she saw Ava coming, her laughter stopped, and all mirth left her expression. What replaced it was a look of loathing, of almost cartoon-like hatred, and Sarah half expected smoke to come out of Sondra's ears. She laughed to herself, then watched as Sondra moved a couple of inches closer to the steps and, covertly, without looking down, slid her foot into Ava's path. Sarah stopped laughing. Everything slowed down, as Ava, who did not notice what Sondra was doing because she was examining the drawings she had done on her program, stepped forward. Sarah opened her mouth to call out to Ava, but no sound came.

Ava stopped, half a step from Sondra's foot, as Geo's voice called to her from the other side of the lobby. She turned and frowned at him. "Mama's looking for you," she said, and skipped off in his direction. Sarah watched as Sondra retracted her foot, looking disappointed.

1976

The next morning, Saturday, Regina was awakened by the sound of her own muttering. She got up carefully from the bed, trying not to wake Sarah. She grabbed the dress she had left hanging over a chair the night before, her purse, and her shoes, and crept out of the room. In the bathroom, she dressed and brushed her teeth, then stepped out into the hallway and listened. No one in the house was stirring. She crept down the steps and when she got to the front door she stopped. It seemed to her that there was something on the other side of the door that she didn't want to see, something that would tear her up, but she couldn't think what. "Maybe it's gone rain," she muttered to herself, and then wondered why rain would stop her. "I guess if I just take a umbrella I be alright." She grabbed an umbrella from the umbrella stand and went out the door.

On the bus, people looked at her sideways, as if she were crazy or something. When she noticed a couple of teenagers pointing at her and whispering, she thought they must be looking at something out the window behind her.

She got off the bus at the corner of Fifty-First and Baltimore, and when she stepped out into the street a car slammed its brakes and honked loudly.

"Get your crazy ass out the damn street!" the driver yelled, slamming his hand against the steering wheel.

Regina gave him the finger, then stepped back onto the curb and waited for the light to change.

Baltimore Avenue was a wide, busy, two-way road, much more heavily trafficked than Radnor, and louder for it, with cars and trucks rolling up and down it in constant succession. The houses along Fifty-First and Baltimore were narrower than those on her own block, but taller, standing three stories high and, because of their lack of width, there seemed to be many more of them, all crammed together along the block like books on a shelf.

She walked down Fifty-First Street, looking for the house number she'd gotten from the phone book the night before, under the listing for Charles Ellis. A couple of times, she got confused, and thought she was back on her own street, and wondered why the houses looked so different. Finally, after walking up and down the block twice, she found the correctly numbered row house, with a green awning and, hanging over the front porch railing, flower boxes full of violets. She walked up the front steps, the metal point of her large umbrella dragging against the cement. She stepped up onto the porch, rang the doorbell, and waited. She remembered that Lena always used to get up early on weekends and do all her cleaning before her family could get in the way. Regina used to see her all the time, out on her front porch in the mornings, beating out rugs and sweeping. That was so many years ago, though, and she wondered whether Lena, who was older than she was, still had that kind of energy. She didn't have to wonder about it long. After just a few seconds, the front door opened and Lena stood there, holding a dustcloth and some furniture polish, squinting at her through the screen door that still separated them.

"Regina?" she asked, sounding surprised.

"Hello, Lena," Regina said. "I'd like to talk with you. Can I come in?"

Lena hesitated.

"I'm sorry to drop by unexpectedly," Regina said, and she realized she was speaking unnecessarily loudly, so she lowered her voice. "I know it aint good manners. But what I need to say ought to be said face to face. It won't take long."

Lena stood there a long moment and then, finally, the screen door opened, and she gave Regina a strained smile. "Of course," she said. "Come on in."

Inside, the house was as narrow as it appeared from the outside. Regina propped her umbrella against the wall and followed Lena down a hallway, past rooms lit only by the new daylight coming in through the windows. It had been a long time since Regina had been inside anybody else's house, besides the houses she worked in. She eyed the furniture, which was at least a decade newer than anything she owned, and well-kept, cared-about in a way she herself had not cared about any item in her own house in seventeen years. All along the walls, there were framed photographs of the Ellis family, of Chuck and Lena and their children and, Regina supposed, their grandchildren, of whom there appeared to be many. She got confused again and wondered why Chuck and Lena looked so old in the photographs. They were both around her age. Then she remembered that she was old, too, and that many years had passed since she had known them.

They entered the kitchen, which was very warm, and which looked very like the kitchen of the house Lena and Chuck had lived in on Radnor Street. This did nothing to help Regina's confusion. "It's now," she muttered to herself. "Not then." She took a seat at the table and Lena offered her lemonade.

"No, thank you," Regina said. "Your lemonade taste like shit, Lena. It always did. And I aint gone stay long, anyway."

Lena frowned and sat down at the other end of the table.

Regina didn't know what she had come there to say. She knew that in the last couple of days, ever since she'd found out that Chuck had been in the house, she had thought about Lena a lot, after not thinking about her much at all for nearly two decades. She had wondered how she was doing, what her life had turned out to be like, and she had felt compelled to reach out to her. Now, sitting there at the table with her, she decided she must have come to talk about George and Chuck. "Twenty-some years ago, I sat in your kitchen—not this one, but one that looked a lot like it," she said, more for herself than for Lena, "and you asked me about our husbands. I guess you remember that."

Lena nodded. "Yes. I remember."

"Well, back then I wasn't ready to talk about it, I guess." She paused, trying to remember whether or not she had been ready to talk about it then. "No, I definitely wasn't," she said. "I never have been ready. But I'm ready now."

Lena looked down at her hands in her lap. "Maybe I aint ready to talk about it no more," she said.

"Well, then you aint got to say nothing," Regina told her. "Just shut up and let me say what I got to say."

Lena sighed. Nodded.

"Back then, I was trying not to think about it. All them years, from way back when me and George was first going together, I tried not to. And I did a good job of it, too." She felt her head clearing a little and what she was saying made more sense to her. "I managed to push it back, way back, in my mind, and not look at it. But that changed when we moved onto Radnor Street and George met Chuck."

Lena shifted in her chair.

"After that it was harder to ignore it, to not see it. Shit, it was plain as day." She laughed, loud and deranged-sounding, even to her own ears.

Lena looked a little scared.

"Still, I wasn't gone talk about it and let it be real," Regina went on. "I had three children and a house to take care of, so I kept it in. And I hated George. *Hated* him."

She remembered watching George with Chuck one Thanksgiving, them laughing and whispering together, and she being filled with loathing, stuffed with it like the turkey, and how it had felt as if she wouldn't be able to hold it in, that it would bust her open at her seams, and spill out like the dressing from the bird's opened-up carcass.

"I held it in for so long. Even after their *friendship* ended, I still felt like Chuck was there, that George still thought about him. And I kept on hating him." She sighed, and shook her head. "When my son died—" she stopped. Her son hadn't died. What was she saying? But he had, hadn't he? "I went crazy. I lost my mind. I wanted to die myself. But I remembered I still had two children to provide for, so I pulled myself together best I could, and I kept on keeping George's secret, because providing for them still meant doing that. You understand what I'm saying?"

"Yes," Lena said. "But I already figured all this, Regina."

"Well, you aint figured what I'm gone say next, so you just sit tight," Regina said. "Lately I been thinking, wondering why I'm still keeping it. My children is grown. My house is paid for. But here I am, still keeping it in, and still hating George. Why didn't I confront him once Ava and Sarah was old enough to take care of theyselves? Why didn't I toss him out on his sorry ass?"

Lena looked as if she were thinking about the question, trying to figure it out. Finally, she said, "Why didn't you? Why don't you?"

"Because hating George is who I am now!" Regina said, slapping her palm on the table to stress the point, and causing Lena to jump. "My anger, my disgust, is everything to me! These past years, I aint gave a damn about hardly nothing. I aint took care of myself, or my house. But I took good care of my hate for my husband. I nurtured it, kept it feeling new, looking shiny. It's the most well-kept thing I own."

Lena stared at her, the lines around her mouth deepened.

"But now I'm old and sick and mean," Regina said. "You see this hardness in my eyes?" She leaned forward and opened her eyes wide so Lena could see. "I'm tired of it," she said. "'Cause, you know what? It aint no joy in it, Lena. Not one bit. And it aint never been none. So, why I'm doing it? Why I spent all these years doing something that aint brought me a lick of joy?" She laughed, and this time it didn't sound crazy, at least not to her own ears. "I see now what I got to do," Regina said. "I either got to leave, or let it go. And since I'm too damn old to leave, I'm letting it go. Right here, right now. I came here and tell you that, Lena. In case it helps you in any way."

Lena just sat there, not saying anything, with a look on her face that was half surprised and half thoughtful, as if she were still trying to figure out what Regina was talking about, still trying to make sense of her sudden appearance, but still understood everything she had said.

Regina stood. "Thank you for letting me barge in on you, Lena."

"Regina," Lena said, getting up, too. "I want you to know I never agreed with Pastor Goode, or believed in what he did to you and your family. The only reason I didn't get in touch with you after your son was killed was because of Chuck and George. I just wanted to keep my distance from that. But I always hated what the pastor was doing. It's the reason I told Chuck we had to leave that block, because I couldn't stand to watch what was going on over there. Y'all didn't deserve that."

"Thank you. I appreciate you telling me that."

"I been at Blessed Chapel since I was a child. Since way before Ollie Goode became pastor. His uncle, the pastor before him, wasn't like that. He was a kind man."

"You mean his father?"

"No. Arthur Goode was Ollie's uncle, his father's brother," Lena told her. "Ollie's father died when he was young, and his uncle took him in."

"I aint know that," Regina said.

Lena shrugged. "Well, he don't talk about it much."

"How'd his father die?" Regina asked.

"In jail," said Lena. "A cop shot him. They said he was trying to escape. At least that's what I heard. I don't know nothing about it firsthand."

"Lord."

"Anyway, I just wanted to make sure you know that I—that Chuck and I—been praying for y'all all these years. And if you ever want to come by again, Regina, just to talk, I hope you know you welcome to."

"Thank you," Regina said. A few minutes later, on the bus ride back home, her mind began to unclutter itself. The confusion and craziness of Saturday morning began to drop away and, several hours earlier than usual, her sanity returned.

Ava slept long into the morning and she awoke feeling deeply rested, as though she had slept for days, or months, or years. She showered and dressed hurriedly, eagerly, filled with a sense that the day ahead held great things. When she got downstairs, she saw the front door open, and she went out onto the porch. Paul was on the sidewalk, cutting the hedges. He looked up when he heard the screen door knock shut. "Morning," he said.

Ava leaned over the porch railing. It was a magnificent day, the sky watercolor blue over white, with just enough cloud-wisp brushed in at the edges to balance the heavy color of the almost-too-yellow sun. The grass in the yard was a million strokes off the corner of a thin brush soaked with green, and the sunlight reflecting off the tips of the grassblades was like daubs of oily white, carefully, painstakingly placed. Each flower in the garden Helena had planted was a fat drop of lush pigment, lemon-yellow or vermillion, hot orange or rose or purple, and some of them seemed to spill into each other, as if they were made by an excited hand, tiny beads of orange dotting the edges of violets, and specks of purple clinging to buttercup petals. Ava watched Paul at the hedges, bare-armed and bay brown, and looking like a field hand from a Spanish fresco, superimposed against the backdrop of a city block, the size of his hands and the amount of sweat on his forehead exaggerated just enough to show that he was hard-working, a good, strong kind of man, the lines across his forehead etched in with the sharp edge of a palette knife, like the lines of the group of row houses that stood solidly behind him, sturdy and not changing, solid and achromatic, a constant captured in grays. The screen door opened and Helena appeared. Her skin was a saturate of all color, her body a chroma made up of angled brushstrokes, her bare shoulders like drops of oil-black thrown against the canvas in a fever, precarious and lovely.

"I'm leaving," she said to Ava. And then, louder, so Paul could hear. "I'm leaving. I've decided to leave."

Paul looked up at her. She looked from Ava to him. None of them said anything.

Suddenly a voice, loud and bellowing, filled the warm morning air. "Sinners, hear the name of the Lord and be afraid!" Ava turned and saw Pastor Goode crossing the street, followed by a small group of people. "The Lord will not let your evil go unpunished. He will hold you to account."

"Oh, here we go," Paul said, holding the hedge clippers aloft of the hedges.

"How many times will they flout the Word of God so boldly?" Goode stopped in the street in front of the Delaney house and the crowd, which included Doris and Dexter, Hattie, and Antoinette, stopped with him. He raised his hand and pointed his finger right at Helena, and the crowd turned its collective head and looked at her, as he said, "That woman is a homosexual and a home-wrecker!"

There were gasps from the crowd. Doris frowned and shook her head, while Hattie gripped her husband and held on to him as though an earthquake might come and shake the block to rubble any second.

Paul looked around at Ava and Helena, and back at the preacher as if he were crazy. Ava saw Helena sigh deeply and fold her arms across her chest. The screen door opened and George came out onto the porch, followed by Regina and Sarah.

"What's all this?" George asked.

"That woman," Pastor Goode hollered, still pointing at Helena, "was thrown out of the school where she was a teacher, down in Baltimore, for committing unnatural acts with the mother of one of her students. A *married* woman!"

The gasps this time came not only from the crowd, but from the porch. Sarah put her hand over her mouth and stared with wide eyes at Helena.

"She got run out of Baltimore," the preacher said. "Disgraced. And now look who takes her in."

Dexter yelled, "That don't surprise me a bit!"

"Well, I want her gone!" Pastor Goode bellowed. "I want them all gone! Off this block! Out of this neighborhood!"

"Gone!"

"But I don't think we gone have to wait much longer," Goode said. "'Cause they starting to turn on each other now. It was Ava who came to me last night and suggested I look into this woman's past."

Everyone on the porch, and in the street, looked at Ava.

She shook her head. "He's lying."

"May the Lord strike me down right here, right now, if it aint the truth!" Goode yelled. He looked around at the crowd. "And y'all know when the rats start leaving the house, it's about to fall."

Paul paced the living room, looking shocked and angry, the veins in his forehead bulging. "Where do that fool get off?" he asked, looking around at them all. The street sermon had ended, Goode having made his point and returned to the church. "He think he can just say whatever he want about people, just make up lies, and get away with it?"

Regina and Sarah were sitting on the sofa, and Ava was sitting on the arm. George was standing in the doorway, his arms folded across his chest. None of them said anything.

"Y'all don't believe that bullshit, do you?" Paul asked, looking around at them.

Nobody said anything.

"I guess y'all think Ava put him up to it, too?"

"I would never do that," Ava said.

"I know you wouldn't," Paul said, laughing at the absurdity of it. "I know that man is crazy. Y'all know it. He just made all that up to get to us."

"He's not lying," Helena said. She was leaning against the mantle, looking shaken. "At least not about me."

"Yeah, he is," Paul said, sounding sure. "He's always doing this; calling people devils and making up crazy shit. I told you, he out his mind."

"It's the truth, Paul," she said. "I had a relationship with the mother of one of my students. The school found out about it, long after it was already over, and they fired me."

Paul shook his head wildly from side to side, as if he were trying to push away the thought.

"Listen to your sister, Paul," Regina said. "You aint listening to her."

"I aint listening, 'cause she aint making no sense," he said. He looked at his sister. "If it's true, then the woman must've made you do it, she must have—"

"She didn't make me do anything," Helena said, taking a step toward him. "I did it because I wanted to."

Paul took a step back. He looked around at them all again, then back at Helena. "No," he said. "You aint like that, Helena, you aint that way."

"Yes, I am," she said.

"It's because of that girl," he whispered. "It's because of what that girl did to you when we was kids."

"What girl?" Ava asked.

Paul looked at her. "The girl I..." He stopped. He looked at Regina and Sarah and George. "I walked in, and saw I her. She was doing things to my sister, she was hurting her. That's why I grabbed her, that's why I pushed her. I didn't mean to—" He stopped again.

"To what?" Regina asked.

Paul shook his head, stared down at the floor.

"What's he talking about?" Regina asked Ava.

"You have to tell them," Ava said to Paul.

Paul had the hardest time raising his head. It felt like a pile of bricks on his shoulders. When his eyes met Regina's, shame flooded through him. "I killed somebody."

Regina's eyes went wide.

George said, "What the hell you mean, you killed somebody?"

"I mean I killed somebody, Pop. A girl. When I was fifteen. I didn't mean to do it."

Regina looked at Ava. "You knew about this?"

"Not until a couple of days ago."

"I didn't mean to do it," he said again. "She was hurting my sister." He looked at Helena. "She was hurting you. And now you confused."

Helena shook her head.

"Why you shaking your head like that?" Paul asked her, looking and sounding panicked now. "Don't shake your head like that."

"She wasn't hurting me," Helena said. "I liked what she was doing. She wasn't hurting me, Paul."

"Oh, Lord," Regina said. "Oh, Lord."

"You came in and saw us, and it *seemed* that way to you, but that's not how it was. I tried to say something, to tell you, to stop you. But it all happened so fast."

Paul put his hand over his mouth and retched, a dry-heave, and he doubled-over, losing his legs and falling on his knees to the floor. Ava hurried to his side, knelt down beside him, putting one hand on his back and the other on his arm.

"Afterward, I was afraid to tell you," Helena went on. "I thought you would hate me. I've carried it around all this time."

Paul did not think he could stand. He stayed there on his knees, with his forehead against the floor and his eyes squeezed shut, telling himself to wake up, that this was a dream, or a delusion, and that she was not really saying these things. It wasn't possible that he had killed that girl for nothing. She had been hurting his sister. He had been trying to protect his sister. He had not meant to kill the girl, he had never meant to do that, but he had grabbed her and pushed her because she had been hurting his sister. Doing things to her. Wrong things. Through all these years, the one thing that had made it possible for him not to hate himself—not to forgive himself, never that, but to not hate himself—was knowing that he had been trying to protect his sister.

"That's why I tracked you down. That's why I came here," Helena said. "To tell you."

Paul raised his head off the floor, and looked up at her. She stood there, with tears pouring down her face. He wanted to grab her. Shake her. But she was too far away, and he did not think he could stand.

"I'm sorry," she said.

He needed to get up, to get out of there. He did not know what would happen if he didn't get out of there. He put his palms flat against the floor and pushed himself up. He did not look at her again. He turned and left the room, walked into the foyer and up the stairs. In his bedroom, he took a small suitcase from the top of the closet and packed a few things—clothes and shoes for work, his hair pick. He went to the bathroom and got his toothbrush and razor. Every second he felt angrier, more ready to scream, to kill somebody, to kill *her*, and he knew he had to hurry and get out of there. He shoved his wallet into his back pocket and ran back down the stairs. From the corner of his eye he saw her still standing there in the living room, and Ava still kneeling on the floor, and all of them watching him, but he did not turn his head. He went out the front door, and when the screen door caught shut behind him, he thanked God that he'd got out of there without doing something crazy.

After Paul left the house, Helena shut herself up in Sarah's room. The family remained gathered downstairs. George sat on the sofa now, while the women paced around the room, circling the furniture and talking in hushed voices.

"I can't believe it," Sarah said, shaking her head.

George was surprised, too. He'd been so busy worrying what Helena might see in him that he hadn't imagined that she could be hiding the same shame. If she was even ashamed about it. Maybe she wasn't. After all, she'd confessed it in front of all of them. Goode had opened the door, but she could easily have lied, especially knowing their history with the pastor and that no one in that house really wanted to believe anything Goode had to say. She could have gotten out of it if she'd wanted to, kept her secret hidden. But she hadn't.

"I guess you never really know about people," Regina said.

George looked up at her and waited for her to turn and glare in his direction, but she didn't.

"What I can't understand," Sarah said, "is why Pastor Goode said that about Ava telling him to look at Helena's past. Why would he say that?"

Regina shrugged. "Why do that man say any of the things he say? He always hated Ava, from the day he met her."

"But he aint never *lied* before," Sarah said.

"What you mean he aint lied?" George asked. "You think the devil's in this house?"

"No. But he thinks so. It aint really a lie, because he believes it. That's my point. He must believe Ava told him that."

"You trying to make sense of that man's ranting and raving?" Regina asked her. "That's what you trying to do?"

Sarah shrugged. "I don't know."

Ava was sitting on the arm of the sofa, not saying anything.

Sarah sighed. "I just can't believe it," she said again. "But, now that I think about it, I guess she is a little bit...boyish."

Regina frowned. "Helena is still a guest in this house, and we gone treat her with respect as long as she here."

George felt bile collecting in his stomach and rising up into his throat. "Since when you so forward-thinking, Regina?"

"I aint said nothing about being 'forward-thinking.' But she aint my daughter, so it aint none of my business."

"You—"

"This aint about us, George," Regina said.

He peered at her. There was a look in her eyes he hadn't seen in years. Usually she was all set to bicker with him, poised, morning, noon and night for a fight. Whenever he entered a room, her shoulders tightened. Whenever he spoke, she got her mouth ready to argue. But not now. Now she stood there looking as though a fight was the last thing she wanted. George didn't know what to think.

"What if it *was* your daughter?" Ava asked.

George felt a squeezing in his gut.

"What's that supposed to mean?" Sarah asked.

"What if I was like that?" Ava said. "A lesbian."

George shook his head. He didn't want to hear this. He *wouldn't* hear it. "That aint funny, Ava," he said.

"I'm not trying to be funny, Daddy."

Regina said, "Oh, Lord."

"Are you a lesbian?" Sarah asked.

Ava shrugged. "Maybe."

Sarah rolled her eyes. "You aint no damn lesbian, Ava. Those women don't have husbands."

"Neither do you," Ava said.

Sarah glared at her, but didn't say anything else about what lesbians had or didn't have.

"What you need to be thinking about right now," George said to Ava, "is Paul. Where you think he went?"

Ava shrugged. "His cousin's, maybe. I don't know."

"You don't even care? He still your husband, aint he?"

"I don't think he will be for much longer," she said.

"What you saying?" Regina asked. "You and Paul splitting up?"

"I'm saying I don't want to be married to him anymore."

Sarah looked disgusted. "You never deserved that man."

"Who deserves him, then?" Ava asked. "You? Did you wish for Paul, too?"

"Y'all stop this right now!" Regina said.

George got up.

"Daddy, don't leave," Ava said.

He ignored her, headed for the door.

She grabbed his arm. "Let's see what happens if you stay," she said, "just this one time."

But George didn't want to know what would happen. He wanted to get away from there before Regina remembered she was an angry, evil old woman and started blaming him for what Ava might be, the way he was already blaming himself.

Ava waited a while before knocking on Sarah's door. She knew that Helena needed space, and time to sort through what had happened. She needed those things herself. After her father fled, yet again, from the house, she went and sat alone on the back porch, on the top step where Helena always sat, and thought long and hard about this woman who had come into their house and into their lives and thrown everyone and everything out of whack. She hadn't been surprised when Helena had confessed to the scandal in Baltimore, in fact she knew the moment Pastor Goode said it that it must be true. Although Ava had not considered it before, the idea that Helena had loved a woman, had loved her *that way*, and that whatever feelings had developed between she and Ava weren't entirely new to her, seemed a given now. Not because she was a little bit boyish, as Sarah had said. But because she was a little bit unconventional in every way, a little bit off-center of what every other woman Ava knew was like. A little bit bolder, a little bit more sure. A little more curious, and a little less concerned with other people's opinions of her. A little bit like Ava herself.

The memory of the girl in the pastor's nook had made itself solid in Ava's mind, and she knew now that it was Ellen, Miss Maddy's daughter, whose mouth had been pressed against hers in that tiny space. They'd snuck in there on their way from the bathrooms back to Sunday service.

Ellen had looked at Ava with so much light in her large eyes that the small, dark room seemed to light up from within her. Ava was suddenly filled with an impulse to put her mouth on the girl and she did just that, moving quickly forward and pressing her lips against Ellen's.

It was not the first time, either, that she had kissed another girl. The summer before, when she was twelve, she had been kissed by her sixteen year-old day camp counselor, a beautiful girl with skin like honey. But she had been a little scared then, a little tentative. That time with Ellen she was neither. The sensation of her warm lips against Ava's made her dizzy, and so full of desire that she put her hands on the back of Ellen's white dress, on her lower back, and pulled the girl into her. Ellen opened her mouth and Ava felt the wetness of her tongue flick against her bottom lip. Ava opened her mouth too, and their tongues touched and played as the preacher boomed from the pulpit, "Get thee behind me, Satan."

When she'd slipped past her brother on her way back to her seat at the pew, he looked at her suspiciously, and she knew that he knew she'd been up to something. But she never told him about it, because she never had the chance. He was dead only a few days later, and with him all of that, and all of everything else she had been, had faded away.

Ava sat out on the back steps for a long time, for hours, and when she couldn't stand it any longer she went upstairs and knocked on Sarah's door. After a moment, Helena said, "Come in, Ava."

Ava entered the room and found Helena tossing clothes into her suitcase. "You're packing."

Helena glanced over her shoulder. "Yes. I've imposed myself on your family long enough."

Ava sighed and sat down on the bed. She had no intention of letting Helena leave like this, just walking out like a stranger the way she had walked in. It meant something that she had come there and Ava wasn't ready to let her go. "Were you able to get a hold of Paul?" she asked. Earlier, she'd seen the light blinking on the telephone in the kitchen and knew that Helena was using the upstairs phone.

"No. I called our cousin's place but the line is disconnected. I hate leaving with things so bad between us."

"Then don't," Ava said. "Stay a little longer. I'm sure Paul will call in a day or two, even if it's just to speak to me. If you're still here, maybe he'll talk to you."

"What if he won't?" She dropped a skirt into her suitcase and stared at it. "I guess I deserve it."

Ava shook her head. "You were only a child. How could you have known what to do, what to say?"

Helena continued to stare down into the suitcase, and after a long moment of silence, she said, "I still remember the moment he walked in on us, the look on his face when he thought…when it seemed to him that she was hurting me. He really was just trying to protect me." She sighed. "But she wasn't someone I needed protection from. She was a sweet girl. A gentle soul. Afterward, after they took Paul away, I couldn't stop thinking that she was dead because of how something had seemed. Not how it really was. I decided then that I would never be satisfied with how anything seemed—a situation, or a person. That I would always look deeper and try to see what was really there. I became obsessed with the idea of knowing things, and knowing people, really knowing them, underneath. Some people find it obnoxious, like your father. But it's how I cope with what happened."

Ava remembered that first moment at the front door on that Saturday morning, and later when her eyes had met Helena's across the kitchen table, and again when Helena had held out the drawing to her, and she realized that each of those times, and all the others since, when she had looked into Helena's eyes she had seen, looking back at her, what Helena saw— what she saw because she had been looking for it. The reflection of her real self.

"Well," Helena said. "There's no use crying about any of this now. It's long past able to be fixed. The only thing to do now is try to get past it, to move on, finally, which neither I nor my brother have been able to do these past eighteen years."

As Helena talked, Ava watched her face and could see the strength in it, the determination to be tough, and she thought how lovely Helena was, and wondered why she had ever thought of her as plain. Then, for no reason she understood at that moment, Ava went and stood close to Helena, and put her hand on her shoulder. And right then Helena cried. Tears suddenly streamed down her face. Ava was already right there and Helena turned and put her head on Ava's shoulder, and Ava held her. She cried silently, only the sound of her breathing meeting Ava's ear, close and quiet. Ava closed her eyes and listened, and heard the tiny sound of teardrops falling on her shoulder. She felt the pump of Helena's heart against her, the expanding and contracting of her chest as air filled and left her lungs. She smelled the bar-soap clean of her skin and the salt in the traces of sweat on the back of her neck. And although she had never been so close to Helena before, it all seemed so familiar. She knew then why she had gotten up and gone to her, how she had known before the tears had come that they would come. It was because, over these many days, as Ava had taken in the things around her, had come to see the colors and taste the tastes, she had also been taking in Helena. With the easy excuse that she was paying more attention to everything, she had indulged herself in the qualities of this woman, had heard and felt and smelled and tasted her as surely as she had tasted the butter that night. It was only that the melting of Helena on her tongue had been slower.

"Stay," Ava said.

Helena moved away from her, sat down on the end of the bed. "I can't."

"You were thinking of not going to New York at all."

"That was before."

Ava nodded, understanding. "I'm sorry I kissed you," she said. Then she laughed. "I'm starting to sound like a broken record. And, anyway, it's a lie."

"Ava, when I left Baltimore, I told myself that I would never do anything like that again. Fall for someone's wife."

Ava grinned. "So, you haven't fallen for me, then?"

Helena didn't look the least bit amused. "You're *my brother's wife*."

"You mean the brother who just left here completely disgusted with who you are?"

"It's not that simple," Helena said, getting up off the bed. "You know that." She crossed to the dresser and took out a pile of clothes, and put them into the suitcase. As she turned to go to the dresser again, Ava got between her and it, and closed the drawer. "Get out of the way," Helena said.

"No."

Helena peered at her. "Is this the new you?"

"It's the old me," Ava said.

"Well, I don't like it."

Ava laughed. "I don't believe you."

Helena's eyes flashed anger, but only for a moment. Then she sat down on the bed again. Ava sat down beside her, close. The moment their shoulders touched Ava felt a sudden, searing pain in her temple. She took a deep breath and waited for it to subside. When it did, she said, "Stay."

Helena sighed, nodded. "Alright. But just until we hear from Paul."

Chuck lay on his back on the choir-room couch, bare-chested, the light coming in through the stained-glass window falling in colors on his face. George lay curled next to him on his side, watching his closed eyes moving beneath his eyelids.

"What you thinking about?" George asked.

Chuck smiled, his eyes still closed. "Nothing. Just us."

"That's something to smile about?"

Chuck opened his eyes. "I think so. You don't?"

George sat up, then stood. He crossed the room to where his clothes were lying on the floor and picked up his drawers and pulled them on. Then he dug into his pants pockets and pulled out his cigarettes. Chuck sat up, too, and watched him light one and take a long drag. "Let's go away," he said. "Let's go to New York. I got a cousin lives up there, and he know a lot of good places to go. We could spend a weekend."

George laughed, shook his head. Where was he supposed to tell his family he was going for a whole weekend? 'Out' wouldn't cut it. "Where you gone tell Lena you going?"

Chuck shrugged. "I don't know."

"Yeah, I guess you don't," George said, hearing the disdain in his own voice. "I don't like New York no way. It's filthy."

"Philly aint?"

"Maybe," George said, "but I'm already here."

Chuck got up and went over to where George was sitting on the floor. He sat down beside him and put his arms around his shoulders, and kissed his cheek. "I'm just trying to make you happy. Be like a real couple, and go places together."

"We aint a real couple," George said. "We two men, fucking."

Chuck frowned. "That's all? This aint nothing more to you than that?"

"Shit," George said. "You sound like a damn woman."

Chuck moved away and George felt a sting in his chest. He wanted to say he was sorry, but those words never came easily to him. And, anyway, he had nothing to be sorry for. Chuck was the one being stupid, talking about them as though they were a couple, like Ossie Davis and Ruby Dee, or some shit. It was better if they just stopped this now, this pretending, this foolishness, before somebody stood in the middle of the street and preached a sermon about *them*.

He watched as Chuck pulled on his clothes in the stained-glass light. When he was dressed, he looked at George. "You gone call me later on?"

George shook his head.

Chuck didn't say anything. When George looked up at him, his eyes were wet. "This aint what's supposed to happen," Chuck said. "This supposed to work, some kind of way. If it don't, then I don't know what else to try. I don't know where else to look for my life."

George took a drag off his cigarette. "I got urges. Needs. I aint pretending otherwise. But all this is something else, and I don't want it. It aint right."

"But I love you," Chuck said.

"Don't even say that."

"It's the truth, George. I—"

George lunged at Chuck, grabbed him by the collar of his shirt. "Don't say it, goddamnit. I don't want to hear no more of this faggoty shit. You hear me?"

"Yeah, I hear you," Chuck said.

George let go of him. He grabbed his clothes and put them on, hastily, almost frantically, wanting to get out of there fast, before the thing in him that made him do these things, that made him return, time and time again, as hard as he tried not to, to this secret, shameful life, could take hold of him again.

One evening, a couple of days after Paul left, Sarah was in the kitchen, cooking beef stew and thinking about all the things that had happened that summer: Helena's arrival, her time with the fire-eating man, Ava's strange behavior, Chuck Ellis showing up in their living room, Helena's revelation, and Paul's disappearance from the house. She knew that it all had to mean something. She thought about the ghosts and wondered if death was coming, if that's what all of it was really about, all this upheaval.

She could hear Helena moving around in her bedroom upstairs. She still found it hard to believe the truth about her exodus from Baltimore, hard to believe that she was *that way*, when she had seemed so normal. She wondered if Helena had ever thought of her that way, even if for a moment. She doubted it. It was only Ava who held Helena's attention, and she imagined now that Helena's feelings for her sister included *those kinds*, that she loved Ava just as Kenny Goode had. And, just like Kenny, that she had no such feelings for Sarah herself. Not that it mattered, anyway, because Sarah wasn't that way. Neither was Ava, no matter what she'd said the other day. Sarah sighed. Really, with Ava, who the hell knew?

Regina came into the kitchen then. "What you fixing?"

"Beef stew," Sarah told her.

"Where Ava and Helena?"

Sarah shrugged. "I don't know. Probably somewhere together." She threw the onions into the pot, and stew splashed onto her blouse.

Regina frowned. "What's wrong with you?"

Sarah shook her head. She didn't want to talk about it, any of it. But she couldn't help herself. "She took her from me. She was my friend, and Ava took her from me."

Regina's eyebrows drew close together on her forehead. "*Took*? Is she a person or a pair of pantyhose?"

"You don't understand, Mama," Sarah said. "I wished for her. I was so lonely. I prayed for somebody to come. And she came."

Regina looked hesitant. "What you saying? You got those kind of feelings about her?"

"No," Sarah said. "Of course not. I'm not saying *that* at all."

Her mother looked relieved. "I was starting to think it's something in the water."

"But she was my friend," Sarah said. "My only friend. And Ava took her from me."

Regina breathed a long, heavy breath, and sat down at the table. She looked up at her daughter. "Sarah, listen to me. Put that spoon down, and listen to me."

Sarah put down the spoon.

"You don't need to be praying for nobody to come to you here in this house," Regina said. "You ought to be out there in the world trying to make some kind of real life for yourself."

Sarah shook her head. "That's not the point, Mama."

"I know it must be hard living in Ava's shadow," Regina said. "But it don't reach everywhere. I promise you, it don't. You just need to find out where it stops and go a little farther than that."

Sarah shook her head again. "I can't."

"Why?"

She started to say that it was because she didn't want to leave her family, or that she didn't want Pastor Goode to feel like he was winning by running her off. But those words wouldn't come. In their place came the truth. "I'm afraid."

"Of what?" Regina asked.

"Of the world. What if nobody out there sees me?"

Regina got up from the table and stood in front of her daughter, took Sarah's hands in hers. "It's the easiest thing in the world to sit back and blame other people for how your life turned out. I done that for years. But it don't serve no purpose, 'cause in the end all you gone get is a life that went ahead and turned out while you was busy pointing fingers, and by then it'll be too late for you to do anything about it."

Sarah knew her mother was right, but it was too hard to change now. It *was* easy to blame Ava, and even easier to blame the pastor, and maybe it was their fault. It didn't matter, though, because it was her life that was passing by, thirty-two years of it gone already, nearly two decades of it spent hiding in this house. She thought about the fire-eating man. Maybe he had seen her. Maybe he meant the things he said.

"Mama, there's a man," Sarah said. "His name is..." She shook her head. "I don't even know his name. He invited me to come and see him do a show tonight. Now."

"So, why you here?" Regina asked. "Go."

"But what if he—"

"Go," Regina said again. "Go. Go. Go."

Sarah was halfway up the block between Radnor and Chestnut when she saw the twenty-one bus pull up to the stop. She ran to catch it, waving her arms so the driver would see her, but he pulled out from the stop. "Wait!" she called. "Wait!" The bus stopped with a loud screech of brakes and she hurried up onto it, breathing hard.

"I almost didn't see you," said the driver.

She paid the fare and took a seat near the middle of the bus, which was more crowded than she had expected. She checked her watch. It was already eight-thirty. There was no way she would make it all the way to Penn's Landing before nine. Maybe the show would run longer—maybe, because it was his final performance, he would want to make it last. Maybe he would linger a while after, talk to the people who had come to see him, say goodbyes. Surely she was not the only person he had invited.

She sat on the bus feeling fidgety and anxious. She wished she had left sooner. She wished she hadn't wasted ten minutes changing clothes and putting on eye-shadow. She wished she hadn't wasted thirty-two years being afraid.

The bus made damn near every stop between Fifty-Ninth and Front and by the time Sarah got to Penn's Landing, the fire-eating man was nowhere in sight. She hurried down the length of the landing. She stopped to ask a couple passing by if they had seen the show, but they had not. The next couple of people had, and she asked whether they knew if the fire-eating man was still down here somewhere, but they didn't know. She walked over to Market Street, and then back, past Chestnut again and all the way over to Locust, but saw no sign of him. Finally, she returned to the spot where they had sat that day when he had offered her peanut butter. She sat on that bench and looked out at the water.

The night was very warm, very still, and she felt that now that she had got here time had slowed down. She looked toward the city and the lights in the tall buildings didn't flicker. She wished he would come. She thought about what Ava had said, that people really did see her, and she wished it were true.

A homeless man walked by and leered at her. It was getting darker. She was too late. He was gone. She wished she'd asked his real name or where, exactly, he worked security, but she had been too busy worrying about what Ava was taking away from her, so consumed with turning a lie into the truth—a lie that, she could see now, had never really mattered much anyway—that she hadn't bothered. Now she would probably never see him again.

When she left Penn's Landing, the bus wasn't coming, so she walked west toward home. She passed couples walking hand in hand, and friends in groups, laughing or whispering confidences to each other. The bus ride back to West Philadelphia was a little faster, with more people heading into Center City on a Saturday night than away from it. Through the large windows of the bus, she watched the city skyline, and wondered if the fire-eating man was inside one of those buildings. She wondered if he was thinking of her the same way she was thinking of him right now, if he was remembering their brief time together—the peanut-butter sandwich, the way she'd leaned into him as he'd held the fire before her, the sun on the Delaware River as they'd sat together by the water. And she decided, this once, because she didn't see how it could hurt, to believe with all her might that he was.

Regina sat out on the front porch, looking out at Radnor Street. Night had fallen and the streetlights glowed pink and purple and soft orange. She could hear teenagers on darkened porches, laughing and singing along to their radios, the sounds of popular rhythm and blues songs hanging in the warm summer air. She looked down the street, at the church, and she could see the light on in Pastor Goode's office. He was in there all the time, it seemed. He had no family anymore. His wife had had a stroke and died less than a year after their son. Regina wondered what he was in there plotting now. He was surely incensed that Helena hadn't left immediately after his performance in the street. Paul had gone, though, and she figured that had made him very happy.

She wondered why it had come to this, why something that had been so good at first—their lives on this block, their relationships with these people—had gone so terribly bad. Ava's defiance of the pastor had been the beginning of it, but the death of their sons had set the worst of it in motion. Goode had blamed them, hadn't been able to see reason. Regina had never understood it. She had loved her son as much as he had loved his, had been torn to pieces by the loss of him, but she had not looked for anyone to blame.

The light in Goode's office flickered as a shadow moved past the window. Regina got up, intending to go to the porch railing and get a closer look, but without even thinking she went past the railing and on down the steps, on to the sidewalk. She was determined, although she wasn't sure about what, exactly. When she got to the back door of the church, she tried it and it opened. She went inside, and in the dimly-lit cool of the sanctuary, she was met by the familiar smell of old bibles and hymnbooks. She marveled at how the sense of smell could instantly transport you to another time, and her skin tingled with memory as she recalled Sunday morning services, and Saturday morning meetings, evening prayers, and bake sales. Her hands found the back of a pew in the dim light, and the feel of the wood against her fingertips erased, for a moment, the seventeen years that had passed since she had last been in here, singing and giving praise, her family all around her, her friends close, her God even closer. She had never disconnected herself from the Lord, and still prayed every day and night, but here, in this church, her experience of God had been bigger, more, wrapped up like a gift in the sounds of lifted voices and stomping feet, in the sight of soft, stained-glass light through the picture windows, in the feel of friendship and community all around her. She had left a piece of herself behind here, the piece that was a part of something bigger than Regina, bigger than just family, or just friends, or just God, but was all those things together, and more.

She was pulled from memory by the sound of creaking floorboards and she made her way through the sanctuary to the pastor's nook, just behind the pulpit. The door was open and light spilled out onto the altar. Regina peered inside and saw Pastor Goode pacing the floor. She watched him in silence for a moment. His shoulders were hunched, his head down, his eyebrows drawn tight together on his forehead. He looked like an old lion in a cage, trapped and troubled, too proud to rest and too tired to roar. Regina remembered him again as a young man, handsome and quick to smile, and she tried to see some of that person in him now, but could not.

She reached up and knocked gently on the doorframe. The pastor looked up, surprised, and when he saw her, his light eyes grew dark. "You aint welcome in here, Regina."

Regina had not expected to be welcome in the first place, so she entered the room anyway, without hesitation. "It's time you and me had this out."

Pastor Goode watched her for a moment, his eyes taking her in, and she was sure he was thinking of the woman she used to be, all those years ago, and not finding much of her left, just as she had seen nothing of his younger self left in him. "It aint nothing to 'have out'. You on the side of wrong, and I'm on the side of right. Right don't need to have it out with wrong, right just needs to—"

"Oh, stop it with all that damn sermonizing!" Regina yelled, her voice echoing through the quiet church. "Talk like a normal person for change!"

He folded his arms across his chest.

"You used to be one of those," she said. "A normal person. We used to like each other. Remember? We was both parents of young children, both devoted to the church. We had a lot in common at one time. I didn't even know it then, but even our tragedy was the same. My father was killed when I was a child. By white men. Just like yours."

Pastor Goode moved to the window and leaned against the sill.

"I know what that feels like," she continued. "I know what that do to your soul. That's the reason I snapped when my boy died. I didn't know it, but I was already on the edge, and it wasn't gone take too much to push me over. What happened to Geo was more than enough. I never got over what they did to my father. I never will."

Goode sighed and gave her a bored look. "You done?"

"I know it's hurting you," she said. "I know it's eating you up and has been all this time. You lost your father and your son. Just like me. I *know*."

He shook his head, mumbled something to himself that she couldn't make out. Then he leaned his head back against the window, stared up at the ceiling. "You want to know what happened to my father?"

"I already know," Regina said. "Cops killed him."

"That's right. He died in jail. You know the reason he was in there in the first place?"

She shook her head no.

"The reason he was in jail was because somebody attacked a woman out in the suburbs near where we lived—somebody who was tall and skinny and black, just like him. The woman who was attacked identified my father as the one that did it. But it *wasn't* him that did it. I know that 'cause he was home with me and my mother when it happened. We was eating dinner. Biscuits and black-eyed peas—I never will forget it. My mother told the police that, but they didn't believe her because she was his wife and bound to lie for him. So they took him, locked him up. He was in there three days when we got the call that he'd tried to escape and they shot him."

Regina remembered, as she and her mother and siblings had lain hidden under their neighbor's beds, the sounds of gunshots heavy as thunder in the air.

"But that's only half the story," Goode said. "My father was a drifter most of his life. He moved around from place to place, farm to farm, city to city, looking for work. He didn't like to feel stuck, he liked to be able to get up and go when he needed to. When he married my mother and they had me, that didn't change. We was always moving, never stayed in one place more than a few months. We never got to know our neighbors. I never made any friends, 'cause if I did I'd just have to leave them, and I got tired of being sad about it. We never joined a church. When my father was arrested, we had lived in Virginia for seven months, and we didn't have anybody to turn to. There wasn't no neighbors who could say that he was at home when that woman was attacked, because no neighbors ever stopped by. There wasn't no church to rally behind him. No reverend to vouch for his character. There wasn't nobody to help him. After he was killed, and my uncle took me and my mother in, I saw the safety of his community and his church around him, and I wanted that for myself. I decided right then, at fourteen, that I would never be without those things. And that, if I could, if the Lord called me to, I would make sure that nobody I knew went without them, either. And I have done that. I have spent my whole adult life doing just that."

"Bringing people together in community?"

"That's right. These people need me. They need me to protect them and support them and keep them close to God, and that's what I do."

"Is that what you did for Grace Kellogg?" Regina said. "Is that what you did for us?"

"I tried to. I tried hard as I knew how. It aint my fault your daughter has the devil in her. I tried to put her on the Lord's path, but she aint want to go that way. So it was my duty to protect the rest of my flock from her influence."

"You might have started out wanting to help people, to keep them safe," Regina said. "Maybe that's true. But somewhere along the way you decided that meant controlling everything they do. It stopped being about the Lord and started being all about Ollie Goode."

He shook his head. "You don't know what you talking about. I'm gone ask you one more time to leave."

"I told you I'm gone leave when I'm ready," she said. "And I aint ready. I got one more thing to say. And that's this: we are responsible for what happened to Geo. *I* am responsible for it. Because, no matter what happened, no matter who did the killing, I was his mother, and it was my job to protect him, to keep him safe. I didn't, so the blame is mine. But I aint to blame for what happened to Kenny. Nobody in my family is to blame for that. The Lord wasn't bringing down no judgment on us that morning. I don't know why it happened, but I know it wasn't that. We loved your boy, we let him breathe and be hisself, the way you never did. He loved us. And dedicating your life to making our lives miserable is the worst thing you ever could have done in his name."

Goode stood there, shaking, glaring at her, and saying nothing.

"Now," Regina said, "I'm gone leave. 'Cause I'm ready."

1959

Maddy and Doris sat on Regina's front porch, all of them drinking iced tea and planning the next week's block party. Ava came out of the house and ran down the front steps without saying a word to anybody.

"Ava!" Regina called to her.

Ava stopped.

"I know you aint just walk past Miss Maddy and Miss Doris without saying hello. What's the matter with you?"

"Hi, Miss Maddy," Ava said. "Hello, Miss Doris."

"Where you going, anyway?" Regina wanted to know.

"Nowhere," Ava said. "Just over to Ellen's."

"Well, y'all have a good time, baby," Maddy said.

Ava smiled and ran off.

Regina thought she saw Doris frown before she turned back to her iced tea.

"I know you got something to say about what Ava did, Doris," Regina said. "So go ahead and say it."

Doris shrugged. "Well, maybe I do have something to say."

"Big surprise," said Maddy.

"Go on, then."

"I think your daughter got a point," Doris said.

Maddy leaned closer to Doris. "Say what?"

Doris frowned. "You heard me."

"I heard *something*. Aint no way it coulda been you."

"Hush, Maddy," Regina said, and looked at Doris. "What point you think she got?"

Doris looked around, as though checking to see if anybody was listening. There were people sitting out on their porches nearby, but no one was paying any attention to Doris. Still, she lowered her voice a little and said, "That the pastor got too much power around here."

Regina and Maddy exchanged a look of skepticism.

"I been thinking about it for a while," Doris said. "Ever since that whole mural idea came up in the first place. I never thought we should have one. I think it's tacky. But Pastor aint ask me. Matter fact, he aint even ask the elders, and some of them been in that church longer than he been alive. He just decided it all on his own. Well, I didn't think that was right. But everybody just went along with it, even people I know for sure didn't want it.

And it just got me thinking." She looked around again. "Now, I sure don't condone what that child did, putting us all in chains up on the church like that. That was disrespectful. She always been too wild, if you ask me. But she do got a point, is all I'm saying."

Maddy reached over and pinched Regina's arm.

"Ow. What you do that for?"

"I wanted to make sure I aint dreaming this."

"So, why you pinch *me*?"

"Oh," Maddy said. She held out her hand. "Pinch me."

Regina slapped her hand away.

"Lot of people don't seem to agree with me, though," Doris said.

This was not news to Regina. In the week since Ava's stunt with the mural, not a day had passed when somebody hadn't told her that her daughter had crossed the line. Vic Jones had even repeated the pastor's sentiment, that Ava had the devil in her. Malcolm hadn't said anything about what had happened, but he also hadn't come by even once in the last week. At church that morning, he had greeted Regina and George unenthusiastically, nodding as he went by, towards a pew a few rows behind them, not sitting with them as he almost always had before.

For every two people who reacted the way Malcolm had, though, there had been another one who seemed to share Doris' view.

"Sometimes I think Pastor Goode wants to have too much control over folks," Jane Lucas told Regina one afternoon, as they walked together from the bus stop to their block. "He likes to judge people, but the bible says that's the Lord's job."

Regina sighed. "Well, Ava aint never liked him. And, tell you the truth, I don't think he ever liked her."

"What he got to not like about a little girl?"

"I saw it the first time he ever laid eyes on her," Regina said. "People react to Ava in strange ways, you know, they always have, so I didn't think a whole lot about it at the time. But I think he had a feeling he wasn't gone be able to control her."

"So, you agree he's trying to control people?"

"I don't know," Regina said. "But you remember Grace Kellogg?"

Jane nodded. "Of course."

"Well, I always thought that wasn't right. I didn't think she should have been throwed out the church like that. But what really bothered me was how everybody turned on her, just because the pastor said she wasn't welcome no more."

"I never did," Jane said. "I still speak to her to this day."

"So do I," said Regina. "And my children still visit with her every now and then. But did you ever tell the pastor you thought what he did was wrong?"

Jane shook her head. "No, I didn't."

"Well, I did," Regina said. "And he aint like it one bit."

She had gone to him that day after the Easter Bazaar and told him that she didn't think Grace deserved to be kicked out of Blessed Chapel. "We all sinners in one way or another, Pastor," she had said. "Aint the church supposed to be there for us even when we don't do right? Especially then?"

"I gave Grace a chance to repent," he said. "She refused to. Said she didn't regret what she had done. It's my job to protect this congregation from bad influences, from people who would turn them away from God." He had been calm and polite, even pleasant, in his voice and demeanor, but there had been something very final in his tone, something that had let Regina know that he had made up his mind and that was that. She hadn't liked it, but she hadn't argued, because she wasn't raised that way, wasn't taught to argue with a man of God. That had been her way of dealing with him ever since. Whenever she disagreed with him about something that she thought was important, she told him so, but when he went ahead and did what he wanted to do anyway, she never challenged him.

Ava had, though. Ava always had.

She said goodbye to Jane Lucas when they got to her house, and then continued home, and when she got there she found Ava in her bedroom, on her bed with her drawing pad in her lap. She came in and sat beside her, and put her arms around her daughter, and kissed her face. Ava didn't look up from her drawing, but she leaned into her mother a little.

"You an amazing child, Ava," Regina said.

"I'm not apologizing to that preacher."

"I aint trying to get you to apologize. I don't even think you ought to."

Ava looked up from the drawing. "Good," she said. Then she shrugged. "It wouldn't make a difference, anyway. 'Cause I'm really on his bad side now."

Sarah had never said anything about Sondra and Ava at the top of the stairs. She knew that Sondra had always hated Ava, since they were little. While that childish dislike barely resembled the loathing she saw in the girl's eyes that day after church, she told herself, then and for weeks after, that Sondra would never really have done it, that she would have snatched back her foot before Ava tripped, that she did not really want to hurt Ava that much. And that her own failure to warn her sister, then, her hesitation, was not as evil as it felt. She tried not to think about the steepness of that stairwell.

Sitting at the dinner table a few days later, she imagined what her family would say if she told them, what they would think if they knew she had just stood there, had watched her sister walking into danger, and had not said a word. She kept silent.

Every time Ava left the house, Sarah worried. She took to jumping up whenever she saw her sister headed for the front door, asking where she was going, and wouldn't she rather stay inside and play cards or something. After the sixth or seventh time, Ava rolled her eyes, annoyed. "Why you so interested in me all of a sudden? You never cared before."

"I *care*," Sarah insisted. "*Of course* I do."

Ava frowned and left.

Sarah waited. She sat and waited until Ava came back, and each time her sister walked back in through the door, Sarah felt relief course through her.

One evening, she passed Ava's room and saw her standing in front of the mirror, brushing her hair. She was wearing a skirt, and dress shoes.

"Where you going?"

"To a party," Ava said. "And, no, I don't want to stay home and play Old Maid."

"Mama and Daddy are letting you go to a party by yourself?"

"No. Geo and Kenny are going, too."

Sarah went to their brother's room and found him practicing dance moves in front of the mirror. Kenny was sitting on the bed, reading a comic book. He had eaten dinner at their house for the second day in a row.

"You live here now?" Sarah asked him.

He looked up from his comic, his face turning pink.

"Leave him alone," Geo said.

"I thought your father didn't want you over here anymore," said Sarah.

Pastor Goode had forbade him to go into the Delaney house, in case the Lord rained down fire on it or something. Kenny didn't seem bothered about it. "I like it better over here than at my house. Especially when my mother aint home. She's in Jersey at my grandparent's house, and my dad can't cook for shit."

George walked by and stopped when he saw Geo in front of the mirror. "Where you think you going?"

"Party. Mama said we could."

"You cut them hedges?"

Geo frowned. "I forgot. I'll do it tomorrow."

"Yeah, you will," George said. "And you gone be up bright and early, too, 'cause you aint going to no party."

"But mama said—"

"I don't care what Regina said. I'm your father and I say you aint going."

"Father?" Geo said, quietly but still loud enough to be heard. "I don't know what kind of father you supposed to be."

George took a step into the room. "What you say?"

Geo glared at him, his face hard and angry like Sarah had almost never seen it. He shook his head. "I aint say nothing."

George peered at him and for a moment Sarah was sure Geo was going to get it. But then their father turned and walked out of the room.

Geo turned back to the mirror and stared at himself for a long moment, before picking up his brush and brushing his hair.

"We aint going?" Kenny asked.

"Hell, yeah, we going," Geo said.

Sarah shook her head. "You can't. Daddy just said—"

"I was right here when he said it. I don't need no playback. We going, and that's all."

She thought of threatening to tell, but considering the look he'd given their father, she decided against it.

He looked at her reflection in the mirror. "Come with us. It's gone be fun."

She hated parties. So many people not seeing her at the same time. "Will Sondra be there?" she asked.

He laughed. "Nobody invites Sondra nowhere."

She nodded, a little relieved. "Oh. Well. Just keep an eye on Ava, okay?"

He turned around and looked seriously at her. "Why? What's wrong with Ava?"

"Nothing, Geo. I'm just saying, look out for her."

"I always do."

That evening, Sarah sat on the sofa, watching television and waiting for them to come back. Their curfew was nine o'clock. At eight-forty-five, she went and stood on the front porch, looking up and down, up and down the street. Nine o'clock came, and then went. She walked down to the sidewalk and looked both ways up and down the block. At nine-fifteen, Ava rounded the corner at Fifty-Ninth and came down the street. When Sarah saw her, she ran back into the house and sat herself down in front of the television again. Ava came in, looking sleepy.

"How was the party?" Sarah asked.

Ava shrugged. "Kenny tried to kiss me," she said, sounding bored.

Sarah frowned. She turned off the television and walked past Ava up the stairs.

"What's wrong with you?" Ava asked.

"Nothing," Sarah said, annoyed. She opened her bedroom door, just as Ava opened hers. "Where's Geo, anyway? It's past your curfew."

Ava yawned. "He can't be that far behind me," she said, and she went to bed.

She didn't know she was dead. She was standing in the foyer of her house, but it was colder than it should have been and there was little light. Geo was sitting cross-legged on the floor, his head leaned back against the wall, staring up at the ceiling.

Why's it so cold, Geo? She rubbed her arms, but couldn't feel it.

Is it? Geo asked.

Yes. She looked around. It was definitely their house, but there was something off about it. It was eerily quiet, devoid of any sound but their voices, no noise coming from the other rooms or from outside. *I don't like it. Let's go back to the way it was.*

I can't.

She looked at him, rubbed her unfeeling arms again. *Yes, you can. Let's just go back. It's too cold now.*

He looked at her for the first time, and his eyes were very dark and very empty. *I can't go back cause I aint nothing now. I aint got nothing to go back in. My thing is broke. My thing that I was in before I came here. It got broke and that's why I'm here.*

What about my thing? Ava asked.

Your thing aint broke. You can go back. You aint here because your thing got broke, so you can go back.

I don't want to go back.

You have to, Ava.

She felt herself being pulled, as if there were a hook right behind her navel and something was tugging at it. She reached out for her brother. Geo hesitated, then reached out for her hand. Their fingertips touched.

The next thing she knew, she was looking up at her mother.

"Mama, where is my brother?" she asked. "Where is Geo?"

Ava was still in her bed, still and quiet under the covers, though the room was getting hot. Regina had gone up there because neither Ava nor Geo had come down to breakfast, and neither had answered when she called to them from the bottom of the stairs. Regina had entered Ava's room and found her still in bed, and tried not to think about how strange it was that Ava was still sleeping, Ava who was often up at dawn, drawing or painting at the sunrise. Regina called her daughter's name and gently shook her, but Ava did not wake. And there was a moment. A moment Regina would remember for the rest of her life, when she knew Ava was not there, not in her body, which lay still beneath the covers, not in the space around her, not in the house, not in the world. Ava, her Ava, who, when Regina had once been overwhelmed with sadness and had broken down in tears while sewing up a hole in a sock, had, at two years old, climbed into her mothers lap and said, clear as morning, "Mama, I am here with you," was no longer here, no longer with her. In that moment, the air in the getting-hot room got hotter, thicker, heavy like cooking grease, and Regina could not draw a breath. She grabbed Ava by the shoulders and shook her harder, the weight of the moment closing in on her, congealing, molding out a sticky place for itself in reality, and she shook Ava and shook her, her own face contorted in the effort, her own soul starting to split open at its corners and bleed, and then, in the quiet, in the still, that moment passed and Ava awoke, with a start and a sharp intake of breath, and looked at her mother the way she had first looked at her, a few seconds after being born, as if to say, "How did I get here?" And Regina, just like she had done that first time, held her daughter against her heart and trembled. After another few seconds, Ava pulled away, and looked at her mother just as she had as a newborn baby, and said with words this time what she had expressed without words then. "Mama, where is my brother?"

George Jr. was not in his bed when Regina rushed into his bedroom with Ava on her heels. They went downstairs to see if he had slipped by them when Regina was in Ava's room, but Ava knew he wouldn't be there, though she could not tell her mother that.

"He must have gone to that damn party last night," George said, seemingly concerned only with his son's lack of adherence to his instructions and not the question of why, if he had gone out, he had not yet returned. "I'll take care of him when he gets back."

"I'm going to get him," Regina said.

Ava wanted to tell her not to go looking for Geo. That finding him would be worse than these moments of mere confusion, these moments when he was simply absent from the house, but maybe still existed, these moments before the answer came, and that once it came it would come forever, over and over every day and night. But Regina was trading her slippers for her shoes and moving for the door.

"Mama," Ava said, and Regina turned to look at her, but Ava couldn't say anything else before the scream came. It came through the open window at the front of the house, the big one Regina had opened to let in some air, and it slid into the house like smoke sometimes did when Mr. Liddy sat smoking his pipe on his porch. Regina opened the door and ran outside.

Another scream pierced the air and Vic and Malcolm ran by the house towards the church. Ava could see other people running that way. Regina moved to go down the front steps and Ava was there beside her, holding her back.

"Mama," she said again, and nothing else came out.

Regina pulled away and walked off down the street towards the crowd, slowly, with Ava right beside her, while others ran past them towards the church, drawn by the screams that were rising into the air every few seconds now. The crowd was crowded in such a way that they could not see what they were screaming about until they were right there, squeezing past the broad shoulders of Malcolm and Vic. There on the ground were two dead bodies. Kenny Goode was lying on his stomach with his cheek against the ground, his light eyes staring blankly at the shoes of the gathering crowd, a deep red gash at his throat. A few feet away from him, curled up in a ball like a tiny child, and leaning against the back wall of the church, was Geo. He was badly beaten, his face bruised and cut and bloodied, his lips busted, a spray of his blood staining the white paint that covered what had been, for a very little while, Ava's mural.

When Regina saw her son lying broken on the ground the whole world disappeared. For a moment, all her senses failed, and she could not hear the screams of the gathered crowd, or feel the disrespectfully-bright sun on her arms, or see the horror, laid out like a gruesome diorama before her. For a moment, it hadn't happened. In place of what was real, she saw what was desperately needed—Geo running up the street on long, strong legs, laughing. When that moment passed, though, when it cleared away like a leaving fog, she was assaulted by what was really there. The screaming, like sirens following each other around in circles on the air. The sun, a perfect, terrible warmth against her skin. And her boy, bashed up and discarded like an outgrown toy, lying in a heap against the church. The sight of it punched through her, knocking her back, and her legs gave out. She dropped to the ground, her knees smashing hard against the hot asphalt. Beside her, Ava stooped down, tried to help her to her feet, but Regina pushed her away and crawled on all fours across the few feet that separated her from her son, as people stumbled over each other trying to get out of her way. She got to the place where Geo lay, and she reached out and put her hands on either side of his swollen head, and when she felt a squishiness beneath her fingers, she felt something snap and come apart inside her. She heard a sound come up out of herself, like the growl of a feral thing, a terrified, trembling sound, and all the people around her became dangerous. She threw her own body over her son's, shielding him from them. "I got you," she whispered to him, as she rocked him back and forth in her arms. "Mama's got you now."

Ava was looking down at her mother and brother on the ground, and although she didn't see him arrive, she knew the moment Pastor Goode appeared on the parking lot. A hush fell over the gathered crowd, like none but the pastor or Jesus himself could affect. When she looked up, she saw him standing over Kenny's body, his face like a changing mask, first confused, then shocked, then horrified, then overcome. His bottom lip trembled and for a moment it seemed his legs might give out too. He stood there, teetering, as Vic and Malcolm stood with their bodies in almost-motion, their arms out, ready to catch him if he fell. He didn't. He looked over at Regina cradling Geo in her arms, then back at Kenny again, and Ava could see his mind working, his eyes flashing through possibilities, the way they had when Ava had sat in his office watching him writing the end of his sermon. Now, as then, Ava thought, he was trying to decide what God had to do with it. And she knew the moment his eyes met hers that he had made up his mind.

"This is the Lord's judgment," he said, his eyes wide as he raised his hand and pointed at her. "This is his judgment on you."

Every head turned towards Ava at once, even Regina's.

"I told y'all something was gone happen," Goode said, glaring at Ava. "I said the Lord would send down his wrath on this family, and he has! This is his punishment for your arrogance and your blasphemy! And *my son* got caught in it!" He looked down at Kenny again, and his voice was wet and quivering. "I told him to stay away. I *told him*!"

Ava wanted to say something, like how absurd it was to suggest that God had punished her by letting her brother be killed. That it was a ridiculous, bizarre thing to say. But besides her mother, who was shaking her head, no one in the crowd seemed to appreciate the absurdity, the downright craziness of it. Most of them were staring at her as though she might sprout horns from her forehead at any moment.

Pastor Goode grabbed Vic by the collar of his bathrobe. "Didn't I tell y'all?" he said, his face close to Vic's. "Didn't I?"

Vic nodded. "You said so, Pastor. You said something was gone happen."

Goode turned Vic loose and crouched down on the ground beside Kenny, laid his head on the boy's chest and sobbed.

Vic turned and glared at Ava. "You the one caused this." Vic looked at Malcolm, who nodded his agreement. Then Vic and Malcolm both looked around at the rest of them. Sister Hattie nodded, too, her hand over her mouth. Antoinette clutched her sister's hand. Miss Liddy looked at Ava and shook her head. "Lord," she said, "Oh, Lord."

"Y'all talking crazy," Miss Maddy said.

Miss Lucas shook her head. "The Lord don't work like that."

But no one else seemed to hear them, or to care if they did.

Ava watched them, these people she had known almost her whole life, who had eaten in her mother's kitchen and worshipped beside her family for nearly a decade, watched them, right there on the parking lot, as they turned away from her family right before her eyes.

1976

George made a promise to himself on the night he left Chuck at the church that he would never go back. That the years of stealing around, of debasing himself and everyone who loved him, would end right there and then. He vowed never to see Chuck again, nor Butch, nor any of the other men with whom he had lain himself down in shame, like hogs in shit. He didn't want to go home, either, in the evenings after work, didn't want to look at his family and see the ways he had failed them. Instead, he walked. Leaving work he headed farther east, towards the city, seeking invisibility in the shadows of the tall buildings, anonymity on the crowded sidewalks. Walking among businesspeople, shopgirls, and construction workers, he might be just an ordinary person, a holder of no secret any worse than any of theirs, a caring husband and father, a trustworthy friend, a loved son. No one could say he wasn't all of those things, this perfectly normal-looking man in his city-worker's uniform.

He walked for hours every day for more than a week, as far as his legs would take him without too much protest, and when he was good and tired, and night had fallen entirely, he would stop for a bite somewhere, and then hop on a bus or find an el station and head home. One evening, he stopped in a little pizza joint and ordered a slice, and as he sat eating in a corner he looked up and saw a boy sitting a few tables away, staring at him. He was around nine, light brown with kinky, reddish hair, and he reminded George of a boy he'd known back in Hayden, a boy he tried never to think about. He looked away, closed his eyes and tried no to let the memory seep into him, but it came anyway, pulled him with it from his seat in the pizza place to a back porch railing in Hayden, Georgia.

It was a chilly day, windswept and leafy. George, then ten years old, sat watching two cats fighting in the grass behind his house. Red came around, carrying a jar with a garter snake in it. "I caught it under the bed," he said, grinning and proud. "I'm gone take it out to Els Field and turn it loose. Come on with me."

"I can't. I'm waiting on my daddy to get home."

His father was stopping by the dump on his way home, which meant he'd be making art that night, and George would be able to stay up late and watch him, and tell him stories.

"It won't take that long," Red said.

George liked Red, when he wasn't being mean, wasn't showing off for other kids the way he sometimes did. And he was bored, sitting there waiting for his father. He looked down the road and didn't see his father coming yet. He could usually see him when he was a quarter of a mile away. He hopped down off the porch railing and called through the back window into the house, "Mama, I'm going to Els Field," and then hurried down off the porch before she could come out and tell him he couldn't go.

They walked down back roads to Els Field. Years ago there had been a factory there, but now it was only a shell, with broken windows and overgrown plant life. Red stood on top of a rusty steel drum and opened the glass jar, tossing the snake out into the high brush. For a moment, it coiled in the air like a paper spiral.

"You ever been in there?" Red asked George, pointing at the factory.

George nodded. "Couple times."

"I want to see inside."

"It aint nothing in there to see."

Red shrugged. "Still."

They walked down a short, overgrown path to a side door, and Red pushed it open. Inside, the place was empty and caked everywhere with dust, and full of broken glass from all the busted windows. The glass shimmered in the light streaming in from outside. From a corner, a field mouse scurried across the floor and squeezed itself into a hole in the wall.

"You right," Red said. "It aint nothing to see in here. I can see mice at home. I bet it's scary at night, though."

George agreed, then turned to go.

"Hold up a minute," Red called.

George stopped, and looked at him.

"You want to do something?"

George frowned. "It aint nothing to do in here."

"You want to see each other's dicks?"

George blinked. Hesitated. It might be a trick, he thought. Sometimes Red was mean that way. He liked to put bugs down the backs of girls' dresses and gum in their hair and all that kind of foolishness. But the possibility that it wasn't a trick intrigued George. He'd never seen another boys' dick, and he wanted to. "I guess," he said.

Red grabbed his wrist and pulled him farther into the factory, back towards the end of a long corridor. They stood there looking at each other. "You go first," Red said.

George shook his head. "No. You."

Red unzipped his pants and let them fall down around his knees. His white drawers were dingy and the elastic band was almost too stretched out to hold them up. He pulled them down, too, and stood there facing George, his small, reddish-brown penis hardening before George's eyes. "Now you."

George pulled down his pants, his own erection already pressing eagerly against his zipper. For a moment they stood there, just looking at each other, then Red reached out and touched the tip of George's penis. A breath caught in George's throat. Red's eyes widened. He took hold of it then, rubbing it from shaft to head, and George closed his eyes and let the pleasure melt over him. No one had ever touched him down there before and it was so much better than when he did it himself.

He heard a flurry of movement and opened his eyes, expecting to see another mouse, but instead he saw his father, standing down the corridor, staring wide-eyed at him, a look of horror and revulsion on his face.

George scrambled away from Red, who said, "No, don't quit. It feels good, don't it?"

His father had closed the distance between them before he knew it, and was reaching out and grabbing him by the throat, throwing him down on the hard floor. George heard Red running away, his bare feet slapping hard against the ground. His father looked enraged, his face contorted into something monstrous, and he slapped George hard across the face and head, over and over. Then he grabbed the boy by the shirt, and shook him, growling at him through clenched teeth, "I didn't raise you to be no filthy queer. I work myself to death every day to give you a life, and this what I get?"

"No," George cried. "I'm sorry, Daddy."

"What did I do wrong?" his father asked. "Huh? What did I do?"

The chewed pizza in George's mouth tasted cold and oily, and he couldn't swallow it. The reddish boy was still staring at him, and George began to wonder if he was really there, and not some ghost come to haunt and torment him, to make him remember that day in the factory, that day when his father had stopped loving him. After that, nothing between them was the same. There was no more hitting, no more epithets hurled, no more mention at all of what had happened. But the days of watching his father turn broken things into art ended all at once.

George peered at the reddish boy and thought about all the times he had returned to that old factory, with other boys and, later, men, all the times he had recreated that awful scene, only without his father bursting in, and all the times he had recreated it in other places, in Butch's basement, in the church with Chuck, his father's disgust always there even if the man himself was not. He wished he could go back and undo it. He wished that about so many things, but that thing more than any other. He wished Red had never come up to him as he sat on that porch railing. "You ruined everything," he whispered to the reddish boy, who only blinked at him. George got up from his seat and closed the distance between himself and the little boy and stared down at him, shaking his head. "You opened that door, and after that I couldn't shut it."

The boy looked up, wide-eyed at him.

He felt a hand on his shoulder and when he looked a man was standing there, frowning hard at him. "What you say to my son?" he asked.

George looked down at the boy, and saw now that he wasn't Red, or a ghost of any sort, but only a kid with rust-colored hair. George swallowed, shook his head. "Nothing," he said to the father.

"Well, get away from him, then," the man said, putting himself between George and his son.

George turned and left the restaurant, and made his way over to Market Street, and the el that would take him home, not because he wanted to be there, but because he had nowhere else to go.

Ava was painting on the back porch because the house was hot, too hot. She had gone to work that morning an hour early, and had spent that time, as well as her lunch break and an hour after work, tucked away in corners of the museum, wrapping herself in paintings, in color that stretched out for hours. Into the planes and angles of Fernand Leger's *Animated Landscape*, she had folded herself. Into the contours and curves of Georgia O'Keeffe's *Peach and Glass*, she had balled herself up. On the edges of Paul Cezanne's *Mont Sainte-Victoire*, she had perched and observed the world below. On her way out of the museum, coming down the steps, she'd seen Ben Franklin Parkway as she hadn't seen it in seventeen years, the wide boulevard lined with trees whose green was lush and stark against the blue-white sky, and whose domed and columned edifices—the Basilica of Saints Peter and Paul, the Free Library of Philadelphia, the Franklin Institute— contrasted with the many-windowed office buildings that winked from the city skyline, out of which City Hall rose. When she'd gotten home, she'd helped Sarah and Helena with dinner, and while eating she'd planned the painting she would make, designed it in her mind from top to bottom. The skyline had inspired her and she thought to set that inspiration down on canvas. When dinner was over, she'd wanted to bolt from the kitchen, but she forced herself to be considerate and help with the dishes. When every-thing was clean and put away, she dragged the easel, and her case full of paints and brushes, out onto the back porch. She stayed out there for hours, as the sky darkened. She could hear her family moving around inside, but for a long time no one disturbed her. As she painted, her head throbbed. It had been throbbing on and off all day. She kept painting, determinedly, as though it would help. Hours later, Helena came outside, and when she peered at the image on the canvas she said, "It's you again."

"I meant it to be the city skyline," Ava told her.

Helena tilted her head to one side and squinted at the painting. "It's not."
"Hmm."

The day before, Ava had begun to draw a picture of a butterfly alight on a flower in the garden, and had ended up with a sketch of herself, watching the butterfly. Now she stood back from the canvas and examined yet another unintended depiction of herself, this time with no hint of the scene she had set out to paint, only her visage looking out from the canvas.

"Well," Ava said. "That is interesting, isn't it?"

Helena nodded. "Any word from Paul?" she asked, leaning back against the porch railing.

"No," Ava said, dipping her brush in brown.

Helena frowned. "You're not very upset about him being gone, are you?"

"I hope he's safe," Ava said, "and that he's not hurting too much. But no, I'm not upset that he's gone."

Helena went and sat down on the steps, lit a cigarette and stared out at the garden. After a few minutes, she said, "It's because of me. You're angry with him for keeping that secret from you. But it's my fault there was ever a secret to begin with."

Ava shook her head. "That's only part of it," she said. "I've actually been thinking a lot about Paul."

"Have you?"

Ava put down her brush and palette, and sat down beside Helena on the step. "So much has happened to me in these last few days. So much memory returning, so much emotion filling me up. Everything feels so much more..." She sighed. "So much *more*. You know?"

Helena nodded.

"Everything," Ava said, "except Paul. My feelings for Paul haven't changed. They haven't gotten bigger, or heavier, or...more red."

"Maybe they will," Helena said.

"I've been waiting for them to. I've been waiting to feel something so intense that I couldn't deny it. But I haven't. I don't feel any less about him than I did a few days ago, but a few days ago it was enough. It's not anymore. I don't love Paul." She thought Helena would argue, would try to convince her that she did still love her brother, for his sake, but Helena was silent. In the light of the moon, Ava could see Helena's eyes, fiercely green against the dark, watching her, half afraid of what she might say next, and half eager to hear the words. "Of all the things I have felt these last few days, of all the things I feel now, there is nothing I feel so intensely, so thoroughly, as I feel you."

Helena shook her head no, the way she had when Ava had kissed her a few nights ago, and Ava thought she would get up and leave, but this time Helena did not move away. She moved closer. She leaned her body into the empty dark that separated them and kissed Ava, hungrily, and put her arms around her waist and pulled her closer still. Ava met the kiss with an equal rush of passion, and her tongue tasted red and coffee and butter, and every good thing. They kissed and kissed, for many minutes, there on the back steps, kissed until their lips were raw, and long after that. It was late when they went into the house, upstairs, and in the hallway Ava said, "Sleep with me."

Helena shook her head. "I can't. Paul—"

"I mean sleep," Ava said. "Just sleep."

Paul had been gone from the Delaney house for two whole days. He was staying at Tyrone's place in North Philly, but he'd barely seen his cousin at all. He'd requested night shifts at the cleaning company, less for the money than for the distraction, thinking that dirty windows and toilets would keep his mind off much worse things. They didn't. In every window pane, every shiny surface, he saw the face of the girl he had killed, killed for *nothing*, trying to protect a sister who hadn't wanted protecting in the first place. He wished that he had been the one who died that day, twenty years ago. He wondered if that girl would have grown up to be something. Something more than he had turned out to be.

During the few hours that he slept on his cousin's floor each morning, his mind, his conscience, gave him a reprieve from the image of the girl, and in those moments he dreamed about Ava. He saw her the way she was before, without the emotional eruptions and fainting spells, when she was steady and easy, and they were happy.

It was all connected to Helena, this misery he felt now, though he didn't know exactly how her presence had caused the changes in Ava. He only knew that after she came, everything had come undone. His life had crumbled in the wake of his long lost sister's return. He hated her for what she was, for what she had let him do, but most of all he hated her for coming back, for showing up on his doorstep, for not having the decency to just stay away, to let the lie remain, for not caring that the truth would be so much harder for him to live with.

He figured that after he left, she would go on up to New York like she'd planned. He gave it a couple of days, knowing that his in-laws weren't the kind of people who would just toss her out, that she might need a couple of days to clear out. Then, when he was sure she would be gone, he went home.

It was late, and coming up the street he saw no lights on in the house. As he got closer, a figure crossed the street in front of him, and in the glow of the streetlamp he saw Pastor Goode.

"What you doing back here, brother?" Goode asked him, standing in his path.

Paul shook his head. "I aint your brother. And if you got half a bit of sense in your head, you'll get out of my goddamn way."

"When I saw you leave, I thought maybe you had a chance," the pastor said. "Maybe you wasn't being controlled by the devil like the rest of them. But I guess I was wrong, 'cause here you are again."

Paul felt anger rising in him. In all the years he'd lived on this block, he'd thought of the preacher mostly as a crazy old man, a bible-thumper gone mad, seeing Satan in ordinary people trying to live their lives. But now, after the sermon in the street, he could see that Goode was more than just crazy, that he had a plan, and that plan was to push and push until somebody in that house broke. He didn't seem to care who it was.

"Look, preacher," Paul said, trying to keep his voice steady, trying to keep the rage from spilling over like lava and burning up everything in its path, "I been listening to your nonsense for five years. I still remember that day you told me to get out while I still could, not to get mixed up with these people. What you didn't understand then, and what you still don't understand, is that one of these people is the woman I love, and I aint going nowhere without her. I aint ever heard you say nothing that was gone change that, and I doubt today's gone be any different, so I'm telling you to step aside before I lose my mind and go upside your goddamn head."

Goode moved and Paul went by him.

"Your sister is trying to seduced your wife," the pastor said, his words as cool as sudden autumn in the hot summer air. "Does that change it?"

Paul kept walking and the preacher followed.

"You don't even know what's been going on in there, do you? I don't know if it's because you work too much, or because you that naïve, or because you just plain stupid, but somehow she managed to do it right under your nose and you aint see it. She making a damn fool out of you."

"I don't need nobody to make a fool of me," he said. "I been doing that fine by myself. You giving it a good shot, though."

Goode caught up to him and grabbed his arm. "Look at me, boy!"

Paul turned around and peered at the old man. "What the hell you want with me?"

"I am trying to give you back your dignity," he said. "I am trying to tell you that your sister is trying to corrupt your wife. I am telling you that so you can do something about it."

"I'm gone kill you," Paul said. "I swear to God, I'm gone kill you with my bare hands right here on this sidewalk if you don't shut your filthy mouth." He jerked hard out of Goode's grip and the old man lost his balance and nearly fell over. He grabbed hold of a parked car and steadied himself.

"I am prepared to die doing the Lord's work," he said.

Paul laughed. "How come everything you say, and everything you do, is the Lord's work? When you taking a shit—that the Lord's work, too?"

Goode smiled. In the light pouring down from the streetlamp, he looked like a haunted man. "You ignorant, boy, but you aint dumb. I know you see it."

Paul didn't want to, but he thought about how close Ava and Helena had gotten over the last few days. He thought about Helena telling him that Ava was full of passion and intensity and that he just couldn't see it. "I aint one of your sheep," Paul told the pastor. "You can't make me believe a bunch of nonsense just by telling me how dumb I'd be if I didn't believe it, or how I'm going to hell if I don't."

"She told me herself. Your wife. She came to me and told me all about it out her own mouth. She said that woman's been after her since the day she got here."

"You a damn lie. I didn't buy that story when you yelled it from the street and I aint buying it now."

Pastor Goode watched Paul, his eyes moving over the younger man's face. Then he glanced towards the Delaney house. "She's still in there, you know. She aint left. Why would she? With you gone, she got your wife all to herself."

1959

It had been several hours after the police left, on the morning they found Geo and Kenny dead, that Ava realized her brother was with her. She was sitting alone on the back porch, wondering why she was not crying. The sight of his dead body had shocked her, but not nearly as much as it should have. She had been so occupied with her mother's pain that she had not realized at first that her own pain was so slight, so almost incidental. Sitting there alone in the smoldering hot sun of the afternoon, though, Ava had felt Geo's presence. It was so palpable that she turned, confused, and looked behind her, half expecting to see him sitting there, before she remembered he was dead. But the feeling that he was there did not go away. She stood there, trying to understand what was happening. "Geo," she whispered into the sticky summer air. "Are you there?"

When the answer came, it came from within her, a surge of thought and emotion that felt familiar and foreign all at once. And she knew. It was as though they were in their mother's womb again, so close was his soul to hers. The rush of it was such that it made her knees buckle, and she dropped to the wood-planked porch, small splinters penetrating the skin of her bare knees. She closed her eyes and thought, "Geo, are you there?" The response was the same, the same rush of confused thought and emotion, but no language occurred to her, no answer came in words.

She could not tell her family that Geo was not gone, that his body was broken, but that he, his real self, his soul, was still there. They would have thought she meant it in a sentimental way if she told them that he was with her, as if she were keeping him alive in her heart, and she couldn't bear to have the experience of having her brother's soul side by side with her own in her body reduced to some corny sentiment like the few people from the block who came to the funeral wrote in the cards they handed her with somber looks and hand-squeezes. She wanted to tell her mother, at least, that Geo was sharing her body now, thinking it would bring her some comfort, but Regina had ceased being someone you could hold a conversation with when she carried his body back up the street to their house. Ava didn't even consider telling her father, or her sister. So, she was on her own to sort out what it meant that she and her brother were sharing her body. And it wasn't easy. Sometimes, in the days following the killings, Ava felt the urge to pee, and then found herself facing the toilet with her jeans unzipped, not knowing what to do.

On top of that, she was suddenly interested in yellow cake, which she had never liked, and uninterested in coffee, which she had always liked before. Only Sarah noticed anything different about her. Ava was brushing her teeth one morning and looked into the bathroom mirror to see Sarah standing behind her, looking annoyed.

"What?" Ava asked, splattering toothpaste on the mirror.

"You're brushing your teeth like Geo. Up and down instead of side to side. Geo brushed his teeth like that."

"Oh."

"You're not going to try to be like him now, are you?"

"I was always like him. We're twins."

Sarah rolled her eyes. "You know what I mean."

"No, really, I don't."

It was hard sharing a body with her dead brother's soul. What had happened to Geo had broken him. Not just his body, but his spirit. Being murdered had fractured his soul, so that he was little like the brother Ava had known. He was always scared, and Ava often had the feeling now of being consumed with fear. The fear often came upon her without warning, so that she might be buying something at a little store and jump at the sound of the bell as the door opened. Or she might be walking down the street, on her way home from school, trying to ignore the evil looks being hurled at her by the Brown sisters from their porch, and the sound of a car horn would frighten her almost to tears. A few weeks after Geo's death, at the dinner table, Sarah dropped her fork onto her empty plate, and the clang caused Ava to scream.

Over weeks, Geo's soul became less easily frightened, but in place of that panic came a solid disinterest in the world and the people in it. Ellen and Jack Duggard, and Rudy Lucas, were the only friends she still had, the only kids whose parents would let them go near her, but she felt less excited to see them now, less eager to spend with them the long summer days that came.

Ava's own soul was hard-pressed to hold up under the weight of the busted-up soul of her brother. Painting helped. In the months that followed Geo's murder, she painted endlessly, spent every dollar her parents gave her for school supplies or clothes or toiletries on canvas and brushes and paints. At first, she painted abstracts. Colors and shapes that seemed to represent the things she was feeling, the bewilderment, the unsteadiness. But soon that wasn't enough, and she began to paint what was happening around her, as horrible as it all was. She painted her mother in bed, with dry, cracked lips and an empty look in her eyes that seemed to beg death to take her, too. She painted her father, his shoulders rigid with grief. She painted Sarah surrounded by the dishes she was always washing, and the broom she was always pushing around the floors. Finally, she started painting herself, sometimes laughing, sometimes crying, other times with her full lips pursed as if trying to decide whether to laugh or cry, often naked with unkempt hair, and always with smoldering fire in her dark eyes. She filled the house with art. Her father and grandmother, the latter having gotten on a train from Georgia within two hours of receiving the phone call telling her that her only grandson was dead, complained about what they called the *disturbing pictures* of Regina, and hollered about the naked ones of Ava, demanding she stop hanging them above the mantel and in the foyer and everywhere else all over the house. Mother Haley was scandalized when Miss Maddy came by to drop off a pecan pie for Regina, hoping her favorite dessert would get her eating, and caught sight of a painting of Ava, naked and brown as a raw pecan, with hard nipples and wiry pubic hair and a fire like the devil in her eyes, holding a huge paintbrush that dripped dark red paint down her hand and arm. Maddy had gasped when she saw it, her eyes wide. Mesmerized, she did not look away until Mother Haley said, in her best normal voice, "Come on bring that pie into the kitchen, Maddy."

Later, Mother Haley screamed at Ava. "Stop hanging those filthy pictures all over this house! You trying to get rid of the last little bit of friends y'all got around here?"

By then, nearly everyone on the block had turned against them. The fact that nobody seemed to know anything about the murders, that there seemed to be no reason for them, reinforced the idea that it had been the Lord raining down a judgment on Ava, and poor, innocent Kenny getting caught in the torrent.

Ava didn't care what their neighbors thought, not even Miss Maddy, who, along with Miss Lucas, were the only people who still called themselves friends of her family. She looked at her grandmother with disinterest from her seat in front of her easel, where she was painting her father with wood-like skin. "This aint your house, Grandma. This is my mother's house. If she wants me to stop hanging my art, then I will."

"Regina don't know what day it is, let alone what's hanging on the walls!"

Ava shrugged. "Well, then."

"It's your father's house," Mother Haley said. "And he don't like them, either!"

Her father came later. Ava was surprised by his calm voice and demeanor. "Can't you just stop hanging them where everybody can see them?"

"It's art, Daddy. It's supposed to be seen."

"People don't like walking into a house and seeing the family's thirteen year-old daughter sprawled naked everywhere they turn." His calm had gone, and he was hollering, his hands balled up in fists at his side. "Now, I'm not going to tell you again to stop it!"

Ava didn't stop painting the pictures, but she did stop hanging them where the very few people who came by could see them. She hung them all over her bedroom, until no sliver of the pink and green wallpaper could be seen underneath. When she ran out of places to hang her paintings, she started stacking them in the corners of the bedroom. Seeing herself, seeing herself everywhere she looked, helped her to remember who she was when Geo's broken soul surged up within her and pushed aside her own self. When she felt the fear and anxiety she knew was his, she quickly turned to see herself, and the fear subsided, and her own emotions returned. When she was away from home, and not able to get to a painting of herself quickly enough, she would look for her reflection in any shiny surface, and that often worked, but not as well. When she couldn't see herself at all, Geo's feelings would overwhelm her, and his fear and anxiety would become real for Ava, even though it was connected to nothing.

It became a slow battle. Over time the paintings helped less and less. Geo's fear was otherwordly and Ava began to weaken beneath it. Lost in their own grief and guilt, no one in the family noticed, except Mother Haley, who liked the change and said nothing.

1976

Ava dreamed she was walking with Kenny Goode. They were on a dark street that seemed to go on forever ahead of them, streetlights glowing far into the distance.

"Where's this party, anyway?" Kenny asked her.

"Wanda's," she said, in a voice that was not her own.

Kenny laughed. "You still trying to get in that girl's pants?"

Ava laughed, too. "I'm trying to get wherever she's gone let me get."

They skipped ahead in time, and suddenly they were farther down the street. Somebody called out to Ava from behind. "Hey, Geo!" Ava turned, and saw Sondra and Lamar coming up the street. She kept walking, Kenny close at her side. "Geo!" Lamar called again. "I know you hear me, nigger!"

"Let's just keep going, Geo," Kenny said. "You know Sondra and Lamar always want to start something."

Ava was afraid. She put her hands in the pockets of her jeans so Kenny wouldn't see them shaking. She quickened her pace, and Kenny followed suit. Ahead of them, a large white dog ran across the sidewalk, disappeared behind parked cars. Time skipped ahead again, and Ava and Kenny were coming up beside the church. Kenny grabbed her arm and pulled her into the alley behind it. They hurried down the narrow passageway, at the end of which there was a bright light. Behind them they heard Sondra yell, "There they go!" and suddenly there were footsteps running toward them. They ran toward the light, into it, and came out behind the church. Sondra and Lamar were there waiting for them.

"Yo, man, why you running?" Lamar grabbed Ava's arm and she jerked away from him.

"What you want, Lamar?" Kenny asked.

Lamar pushed him. "Shut up, preacher boy. Aint nobody talking to you."

Sondra looked at Ava. "Where your sister at?"

Ava didn't say anything. Inside her pockets, her hands were still shaking. She clenched her fists and willed them to stop. She didn't want them to see that she was afraid.

Sondra got up in her face. "I asked you where Ava at."

There was a flash of light, and Lamar was behind her, holding a knife to her throat.

Kenny said, "We don't want no static with y'all."

"Didn't we tell you to shut the hell up?" Sondra said.

Ava elbowed Lamar in the gut and he groaned and stumbled back, dropped the knife on the ground. She lunged at him, swinging, but he ducked and punched her in the kidneys. Sondra ran up and hit her hard in the face, and she fell against the back wall of the church. They kept coming. A searing pain ripped through her ribs, then her gut, then her side. Another hard blow to the face whipped her head around, slamming it into the wall, and the night turned red before her eyes.

She awoke to the taste of blood in her mouth, Geo's blood, and she winced in pain and shock and sat up in the bed. In a moment the blood-taste was gone. She swallowed hard and took a deep breath, tried to get her bearings in the dark room. Her head was spinning; the faces of Sondra and Lamar blinking in and out like images in a broken viewfinder. Fear and dread came over her. She knew that they were both gone, past hurting her or anyone else. Lamar was on death row out in Kentucky somewhere. Her mother had read about it in the paper more than a year ago. And Sondra was already dead, succumbed to some kind of cancer before she was thirty. They'd heard the screaming from next door when the news had come, Miss Doris in hysterics. Nevertheless, a sense of alarm took hold of her, and seemed to move around like a live thing in the dark room. Ava blinked, and saw, standing in the doorway, a dark silhouette. "Geo?" she whispered.

He looked small in the light coming in through the window, diminished in the darkness. The pain coming from him was palpable. It hummed in the air. He did not move or speak. Ava sat up in the bed. He took a step forward and she saw that he was not her brother. She reached over and shook Helena awake.

"What is it?" Helena asked, groggy.

"My husband is here," Ava said.

Helena flicked on the lamp by the bed and everything came into the light. Paul looked from his wife to his sister, his face so mangled with pain and rage it was like a mask, nearly unrecognizable.

"Paul," Helena said, "You came back."

Paul looked at his sister. "That's my wife," he said. "That's *my* wife."

Helena got out of the bed.

"That preacher was right about you," Paul said. "It's bad enough what you did to some teacher's husband down in Baltimore, but you'd do the same to your own brother? You some kind of animal that can't control itself? Or maybe you just like hurting people."

She shook her head. "No. I'm not…we're not…" She couldn't even get the words out. "We were sleeping."

"Since when y'all sleep in the same bed?"

Ava got up and took a few steps toward him. "I'm going to tell you the truth, Paul."

"Ava," Helena said. "Don't."

Paul laughed. "I think I already heard more truth today than I can handle. I don't need to hear no more. I can see for myself." He pointed at Helena. "I guess I aint surprised that she would do this. But why would you, Ava? This aint you."

"It is me," she said.

He peered at her. "Wasn't I good to you?"

She nodded.

"But it wasn't enough?"

"Paul, this is not about you being enough or not enough," she said. "I know this is hard to understand, but you were never married to *me*. I wasn't there."

He shook his head. "That aint true. Where you getting this crazy shit from? You aint been yourself this last week or so. You been going crazy or something, Ava. But it don't matter. 'Cause I still love you."

"I don't love you," she said. "*I* never loved you, Paul."

For a moment, everything stopped. No one spoke or moved, or breathed. Just as it hit Ava that she should take that back, say that some different way, she saw the look in Paul's eyes and knew it was too late. He lunged towards her, and past her, crossing the room in one bound and grabbing Helena by the throat. He pushed her down on the bed and crouched over her, his thick hands squeezing her windpipe as she clawed at him, struggling for breath. Ava wrapped her arms around his neck and tried to pull him off. Paul took one hand off Helena's throat to push Ava off, and Helena was able to get half a breath, and with it the strength to hit Paul across the face, stunning him for a second, long enough to get loose from his grip and push him off her onto the floor. Ava reached for Helena, and together they tried to get past Paul, hurrying towards the door, but Paul reached out and grabbed Ava's ankle and she fell face first onto the floor. Now his hands were around Ava's throat, squeezing. She struggled to fight him off, clawing at his hands and face. His eyes were blank and empty as he looked down at her. "Why did you have to come here?" he said, through clenched teeth, and she knew that in his rage he did not realize it was her that he was choking. Helena was on his back, trying to pry him off of Ava, but he was too strong in his fury. Ava felt her herself losing consciousness. A hush fell. Her lungs burned. Greens and yellows and, especially, reds, appeared before her eyes. She thought of her brother, and she wondered if it had been like this for him, in that last moment: quiet and bursting with color.

This time Ava knew she was dead. She was standing alone in the foyer of the Delaney house and the hum of her brother's presence was so palpable that she thought she could reach out and touch him.

Geo?

He appeared suddenly in the doorway to the dining room. He looked small, not at all like the tall, broad boy she thought she remembered. He looked at her with eyes like pools of oil, shiny and dark and wet. His voice came out in a whisper. *They killed me because of you, Ava.*

I know, she said.

He came into the middle of the foyer and sat down on the floor beside her feet, cross-legged, and stared up at her. *You too wild*, he said. *You too much.*

She sat down beside him. Up close, he looked more like the brother she had known, round-faced, his thick hair like a swatch of wool on his head. She reached up and touched it, and it felt just the same as it used to. *You've been here with me all this time*, she said.

He nodded. *Looking out for you like I always did. Keeping you from being wild. From being too much. So they won't kill you.*

You made me talk to the pastor. That was you.

She need to leave here, he said. *She making you too much again.*

Ava sighed, and shook her head. *You have to go, Geo. You have to let me be.*

I protect you.

I don't need your protection. I don't want it.

They'll kill you if you too much.

They're gone. They're dead and gone. They can't hurt me.

Not them.

Who, then?

He leaned close to her and whispered. *Everybody.*

She sighed a long sigh. *I would rather die than lose myself again.*

He stared at her. His whole self trembled.

Go, she said. *Rest.*

Rest? He looked comforted by the idea.

Ava stood up and reached out her hand to him. Geo hesitated, then took her hand and let her help him up off the floor. He stared into her face, his eyes searching hers. *Don't be mad at me.*

She shook her head. *No.*

Be careful.

Yes.

He turned and started walking away, towards the back of the house.

Geo.

He stopped, looked back at her.

Thank you.

He came back, put his arms around her. She could feel all the weight of him, and she held him tight and close, buried her face in his chest, smelled the butterscotch he always ate, breathed it in, filled up her lungs with it. In another moment, he turned out of her embrace, and was gone.

Paul was crouched in a corner of the bedroom he had shared with Ava for the last four years. He was down on his knees, staring at his wife's lifeless body on the floor. He didn't understand what was happening, how he'd got there. He watched Helena, who was kneeling over Ava, her mouth pressed against hers, blowing breath into her body. Paul tried to put it all together, but only pieces, fragmented things, occurred to him. He had been coming home. Goode had been talking crazy to him out in the street. And then his hands had been at Ava's throat, squeezing the life out of her. He shook his head, hard, tried to clear away the fog that clung to his brain. "Ava," he called. She did not answer.

Helena's hands were shaking. Her lips trembled on Ava's lips.

"Please, God," Paul whispered. "Not again." He dropped his face into his hands and screamed.

The first thing Ava heard when she woke up was Paul's screaming, but the first thing she saw was Helena's face, looking down at her, tear-stained and determined, her mouth so close that the first breath Ava inhaled was hers. The trace of a smile crossed her lips as she thought to herself that it was Helena, again, who was bringing her back to life.

In the first hours after Geo left, Ava felt a deep and heavy sense of lone-liness, and the anguish that had eluded her seventeen years before, when she saw him dead and broken on the ground, finally came. All through the night she cried, let herself be lost a while in grief and sorrow, and anger. She cursed the names of Sondra Liddy and Lamar Casey, but even in her pain she knew it was a waste of energy. They were dead and gone, and there was nothing to be done about them now. Still, she cried. Cried alone, like a sick dog, shut up in her room, growling at anyone who came near.

During a lull in her wailing, Paul came into the room, said something about being sorry and that he was leaving and that he hoped she didn't hate him. Weeks later she would tell him that she didn't, and that she was sorry, too. When he left, she saw, through the open bedroom door, her family, standing in the hallway, looking anxious and protective, even Sarah.

She fell asleep crying and dreamed of nothing. When she awoke it was morning, and the room was hot, the sun streaming heavy and lush through the window. The loneliness had gone, and in its place she felt complete. Her first thought was of Helena, and she got out of bed and hurried down the hallway, and burst into Sarah's room. Sarah sat up in her bed, and squinted at her through tired eyes.

"Where's Helena?" Ava asked her.

"Gone. She left last night with Paul."

Ava looked around the room. Helena's things were gone.

Downstairs, the house was warm, but not hot the way it had been for days. The hum of unsettled things that had risen up, that had clung heavy and greasy to every surface, had faded away. The sense of ghosts had gone. Ava went into the living room and stood at the front window, peering out. The congregation of Blessed Chapel was heading to Sunday service the same as always. They moved up and across Radnor Street, the women in their linen dresses and wide-brimmed hats, the men in their short-sleeved dress-shirts and wide ties, the children in shoes that snapped against the concrete sidewalk like fingers snapping to the choir music that wafted through the air. Ava watched as a little girl in a dress with lacy collar and cuffs stopped in the middle of the street and spun, the pink of her skirt making a twirl of blush around her. She saw Doris and Dexter Liddy walk-ing down their front steps, Doris' dyed-red hair peeking out from under her blue-feathered hat. Across the street, Malcolm Hansberry waved to them as he came out of his front door. As she stood there watching, she saw Hattie Mitchell and Clarence Nelson and Antoinette Brown, and she was struck by the fact that so many people had stayed on this block for so many years. Most of their children had grown up and moved away, but they remained, attached to the community and church they loved and felt part of. As they made their way to the church, Ava thought how strange it was that nothing outside her house had changed in the last week, while to her almost every-thing and everyone inside it felt different.

She left the window and went to the kitchen, suddenly craving coffee and butter. She put coffee on, and made toast, and she was getting the but-ter from the refrigerator when the doorbell rang. Despite the week she'd had, the sound was as strange and unexpected as ever, only now she hur-ried, interested and eager, to see who was there.

When Ava pulled open the door, Helena turned, and this time Ava did not feel the rush of confused emotions, or the overwhelming urge to reach out. This time she felt joy, all by itself, pure and unbemused. She stepped out onto the porch. "I thought you left," she said.

Helena nodded. "I took Paul to our cousin's."

"All your things are gone."

"Well, I couldn't stay here forever, Ava."

Ava knew that, understood that, but she didn't like it one bit. She was getting her mouth ready to say so, when Helena said, "I took that place out in Wynnefield."

"You didn't!"

Helena laughed. "I did."

Ava came forward and threw her arms around Helena, and Helena held her, too, so tightly that she could hardly breathe, but she didn't care, be-cause just breathing wasn't the most important thing. After a long, long moment, Helena said, "People are watching us."

"Good," Ava said. "This is just the kind of thing they need to see."

They stood there like that for a long time, wrapped up in each other, and for the first time since she was thirteen years old, Ava felt free.

1983

Regina lay awake in her bed, on a cool Saturday morning in September, listening to the sound of death coming up the stairs. When George's illness had advanced to the point of no return, she had moved him out of his bedroom and onto the sofa-bed, at his request, because he didn't want to spend his last days alone in that room, he'd said, where he had hidden himself so much over the years. So, it was from the living room that the sound came, the death growl, that morning. It was very early, just dawn, and the light coming in through Regina's window had a pinkish hue. She thought about her father, and her son, and she wondered where they were now, and what awaited her husband. All her life she had believed in heaven, but lately that idea had made less sense to her. It was too random, death, too indifferent, to possibly lead anywhere as *ordered* as a perfect, pearly-gated heaven.

She considered getting up and going downstairs, sitting beside George and holding his hand. In the last few years, with their children gone from the house, the two of them had made something of amends, an unspoken agreement not to despise each other anymore. She had let him go on and live his secret life without interference or questions or dirty looks. And he, in turn, had done his best to reconnect with her, to rediscover some small part of the love they had shared so long ago. They'd almost become friends again, the two of them creeping around that old house, cooking and watching television together. "We almost like a old married couple," George had said. Regina had laughed. "Almost."

She decided against going downstairs, though, that morning, as she heard him breathing his dying breaths. Not because she didn't care. Not because she didn't love him or because she thought he deserved to die alone. But simply because she was afraid to. She had seen death up close too much already, and it had made her sick and crazy once before. She thought it best to keep her distance from it now, as best she could. In the pink light coming in through the window, Regina whispered a prayer for her husband, and listened as he passed away.

George's senses were the first parts of his soul to die, so that the boundaries of one passed away into the others, and for a few of his last moments in the world he could see touch, and hear smell, and feel taste. As he lay sunken in his sickbed, undignified and emaciated, little more than a pile of twigs, a cricket of a man, on the threshold of a shameful death, he suddenly remembered his boyhood. Down Georgia. Where he once ran barefooted in tobacco fields, his feet barely touching the hot ground, his face to the sun. As he lay in his bed, now too weak to move, the crumbly smell of Georgia bird songs danced before his clouded eyes. The salty tastes of down-south sunsets were loud on his lesioned skin. And he remembered knowing he was good then. A good boy who did what he was told and helped his mother with the washing and knew God. He remembered climbing trees and how his skinny legs looked like two more branches as he sat high and leaned his head against the breathing trunk. He had known then that he was part of creation, made by God with intention, pure and right as grass and bees. He did not know the moment when he had forgotten it, the moment when his desire for other boys' mouths and hands and *things* started to mean that he was not good, not something the Lord had made. He had spent his life since moving from moment to moment between longing and shame, and as he lay on his deathbed he could no longer remember or understand the self-hatred he had carried for so long a time. He could no longer taste the scorn, once like a stew on which he had gorged and fattened himself almost all the days of his life. But he could remember the taste of Chuck's quiet eyes, and the ruddy smell of Butch's voice. He could hear Robert's smooth skin now, and see James' silly and abundant heart. And the same for all of them. Louis. And Bud. And Tony. And Richard. And Red. And the boy with the cigarette behind his ear and the eight-shaped scar above his lip, who never said a word but smiled almost to laughing the whole time they were together. And the man behind the shed by the train tracks, who shuddered and cried like a child when he came, and held George to him for hours in the dark. And so many others. He remembered them now, not with the deep hatred of himself with which he had always tried to forget them, a deep hatred which his dying mind and body could no longer clearly recall, but with as much joy and light as the coming of sure death would allow him. They had all been so beautiful, black and soft, brown and wiry, red and lithe. Southern boys the color of Georgia earth, who had run in the same tobacco fields, with their faces to the same sun and the sounds of birds on their same skin. They had been more than his lovers, more than secret tousles in tree-hidden places. They had been his kin, too, they had been *of* him, and of God. In his last moments, he did not have to wish that he had seen that truth before, that he had understood more, that he had loved them better, and himself. When the shame fell away, ashenly, quietly forgotten, it was as if he had always known, and that trick of memory was a tender mercy before he died.

Sarah stood by her bedroom window, watching the sun coming up pink and soft on the horizon. Beside her, her husband leaned his shoulder into hers and said, "Pretty, huh?" raising his eyebrows toward the sky. "Maybe it's a sign from your Daddy."

Sarah thought the sunrise always looked like that on September mornings, but she knew he was trying to comfort her, so she nodded and tried to smile.

Regina had called only a few moments ago to tell them that George had passed away. Sarah wanted to cry, but she couldn't, no tears would come. For the last few weeks of her father's life, she had helped her mother tend to him: feed him and clean him, and keep him company. A few times, in the last days, she had wanted to say things to him, things she knew she should say before he died because if she didn't she'd spend the rest of her life regretting it, but she didn't say them. The last thing she said to him, the evening before the morning he died, was, "I'll come by and read you the funnies tomorrow."

"I'm gone get dressed and go on over to the house," Sarah told her husband now.

He nodded. "Alright."

She sighed. "Mama said Ava is coming down from New York right away. Helena, too." She glanced at him.

"Well. You want me to call off work?" he asked. "So I can be there for you today?"

She shrugged. "You don't have to."

He put his arms around her. "I will."

Sarah rested her head against his chest.

"You can go ahead and cry if you want to," he said. "I got you."

"Maybe I will."

But she didn't. Instead, she looked out at the pink sky and said a silent prayer for her father.

Ava and Helena took the train from New York City and then the el from the train station and as they walked the rest of the way to Radnor Street, Ava said, "I wish he'd told me. I wish he hadn't had to get sick for me to find out."

She'd said it half a dozen times since her father had been diagnosed, and Helena said now what she'd said each time before. "I guess he never came to terms with it himself."

Even after Ava had moved to Wynnfield with Helena, even when the two of them had moved together to New York, George had continued to keep his secret from her. He had accepted her relationship with Helena, begrudgingly, once he was sure there was nothing he could do about it, but he had never revealed to either of them the truth about himself. After he got sick, Ava had asked Helena whether she had ever suspected, and Helena said she'd known from the day she met him, that Saturday morning in the foyer when he'd been unable to look her in the eyes for fear of what she might be able to see. She hadn't ever told Ava, she said, because it wasn't hers to tell.

"I hope," Ava said now, "that he made some peace with it before he died."

They turned the corner onto Radnor Street then, and found the block buzzing with activity. News of her father's death that morning had brought people out onto their porches, no doubt inspiring lengthy exercises in speculation across banisters and at curbsides. In the last seven years the harassment of Ava's family had ceased, maybe because once Ava and Paul and Sarah had all left Pastor Goode had decided he'd done enough, or maybe because he was just too tired to care anymore. He'd died of a heart attack three years ago.

As Ava and Helena walked down the street, a hush fell over the block and every head turned and watched them. Dexter Liddy folded his arms across his chest. Malcolm Hansberry leaned out over his porch railing and glared. Clarence Nelson shook his head, slowly, from side to side. Vic Jones spit into his front yard. Hattie Mitchell stared wide-eyed. Doris Liddy twisted her lips into a frown of near-cartoonish severity. Ava remembered that when she was a child they had watched her, too. Everywhere she went on that street, and in that church, eyes had followed her. Back then it had been wonder, an attraction to whatever they saw in her that seemed bigger, brighter, more than what they knew. She looked out at them now, each of them displaying their own exaggerated but silent disapproval, and she suddenly remembered their love. Their love, all warm and eager and sure. Though it had ended long ago, their love had helped her become who she was. As a child she hadn't understood that, but she knew it now. Seeing herself in their eyes had helped her understand that she was special, and because she understood it she had been free to *be* it, the same way seeing herself in Helena's eyes had helped her get free again. Silently, she thanked them.

As she came up the front steps of the Delaney house, the flowers in the front yard screamed orange and red and yellow at her. They were the indirect descendants of the flowers Helena had planted there years ago, Regina having re-planted them each following spring. Ava looked down at the flowers, the fat bursts of happy pigment against the drab old house, and she felt giddy with color and promise.

Acknowledgements

This book has been a long time coming. I started it in college, more than sixteen years ago, and though it has changed and been reimagined so many times that it looks nothing now like what it was then, its heart, its pulse of family and community and womanhood and queerness has never changed. Over so many years, there have been so many people who have helped it along on its journey. Some of them are: my college writing teacher, Geeta Kothari, without whom I would not be the writer I am now or the writer I might someday become; Lighthouse Writers Workshop, for their support, encouragement and flattery; Lisa Volk, for her friendship and patronage; Nico Amador, for his editing help; and all the family and friends who have been waiting so long to read this book. Your anticipation helped fuel me. Thank you.

Mia

CPSIA information can be obtained at www.ICGtesting.com
Printed in the USA
BVOW01s2246090614

355911BV00004B/318/P